D1743151

LITERARY
SAN ANTONIO

LITERARY SAN ANTONIO

Edited by Bryce Milligan

TCU PRESS • FORT WORTH, TEXAS

Copyright © 2018 TCU Press (compilation)
Introduction and headnotes copyright © 2018 Bryce Milligan

Library of Congress Cataloging-in-Publication Data

Names: Milligan, Bryce, 1953- editor, author.
Title: Literary San Antonio / edited by Bryce Milligan.
Description: Fort Worth, Texas : TCU Press, [2018]
Identifiers: LCCN 2017049443 (print) | LCCN 2017052285 (ebook) | ISBN
    9780875656939 | ISBN 9780875656878 | ISBN 9780875656878?q(alk. paper)
Subjects: LCSH: San Antonio (Tex.)--History. | San Antonio (Tex.)--Social
    life and customs. | San Antonio (Tex.)--Intellectual life. | San Antonio
    (Tex.)--Poetry. | San Antonio (Tex.)--Fiction.
Classification: LCC F394.S2 (ebook) | LCC F394.S2 L73 2018 (print) | DDC
    976.4/351--dc23
LC record available at https://urldefense.proofpoint.com/v2/url?u=https-3A__lccn.loc.gov
    _2017049443&d=DwIFAg&c=7Q-FWLBTAxn3T_E3HWrzGYJrC4RvUoWDrzTlitGRH
    _A&r=O2eiy819IcwTGuw-vrBGiVdmhQxMh2yxeggw9qlTUDE&m=DBKo1qICJpwdbt3l-
    D0jRNnL8kPp5n6UE4XuA-KZcls&s=68aFyEA4TxktLriRhIaLFv9l6HVMX3o5LjHW63Iec-
    mc&e=

TCU Press
TCU Box 298300
Fort Worth, Texas 76129
817.257.7822
http://www.prs.tcu.edu

To order books: 1.800.826.8911

Cover photo/Siggi Ragnar
Jacket design/Vicki Whistler
Book design/Margie Adkins Graphic Design

Note to readers: We have retained the style of the original pieces in spelling, italics, capitalization, and use of accents.

This volume is dedicated to
Mary Guerrero Milligan,
una verdadera hija de este pueblo
who taught me to love it.
This volume would not exist without her.

With special thanks to
Roberto Bonazzi, Rosemary Catacalos,
Naomi Shihab Nye, Camille Rosengren,
and Kathy Vargas,
wise guides all,
for their enduring support.

In memory of
Angela De Hoyos,
pioneering publisher and poet,
friend and mentor,
who named San Antonio
"ciudad-reina de la frontera."

Contents

INTRODUCTION:
THREE CENTURIES OF WRITING IN AND OF SAN ANTONIO

BRYCE MILLIGAN

THE DEPTH AND DIVERSITY OF SAN ANTONIO'S culture/cultura, and the charm of its cultural ambiance, have been remarked upon since the middle of the nineteenth century. Water in abundance certainly drew the first inhabitants to the area—indigenous peoples, colonizers, and settlers alike—but it was the multiethnic, multilingual, cosmopolitan culture of the city that drew writers and artists. In her introduction to Robert Sturmburg's 1920 *History of San Antonio and of the Early Days in Texas*, no less than the "savior of the Alamo" Adina De Zavala wrote: "It has long been a dream of mine to see raised up, before I die, a school of loving and appreciative writers and artists who will do justice to the wonderful history, legends and romance of Texas, and her most attractive city: San Antonio, the beautiful." We believe that Adina would be pleased with the present volume.

In truth, there were writers of all descriptions present in San Antonio throughout the eighteenth and nineteenth centuries—essayists, naturalists, historians, travel writers, playwrights, poets, fiction writers, songwriters, journalists. Virtually all of their writing is of interest, often downright fascinating, but not all of it qualifies as "literary." (Some frontier poets, reaching for literary heaven, fell so far short of that mark as to redefine the depths to which bathos can descend.) And yet, it was the history, culture, geography, and climate of the region, reported back to readers in more refined realms, that made the region and the town so appealing to visitors, whether they were writers or not. Explorers, soldiers, missionaries, and travelers like Álvar Núñez Cabeza de

Vaca (1542), Father Damián Massanet (1691), Father Isidro Félix de Espinosa (1709), Father Francisco Celiz (1718), Father Bartolomé García (1760), Father Juan Agustín Morfi (1779), Zebulon Pike (1806), Mary Austin Holley (1833), and Frederick Law Olmsted (1856)—all published diaries, reports, or travelogues announcing to the world that they had discovered someplace very special. Writing by Spaniards drew more Spaniards, culminating in the arrival on March 9, 1731, of *los isleños*, fifteen families from the Canary Islands who created the first civil government in the village they called San Fernando de Béxar. Mexican reports drew Mexicans. American reports drew Americans. Frederick Law Olmsted, a very well-respected travel writer in his day, visited the city in 1852. He published this portrait of the city, guaranteed to pique the interest of other travelers and potential settlers:

> We have no city, except, perhaps, New Orleans, that can vie, in point of the picturesque interest that attaches to odd and antiquated foreignness, with San Antonio. Its jumble of races, costumes, languages and buildings; its religious ruins, holding to an antiquity, for us, indistinct enough to breed an unaccustomed solemnity; its remote, isolated outposted situation, and the vague conviction that it is the first of a new class of conquered cities into whose decaying streets our rattling life is to be infused, combine with the heroic touches in its history to enliven and satisfy your traveler's curiosity.

Olmsted's description of San Antonio as civilized, charming, and exotic was serialized during his journey—in the *New York Daily Times*, soon to become the *New York Times*. Then, as now, it had a national readership. He followed it up with a best-selling book in 1857.

The point being that the written word had a considerable role in creating the city as we know it. And some of those written words were, indeed, literary. Thus this collection defines "literary" not solely in terms of the traditional genres of fiction, poetry, and creative nonfiction, but is broadly inclusive of writing that has defined and helped to shape the city, no matter its genre. Early inhabitants came to San Antonio for its abundant water and lovely environment. Tourists have come for its history and culture. *Literary San Antonio* gathers some of the early written accounts that describe both the environs and the history of San Antonio together with creative literature written by residents (some of them very brief residents) of the city. We have chosen to include only work that is set in the city or its immediate vicinity.

A Few Words on the Alamo

Without doubt, from many perspectives, it was the 1836 Battle of the Alamo that defined San Antonio for all time. All over the globe, reports of the "American Thermopylae" drew emotional responses in the press, almost immediately. Only seven years after the battle, in September 1843, the first international tourist arrived to view the scene. William Bollaert, from England, recorded a conversation with "an old Mexican woman" in which she recalled that the Alamo had not always been merely a scene of carnage and heroism:

> Ah, Señor, had you but seen thc Alamo on a feast day, as I have seen it, not like it is now, in ruins, you would have been delighted. . . . The front of the church was so beautiful. On one side of the doorway stood San Antonio, on the other San Fernando with other saints. The bells rung a merry peal; they were broken up and thrown into the river . . . the enemy not being able to melt them into bullets. I never look into the ruins of the church without shedding a tear; not half the walls are now to be seen. . . .[1]

The Alamo is a cultural lodestone for Texas writers in general, and it would be quite easy to fill numerous volumes with nothing but literature generated by the Alamo, written by Texans living outside of San Antonio. From inside the city limits the literary view is, we would like to think, more nuanced, even if the topic can still set off pitched political battles. We have included only a very few accounts that will give the reader a sense of the Alamo's evolving symbolic value and cultural relevance. And yet, references to the Alamo will be found throughout the entire book, occasionally from writers for whom it was a symbol of oppression.

Culture before Writing

To begin at the beginning, we have opened *Literary San Antonio* with a song in one of the many indigenous Coahuiltecan languages that flourished—for millennia—all across South Texas. The presence of Clovis arrow and spear points in the Olmos Basin, near the headwater springs of the San Antonio River, and cave paintings slightly further west, indicate that this area has been occupied for up to 15,000 years. We do not know exactly when the peoples speaking Coahuiltecan dialects arrived in the area, but prior to the arrival of the Spanish, the populations of northern Mexico and South Texas appear to have been relatively stable for several centuries. The inclusive term "Coahuiltecan" covers, according to some scholars, at least seven distinct but interrelated language groups, consisting of hundreds of clan-based languages and dialects.[2] The Coahuiltecan population in 1690 is estimated at between 85,000 and 100,000 persons, occupying southern Texas, northeastern Coahuila, and portions of Nuevo León and Tamaulipas.

The song presented here is in Comecrudo, a Coahuiltecan language used in the region immediately south of San Antonio, which would have been understood by other bands like the Payaya. This song was originally collected in 1886 from elders of that band living at the time along the Rio Grande. The vicinity of San Antonio proper was populated mainly by the Payaya band. The Payaya were fairly numerous community-based hunter-gatherers who lived in a place so plentiful that relocation in search of food was rarely required. In 1760, Father Bartolomé García wrote his *Manual* in Spanish and Coahuilteco for convert servers at the Catholic Mass in the San Antonio missions, which is the primary source for all that is known of this particular language. (García's manual does *not* pass for literature.) Although we know that the Payaya spoke Coahuilteco, we have only one word that is definitely associated with the Payaya alone—*Yana wana (Yanaguana),* their word for the San Antonio River.

The first European to encounter the Payaya was Álvar Núñez Cabeza de Vaca, who was shipwrecked on Galveston Island in 1528. He made his way across south Texas, along the Rio Grande and then to San Miguel de Culiacán on the Gulf of California, arriving there in December 1535. Cabeza de Vaca's *Relación*, published in Spain in 1542, is a remarkably detailed account of his encounters with indigenous peoples, and certainly qualifies as the earliest written literature of the region. Alas, Cabeza de Vaca passed among the Payaya some one hundred miles south of San Antonio and thus his text passes from our focus.

Having been described by Cabeza de Vaca as both numerous and relatively passive, the Payaya were targeted by Spanish missionaries as being ripe for conversion. In fact, the Payaya were the primary reason that Spanish explorers and missionaries visited the area in 1691 and 1709, and were the people for whom Mission San Antonio de Valero (the Alamo) was established in 1718. It should be noted that the "Spanish" missions, the intricate system of irrigation *acequias*, even the Cathedral of San Fernando, were all built with mostly indigenous labor.

The arrival of the Spanish in North America set many things in motion. The Apaches and Comanches acquired horses from the Spanish and became mobile. Throughout the eighteenth century, the Comanches drove the Lipan Apaches south and east. Several Comanche bands raided far south into Mexico, including the Peneteka (Pehnahterkuh, "Wasp People" [indicating their speed as raiders]) who settled in the Texas Hill Country around 1740. It was they who drove the Lipan Apache band known as Tche shän (the "Sun Otter People") south of San Antonio. Almost a dozen bands of Lipan Apaches lived in Central and Southern Texas throughout the late eighteenth and early nineteenth centuries, but only a few adapted to mission life. Many of the local Coahuiltecan bands, including the Payaya, accepted the relative safety of the missions, where they could escape the depredations of both the Apaches and Comanches. They could not escape, however, smallpox and other European diseases which ravaged their numbers.

In 1768, the San Miguel de Linares de los Adaes Mission and Nuestra Señora del Pilar Presidio in far East Texas were abandoned and their Christianized Indian residents, Adaes and other Caddoan bands, were removed to San Antonio. This was recorded in a fascinating work by Father Juan Agustín Morfi, "Memorias de la Provincia de Texas," published as *History of Texas: 1673-1779,* edited by Carlos Castañeda (Quivira Society, 1935). Written in 1780-82, Father Morfi recorded his observations of many tribes throughout Texas, especially the Indian residents in the missions of San Antonio. Beginning in 1772, the management of the San Antonio missions was transferred from the College of Querétaro to the College of Zacatecas, which was entrusted with the task of closing the missions. By the 1790s, all five San Antonio missions had been secularized and abandoned, although individual priests continued to say Mass at several of them for years afterwards. The extensive mission records remained, and are today part of the Bexar County Archives. Records of baptisms, marriages, and funerals, as well as the inventories of the possessions and peoples of the missions are very instructive. When it was secularized, Mission San Antonio de Valero listed its resident Indians as including Lipan, Sana, Muruame, Copan, Payaya, Karankawa, Jarame, Yerbipiame, Pacuache, and Papnac. Other missions included dozens of other tribes and bands from all over the region. Marriage records show not only inter-tribal unions, but marriages uniting indigenous men and women with Spaniards and Mexicans. Indigenous family names vanished (Indians were given Spanish names upon baptism), and indigenous languages went extinct, but it would be a huge mistake to say that the Indians of South Texas vanished from history. A caste system did in fact separate supposedly "pure Spanish" families from the rest of the population well into the nineteenth century, but even so, marriage into an established family more or less automatically improved the caste into which one was born. Inevitably, by 1800 the base population of San Antonio was composed predominantly of Indians with Hispanic names, or mestizos, most of whom were more indigenous than Spanish or Mexican.

In San Antonio, tribal and band names may have faded from memory, but the people certainly did not. Remnants of indigenous cultural awareness have played a constant if minor role in the development of the literary self-image of San Antonio's Mexican American population, and today there are active efforts to reclaim what was lost.[3]

"They came for the water…"

Not surprisingly, the Comecrudo song that opens this collection gives praise to water. So also, nonindigenous priests, poets, and passersby have, for over three centuries, commented on the magnificence and beauty of the springs that give rise to the San Antonio River, often in terms little short of amazement. Father Espinosa, writing in 1709, described a river that "could supply not only a village but a city." Novelist and priest Anthony Ganilh wrote in the 1830s of "... the district of Bexar, and the river San Anton, which may be considered as destined to become the paradise of North America." Frederick Law Olmsted would classify the San Antonio springs as being "among the gems of the natural world. The whole river gushes up in one sparkling burst from the earth. The effect is overpowering. It is beyond your possible conceptions of a spring. You cannot believe your eyes, and almost shrink from sudden metamorphosis by invaded nymphdom."

Olmsted's use of the word "nymphdom" may raise a modern eyebrow, but it was not unjustified at the time. The cover illustration of *Frank Leslie's Illustrated Newspaper*, January 15, 1859—a very popular national publication at the time—showed a number of young women frolicking in the river, *sans* clothing, with this description: "The temperature of the water is the same throughout the year, neither too warm nor too cold for bathing, and not a single day passes without the inhabitants indulging in the favourite and healthy exercise of swimming, which is practised by everybody, from morning till evening; and the traveller along the shores of this beautiful river will constantly see hundreds of children, of all ages and colour, swimming and diving like so many ducks."

Abundant water rising in a pleasant valley created a fertile landscape, rich with water, pecans, and wild game. The "Blue Hole," the once-huge headwater spring of the San Antonio River, rises at the southern end of the Olmos Basin. Dr. Karen E. Stothert, in *The Archaeology and Early History of the Head of the San Antonio River*, describes this idyllic basin as lying "between the oak-juniper-hickory woods common to northern Bexar County and the Texas Hill Country, and the mesquite and dry brush country characteristic of southern Bexar County, the Coastal Plain and the Rio Grande Plain. . . . Such rich diversity makes this area of Texas the 'biological hub' of the northern half of this hemisphere."

Who would not want to live here?

San Antonio writers to this day celebrate the water that gave rise to the city, as Texas Poet Laureate Rosemary Catacalos does in her justly famous poem:

Homesteaders

for the Edwards Aquifer

They came for the water,
came to its sleeping place
here in the bed of an old sea,
the dream of the water.
They sank hand and tool into
soil where the bubble of springs
gave off hope, fresh and long,
the song of the water.
Babies and crops ripened
where they settled,
where they married their sweat
in the ancient wedding,
the blessing of the water.
They made houses of limestone
and adobe, locked together blocks
descended from shells and coral,
houses of the bones of the water.
And they swallowed the life
of the lime in the water,
sucked its mineral up
into their own bones
which grew strong as the water,
the gift of the water.
All along the counties they lay,
mouth to mouth with the water,

fattened in the smile of the water,
the light of the water,
water flushed pure through the
spine and ribs of the birth of life,
the old ocean,
the stone,
the home of the water.[4]

San Antonio's first Poet Laureate, and later the Poet Laurcate of Texas, Carmen Tafolla finds that:

This river here
is full of me and mine.
This river here
is full of you and yours.
…
Right here,
the stories and the stillness
of those gone before us
haunt us still [5]
…

Early San Antonio Newspapers

Presumably, printing presses existed in San Antonio during the Spanish and Mexican eras for government and church use, but we have no physical evidence to prove it. Local and regional news was most often announced by a *pregonero* (an official town crier) who regularly read aloud all official decrees and other public communications.[6]

The first documented printing press to arrive in Texas came with José Álvarez de Toledo y Dubois in May 1813, but it was probably never used on Texas soil. The press was hauled back to Natchitoches, Louisiana, almost at once because the type had already been set there. That press was used to print a single issue of the two-page *Gaceta de Tejas* in 1813. The *Gaceta de Tejas* was in Spanish and carried the motto "La Salud del Pueblo es la Suprema Ley" ("The Safety of the People is the Supreme Law"). A second paper, *El Mejicano*, edited by William Shaler and José Álvarez de Toledo, was bilingual. Appearing in June 1813, it too was published in Natchitoches and was aimed at Texan readers. Copies of *El Mejicano* are known to have been distributed in San Antonio.

When the first post-independence governor of Texas, José Félix Trespalacios, arrived in San Antonio on August 25, 1822, he found that the government offices were severely lacking in basic necessities. He ordered a printing press from New Orleans and sent his aide, Juan Almonte, to bring it back. Almonte arrived in San Antonio with the press, very likely a Washington hand press, in early April 1823.

On April 9, 1823, a bilingual prospectus for the *Texas Courier/Correo de Texas* was printed in San Antonio. The "publisher" was an American named Ashcroft, who was known to have printed public notices for the municipal government, and may have been Trespalacios's printer. Whether the press brought to the city by Trespalacios was used for the *Texas Courier/Correo de Texas* is unknown, and no copies of the paper are extant. Whether or not the paper was actually printed and distributed is unknown. However, Ashcroft boldly headlined his prospectus to "the Advocates of Light and Reason, the friends to the Province of Texas, and the Mexican Empire." Given Trespalacios's political inclinations, it is almost certain that he was behind the *Texas Courier/Correo de Texas*. Only two days after his arrival in San Antonio, he had announced to the *ayuntamiento*, the town council: "Sois libres: en tal concepto bien podeis criticar mis hechos sin temor de ser incomodados ni en buestras personas ni en btra opinión" ("You are free: Thus you may criticize my deeds without fear of inconvenience to either your body or your opinion.")

San Antonio's first successful newspapers appeared in the 1850s: the *Western Texan* and *El Bejarraño*, which was dedicated to "los intereses de la población México-Tejana." Interestingly, *El Bejarraño* took a very early stand for teaching Spanish in Texas schools. The *Daily Ledger and Texan* was founded in 1860, the *San Antonio Express* (later the *Express-News*) was founded in 1865. Most of these newspapers, at one time or another, published work by local poets. In the English language papers, the poems were routinely patriotic paeans to (Anglo) Texas, with occasional vitriolic diatribes against Mexico and Mexicans. Most poems were published anonymously, although it can be assumed that many were written by the editors of the papers.

San Antonio and Early Texas Creative Writing

The best-known early Texas poet was also one of the worst poets to ever set pen to paper—Hugh Kerr. Fortunately for San Antonio's literary reputation, he spent only a couple of years here. Kerr was the author of *A Poetical Description of Texas, and Narrative of Many Interesting Events in that Country, Embracing a Period of Several Years, Interspersed with Moral and Political Impressions* (New York: self-published, 1838). Sam Dixon was the author (and publisher) of the first work of literary criticism to be published in the state, *The Poets and Poetry of Texas* (Austin: Dixon & Co., 1885). Dixon's comment on Kerr: "I cannot conceive of anything more crude." Or as one reviewer put it, "O Kerr, Kerr, Kerr, what'd you write those poems fur?" Forty years later, critical opinion was not much changed. University of Texas Professor Leonidas Payne wrote in his *A Survey of Texas Literature* (Chicago: Rand McNally, 1928) that "Little need be said of the early poetry written in Texas. . . . It is almost devoid of artistic merit."

Fiction was written mainly about Texas rather than in Texas until late in the nineteenth century. The first novel we know of to be set in Texas was by an anonymous French writer, *L'Héröine du Texas*. It was about exiled supporters of Napoleon Bonaparte seeking to establish a French colony in Texas. The novel was published in Paris in 1819, but was virtually unknown in Texas until it was translated in 1937. Another pre-Alamo novel set in Texas was written by a Massachusetts minister, Timothy Flint. *Francis Berrian, or the Mexican Patriot* (Boston, 1826) was mainly a fictional diatribe against Catholicism. Flint never set foot in Texas. Then there was *Mexico Versus Texas, a Descriptive Novel, Most of the Characters of which Consist of Living Persons,* by "a Texian" (Philadelphia: N. Siegfried, 1838), which was very likely written in San Antonio. Four years later, it was republished as *Ambrosio de Letinez, or The First Texian Novel, Embracing*

A Description of the Countries Bordering on the Rio Bravo, with Incidents of the War of Independence (New York: Chas. Francis & Co., 1842). This time the author was given as A. T. Myrthe. A century later, some minor literary sleuthing by Sister M. Agatha Sheehan revealed that "Myrthe" was a pseudonym for a Catholic priest with a bent for writing romantic fiction, Anthony Ganilh—another Frenchman, but one who had actually spent a decade in Texas, much of it in San Antonio.

Certainly there were journalists, diarists, poets, and singer-songwriters in San Antonio throughout the nineteenth century, but the first "creative writer" with a national reputation to be associated with the city was the Georgia poet and flutist Sidney Lanier, who arrived in 1872. Lanier was suffering from consumption, and the climate of San Antonio was reputed at the time to be excellent for recuperating consumptives. Thus the town was swarming for a time with America's dying elite, Lanier among them.

Lanier was positively taken with the place. He joined the Alamo Literary Society and spent many a pleasant afternoon in George Henry Kalteyer's Eagle Drug Store on Military Plaza, drinking sodas and reading the latest newspapers. (Kalteyer founded the Literary Society in 1871 and was apparently overjoyed when a real, published author showed up on his doorstep.) Lanier undoubtedly perused the bookstore of Sidney P. Gamble, on West Commerce, and that of Julius Berends at 220 E. Commerce Street;[7] he accompanied the Beethoven Männerchor on his ebony-and-silver Boehm flute; he gambled in San Antonio's "glittering palaces"—some of the swankiest saloons between New Orleans and San Francisco. Whether or not he visited any of the town's hundred or so bordellos we cannot say, but all in all, Sidney Lanier was charmed to his toes. San Antonio, he wrote, was "so European." It even had ice. On the other hand, as Lanier pointed out, there was still, in 1872, the possibility that the unwary might be captured and ransomed by Indians just beyond the city limits, which gave San Antonio an exotic—and dangerous—appeal which Paris would have been hard put to match.

Lanier wrote *San Antonio de Bexar: An Historical Sketch,* which found its way into the hands of book dealer William Corner, who published it in 1890.

Amazingly, the little book was reviewed in London, Paris, and New York, letting the literary world know that there was a positively cosmopolitan, cultural oasis gleaming in the middle of Texas.

The next major writer to visit San Antonio did not stay long, but his visit certainly made an impact. Oscar Wilde spent a few days at the Menger Hotel in 1882, during a lecture tour. The *San Antonio Light* described Wilde as wearing a "velvet jacket, with a white waistcoat, blue cravat, white lace ruffles about his neck and sleeves, light drab knee-length trousers, scarlet stockings and black slippers with large silver buckles." He must have seemed a rare bird to the shopkeepers and cowboys on Commerce Street. Wilde was quite moved by the missions (*every* tourist visits . . .), praising "their picturesque remains of tower and dome, and their handsome carved stonework." He thought San José to be "the finest example of beautiful architecture . . . in all of the Americas," but he thought that Texans had let the Alamo fall into a "monstrous" state. Accuracy of social observation was one of Wilde's best assets, which he exercised when he reported that "men in Texas cannot survive more than an hour between beers."

The next major writer to arrive was another Sidney—Sydney Porter, otherwise known as O. Henry, though he would not take on that appellation until he was long gone from San Antonio and was, in fact, sitting in the federal penitentiary in Columbus, Ohio, having had the bad luck to be caught with his hand in the till of the bank where he worked in Austin. Porter had started up a satirical newspaper in Austin called the *Rolling Stone* in 1894. Shortly thereafter he moved the paper to San Antonio and hooked up with one Mr. Ryder-Taylor, the self-proclaimed former amanuensis of no less a personage than Charles Dickens. That Dickens was himself unaware of this fact was par for the course among frontier journalists. Stephen Crane, author of *The Red Badge of Courage,* was also in San Antonio in 1894, and he described it in the same glowing terms as had Sidney Lanier twenty years prior.

O. Henry spent most of his time at 903 South Presa Street in San Antonio, where he had moved the editorial offices of the *Rolling Stone.* The character of the editors is made clear from their stated editorial policy, which read:

The politics of *The Rolling Stone* is Independent, with an inclination toward Presbyterianism, and the theory that the world is supported on the back of a mud turtle. Our platform might be stated in the following words: We believe in treating everybody square all around, backing the winning horse, and closing all open accounts with a note when hard pressed. We will hew to the line, provided the chips fall our way.

Needless to say, the chips did not fall O. Henry's way, which is why his hand was in the till in the bank in Austin. Nevertheless, O. Henry contributed significantly to the literary reputation of San Antonio, setting six of his finest stories in the city, including "The Enchanted Kiss," "A Fog in Santone," "The Higher Abdication," and "Hygeia at the Solito." The city fathers, eager to associate themselves with such literary fame, renamed the Commerce Street bridge after the author.

The Mexican Revolution and Latino Literature in San Antonio

San Antonio has always been a cultural crossroads, not to mention being a geographical stopover whether one was headed west to California or south to Mexico. Aside from the cultural ambiance and the pleasant weather, San Antonio became a very interesting place for writers due to events transpiring in Mexico. The "wind that swept Mexico"—the Mexican Revolution—created an inter-American awareness that change was possible, that even the most rigid caste system could be overthrown, that the most mercenary economic exploitation could be remedied, that *los pobres de la tierra*—as José Martí had proclaimed in Cuba decades before—could rise up and shake the towers and temples of the rich.

In Mexico, and consequently in San Antonio, things really began to heat up just after the turn of the century. The Flores Magón brothers (Jesús, Ricardo, and Enrique), publishers of the opposition newspaper *Regeneración*, were jailed repeatedly for running antigovernment editorials. They fled Mexico City and set up their newspaper in San Antonio in 1904. The brothers published a book entitled *La Sucesión Presidencial en 1910* in 1908; its author was Francisco Madero.

Two years later, Madero ran against Porfirio Díaz for the presidency, but Madero spent much of the campaign in the San Luis Potosí jail, until he escaped into exile here in San Antonio—together with most of his family. They lived in the Hutchins Hotel, 205 Garden Street, and at various other locations, including 437 S. Main and 421 S. Presa. Another revolutionary, Venustiano Carranza, also arrived in San Antonio in 1910 and lived at 140 North Street, then at 520 S. Presa. Later, Carranza would serve as president of Mexico from 1915 until he was assassinated in 1920.

In 1910 Madero released his *Plan de San Luis Potosí*, calling for an armed rebellion to begin on November 20. It is important to reiterate that this book, which literally called the Mexican Revolution into being, was written and published in San Antonio, printed on Santa Rosa Avenue. The call was heard throughout Mexico. Over the next five years, revolutionaries like Pancho Villa and Emiliano Zapata drove from power one of the cruelest and most powerful dictators in the world—and suddenly anything seemed possible. The rise of flamboyant characters like Villa and Zapata drew journalists like flies, including John Reed, whose book *Insurgent Mexico* was partially written and edited in the San Antonio's Menger Hotel.

Assassination attempts against the Flores Magón brothers forced them to begin publishing on the run—in El Paso, St. Louis, and elsewhere, but what they had begun in San Antonio took on a life of its own. Throughout the teens and 1920s, Santa Rosa Avenue was lined with expatriate Mexican printers and publishers. In 1913, for example, the newspaper *La Prensa* was founded here by Ignacio E. Lozano. It continued until 1962, a full fifty years, and was considered to be the most influential of all Mexican exile newspapers. This is very important for the topic of San Antonio writing because *La Prensa* ran a weekly literary section with stories, poems, and reviews, entitled *Lunes Literario*. For the first half of the twentieth century, this was one of the primary publication vehicles for both Mexican and Mexican-American writers. Lozano's publishing house, Casa Editorial Lozano, was the largest in the United States owned by a Mexican American, publishing hundreds of titles every year.

The presence of so many Mexican intellectual exiles in San Antonio had a long-lasting political effect on Mexican Americans here. Printer, publisher, and journalist Rubén Munguía—in whose print shop future congressman Henry B. Gonzalez worked as a teenager—once wrote that the "results of their labor were slow coming, but in the 1950s great changes took place and the children of *La Prensa's* early readers began to flex their muscles."

For Mexican-American women writers, newspapers were virtually the *only* opportunity for publication. Feminist poet and journalist Sara Estela Ramírez was a teacher, editor, political and labor activist, and a founder of the Partido Liberal Mexicano (PLM). Ramírez founded the Laredo-San Antonio newspaper *La Corregidora* in 1901, which she saw as a news link for Mexicans on both sides of the Rio. She also founded a feminist literary magazine, *Aurora*. She was well known in San Antonio as an organizer and a literary figure.

Many of the Latina/Chicana writers who came of age in the 1960s or shortly thereafter have described their female role models as belonging to the generation prior to that of their parents. Numerous *abuelita* (grandmother) poems and stories depict strong-willed survivors, women who had, somehow, acquired a yearning for independence and education decades before the women's movement of the 1960s. It is thought that this awareness stemmed from growing up with the strident rhetoric of the feminism debates that raged in the pages of San Antonio's *La Prensa* throughout the 1920s and '30s. This debate pitted the traditional views held by the paper's male editors against the emerging feminism of its many female editorial writers (notably Antonieta Rivas Mercado), short fiction writers, and poets. The community of intellectual Mexican exiles in San Antonio, called "el México de Afuera" by Ignacio Lozano, became a microcosm of the larger implications of this debate. One of their outlets was *La Mujer Moderna,* published in San Antonio by Teresa and Andrea Villarreal and the Club Liberal. As Professor Juanita Luna Lawhn has pointed out, "by the second half of the 1920s, the selection of feminist essays published in San Antonio in the *Sección del Hogar y La Sociedad* (of *La Prensa*) broke the silence of the women of *El México de Afuera*." Similarly, the "*crónicas femeninas*" of María Luisa Garza (writing under the pseudonym Loreley), published in the Texas-Mexican newspaper *El Imparcial de Texas*, along with her feminist novels published by the Quiroga Company of San Antonio, were very popular among Latinas of this generation on both sides of the border.

Emma Tenayuca, born in San Antonio in 1916, became the living embodiment of the revolutionary spirit when, in 1938, she led over twelve thousand Mexican American workers in a labor strike that paralyzed San Antonio and much of South Texas. Known for her fiery rhetorical skills, she was a brilliant political writer. Like Ricardo Flores Magón twenty years before, she identified the Mexican revolutionary overthrow of political oppression with the fight facing Mexican Americans against capitalist exploitation of labor. We have included one of Tenayuca's essays here that prefigures by thirty years both Cesar Chávez and Martin Luther King in her call for civil rights.

Graham Greene arrived here in 1939, as the Mexican Revolution was winding down. He stayed in the Plaza Hotel (now the Granada, a home for the elderly) on the river at South St. Mary's Street. Greene described the city as "Edenic" and particularly enjoyed "loitering on a bridge above the little tamed river." He found San Antonio a peaceful respite from what was going on in the rest of his life. Greene was headed for Mexico, supposedly to escape from a libel suit against him which 20th Century Fox Studios had filed on behalf of Shirley Temple. This was the 1930s, and Shirley Temple was not someone to mess around with. But whatever the reason, Greene headed into Mexico and came back with one of his greatest works, *The Power and the Glory*. He also wrote what has been described as one of the best travel guides ever written, *Another Mexico*, published in England as *The Lawless Roads*. In this work, he describes San Antonio as being half Mexican and half Will Rogers. Greene definitely fared better than Ambrose Bierce, who stopped in San Antonio in November 1913 before riding into Mexico "to see the fighting." Never seen in the flesh again, Bierce inspired Carlos Fuentes's 1985 novel, *The Old Gringo*.

The Rosengrens' Story

Meanwhile, another literary legend was in the making. That story begins in Chicago, where Frank and Florence Rosengren ran a rare bookstore. The Rosengrens had one child, Frank Jr., affectionately known as Figgi. After the Rosengrens returned from a European book-buying tour in 1934, they discovered that Figgi's bronchial condition was such that a relocation was required at once. One of Rosengren's best customers throughout the 1920s had been

Harry Hertzberg, a founding director of the public library here, who described San Antonio to Florence as "one of the most beautiful and healthiest places on earth." Thus the good air of San Antonio called yet another writer south.

Rosengren's Books opened in 1935 on the sixth floor of the Milam Building downtown, one of the first office buildings in the country to be fully air-conditioned. When the shop opened, San Antonio book lovers must have imagined they had all died and gone to some sort of bibliophilic heaven. The shelves were packed with first editions of works by Johnson, Blake, Shelley, Keats, Fielding, Richardson, and Goldsmith. Tennyson, Brontë, and Yeats were considered "moderns," but were acceptable. There was even a first edition King James Bible.

The Rosengrens soon found, however, that collectors like Hertzberg were, in Texas, rarer than the books they sought. About six months after opening, they moved the store down to street level, still in the Milam Building, and began selling new books as well as their beloved rare volumes. Their taste in new books was equal to their expertise in rare works, and it was a mark of distinction for an author to have a book on their shelves. This was a time when booksellers actually read books, and one could be certain that if a book did not meet with Frank and Florence's approval, it would not be found on their shelves, no matter what its sales potential.

During the height of the Depression, however, retailing new books did not make much money, so Florence began renting books as well. This was often the only way San Antonio readers could get to read new titles, since the public library was so impoverished that it had stopped buying new books. In quick order, Rosengren's Books became a cultural oasis in South Texas, frequented by professors, writers of every sort, politicians of every stripe, artists, musicians, and most important, readers.

When poet Robert Frost spent the winter of 1938 in San Antonio, he enjoyed many afternoons in Rosengren's, leaving behind him a photograph signed "Wishing to be remembered in the best of bookstores." He was, as the photograph hung in the store for the next forty-nine years, until it closed in September 1987.

Before she died, Florence left a great many of her signed books to the library at Incarnate Word College. The inscriptions in those books give some idea of what Florence did for San Antonio. Willie Morris wrote that Rosengren's was "one of the finest and most admirable bookstores in America." *Texas Observer* founding editor Ronnie Dugger called Florence "the chief guardian of civilization from here to Mexico City." None other than J. Frank Dobie wrote, "Whenever I come to see you, I want to write another book. You give me good medicine." Larry McMurtry loved the store and made certain to have signings there for each of his new books until it closed.

Not a few San Antonio writers either grew up in the store, came of age in the store, or met their spouses in the store. Figgi Rosengren (writing as Frank Duane) himself grew up to write several nationally-produced plays, including "Walls Rise Up," "Guitar," "A Delicate Question," and "Jimmy and the River." Figgi met his wife, Camille, at a book party. Perhaps San Antonio's best known writer during the 1950s was novelist, short story writer, poet, and dramatist Josephina (aka Josefina) Niggli, who wrote her major novel, *Mexican Village*, while living in San Antonio and occasionally working at Rosengren's at the end of World War II.

The Chicano Movement in San Antonio

The Chicano poet Alurista, one of the founders of the Chicano literary movement in the late 1960s, referred to San Antonio throughout his career as *el corazón de Aztlan*, essentially the heart of Chicano culture.[8] Of course, Chicano writers came from all over the country, but Alurista was right, the heart of Chicano literature was San Antonio. It grew from a *pueblo* fully aware of its *mestizaje*—that mixing of Hispanic and indigenous blood and heritage— completely at ease in a bilingual idiom, and with a history intimately connect- ed with political activism, both here and in Mexico. In short, Black writers had their Harlem Renaissance; Chicano writers had San Antonio, San Anto, Yanaguana, San Cuilmas. The *movimiento* here built upon an existing culture with a deep appreciation for oral literature both as entertainment and educa- tion—public and private *declamación* of poetry and the performance of popular history in *corridos* (ballads) were both extremely popular; private *escuelitas* (small "Saturday schools") flourished to preserve and reinforce Mexican traditions and culture, including literature, music, and dance; free public lectures and speeches in Travis Park and San Pedro Park were popular means of exposing children to rhetorical performance and identity politics. The *movimiento* in San Antonio not only produced its own substantial roster of writers, musicians, artists, filmmakers, dramatists, and performers, it drew them from all over the country, and it created pioneering institutions like the Guadalupe Cultural Arts Center, with its major music and literature festivals, juried art shows, sponsored research, and academic conferences.

The first Premio Quinto Sol for Chicano literature went to San Antonian Tomás Rivera in 1970 for his novel, *y no se lo tragó la tierra*, a work which virtually defined Chicano fiction for years to come. This novel, some of which is actually set in San Antonio, portrays in experimentally disconnected vignettes the life of a young South Texas migrant worker. Rivera, a former south Texas migrant worker himself, spent most of the 1970s as an educator in San Antonio. In 1979, he went on to become chancellor of the University of California, where he remained until his untimely death in 1984.

From the beginning of the movement, the hallmark of Chicano/Chicana writing has been a bilingual idiom which involves "code switching" between languages. Hardly an unknown device in English, the technique took on a special importance for Chicano writers. Many of the early masters of code switching were San Antonians and women: Angela De Hoyos, Carmen Tafolla, and Evangelina Vigil.

Chicano literature was certainly one of the most exciting things happening in San Antonio from 1970 through the end of the century. Poet and activist Cecilio García-Camarillo—the "Johnny Appleseed of Chicano publishing"—and his wife, Mia Kirsi Stageberg, began *El Magazín: la Revista del Mexicano de Tejas*. It was a short-lived (nine issues, 1971-1973), slick arts and literary magazine, which proved too expensive to maintain. García-Camarillo followed it up with *Caracol: La Revista de la Raza*, a twenty-five-cent literary and political magazine (printed on newsprint) that ran monthly from 1974 to 1979. *Caracol* became one of the most important Chicano publications of its time, even though it was limited to one thousand copies per month. The editorial board consisted of Cecilio and Mia, poets Angela De Hoyos and Moisés Sandoval,

Alfredo and Susana de la Torre, poet Reyes Cárdenas, artist César Martínez, and future novelist Max Martínez. *Caracol* published the early works of many writers who became mainstays of *movimiento* literature, from all over the country. Perhaps more than any other "little magazine" of the time, it supported women writers and encouraged writers to publish not only in English and Spanish, but in "Tex-Mex"/Caló and Nahuatl (Aztec). In June 1976, *Caracol*, its editorial board, and the national Flor y Canto committee headed by Alurista produced Festival Floricanto Tres, held at the Mexican American Cultural Center, St. Philip's College, Our Lady of Guadalupe Church, Harlondale Civic Center, and Gus García Junior High School. Chicano writers from all over the country came to give readings and discuss the state of the *movimiento*. The 1976 Floricanto was one of a series of such events held across the Southwest, but the San Antonio Floricanto is recalled by many as a particularly crucial moment.

Angela De Hoyos's small publishing company, M&A Editions, and her literary magazine, *Huehuetitlán*, published the first works of several writers, including Tafolla and Vigil. Angela's partner, Moises Sandoval, printed and bound all their publications in their home. Writers like Nephtali De León, Rafael Castillo, José Montalvo, Jesse Cardona, and others coalesced around poet and columnist Ricardo Sánchez's San Antonio bookstore, Paperbacks y Más.

Meanwhile, the Esperanza Peace & Justice Center was founded by a group of activists headed by Graciela Sánchez. Established to advocate for civil rights, LGBTQ rights, economic justice, environmental awareness, and cultural dignity, the Esperanza remains an eloquent voice in support of women, people of color, the LGBTQ community, the working class, and the poor, especially immigrants. The center has also played a major role in preserving westside neighborhoods. Its monthly journal, *La Voz de Esperanza,* edited by Gloria Ramírez, has created an important and unique body of historical material relating to these communities. Bárbara Renaud González broke barriers by becoming a columnist for the *Express-News* and when her novel *Golondrina, Why Did You Leave Me?* (2009) became the first publication in the University of

Texas Press's Chicana Matters series. Numerous writing/performance groups like Mujeres Grandes and Women of Ill Repute Refute came and went (and in some cases came again).

The effect of these individuals' commitment to the arts, especially the literary arts, in San Antonio should not be understated. Sandra Cisneros went on to become the most well known of all Chicana writers. Her novel *Caramelo* became an international bestseller, but she also created the Macondo Foundation, a group of "socially engaged writers," and the Alfredo Cisneros del Moral Foundation, serving Texas writers. Bryce Milligan purchased Wings Press in 1994, which took up where M&A Editions left off, publishing local Chicano/a writers, and expanded it to include over two hundred writers from all over the Americas. In 1995, Milligan, his wife Mary Guerrero Milligan, and De Hoyos edited the first all-Latina anthologies to be published by New York publishing houses, *Daughters of the Fifth Sun* (Riverhead) and *Floricanto Sí: A Collection of Latina Poetry* (Penguin).

Juan Tejeda founded the Conjunto music program at Palo Alto College, and helped to found the Mexican American Studies program there. The director for many years of the GCAC's Tejano Conjunto Festival, Tejeda also wrote *Puro Conjunto, An Album in Words and Pictures: Writings, Posters, and Photographs from the Tejano Conjunto Festival en San Antonio, 1982-1998* (University of Texas Press, 2001). Tejeda and his wife, Anisa Onofre, now publish Aztlan Libre Press. Kathy Vargas, besides being an internationally respected photographer, spent years developing the art program at the University of the Incarnate Word. Her photographs have graced the covers of many books.

An Evolving Literary Community

More than a score of Chicano political, arts, and literary institutions developing in the 1980s and 1990s have been crucial to shaping San Antonio's contemporary arts community, but it must be remembered that San Antonio has *always* been described as having a cosmopolitan culture. Throughout the twentieth century, other streams were flowing. Besides the exciting and often revolutionary Mexican and Mexican-American publishing that occurred here, there were more sedate activities, mainly dedicated to Texas history, folklore, and family memoirs. Joe Oliver Naylor (1893-1955) began Naylor Printing Company in 1921, reincorporated into a book publisher as the Naylor Company in 1935, and produced hundreds of books, some of them quite popular, such as Chris Emmett's *Texas Camel Tales* (1932) or Boyce House's *San Antonio: City of Flaming Adventure* (1949). In 1961, Trinity University purchased Principia Press from Principia College in Illinois, and in 1967 renamed it Trinity University Press. It focused on regional history and academic titles until it was shut down in 1989. The press relaunched in 2002, directed first by poet Barbara Ras, now by Tom Payton. Former *Express-News* reporter and *North San Antonio Times* publisher, Lewis Fisher, founded Maverick Publishing Company in 1996 to focus on regional general-interest nonfiction, producing some forty-five titles. Maverick was purchased by Trinity University Press in 2014.

One of San Antonio's acknowledged midcentury intellectuals—and nothing less than a cultural juggernaut—was artist and writer Amy Freeman Lee. An outspoken liberal art critic with both newspaper and radio columns, Lee was a passionate poetry advocate. In 1941 she took over the reins of the San Antonio Public Library's annual student poetry anthology, *Young Pegasus* (the country's oldest, having begun in 1927), and turned it into a vehicle that continues to inspire thousands of young poets to submit every year. Among those who published in *Young Pegasus Anthology* were novelist Josephina Niggli (in 1928), future mayor Henry Cisneros, and poet Naomi Shihab Nye. At San Antonio College, poet, playwright, and theater critic John Igo was busy inspiring young writers like Rosemary Catacalos, later the first Chicana poet laureate of Texas. Award-winning novelist Robert Flynn was teaching the only university-level creative writing courses in the city—at Trinity University—and one of his students was poet Naomi Shihab Nye. She called the class "unforgettable." Nye, Catacalos, and a few others took up the challenge of being "artists in the schools" in the '70s and succeeded brilliantly at inspiring a generation, even as they wrote their own first books. Meanwhile, New York actor, writer, and rare bookman David Bowen (1930-1998) came to San Antonio in 1966 to help promote HemisFair, opened a rare bookstore in 1973, then started Corona Publishing Company in 1977, which published over one hundred titles.

When it comes to specifically literary creativity, San Antonio has developed a vibrant and well-supported community of writers, publishers, support organizations, academic programs, and performance venues that have created a literary ambiance hard to match elsewhere. Creative writing programs now thrive at both the University of Texas at San Antonio (UTSA) and at Our Lady of the Lake University. UTSA's San Antonio Writers Collection houses the archives of many local writers.

In 2012, San Antonio became the first Texas city to name a poet laureate, when Carmen Tafolla was appointed by then Mayor Julián Castro. The professional selection process involves public nominations, but with a panel of judges from outside the region. Unlike Texas's various "state artist" positions, including poet laureate, the San Antonio poet laureate receives a financial stipend from the city's Department for Culture and Creative Development, along with financial and logistical support for poetry and literacy initiatives created by the poet laureate. The selection process was designed by Rosemary Catacalos, whose long history of advising the city's evolving arts funding mechanisms has proven invaluable. Tafolla was followed as poet laureate by Laurie Ann Guerrero, then Jenny Browne. All three are included in this anthology. One of the permanent initiatives begun during Guerrero's tenure was the establishment of the San Antonio Poetry Archive at Palo Alto College. The state of Texas has named a poet laureate every few years since 1932, predating the US Poet Laureate by five years, but no Texas city had such a position until San Antonio. Following San Antonio's lead, other Texas cities have followed suit. Catacalos, Tafolla, and Guerrero went on to become the first-ever Chicana poets laureate of Texas. Two other San Antonio poets, Jenny Browne and Carol Coffee Reposa, also hold the title of Texas Poet Laureate.

The fact that San Antonio truly is a "literary city" makes it impossible to represent more than a fraction of the city's large number of published writers.

Hilton Ross Greer, the editor of the 1934 Texas anthology *New Voices of the Southwest,* concluded that the task of compiling an anthology inevitably "lays one open to the charge of unforgivable omissions and inexcusable inclusions." Indeed, that responsibility lies with the editor, and here we are, far past the page limit for this little opus, with still so many authors neither mentioned in this introduction nor included in the collection: native son and pioneering naturalist Rudolph Menger; historians and scholars (and often very fine writers) T. R. Fehrenbach, Charles Ramsdell, Frederick C. Chabot, Tomás Ybarra-Frausto, Timothy M. Matovina, Sr. María Eva Flores, Mary Ann Guerra, Jesús F. de la Teja, Gerald E. Poyo, Gilberto M. Hinojosa, Antonia Castañeda, Arturo Madrid, and so many others; activist politician and memoirist María Antonietta Berriozábal; historical fiction writers Margaret Cousins and Marian L. Martinello; novelist David Liss; poet, playwright, critic, and beloved professor John Igo; poet, short story writer, and publisher of Pecan Grove Press Palmer Hall; biographer and critic Ed Conroy; documentary filmmaker, poet, and memoirist John Phillip Santos; poet Frances Treviño Santos; poet Barbara Stanush; short story writer, poet, and folk artist Enedina Casarez Vásquez; poet and activist Trinidad Sánchez; performance poet Anthony "the poet" Flores; fiction writers Pablo Martinez, Franco Mondini, and Rafael Castillo; poet, editor, and short story writer Sheila Sánchez Hatch; poet Victoria García Zapata Klein; children's and young adult authors Jean Flynn, Peni Griffin, Dona Schenker, Xavier Garza, Mary Grace Ketner, and Diane González Bertrand; the anonymous authors of *Los Pastores;* and, well, the list goes on and on and on and I *will* leave some out.

This city, with its winding, still-sleepy river and its story-shrouded springs, its ancient *acequias* and missions—now acknowledged as valued "world heritage" sites—its sacred battle grounds and historic military forts and bases, its several unique neighborhoods and barrios that have produced and been celebrated by generations of writers, its rich heritage of heroism and revolutionary passion, its endlessly celebratory ability to revel in its multiracial, multiethnic, multilingual roots and branches . . . this city is a good place to write.

1. William Bollaert's diary is held in the "William Bollaert Papers, 1841-1849," Dolph Briscoe Center for American History, The University of Texas at Austin. The old woman's mention of the Alamo bells is interesting. In 1772, when the management of Mission San Antonio de Valero was handed over by College of Querétaro to the College of Zacatecas, a complete inventory of the mission indicated no bell tower, but listed three large bells, ranging from 480 to 575 pounds, and four small ones.

2. The best general source on the Coahuiltecans is Thomas N. Campbell's *The Indians of Southern Texas and Northeastern Mexico: Selected Writings of Thomas Nolan Campbell* (Austin: Texas Archeological Research Laboratory, 1988). Much more detailed information can be found in the Smithsonian Institution Bureau of American Ethnology's Bulletins. See Bulletin 127, *Linguistic Material from the Tribes of Southern Texas and Northeastern Mexico* (1940), by John R. Swanton. This single slim volume contains virtually the entire extant vocabularies of the Coahuilteco, Comecrudo, Cotoname, Maratino, Aranama, and Karankawa languages.

3. The Indigenous Cultures Institute (San Marcos, Texas) was founded in 2006 by members of the Miakan/Garza Band, whose family stories reach back to the arrival of the Spanish. Another organization, American Indians in Texas at the Spanish Colonial Missions, was founded in 1994 by members of the Tap Pilam Coahuiltecan Nation to promote economic development, cultural programs, advocacy for rights, and linguistic research and restoration. Directed by Ramón Sánchez, AIT maintains a growing research collection.

4. Originally published in *Again for the First Time* (Tooth of Time Press, 1984; 30th anniversary edition by Wings Press, 2013).

5. Originally published in *This River Here: Poems of San Antonio,* by Carmen Tafolla (Wings Press, 2014).

6. For an in-depth analysis of the role San Antonio played in the evolution of Latino/Hispanic political thought throughout the nineteenth century, including the history of early printing in Texas, see *A World Not to Come: A History of Latino Writing and Print Culture*, by Raúl Coronado (Harvard University Press, 2013).

7. Julius Berends opened his bookstore and stationer's shop in 1854, but sold it in 1874 to one of his employees, Nic Tengg. Tengg had four sons, all of whom worked in the store for most of their lives. A Mr. E. E. Cervantes worked there for seventy-four years, until he was ninety-two. The store shut down in 1962 (?) when the Groos National Bank bought the land and turned it into a parking lot.

8. Aztlan is a place, a concept, and a symbol. As the original homeland of the Aztecs, it has been identified with several places, the most likely being near the Great Salt Lake in Utah. For the Chicano movement of the 1960s-1980s, it was a geopolitical concept encompassing all of the Southwest—all the land stolen from Mexico under the 1848 "Treaty" of Hidalgo. Aztlan's symbolic value was as a spiritual homeland, a value it retains in Chicano literature to this day.

A Comecrudo Dancing Song

Kuana´ya we´mi kewa´naya wer´me
We´wanakua´naya we´mi
E´we paskue´l pe-a-una´ma.
(Deer comes does not leave the mountain)

Nuewa´na kuana´ya, kuana´ya we´mi
Nu´e e´we paskue´l pe´-auna´ma.

Kere name nu´we seyota´-i-ye kerena´mi.
 (word of the singer)

A´xpepola´mla a´x mel,
(water – a gush water – is thrown)
Ape´l xi´, a´ yohue´l.
(clear sky, water-clouds)

Ke´tseyo´ wene´ yawa´ye; ke´tso wana´ye yeketso weni´ gawa´ye.

Yeke´rena wena´payo we´na, yawe´ye ke´rena wena´peyo we´na.
(whirling)

Semeye´no weno´ weka´payo weno´.
(it continues the ground smelling)

Newe ma´eyo´ wena newe´ ela´r eup wema´.
 (is entering on the mountain)
Pa-iwe´uni newe´ mleta´-u pa-iwe´uni
(goes skipping about deer above goes skipping about)

Ewe´ yekerena´ wena´ payo´wen.
(deer being alive)

The Comecrudo Indians were a Coahuiltecan people who lived along the southern Rio Grande. American ethnologist A. S. Gatschet discovered three elderly Comecrudo near Reynosa in 1886 who provided this "dancing song" along with all that we know now of their language. The Comecrudo were closely related to San Antonio's Payaya and other South Texas Coahuiltecan bands, and a song such as this was likely common to most. This text (twenty-three lines total) is the sole example of a poetic text from this region in an indigenous language. Only portions of it are translatable. What is known is provided.

PART ONE

HISTORICAL WRITING

FRANK W. JENNINGS

Frank W. Jennings (1917-2009) was born in Missoula, Montana, but spent much of his long life in San Antonio. He served in the US Army and the US Air Force, retiring as a Lieutenant Colonel in 1972, then working in the Office of the Secretary of the Air Force until 1985. From 1959 to 1985, he wrote the twice-monthly *Air Force Policy Letter for Commanders* (the Blue Letter). Prior to that he had written for the *Air Force News* Service, and was famous for having coined the term "aerospace" in 1957. In 1984, Jennings received the Citation of Honor from the Air Force Association for making a "major contribution to the effectiveness of the Air Force and the national security of America."

In 1988, he began writing articles on San Antonio history for several publications, including the *San Antonio Light*, the *San Antonio Express-News*, and *Texas Highways*, magazine. The editor of this volume spent many mornings with Frank in the 1990s, visiting missions and springs, bridges and historical trees, while discussing the history and the literature of San Antonio. It was Frank's desire to publish the most complete history of the city since the 1959 classic, *San Antonio: An Historical and Pictorial Guide*, by Charles Ramsdell. Frank's *San Antonio, The Story of an Enchanted City* was published by the *San Antonio Express-News* in 1998. He was particularly pleased to be able to include in that book several poems by San Antonio poets.

NAMING SAN ANTONIO

THE EVENTS, AS WELL AS THE MODERN COM-memoration, of two historic days often get confused in our town. The naming of San Antonio and the founding of the settlement occurred on two different days, 27 years apart. The anniversary of the naming of San Antonio, the first time people with Spanish lineage came here, and the birthday observance of the "founding" of San Antonio deserve distinction.

San Antonio was given its name on June 13, 1691, because that was the feast day of St. Anthony of Padua—and the day that a Spanish expedition came to the river they called Rio San Antonio. But San Antonio was not founded until 1718, when its first mission and first presidio were established at San Pedro Springs. San Antonio's 250th birthday, the anniversary of the founding of the settlement, was celebrated in 1968, when San Antonio held its world's fair, HemisFair '68.

Two men wrote accounts of how San Antonio got its name; both men were present at the time. One, Father Damian Massanet wrote in his diary on June 13, 1691:

> On this day, there were so many buffaloes that the horses stampeded and 40 head ran away. These were collected with the rest of the horses by hard work on the part of the soldiers. We found at this place the rancheria of the Indians of the Payaya nation. This is a very large nation and the country where they live is very fine. I called this place San Antonio de Padua, because it was his day. In the language of the Indians its is called Yanaguana. . . . I ordered a large cross set up [on the 14th], and in front of it built an arbor of cottonwood trees, where the altar was placed. All the priests said mass. High mass was attended by Governor Don Domingo Teran de los Rios, Captain Don Francisco Martinez, and the rest of the soldiers. . . . The Indians were present during these ceremonies. . . . Then I distributed among them rosaries, pocket knives, cutlery, beads and tobacco. I gave a horse to the captain [the Payaya chief].

Domingo Teran de los Rios, the leader of the expedition and governor of Coahuila y Texas, mentioned above by Father Massanet, also wrote an account of the discovery and naming of the place:

> On the 13th, our royal standard and camp moved forward in the aforesaid easterly direction. We marched five leagues over a fine country with broad plains—the most beautiful in New Spain. We camped on the banks of an arroyo, adorned by a great number of trees, cedars, willows, cypresses, osiers, oaks, and many other kinds.

This I called San Antonio de Padua, because we had reached it on his day. Here we found certain rancherias in which the Payaya nation live. We observed their actions, and I discovered that they were docile and affectionate, were naturally friendly, and were decidedly agreeable toward us. I saw the possibility of using them to form reducciones [Indians submitting to mission life]—the first on the Rio Grande, at the presidio, and another at this point.

A second expedition to the Rio San Antonio arrived on April 13, 1709. Father Isidro Felix de Espinosa, accompanied by Father Antonio Olivares, came to the northern reaches of New Spain with an expedition led by Captain Pedro de Aguirre, commander of the presidio of the Rio Grande del Norte.

Father Espinosa wrote:

We crossed a large plain in the same direction, and after going through a mesquite flat and some holm-oak groves we came to an irrigation ditch, bordered by many trees and with water enough to supply a town. It was full of taps or sluices of water, the earth being terraced. We named it San Pedro Spring (agua de San Pedro) and at a short distance we came to a luxuriant growth of trees, high walnuts, poplars, elms, and mulberries watered by a copious spring which rises near a populous rancheria of Indians of the tribes of Siupan, Chaulaames and some Sijames, numbering in all about 500 persons, young and old. The river, which is formed by this spring, could supply not only a village but a city, which could easily be founded here because of the shallowness of said river. This river not having been named by the Spaniards, we called it the river of San Antonio de Padua.

Finally, nine years later in 1718, an expedition led by Don Martin de Alarcon, Governor of Coahuila y Texas, reached this same area. The diarist of the group, Father Francisco Celiz, wrote about San Pedro Springs that, "in this place of San Antonio is a spring of water which is about three-fourths of a league from the principal river. In this location, in the very spot on which the villa of Bejar was founded, it is easy to secure water, but nowhere else."

On the first of May 1718, Father Antonio Olivares, a Franciscan missionary, established the mission of San Antonio de Valero which had been founded by the governor "about three-fourths of a league down the creek" from the presidio. Celiz continued:

> On the 5th of May, the governor, in the name of his Majesty, took possession of the place called San Antonio, establishing himself in it, and fixing the royal standard with the requisite solemnity, the father chaplain having previously celebrated mass, and it was given the name of villa de Bejar. This site is henceforth destined for the civil settlement and the soldiers who are to guard it, as well as the site for the mission.
> . . .

So that's how San Antonio was named in 1691 and founded officially on May 1, 1718—the date it celebrates its birthday. ★

———

Works Cited

Almaraz, Felix D. *The San Antonio Missions and their System of Land Tenure*. Austin: University of Texas Press, 1992.

Chabot, Frederick, *San Antonio and Its Beginnings, 1691-1731*. San Antonio: Artes Graficas Printing Co., 1936.

De la Teja, Jesus. *San Antonio de Bexar: A Community on New Spain's Northern Frontier*. Albuquerque: University of New Mexico Press, 1995.

Ramsdell, Charles. *San Antonio: A Historical and Pictorial Guide*. Austin: University of Texas Press, 1959.

Robles, Vito Alessio. *Coahuila y Texas en la época colonia*. Mexico City: Editorial Cultura, 1938; 2d ed., Mexico City: Editorial Porrúa, 1978.

———

Maury Maverick Sr.

Maury Maverick Sr. (1895–1954) was born in San Antonio, the eleventh child of Albert Maverick and Jane Lewis Maury Maverick. Albert owned a real estate and land office in the downtown Maverick Building; Jane ran their Sunshine Ranch and was important in civic affairs. Maury's grandfather was Texas Ranger, politician, businessman, and memoirist Samuel Maverick Jr.; his great-grandfather was Yale-educated early Texas politician and land baron Samuel Augustus Maverick, who fought in the 1835 siege of Bexar and signed the Texas Declaration of Independence. When it comes to Texas lineage, the Mavericks are in a class by themselves.

Maury Maverick Sr. graduated from college and law school at the University of Texas. He was commissioned as a First Lieutenant in the Twenty-Eighth Infantry, First Division, US Army, and received a Silver Star for actions in the Battle of the Argonne. Maury served as US congressman from the Twentieth District (1935–38), where he organized a group of "maverick" legislators who sponsored legislation to "out-New Deal" FDR's New Deal. His 1937 autobiography, *A Maverick American*, was something of a Depression-era bestseller. As the mayor of San Antonio (1939–41), he was long admired for his reform-minded administration. Among the many progressive acts in his life—which included securing WPA funds for the initial development of the San Antonio Riverwalk—he was proudest of the restoration of La Villita, preserving the two-hundred-year-old Spanish village as a modern city grew up around it. "The Wrong Side of the River" is from a WPA-sponsored publication, *Old Villita* (1939). A new edition of *Old Villita* (Wings, 2018), expanded and illustrated by Lynn Maverick Denzer, will help celebrate the Tricentennial of San Antonio.

The Wrong Side of the River,
from Old Villita

Tradition says that during the next few years La Villita—linked inseparably to Mission San Antonio de Valero because it was the *villa* of its soldiers—was a poor little district of adobe huts, whose yards and gardens alone were pretentious. Difficulties beset the struggling, isolated Spanish outpost: shipments of food and clothing, of *pesos* due the soldiers, were few and disappointing when they did come. Yet the plight of the soldiers' families was not emphasized until the morning of March 9, 1731, when fifteen families from the Canary Islands marched in—and were promptly given the title of *Hidalgos*, "sons of noble lineage," by a grateful King who had long despaired of colonizing this wilderness with permanent settlers. The titled *isleños* (islanders) founded the royal *Villa of San Fernando* across the river from the Villa de Bexar, on present-day Main and Military Plazas. At once the newcomers adopted an attitude of isolation, closing their homes to the folk from the "wrong side of the river," thus inaugurating a class distinction that was to rankle for many years.

The Rev. Mother Louis (Morin) of the Ursuline Academy, on Navarro Street, is descended from the Curbellos—one of the original sixteen Canary Island families brought to San Antonio. She said (in 1939) that Señor Juan Curbello built his residence on property later known as Bowen's Island—where the thirty-one-story Smith-Young Tower now stands—and that this district, close to Villita Street, was devoted to small "farms" or gardens where flowers and vegetables were raised. Mother Louis said:

> Villita was built for the soldiers and their wives: the Canary Islanders were considered noble people and the soldiers' families, common people; and the soldiers' quarters were thus in a different place from that given to the aristocratic Islanders of the San Fernando settlement.

Sturmberg, in his *History of San Antonio and of the Early Days in Texas,* wrote:

> In following this narrative it is well to bear in mind that the Mission San Antonio de Valero and the village San José de Alamo located on the east side of the river; and the city of San Fernando and the Presidio de Bexar, located on the west side of the river, constituted two different communities, each having their own civil administration. They even had trouble about their respective water rights for irrigation purposes.

San Fernando was the capital of the province of Texas, and its grandees led a gay, luxurious life as compared with the humble existence on the east side of the river. Gregorio Esparza told of the folk who lived in the *jacales:*

> We were of the poor people. . . . to be poor in that day meant to be very poor indeed—almost as poor as the Savior in His manger. We were not dissatisfied with it. . . . There was time to eat and sleep and look at growing plants. Of food we had not overmuch chile and beans, beans and chile.

Evil days fell upon the people of the San Antonio Valley, rich and poor alike, between 1731 and 1750. The Apaches, stirred to fury by the coming of more white men to their old hunting ground, made raid after raid upon the settlements of the King. Horses and burros were stolen from off the very streets of Bexar, and finally, on June 30, 1745, the warriors planned to burn the presidio and wipe out the twin Villas. A boy of the mission gave the alarm, and at once the soldiers and neophytes of San Antonio de Valero went into action. Castañeda, in *Our Catholic Heritage in Texas, 1519-1936,* Vol. III, describes the event:

> One hundred mission Indians came to the rescue and so stoutly did they attack the invaders that they were soon put to flight. The soldiers and Indians now gave chase.... The fate of Fort St. Louis (La Salle's fort in Texas) might have been the fate of San Antonio had it not been for the timely aid of the mission Indians of Valero ...

A quarrel caused by the policies of a new governor, Carlos Franquis de Lugo, soon developed between the religious authorities of the mission settlement and the civil heads of San Fernando. This controversy became serious when the governor ordered the mission guards removed. Growing ill feeling was climaxed in the autumn of 1736 when the padre in charge at the mission attempted to close the one small bridge over the river that connected the two Villas. It is recorded that the governor, who had heard that even he was barred from the narrow span, crossed the bridge in heated defiance, faced the padre in his cell, and threatened to send the missionary back to Mexico "packed on a mule." Father Mariano de los Dolores, the rebellious priest, was forced to leave the bridge open, but retaliated by closing the church of the mission to San Fernando's faithful. Mission guards were not restored until 1737.

In 1762 Mission San Antonio de Valero was in its zenith. Those dependent upon its bounty drew from the resources of the mission rancho, described as having "one hundred and fifteen gentle horses, one thousand one hundred fifteen head of cattle, two thousand three hundred sheep and goats, two hundred mares, fifteen jennets and eighteen saddle mares." (From *Documentos para la Historia de la Provincia de Tejas*, pp. 163-167.)

In that year the walls of the chapel of the mission collapsed, a symbolic event, for the fortunes of the mission flock were never again to rise. The following year, 1763, a plague decimated the ranks of priests, neophytes, soldiers and settlers. Of this era Sturmberg wrote:

> The decline of the Mission San Antonio de Valero proceeded very rapidly from 1763 on. The savage Indians preferred to follow the French doctrine—preferred the wild and easy life to the orderly life of the mission. The older, converted Indians and their children soon acquired the habits of the soldiers and their families; many of them moved out of the mission into the Villita San José de Alamo and their children married with the children of the Mexican soldiers.

Indications are that by this time the region of La Villita was peopled not only by families attached to the mission, but by soldiers of the Presidio of Bexar, a royal garrison maintained for the protection of the Villa of San Fernando and the older mission settlement. In his diary Fray Gaspar de Solis, in 1767, tells only of soldiers attached to the Presidio. Yet the Villa of San Fernando still frowned upon La Villita as the home of less aristocratic Spaniards, the home, as Rodriguez says, of the families of soldiers. Solis, by the way, wrote a remarkable description of the San Antonio River in this area:

> The road from the presidio is wooded with mesquite, huisaches, pin oaks and oaks. The river contains fish: barbos, piltontes, seafish, sardines, eels and others. In these woods ... are great numbers of cattle and horses, many animals such as deer, wolves, coyotes, rabbits, and now and then a lion, some wild cats, wild boar along the banks of the river, blue ducks, geese, turkey, ... screech owls which do not call like those outside, but have a different manner of screeching ...

The historian Bancroft tells of a 1778 law which dealt a telling blow to the mission and its dependents. The measure provided that all unbranded cattle were the property of the King of Spain and imposed a fee of four *reales* a head for all such cattle slaughtered. Edward W. Heusinger in *Early Explorations and Mission Establishments in Texas* explains that "Since the wealth of the missions consisted in cattle, which it was impossible to herd together and brand, this double-toothed law practically obliged them to pay four reales apiece for the right to slaughter their own cattle raised on their own lands."

Records disclose that in 1785 the two settlements of San Antonio—that on the east side of the river, including La Villita, and that on the west side, the Villa of San Fernando—became one civil unit under an alcalde—a sort of justice of the peace and mayor combined. Until this year, La Villita and all the mission settlement had been under the jurisdiction of the padres.

A movement was now under way for the abandonment of the missions and the secularization of their lands. The Count Revilla Gigedo in his report as Viceroy said, "Neither our acquisitions nor the number of Indians congregated in the actual mission towns do by any means justify the enormous outlay incurred, nor the fatiguing labors undergone by the missionary fathers." In 1790 there arrived in San Antonio refugees from the Presidio of los Adaes, in east Texas, and to these victims of French aggrandizement many of the lands formerly held by Mission San Antonio de Valero were distributed, including, as old land records disclose, lots in the present area of La Villita. By 1793 the mission beside the San Antonio River had been abandoned, and the families who had lived so near it, obedient to its bells, lost their separate identity and became at last simply citizens of Bexar, as this Spanish town was most commonly known.

Speaking of the San Antonio of 1793, Sturmberg wrote:

> On the south side of our present-day Gas and Electric Company's plant where there are two bridges, there was located the principal ford for wagons and riders on horseback. For the convenience of the general public a log was thrown across the narrowest part of the stream. . . . Where Villita Street begins or ends on South Alamo Street, there was the main part of the Villita. After crossing the stream one entered at once into the city of San Fernando. . . . Houses were built closely together; they were all the one-story kind and topped with flat roofs. The construction was the only practical one for warding off the attacks of savage Indians. . . . The combined population of the city and Villita never exceeded 2,000 or 3,000 souls, whilst at times, it fell below those numbers. . . . The peninsula, formed by the river and extending to the Alamo, was called Protero. There was also a collection of houses around the Mission San Antonio de Valero (the Alamo) and extending to the Villita.

And now the "Little Town," safe so long under the protection of the padres and their soldiers, was thrust out into the often turbulent life of the city beyond the river. ★

ZEBULON PIKE

Everyone knows about the 1804 journey of Lewis and Clark to explore the upper reaches of the Missouri River and find a pathway to the Pacific Ocean. Less well known is the 1806-1807 journey of Zebulon Pike (1779-1813) to seek out the headwaters of the Arkansas and Red Rivers. Pike set out from St. Louis, made his way across the plains to the Rocky Mountains (where he named but failed in his attempt to climb Pike's Peak), then headed south toward Santa Fe. Spanish spies in the US had warned General Nemesio Salcedo y Salcedo, commander of the northern provinces of New Spain, that an armed expedition was about to enter Spanish territory. Lieutenant Don Facundo Melgares was ordered to intercept Pike, arrest him and his force, and bring them to Chihuahua, Mexico. A troop of Spanish cavalry found Pike not far from Taos, and escorted him to Santa Fe. Melgares then escorted the Americans all the way to Chihuahua, then north again to San Antonio, eventually bringing him to the US border on the Sabine River near Natchitoches, Louisiana.

Given the Spanish penchant for jailing and often executing trespassers, Pike was expecting the worst. Amazingly, Pike and his men were treated more like guests than prisoners through most of their long journey. They were welcomed in San Antonio with an all-out fiesta. Pike was particularly impressed that governors Herrera and Cordero wandered so freely among their people, dancing with individuals "who in the day time would approach them with reverence and awe."

Pike's reports, published soon after his return to the US, celebrated the beauty and richness of the western lands, as well as the cordiality of the people. The Spanish authorities were aware of the temptation that such reports might present to land-hungry Americans, and so had confiscated Pike's papers. He kept secret notes, however, which were hidden (among other places) in the barrels of his men's muskets, which the Spanish had thoughtfully allowed his men to retain. Pike's writings about the region were largely responsible for the surge of interest in Texas that rapidly led to Moses and Stephen F. Austin's colonization efforts, and ultimately to the Texas Revolution.

An Unexpected Fiesta, 1806

7TH June [1806], Sunday.—Came on 15 miles to the river Mariano [Medina], the line between Texas and Cogquilla [Coahuila]—a pretty little stream, Rancho. From thence in the afternoon to Saint Antonio [San Antonio]. We halted at the mission of Saint Joseph [San José]—received in a friendly manner by the priest of the mission and others.

We were met out of Saint Antonio about three miles by governors Cordero and Herrara, in a coach. We repaired to their quarters, where we were received like their children. Cordero informed me that he had discretionary orders as to the mode of my going out of the country: that he therefore wished me to choose my time, mode, &c. and, that any sum of money I might want was at my service: that in the mean time Robinson and myself would make his quarters our home; and that he had caused to be vacated and prepared a house immediately opposite for the reception of my men. In the evening his levee was attended by a crowd of officers and priests, at which was Father McGuire and Dr. Zerbin. After supper we went to the public square, where might be seen the two governors joined in a dance with people, who in the day time would approach them with reverence and awe.

We were here introduced to the sister of lieutenant Malgares's wife, who was one of the finest women we saw—she was married to a captain [Joaquín] Ugarte, to whom we had letters of introduction.

9th June, Tuesday.— A large party dined at governor Cordero's, who gave as his first toast, "The President of the United States."—Vive la—I returned the compliment by toasting "His Catholic Majesty." These toasts were followed by "General Wilkinson," and one of the company then gave, "Those gentlemen; their safe and happy arrival in their own country—their honorable reception, and the continuation of the good understanding which exists between the two countries."

11th June, Thursday.— Preparing to march to-morrow. We this evening had a conversation with the two governors, wherein they exhibited an astonishing knowledge of the political character of our executive [Thomas Jefferson], and the local interests of the different parts of the union.

13th June, Saturday.— … It may not be improper to mention here, something of father McGuire and doctor Zerbin, who certainly treated us with all imaginable attention while at Saint Antonio. The former was an Irish priest, who formerly resided on the coast above Orleans, and was noted for his hospitable and social qualities. On the cession of Louisiana, he followed the standard of the "king, his master," who never suffers an old servant to be neglected. He received at Cuba an establishment as chaplain to the mint of Mexico, whence the instability of human affairs carried him to Saint Antonio. He was a man of chaste classical taste, observation and research.

Doctor Zerbin formerly resided at Natchez, but in consequence of pecuniary embarrassments emigrated to the Spanish territories. Being a young man of a handsome person and insinuating address, he had obtained the good will of governor Cordero, who had conferred on him an appointment in the king's hospital, and many other advantages by which he might have made a fortune; but he had recently committed some very great indiscretions, by which he had nearly lost the favor of colonel Cordero; but whilst we were there he was treated with attention. ★

Andrea Castañón Villanueva (Madam Candelaria)

In the 1880s and 1890s, journalists realized that the last eyewitnesses to the Battle of the Alamo were dying off. Of course, some eyewitnesses told better stories than others. One of the most sought-after was Andrea Castañón Villanueva, widow of Candelaria Villanueva, who had fought with Colonel Juan Seguin. Madam Candelaria, as she came to be known, claimed to have been born in 1785, making her 113 at the time of her death in 1899. There is some evidence that she was actually born in 1803. There are several newspaper interviews with her, all conducted in Spanish, and the quality of the translators may account for the fact that her accounts are inconsistent in several details. Her accounts also differ with the reports of other eyewitnesses in regard to where Travis, Crockett, and Bowie were located at the times of their deaths. (Compare the account of Francisco Ruiz.)

A popular character in San Antonio throughout the century, Madam Candelaria was known for her generosity, adopting as many as twenty-two orphans and often providing shelter in her hotel for stranded travelers. Few of her contemporaries doubted her tale, and many visitors to San Antonio came specifically to visit her.

The interview below first ran in the *St. Louis Republic*. When Candelaria died later that year, the story was picked up by the *San Antonio Light*, with the headline "ALAMO MASSACRE: As Told by the Late Madam Candelaria. Her Vivid Story of the Great Battle, Where 177 Brave Men Met Death as True Heroes—Colonel Bowie Died in Her Arms—Blood Was Ankle Deep." This version of Madam Candelaria's story was selected because it has the longest direct quotations from this gifted storyteller who had become a tourist destination in her own right.

The Fall of the Alamo
February 19, 1899

Old Madam Candelaria says that she has heard and read a hundred different descriptions of the battle of the Alamo and that not one is correct. Although she is now in her one hundred and sixteenth year, her health is good and her mind is perfectly clear as to events that transpired in the early part of the century. Her great age and the conspicuous and heroic part that she enacted during the famous siege of the Alamo are matters that are well authenticated and beyond all question of doubt. A few years ago, the Texas Legislature appointed a committee to wait upon this very remarkable woman and investigate all the facts connected with her claims upon the gratitude of the state. After examining many witnesses and looking over the records preserved in the old missions, they reported that no doubt could exist as to the fact that Madam Candelaria was inside the walls of the Alamo engaged in nursing Colonel James Bowie at the time the battle was fought and further declared that they believed she was born in the year A.D. 1782. Acting upon this report and prompted by a commendable desire to promptly recognize and reward the services of one who had done so much to aid in the establishment of the old republic, the legislature granted a pension of one hundred dollars a year to this heroic old lady.

Madam Candelaria is still alive and living in a small adobe house at 611 Laredo Street, San Antonio. Nothing pleases her better than to receive a visitor who manifests interest in her story of the fall of the Alamo. She is totally blind and though rather feeble and somewhat slow and hesitating in the use of the English language, she manages through rapid and emphatic gestures, occasionally assisted by a Spanish girl who is constantly by her side, to give an attentive listener a very impressive description of one of the most remarkable battles ever fought in the history of the world. . . .

Though every drop of her blood is Spanish blood, she has never loved Spain, from the fact that her father's family was forcibly moved to Texas from the Canary Islands about the middle of the last century for the purpose of carrying out a colonization scheme concerning which her people were never consulted. . . .

In 1836 she kept a hotel in San Antonio and her house was always at the disposal of Houston, Austin, Travis, Lamar and such other daring spirits as were at the time committing themselves to the cause of Texas freedom. All of the old warriors knew her well and all of them admired her many fine traits of character and her patriotic devotion to the sacred principles, for maintenance of which many of them afterwards sacrificed their lives. James Bowie had been living in San Antonio for several years, where he was very popular with all classes. The Mexicans, who were still attached to the old country, hoped that he would embrace their cause, from the fact that he had married a beautiful Mexican girl. But the alarm was no sooner sounded than this man of peerless valor offered his services to Texas. When Santa Anna suddenly appeared on the prairies, in sight of San Antonio, at the head of a veteran army of ten thousand men, Colonel Bowie was very sick. Hopeful as all are who are afflicted with consumption, he still felt himself able to discharge the duties of a soldier. He went to the Alamo and declared that he would fight as a private. It was not long before he was confined to his cot. General Houston wrote a letter to Madam Candelaria, which she still possesses, asking her to look after his friend Bowie and nurse him herself. All save Bowie himself realized that the hero was in the last stages of consumption.

When Santa Anna invested the city and drew a cordon of troops around the Alamo, Madam Candelaria was inside the walls. She might easily have returned to her home, but her heart was with the patriots and she determined to remain with them and share their fortunes. Bowie grew worse every day. He was never able to sit up more than a few minutes at any period during the time that the battle was going on. He occupied the little room on the left of the great front door and Madam Candelaria sat by his side. When the firing grew hot he would ask his faithful nurse to assist him to raise himself to the window. He would aim deliberately and after firing would fall back on his cot and rest. One evening Colonel Travis made a fine speech to his soldiers. Madam Candelaria does not pretend to remember what he said, but she does remember that he drew a line on the floor with the point of his sword and asked all who were willing to die for Texas to come over to his side. They all quickly stepped across the line but two men. One of these sprang over the wall and disappeared. The other man was James Bowie. He made an effort to rise, but failed, and with tears streaming from his eyes, he said: "Boys, won't none of you help me over there?" Colonel Davy Crockett and several others instantly sprang towards the cot and carried the brave man across the line. Madam Candelaria noticed Crockett drop on his knees and talked earnestly in low tones to Colonel Bowie for a long time.

"At this time," says the heroic old lady, "we all knew that we were doomed, but not one was in favor of surrendering. A small herd of cattle had been driven inside of the walls and we found a small quantity of corn that had been stored by the priests. The great front door had been piled full of sand bags and there was a bare hope that we might hold out until General Houston sent a reinforcement.

[Madam Candalaria:] There was just 177 men inside the Alamo and up to this time no one had been killed, though cannon had thundered against us and several assaults had been made. Colonel Travis was the first man killed. He fell on the southeast side near where the Menger Hotel stands. The Mexican infantry charged across the plaza many times and rained musket balls against the walls, but they were always made to recoil. Up to the morning of the 6th of March, the cannon had done us little damage, though the batteries never ceased firing. Colonel Crockett frequently came into the room and said a few encouraging words to Bowie. This man came to San Antonio only a few days before the invasion. The Americans extended him a warm welcome. They made bonfires in the streets and Colonel Crockett must have made a great speech, for I never heard so much cheering and hurrahing in all my life. They had supper at my hotel and there was lots of singing, story telling and some drinking. Crockett played the fiddle and he played well if I am any judge of music. He was one of the strangest looking men I ever saw. He had the face of a woman and his manner was that of a young girl. I could not regard him as a hero until I saw him die. He looked grand and terrible standing in the door and fighting a whole column of Mexican infantry. He had fired his last shot and had no time to reload. The cannon balls had knocked away the sand bags and the infantry was pouring through the breech. Crockett stood there swinging something bright over his head. The place was full of smoke and I could not tell whether he was using a gun or a sword. A heap of dead was piled at his feet and the Mexicans were lunging at him with bayonets, but he would not retreat an inch. Poor Bowie could see it all, but he could not raise up from his cot. Crockett fell and the Mexicans poured into the Alamo."

On the morning of the 6th of March 1836, General Santa Anna prepared to hurl his whole force against the doomed fort. The *degüello* [bugle call signifying no quarter] was sounded and Madam Candelaria says that they all very well understood what it meant and every man prepared to sell his life as dearly as possible.

The soldiers with blanched cheeks and a look of fearless firmness gathered in groups and conversed in low tones. Colonel Crockett and about a dozen strong men stood with their guns in their hands behind the sand bags at the front. The cot upon which Colonel Bowie reposed was in the little room on the north side, within a few feet of the position occupied by Crockett and his men. These two brave spirits frequently exchanged a few words while waiting for the Mexicans to begin the battle.

[Madam Candalaria:] I sat by Bowie's side, and tried to keep him as composed as possible. He had a high fever and was seized with a fit of coughing every few moments. Colonel Crockett loaded Bowie's rifle and a pair of pistols and laid them by his side. The Mexicans ran a battery of several guns out on the plaza and instantly began to rain balls against the sand bags. It was easy to see that they would soon clear every barricade from the front door, but Crockett assured Bowie that he could stop a whole regiment from entering. I peeped through the window and saw long lines of infantry, followed by dragoons, filing into the plaza, and I notified Colonel Crockett of the fact. "All right," said he. "Boys, aim well." The words had hardly died on his lips before a storm of bullets rained against the walls and the very earth seemed to tremble beneath the tread of Santa Anna's yelling legions. The Texans made every shot tell and the plaza was covered with dead bodies. The assaulting columns recoiled and I thought we had beaten them, but hosts of officers could be seen waving their swords and rallying the hesitating and broken columns.

They charged again and at one time, when within a dozen steps of the door, it looked as if they were about to be driven back, so terrible was the fire of the Texans. Those immediately in front of the great door was certainly in the act of retiring when a column that had come obliquely across the plaza reached the southwest corner of the Alamo and, bending their bodies, they ran under the shelter of the wall to the door. It looked as if a hundred bayonets were thrust into the door at the same time and a sheet of flame lit up the Alamo. Every man at the door fell but Crockett. I could see him struggling with the head of the column and Bowie raised up and fired his rifle. I saw Crockett fall backwards. The enraged Mexicans then streamed into the building firing and yelling like madmen. The place was full of smoke and the death screams of the dying, mingled with the exultant shouts of the victors, made it a veritable hell. A dozen or more Mexicans sprang into the room occupied by Colonel Bowie. He emptied his pistols in their faces and killed two of them. As they lunged toward him with their muskets I threw myself in front of them and received two of their bayonets in my body. One passed through my arm and the other through the flesh of my chin. Here, Señor, are the scars; you can see them yet. I implored them not to murder a sick man, but they thrust me out of the way and butchered my friend before my eyes. All was silent now. The massacre had ended. One hundred and seventy-six of the bravest men that the world ever saw had fallen and not one had asked for mercy. I walked out of the cell and when I stepped upon the floor of the Alamo the blood ran into my shoes. ★

José Antonio Menchaca

Nineteenth-century Texas gave birth to a lot of tall tales. If everything that José Antonio Menchaca (1800-1879) wrote was factual, then he would have undoubtedly been the Forrest Gump of his age. According to Menchaca, from 1813 on, he was in every battle, at every strategy session, a personal acquaintance of Santa Anna, generous to a fault, beyond magnanimous, able to talk down Comanche chiefs, with a staggering verbatim memory for lengthy speeches and conversations, etc. Unfortunately, many of Menchaca's memories—transcribed by a journalist when Menchaca was near the end of his life—feature historical scenes which do not appear to have actually occurred. But in the latter part of the nineteenth century, there was a ravenous market for such tales, and one man's history was, well, his story.

Menchaca was a fourth-generation descendent of one of the soldiers, Antonio Guerra, who marched north from Monclova, Mexico, to found San Antonio in 1718. Over the next eighty-two years, the family bloodline was cited as mestizo, mulatto, and coyote, thus indicating intermarriage with the local Payaya/Coahuitecan Indians. One of Menchaca's grandfathers has the distinction of having been the first person tried for murder in San Antonio, after he shot a rival for his wife's affections. He was acquitted. Menchaca's family owned land in the barrio del sur, along the western edge of what is today the King William historical neighborhood. He was a witness to the local battles between Spanish and Mexican forces during the Mexican War of Independence in 1812-1813. He is remembered mainly for his role in the Battle of San Jacinto, during which he was promoted to captain under Juan Seguin. After Texas gained independence, Menchaca served on the city council and even as mayor pro tem (1838-1839). After 1848, growing Anglo suppression made such public service increasingly difficult. Still, in his later years Menchaca was active in helping to resolve disputes regarding pension discrimination against Mexican American veterans.

Menchaca wrote down a portion of his memoirs, apparently in collaboration with an Anglo-American journalist or secretary, which are preserved in different states, both printed and in manuscript. The first version to be published appeared in 1907 in a San Antonio weekly magazine, the *Passing Show*, entitled "The Memoirs of Captain Menchaca." Frederick Chabot edited and republished the work as a small book from Chabot's Yanaguana Society, entitled simply *Memoirs*. Scholars Timothy Matovina and Jesús F. de la Teja unearthed a long overlooked manuscript version of the second half of the memoirs at the Briscoe Center for American History at the University of Texas, and produced a remarkably detailed, edited edition of the various versions, *Recollections of a Tejano Life: Antonio Menchaca in Texas History* (University of Texas Press, 2013), from which this excerpt is taken.

After the Alamo . . . 1836–1842 San Antonio
from The Memoirs of Captain Menchaca

[A few days after the Battle of San Jacinto] Next morning at daybreak we heard Filisola's buglers play "Boots and Saddles" on their bugles, and Sherman ordered his own buglers to play the same strain. When we crossed the river and came upon his camp, which was just as the sun rose, it was deserted and nothing but the ashes of his campfires was left. They could not have been very far ahead of us, but we were marching a little more leisurely behind them, than they were in front of us. Houston's orders to Burleson and Sherman had been to avoid bloody battles as long as their enemy retreated in the direction of his own country. And to follow him without pressing him too close.

At ten o'clock Sherman ordered a detachment of ten scouts to ride ahead and see how far off the enemy was. They rode about two or three miles and found 1,000 head of beef cattle lying almost exhausted in the road from hard driving, and they concluded correctly that they had been left behind by Filisola in his hurry to get beyond the reach of Texas powder and lead.

The next day's march brought us to the San Antonio Creek [not the San Antonio River] twelve miles west of the Colorado River, where we halted a week. From here we took up our march to Victoria. . . . We remained at Victoria eighteen days, and during our encampment there we were joined by General Rusk, who came up from San Jacinto with 800 men. A short time after his arrival, Rusk asked me if I would like to go with my men and Seguin's to San Antonio and I told him I would. He said, "There is some risk attendant upon the venture as General Juan José Andrade, with 2,500 men and 30 pieces of artillery, is marching in the direction from San Antonio on his way to Matamoros." I told him I did not feel a bit afraid. He said, "If you fall in with him and get captured, let me know as soon as possible by a courier and I will come to your assistance. I have orders not to fight unless it is necessary, but I would like very much indeed to pitch once more into the Mexicans."

On the road to New Goliad we met Colonel Domingo Ugartechea with an escort of five men on his way to get supplies for Andrade's army. He asked Seguin and me which way we were going with our men, and we said to San Antonio. He said, "I wish to see General Rusk, who is at Victoria, and if you will give me a passport through to him and an interpreter, I will give you one through Andrade's lines to San Antonio." Seguin wrote him a passport and called one of my men, Pedro Flores, and sent him with Ugartechea, and he left us his corporal and a written passport to Andrade and we separated, going in different directions. Our companies halted to prepare their dinner at a little house by the roadside about nine miles from Goliad. And very shortly after we had stopped, the corporal left by Ugartechea came to Seguin and me and informed us that Andrade's command was marching toward us. As Andrade's advance guard came up, some of the officers in front accosted the corporal and asked what he was doing among the Texans, and he explained to them. In the meantime, Andrade and his staff rode up, and Andrade then said, "My corporal informs me that you have a passport from Colonel Ugartechea, let me see it." Seguin handed it to him and he read it and said "You and your command can march ahead to San Antonio undisturbed." Andrade's army marched then by us in silence, and our men kept perfectly silent, too, as they passed on in a regular, slow, and orderly manner. They came to a halt at a creek about a mile beyond us, and about an hour afterwards we took up our march.

BACK TO SAN ANTONIO

After three days more marching, we got into San Antonio and made Múzquiz's house headquarters of our division. We found the city almost deserted.

A great many families who sympathized with the Texas cause moved east, and a great many Mexican families, who either from choice or compulsion espoused the Mexican cause, went to Mexico.

We had returned and remained in town about a week when six Comanche Indians with their chief Casimiro rode into town. They were all horribly filthy and as lean and gaunt as wolves. They asked some of the Mexicans who was in command here, and they were told Seguin and Menchaca. Casimiro said he did not know Seguin but he did know Menchaca, and he came to me and asked me how I came on and I told him very well. He then informed me that he was very hungry (all Indians always are) and wanted something to eat. He also asked me if I did not have something to give him. I told him I would give him aplenty, and I took the key to one of Santa Anna's storehouses, which was full of provisions, and told him to follow me there. I unlocked the door and told him to pitch in and help himself. He ate like a hungry hound with his men and, after they had satisfied the immediate ravings of their appetites, Casimiro began to look around the storehouse. He spied a large sack of bread cooked with lard seasoned with salt and he asked to be permitted to take it with a sack of beans and three strings of peppers, which I agreed to. He then turned to go, but before he left, he looked at me in a very strange, pitying manner and said to me, "Menchaca, I feel a great deal of compassion for you and am truly sorry for you." I asked him why this sudden outburst of pity and compassion and if there was any danger overhanging me. He told me that the Indians intended to come into San Antonio, burn the town, and kill all the people. I said, "Casimiro, this is the worst piece of barbarous ingratitude that I ever heard of. The people of San Antonio have never yet harmed the Comanche and have always fed them when they came and asked for something to eat."

He said, "Menchaca, I have twenty horses, two Mexican prisoners to wait on me, and four wives. If you will come and live with me and my band, I will divide equally with you each of these articles."

I told him I was not quite as well fixed with wives as he was, but still I was satisfied to remain where I was. He said, "Do you intend to stay in San Antonio?"

I said, "I live here, Casimiro, and I am going to get my family, which left during the war, and bring them back."

He said, "How many moons will you be gone?" (Indians reckon time by the number of new moons.) I told him it might take me five or six moons to go and return.

He grunted, "Umph! Good!" and asked me if I had any mescal, and I told him a little and that I would give him six bottles. He then wanted piloncillo (sugar), and I gave him fifty of them. And then I said, "Casimiro, recollect what I have told you about killing people in San Antonio and think of my kindness to you and do not harm them." He and his men then went away.

On 10 June 1836, I left San Antonio to go get my family, who were then at Nacogdoches, and arrived there on 20 July. I remained there with them until 15 August and started with them back to San Antoio.

While we were on the road I heard that 1,500 Comanches on 15 August had been into San Antonio and killed a Mexican woman and two girls and then gone down to San José Mission and there killed two very good men and a lady. On the sixteenth day they came back to San Antonio and dismounted in the Cibolo Square and said they wanted to kill all of the people. Casimiro was their chief and after a while ordered them to ride out of town. He was the last to go, and before he left he told a Mexican to tell me that he had been in town and stayed all day with his band, which wanted to kill everybody in town, and that he had ordered them off without letting them carry out their threats. He asked the Mexican if I was in town, and he told him I was gone to Nacogdoches. One of Casimiro's men said it was so because he had seen me when I got to Nacogdoches. Casimiro then left town.

I did not reach home from Nacogdoches until November 1836. Soon after my arrival General Rusk, who had 4,000 men near Lavaca, sent 300 of them to Seguin and me to protect San Antonio from the Indians, squads of whom we sent out on scouts to fight them. Seguin and I were the commanders of this point as officers of the Texas Republic from 1836 to 1838.

Early in the later year a Colonel Henry Wax Karnes was sent by the president of the Republic to relieve us. He commanded until 1839. Karnes always kept a guard to watch the horses at San José Mission, but in March 1839 a band of Indians from Presidio del Rio Grande captured all of the horses and the two guards who were watching them and took them away.

In September 1830 Colonel Karnes was superseded by Colonel William S. Fisher, who moved his quarters to the San José Mission. A short time after Fisher was placed in command, a band of seven Comanche Indians and their chief wanted to make an overture of peace. Fisher told them they would first have to go and bring him all the Mexican or American prisoners they had. And they told him they would go and return with the prisoners in the course of twenty days. He told his interpreter to tell the chief that if he caught him telling a lie, he would kill him and all of the men he caught with him. The Indians left and returned at the end of twenty days and camped at the spot where the market near Main Plaza now stands. There were about twenty of them, including five women and some children but they did not bring any of the prisoners with them.

Fisher was very indignant when he learned that they had returned without keeping their word to bring the prisoners, and so he determined to teach them a lesson. He took his command and surrounded them and killed every man but one among them, who escaped badly wounded by running down the river, swimming across and following down the timber. He did not kill the women and children but kept them as prisoners.

At the end of three months, a Comanche chief came in unattended by his band. His name was Potsanaquahip, and he offered to exchange five Mexican prisoners for the five Comanche women and the children in the custody of Fisher, to which the latter agreed. Potsanaquhip brought in his prisoners, delivered them up, effected the exchange, and retired with his women and children.

In 1840, while General Lamar was president of the young republic, he had an expedition fitted out that March under General Hugh McLeod, assisted the young José Antonio Navarro, whose father has already been mentioned as one of the former governors of San Antonio under the Spanish regime. The expedition numbered 400 men and was sent to attend to some troubles that were going on out on the Texas border near Paseo del Norte.

They went out there and crossed the Rio Grande and marched into Chihuahua but were attacked and captured after a short engagement by Mexican General Manuel Armijo with 3,000 men and taken prisoners to Veracruz. In September of the same year, Karnes was sent back to San Antonio to organize another exhibition to fight the Indians, who were then very troublesome. The exhibition went to San Saba and had a fight with the Indians in which they killed twenty of the Indians and took from them over 100 horses without losing a single man. The Army of Texas then in this place was disbanded and the discharged soldiers permitted to go to their homes as the government was considered to have been established on a firm basis.

But while there only sixty able-bodied American and Texas men, mostly lawyers and professional men and a great many treacherous Mexicans, in San Antonio, we learned that the Mexicans under a General Rafael Vásquez were coming into San Antonio from Mexico. The sixty Americans who organized and were commended by two lawyers, Barnes and John D. Morris, prepared to defend the town. Vásquez came to the edge of town with 1,500 men in March 1842 and sent word to Barnes and Morris that if they would surrender the town without fighting, the people who chose to leave might be permitted to depart unmolested, but if they did not surrender without firing a shot, he would kill every soul among them. Barnes and Morris held a consultation with the people, and finally agreed to accept the terms offered. Vásquez marched into town, and the Texans and other American people all marched out via the Seguin Road.

Vásquez remained twelve days and then retreated on hearing that 1,500 Texans were after him, who passed through the following day after his departure in hot pursuit after him. They, however, did not overtake him and gave up the chase very soon because Vásquez distanced them so badly. He was in a terrible hurry to get back across the Rio Grande and never stopped longer than necessary before reaching its opposite bank. And the Texans returned through San Antonio to the places from whence they came. ★

SANTIAGO TAFOLLA

Santiago Tafolla was born in 1837 in Santa Fe, New Mexico. His father, an officer in the Mexican Army, was killed during an Indian engagement when Santiago was only three years old. His mother died when he was seven. Being raised by a cruel brother was not to his liking, and so, being of an adventurous disposition, Santiago joined a wagon train returning east. He was eleven years old. In almost no time he found himself in Washington, DC, where he was passed from one family to another, gradually making his way west to Missouri and back to DC. Ever enthusiastic about education, along the way he learned English, shoemaking, tailoring, and other skills, and converted to the Methodist Church. In 1855, he joined the US Army at Fort McHenry in Baltimore, and headed west again, crossing the Red River into Texas on December 14 of that year. The incidents related here occurred in 1856, and present an excellent portrait of frontier life in and around San Antonio. Santiago's autobiography, published as *A Life Crossing Borders: Memoir of a Mexican-American Confederate* (Arte Publico Press, 2010), was translated by his grandson, Fidel, and edited by his great-granddaughters, Carmen and Laura Tafolla.

Later in his life, Santiago (James, by this time) became a Methodist minister and for many years held important pastoral positions on both sides of the Rio Grande. In 1881, he became the Presiding Elder of the San Diego Mexican Mission District, the first time the Methodist Church had ever so honored a minister "of Mexican descent." Twice he was elected by his Conference as Clerical Delegate to the General Conference.

from A LIFE CROSSING BORDERS

THERE WAS A CORPORAL IN OUR COMPANY NAMED Prusia. When the captain [Palmer] left on his trip to San Antonio, he put Prusia in charge of the escort that would accompany him. He left Lt. Mason soon after this noon hour. I happened to be a member of the escort. The soldiers had their canteens filled with whiskey when we left. That night we got to the Llano River and the ranch of a German whose name was Martin. He was a butcher and delivered meat to the troops stationed at Ft. Mason. The captain and his family were invited to Mr. Martin's home and we camped about one hundred yards from the house. Before we went to bed there was a lively discussion among the members of the group. Some insisted it was necessary to put a sentinel on guard while others held that this was not necessary. Among those who argued that there was no danger from the Indians was Corporal Prusia himself. I was in favor of having a sentinel for I felt that, as soldiers, it was our duty to do so. I was more sober than the others. The discussion became so heated that they almost came to blows and Corporal Prusia seemed to be more excited than the rest of us.

As it was dark and we had no other light but the fire, we didn't see the captain start toward us to see what was happening. I was the first one to see him but, according to him, he had been listening for some time and knew everything. As soon as I saw him I gave the order "attention." All stood at attention in military fashion as the officers came to into view. Directing himself to the corporal, he said, "I have been observing your behavior for quite a while and feel that I have made a mistake in selecting my escort for this trip. I thought that Corporal Prusia was one of the best soldiers in my company and I am sorry to find out that not only does he disregard his own safety, but by failing to post sentinel, he shows he does not care about the government property under his charge." He was referring to the fact that we had six saddle horses and six mules that pulled the wagon loaded with the baggage, forage, and provision for the trip. He also had reference to the coach that he and his family rode and the two mules that pulled it. Then addressing himself to me he said, "Tafolla, you take charge of the escort." He then turned away and went back to the house.

Since I had argued during our discussion that I would be willing to keep the first watch of the night, I ordered the men to go to bed and I took the first watch. It was about ten o'clock when I started my watch and at twelve o'clock I woke up another man to go on duty, at two another, and at four another one named Muth.

He was one of those opposed to the watch. I warned him not to sit down telling him, "If you do, you'll go to sleep." Mr. Martin had a great number of pigs on the ranch and all night long we had been driving them away from our camp. Among the captain's belongings was a rocking chair which we had taken down. Our provisions were all around the camp, also a sack of corn for the horses and the mules. Muth pulled all of these things as close to the rocking chair as possible, sat down in it, and was soon fast asleep. About five in the morning, I woke up and saw about fifty pigs in camp. They had eaten all the corn, scattered the provisions and were going round and round Muth and the rocking chair. Just about that time, a big pig got under the chair and upset it with Muth still in it. He woke up scared when he hit the ground saying, "What's the matter? What's the matter?" I answered him, "We are left without provisions and forage for the horses and mules." When the captain came by in the morning he heard the news; I told him all that had happened. "Well," he said, "let us get to Fredericksburg where we can buy provisions." The only article of food that the pigs left intact was the coffee. The distance to Fredericksburg was about twenty-five miles and we got as far as Cibolo Creek by night.

The coach driver, Mr. Jefferson, had been a soldier. The next day we arrived in San Antonio. We camped in the government "corral" (an enclosure for stock) which was next to the Alamo, an historic mission that is still in a good state of preservation at the present time and is known to all of us today as the "Cradle of Texas Liberty."

The area occupied by Alamo Plaza now was then a "chaparral" (mesquite brush). Where the Opera building is now and on the North and South side of the plaza, there were a few "jacales" (huts). These were made of adobe (an unbaked brick of mud and straw), and had thatched roofs made of straw, grass or palm leaves. This was in July 1856. The site occupied by the Menger Hotel today was a mesquite chaparral also. Later the same year, they began to lay the foundation for he great Menger Hotel. This was the very first time I saw the city of San Antonio.

That same year, Capt. Palmer got orders to establish Camp Verde on a creek by that name in Kerr County eleven miles from Kerrville, the county seat of Kerr County, and twelve miles from Bandera Town. Both towns were made up of a few houses and a lumber mill. Barracks for officers and soldiers were erected at Camp Verde, a place that was destined to play an important role in the history of the nation.

It was during that time that the captain selected me to run the mail route from there to Fredericksburg, and to the ranch of a German rancher named Zinc who lived twenty miles from Camp Verde. I ran this route every Friday and these were dangerous days for every now and then the Indians would make raids stealing horses and killing people. I do not know why he chose me for the job; perhaps it was because I was of slight build and not too heavy on the horse. Sometimes on a summer day I would make the trip at night on account of the heat. I was the first to hear about the Indian raids over the countryside. Those occurred either before or after I returned to Camp, but I never met any raiding party face to face.

The captain had a reason for selecting me. One night after the six o'clock roll call, he stood before the company and said, "I want a man to carry a letter to Castroville this very night. Who wants to go? Who knows the road? When no one answered, I said, "I don't know the road but take the dare." He said, "I know you will. Get ready and come to my office for the letter." It must have been about nine o'clock when I left Camp Verde for I arrived at Bandera about eleven that night. I woke up one of the white families at that hour and told them I was a soldier from Camp Verde on an important mission to Castroville. The man came out with a gun in his hands, for in those days no one could leave his house unarmed for fear of the Indians. After he convinced himself that I was acting in good faith, he gave me directions about the road.

I went across the Medina River at this point and at a point ten miles away from Bandera, I crossed the Medina River again, traveled along the river and finally came to a place called Mormon Town. There was a colony of some ten or twelve Mormon families in the village. It must have been about 1:30 a.m. when I arrived and I headed in the direction of a house that was all lighted up. Upon coming closer, I heard music and saw that the people were dancing. I went about ten paces beyond the house and called out "hello." At that moment the music stopped and five or six men with fire arms in their hands—came out to me. After meeting me and learning the purpose of my trip, they invited me into the home and started dancing again. There were about fifteen married or single ladies present and about the same number of men. They were having a good time and everyone appeared joyful and happy. An old gentleman who appeared to be a leader called me over to sit by him and said, "We are celebrating a wedding that just took place in our families." He made me feel welcome and asked me if I wished to dance. I thanked him and told him that I had to be in Castroville at the break of dawn. He ordered some one to feed corn to the horse and took me into another room where there were tables loaded with all kinds of delicious foods imaginable. I did not see any liquor nor any signs of intoxication among the members of the party. This impressed me greatly and I formed a good opinion of the Mormon people. I stayed there about an hour. The old gentleman who acted as my host invited me to stop by on my way back.

I arrived at Castroville about six o'clock in the morning. The letter was addressed to a Mr. Vance and I was given directions to his home. He was in San Antonio at the time but I was informed that he would be back soon after the noon hour. I had no money for food for me or for the horse. I tied the saddled horse to a large oak tree and went to walk around the town. It was one o'clock and I began to get real hungry but about that time Mr. Vance came looking for me and handed me the answer to the message I had brought him. I told him then that I had not eaten and my horse had not been fed either and that I had no money. I asked him if he would be kind enough to feed us and charge the expense to the government as I was on government business. He then told me that the letter I had brought him was in regard to a contract with the government about a shipment of corn which would soon arrive at Camp Verde. He ordered food for me and took care of feeding my horse. It was four o'clock when I left town to return to Camp Verde. About nine o'clock at night I passed through Mormon Town and everything seemed very quiet. Between Mormon Town and Bandera I tied my horse and slept for about three hours. When I got back to Camp Verde the "carretas" (big wheel carts) were already unloading the corn. The captain could have saved me from that trip but since he had the authority to do so, he could send a soldier anywhere he wanted to. Now I get the full meaning of the passage of scripture where the centurion tells the Master about his authority (Math. 8:9) ★

Frederick Law Olmsted

San Antonio has been a "tourist destination" since the first British visitor, William Bollaert, arrived in 1843, specifically to view the scene of the "American Thermopylae." Much of the best nineteenth century literature *about* San Antonio was written by travelers. One of the most quoted descriptions of mid-nineteenth-century San Antonio was by Frederick Law Olmsted. He was on assignment for the *New York Daily Times* to write firsthand accounts of life throughout the American south, including Texas. Olmsted, who would later become famous as the landscape architect who designed New York's Central Park, was a close observer of both geography and culture. He arrived in San Antonio in 1852 as part of his thousand-mile journey through Texas. Five years later, in 1857, Olmsted's account was published as *A Journey through Texas: Or, a Saddle-Trip on the Southwestern Frontier.* A century later, historian Arthur M. Schlesinger Sr. would praise Olmsted's reporting as "the nearest thing posterity has to an exact transcription of a civilization which time has tinted with hues of romantic legend."

Olmsted uses the racial terminology of the time, and assumes certain racial stereotypes as accurate. Thus he—indeed, almost all frontier writers—inevitably sound to twenty-first century ears painfully racist. However, we see that Olmsted is horrified at the admittedly racist depredations carried out by Anglo-American against the Mexican American population, calling it nothing less than "wholesale injustice." He seems pleased to point out that most Mexican citizens of Texas "regard slavery with abhorrence." He also suspects that were they to attempt to exercise their voting rights, they would be met with "summary revolution."

from *A Journey through Texas*

Seven miles from San Antonio we passed the Salado, another smaller creek, and shortly after, rising a hill, saw the domes and white clustered dwellings of San Antonio below us. We stopped and gazed long on the sunny scene.

The city is closely-built and prominent, and lies basking on the edge of a vast plain, through which the river winds slowly off beyond where the eye can reach. To the east are gentle slopes toward it; to the north a long gradual sweep upward to the mountain country, which comes down within five or six miles; to the south and west, the open prairies, extending almost level to the coast, a hundred and fifty miles away.

There is little wood to be seen in this broad landscape. Along the course of the river a thin edging appears, especially around the head of the stream, a short ride above the city. Elsewhere, there is only limitless grass and thorny bushes.

These last, making *chapparal*, we saw as we went further on, for the first time. A few specimens of *mesquit (algarobbia glandulosa)* had been pointed out to us; but here the ground shortly became thickly covered with it. This shrub forms one of the prominent features of Texas, west of San Antonio. It is a short thin tree of the locust tribe, whose branches are thick set with thorns, and bears, except in this respect, a close resemblance to a straggling, neglected peach-tree. Mixed with other shrubs of a like prickly nature, as an undergrowth, it frequently forms, over acres together, an impenetrable mass. When the tree is old, its trunk and roots make an excellent fire-wood; but for other purposes it is almost useless, owing to its bent and tortuous fibre. A great value is said to lie in its gum, which, if properly secured, has been pronounced equal to gum-arabic in utility.

By a wall of these thorns the road is soon closed in. Almost all the roads of entrance are thus lined, and so the city bristles like the porcupine with a natural defense. Reaching the level, we shortly came upon the first house, which had pushed out and conquered a bit of the chapparal. Its neighbor was opposite, and soon the street closed in.

The singular composite character of the town is palpable at the entrance. For five minutes the houses were evidently German, of fresh square-cut blocks of creamy-white limestone, mostly of a single story and humble proportions, but neat, and thoroughly roofed and finished. Some were furnished with the luxuries of little bow-windows, balconies, or galleries.

From these we enter the square of the Alamo. This is all Mexican. Windowless cabins of stakes, plastered with mud and roofed with river-grass, or "tula;" or low, windowless, but better thatched, houses of adobe.

The principal part of the town lies within a sweep of the river upon the other side. We descend to the bridge, which is close down upon the water, as the river, owing to its peculiar source, never varies in height or temperature. We irresistibly stop to examine it, we are so struck with its beauty. It is of a rich blue and pure as crystal, flowing rapidly but noiselessly over pebbles and between reedy banks. One could lean for hours over the bridge rail.

From the bridge we enter Commerce Street, the narrow principal thoroughfare, and here are American houses, and the triple nationalities break out into the most amusing display, till we reach the main plaza. The sauntering Mexicans prevail on the pavements, but the bearded Germans and the sallow Yankees furnish their proportion. The signs are German by all odds, and perhaps the houses, trim-built, with pink window-blinds. The American dwellings stand back, with galleries and jalousies and a garden picket fence against the walk, or rise, next door, in three-story brick to respectable city fronts. The Mexican buildings are stronger than those we saw before, but still of all sorts, and now put to all sorts of new uses. They are all low, of adobe or stone, washed blue and yellow, with flat roofs close down upon their single story. Windows have been knocked in their blank walls, letting the sun into their dismal vaults, and most of them are stored with dry goods and groceries, which overflow around the door. Around the plaza are American hotels, and new glass-fronted stores, alternating with sturdy battlemented Spanish walls, and confronted by the dirty, grim, old stuccoed stone cathedral, whose cracked bell is now clunking vespers, in a tone that bids us no welcome, as more of the intruding race who have caused all this progress, on which its traditions, like its imperturbable dome, frown down.

SAN ANTONIO

We have no city, except, perhaps, New Orleans, that can vie, in point of the picturesque interest that attaches to odd and antiquated foreignness, with San

Antonio. Its jumble of races, costumes, languages and buildings; its religious ruins, holding to an antiquity, for us, indistinct enough to breed an unaccustomed solemnity; its remote, isolated outposted situation, and the vague conviction that it is the first of a new class of conquered cities into whose decaying streets our rattling life is to be infused, combine with the heroic touches in its history to enliven and satisfy your traveler's curiosity.

Not suspecting the leisure we were to have to examine it at our ease, we set out to receive its impressions while we had the opportunity.

After drawing, at the Post-office window, our personal share of the dear income of happiness divided by that department, we strolled, by moonlight, about the streets. They are laid out with tolerable regularity, parallel with the sides of the main plaza, and are pretty distinctly shared among the nations that use them. On the plaza and the busiest streets, a surprising number of old Mexican buildings are converted, by trowel, paint-brush, and gaudy carpentry, into drinking-places, always labeled "Exchange," and conducted on the New Orleans model. About these loitered a set of customers, sometimes rough, sometimes affecting an "exquisite" dress, by no means attracting to a nearer acquaintance with themselves or their haunts. Here and there was a restaurant of a quieter look, where the traditions of Paris are preserved under difficulties by the exiled Gaul.

The doors of the cabins of the real natives stood open wide, if indeed they exist at all, and many were the family pictures of jollity or sleepy comfort they displayed to us as we sauntered curious about. The favorite dress appeared to be a dishabille, and a free-and-easy, loloppy sort of life generally, seemed to have been adopted as possessing, on the whole, the greatest advantages for a reasonable being. The larger part of each family appeared to be made up of black-eyed, olive girls, full of animation of tongue and glance, but sunk in a soft embonpoint, which added a somewhat extreme good-nature to their charms. Their dresses seemed lazily reluctant to cover their plump persons, and their attitudes were always expressive of the influences of a Southern sun upon national manners. The matrons, dark and wrinkled, formed a strong contrast to their daughters, though, here and there, a fine cast of feature, and a figure erect with dignity, attracted the eye. The men lounged in roundabouts and cigaritos, as was to be expected, and, in fact, the whole picture lacked nothing that is Mexican.

Daylight walks about the town yielded little more to curiosity. The contrast of nationalities remained the chief interest. The local business is considerable, but carried on without subdivision of occupation. Each of the dozen stores offers all the articles you may ask for. A druggist or two, a saddler or two, a watchmaker and a gunsmith ply almost the only distinct trades. The country supplied from this centre is extensive, but very thinly settled. The capital owned here is quite large. The principal accumulations date from the Mexican War, when no small part of the many millions expended by Government were disbursed here in payments to contractors. Some prime cuts were secured by residents, and no small portion of the lesser pickings remained in their hands. Since then the town has been well-to-do, and consequently accumulates a greater population than its position in other respects would justify.

The traffic, open and illicit, across the frontier with interior Mexico, has some importance and returns some bulky bags of silver. All the principal merchants have their agencies on the Rio Grande, and throw in goods, and haul out dollars, as opportunity serves. The transportation of their goods forms the principal support of the Mexican population. It is this trade, probably, which accounts for the large stocks which are kept, and the large transactions that result, beyond the strength of most similar towns.

All goods are brought from Matagorda Bay, a distance of 150 miles, by ox-teams, moving with prodigious slowness and irregularity. In a favorable season, the freight-price is one-and-a-quarter cents per lb., from Lavacca. Prices are extremely high, and subject to great variations, depending upon the actual supply, and the state of the roads.

...

A scanty congregation attends the services of the battered old cathedral. The Protestant church attendance can almost be counted upon the fingers. Sunday is pretty rigidly devoted to rest, though most of the stores are open to all practical purposes, and the exchanges keep up a brisk distribution of stimulants. The Germans and Mexicans have their dances. The Americans resort to fast horses for their principal recreation.

. . .

The town of San Antonio was founded in 1730 by a colony of twelve families of pure Spanish blood, from the Canary islands. The names of the settlers are perpetuated to this day, by existing families, which have descended from each, such as Garcia, Flores, Navarro, Garza, Yturri, Rodriguez. The original mission and fort of San Antonio de Valero dates from 1715, when Spain established her occupancy of Texas.

The Missions

Not far from the city, along the river, are these celebrated religious establishments. They are of a similar character to the many scattered here and there over the plains of Northern Mexico and California, and bear a solid testimony to the strangely patient courage and zeal of the old Spanish fathers. They pushed off alone into the heart of a savage and unknown country, converted [the Indians] that occupied it, not only to nominal Christianity, but to actual hard labor, and persuaded and compelled them to construct these ponderous but rudely splendid edifices, serving, at the same time, for the glory of the faith, and for the defense of the faithful....

The Alamo was one of the earliest of these establishments. It is now within the town, and in extent, probably, a mere wreck of its former grandeur. It consists of a few irregular stuccoed buildings, huddled against the old church, in a large court surrounded by a rude wall; the whole used as an arsenal by the U.S. quartermaster. The church-door opens on the square, and is meagerly decorated by stucco mouldings, all hacked and battered in the battles it has seen. Since the heroic defense of Travis and his handful of men, in '36, it has been a monument, not so much to faith as to courage.

The Mission of Concepción is not far from the town, upon the left of the river. Further down are three others, San Juan, San José, and La Espada. On one of them is said to have been visible, not long ago, the date "1725." They are in different stages of decay, but all are real ruins, beyond any connection with the present—weird remains out of the silent past.

They are of various magnificence, but all upon a common model, and all of the same materials—rough blocks of limestone, cemented with a strong gray stucco. Each has its church, its convent, or celled house for the fathers, and its farm buildings, arranged around a large court, entered only at a single point. Surrounding each was a large farm, irrigated at a great outlay of labor by aqueducts from the river.

The decorations of the doors and windows may be still examined. They are of stucco, and are rude heads of saints, and mouldings, usually without grace, corresponding to those described as at present occupying similar positions in Mexican churches. One of the missions is a complete ruin, the others afford shelter to Mexican occupants, who ply their trades, and herd their cattle and sheep in the old cells and courts. Many is the picturesque sketch offered to the pencil by such intrusion upon falling dome, tower, and cloister.

The Environs

The system of aqueducts, for artificial irrigation, extends for many miles around San Antonio, and affords some justification for the Mexican tradition, that the town not long ago, contained a very much larger population. Most of these lived by agriculture, returning at evening to a crowded home in the city. These water-courses still retain their old Spanish name, "acequias." A large part of them are abandoned, but in the immediate neighborhood of the city they are still in use, so that every garden-patch may be flowed at will.

In the outskirts of the town are many good residences, recently erected by Americans. They are mostly of the creamy limestone, which is found in abundance near-by. It is of a very agreeable shade, readily sawed and cut, sufficiently durable, and can be procured at moderate cost. When the grounds around them shall have been put in correspondence with the style of the houses, they will make enviable homes.

The San Antonio Spring

There are, besides the missions, several pleasant points for excursions in the neighborhood, particularly those to the San Antonio and San Pedro Springs. The latter is a wooded spot of great beauty, but a mile or two from town, and boasts a restaurant and beer-garden beyond its natural attractions. The San Pedro

Spring may be classed as of the first water among the gems of the natural world. The whole river gushes up in one sparkling burst from the earth. It has all the beautiful accompaniments of a smaller spring, moss, pebbles, seclusion, sparkling sunbeams, and dense overhanging luxuriant foliage. The effect is overpowering. It is beyond your possible conceptions of a spring. You cannot believe your eyes, and almost shrink from sudden metamorphosis by invaded nymphdom.

BATHING

The temperature of the river is just that agreeable elevation that makes you loth to leave a bath, and the color is the ideal blue. Few cities have such a luxury. It remains throughout the year without perceptible change of temperature, and never varies in height or volume.

The streets are laid out in such a way that a great number of the houses have a garden extending to the bank, and so a bathing-house, which is in constant use. The Mexicans seem half the time about the water. Their plump women, especially, are excellent swimmers, and fond of displaying their luxurious buoyancy. The fall of the river is such as to furnish abundant water-power, which is now used but for a single corn-mill. Several springs add their current to its volume above the town, and that from the San Pedro below. It unites near the Gulf, with the Guadalupe, and empties into Espiritu Santo Bay, watering a rich, and, as yet, but little-settled country.

TOWN LIFE

The street life of San Antonio is more varied than might be supposed. Hardly a day passes without some noise. If there be no personal affray to arouse talk, there is some Government train to be seen, with its hundred mules, on its way from the coast to a fort above; or a Mexican ox-train from the coast, with an interesting supply of ice, or flour, or matches, or of whatever the shops find themselves short. A Government express clatters off, or news arrives from some exposed outpost, or from New Mexico. An Indian in his finery appears on a shaggy horse, in search of blankets, powder, and ball. Or at the least, a stage-coach with the "States," or the Austin, mail, rolls into the plaza and discharges its load of passengers and newspapers.

The street affrays are numerous and characteristic. I have seen, for a year or more, a San Antonio weekly, and hardly a number fails to have its fight or its murder. More often than otherwise, the parties meet upon the plaza by chance, and each, on catching sight of his enemy, draws a revolver, and fires away. As the actors are under more or less excitement, their aim is not apt to be the most careful and sure, consequently it is, not seldom, the passers-by who suffer. Sometimes it is a young man at a quiet dinner in a restaurant, who receives a ball in the head; sometimes an old negro woman, returning from the market, who gets winged. After disposing of all their lead, the parties close, to try their steel, but as this species of metallic amusement is less popular, they generally contrive to be separated ("Hold me! Hold me!") by friends before the wounds are mortal. If neither is seriously injured, they are brought to drink together on the following day, and the town waits for the next excitement.

The town amusements of a less exciting character are not many. There is a permanent company of Mexican mountebanks, who give performances of agility and buffoonery two or three times a week, parading, before night, in their spangled tights with drum and trombone through the principal streets. They draw a crowd of whatever little Mexicans can get adrift, and this attracts a few sellers of whiskey, tortillas, and tamaules (corn slap-jacks and hashed meat in corn-shucks), all by the light of torches making a ruddily picturesque evening group.

The more grave Americans are served with tragedy by a thin local company, who are death on horrors and despair, long rapiers, and well oiled hair, and for lack of a better place to flirt with passing officers, the city belles may sometimes be seen looking on. The national background of peanuts and yells, is not, of course, wanting.

San Antonio, excluding Galveston,* is much the largest city of Texas. After the Revolution, it was half deserted by its Mexican population, who did not care to come under Anglo-Saxon rule. Since then its growth has been rapid and steady. At the census of 1850, it numbered 3,500; in 1853, its population

---

* The two towns have nearly kept pace in growth. The yellow fever, it is said, has now given San Antonio the advantage.

was 6,000; and in 1856, it is estimated at 10,500. Of these, about 4,000 are Mexicans, 3,000 Germans, and 3,500 Americans, as well as the officers and the Government. Most of the mechanics and the smaller shopkeepers are Germans. The Mexicans appear to have almost no other business than that of carting goods. Almost the entire transportation of the country is carried by them, with oxen and two-wheeled carts. Some of them have small shops, for the supply of their own countrymen, and some live upon the produce of farms and cattle-ranches owned in the neighborhood. Their livelihood is, for the most part, exceedingly meager, made up chiefly of corn and beans.

THE MEXICANS IN TEXAS

We had, before we left, opportunities of visiting familiarly many of the Mexican dwellings. I have described their externals. Within, we found usually a single room, open to the roof and invariably having a floor of beaten clay a few inches below the level of the street. There was little furniture—huge beds being the universal pièce de résistance. These were used by day as a sofa and table. Sometimes there were chairs and a table besides; but frequently only a bench, with a few earthen utensils for cooking, which is carried on outside. A dog or a cat appears on or under the bed, or on the clothes-chest, a saint on the wall, and frequently a game-cock fastened in a corner, supplied with dishes of corn and water.

We were invariably received with the most gracious politeness and dignity. Their manner towards one another is engaging, and that of children and parents most affectionate. This we always noticed in evening walks and in the groups about the doors, which were often singing in chorus—the attitudes expressive of confident affection. In one house, we were introduced to an old lady who was supposed by her grandchildren to be over one hundred years old. She had come from Mexico, in a rough cart, to make them a visit. Her face was strikingly Indian in feature, her hair, snow white, flowing thick over the shoulders, contrasting strongly with the olive skin. The complexion of the girls is clear, and sometimes fair, usually a blushing olive. The variety of features and color is very striking, and is naturally referred to three sources—the old Spanish, the Creole Mexican, and the Indian, with sometimes a suspicion of

Anglo-Saxon or Teuton. The hair is coarse, but glossy, and very luxuriant; the eye, deep, dark, liquid, and well set. . . .

The common dress was loose and slight . . . It was frequently but a chemise, as low as possible in the neck, sometimes even lower, with a calico petticoat. On holidays they dress in expensive finery, paying special attention to the shoes, of white satin, made by a native artist. . . .

The majority are classed as laborers. Their wages are small, usually, upon farms near San Antonio, $6 or $8 a month, with corn and beans. That of the teamsters is in proportion to their energy. On being paid off, they hurry to their family and all come out in their best to spend the earnings, frequently quite at a loss for what to exchange them. They make excellent drovers and shepherds, and in work like this, with which they are acquainted, are reliable and adroit. A horse-drover, just from the Rio Grande, with whom we conversed, called them untiring and faithful at their work, but untrustworthy in character. To his guide, he paid $24 a month, to his "right bower," $15, to his "left bower," $12 a month.

The old Mexican wheel of hewn blocks of wood is still constantly in use, though supplanted to some extent, by Yankee wheels, sent in pairs from New York. The carts are always hewn of heavy wood, and are covered with white cotton, stretched over hoops. In these they live, on the road, as independently as in their own house. The cattle are yoked by the horns, with rawhide thongs, of which they make great race. A few, of old Spanish blood, have purchased negro servants, but most of them regard slavery with abhorrence.

The Mexicans were treated for a while after annexation like a conquered people. Ignorant of their rights, and of the new language, they allowed themselves to be imposed upon by the newcomers, who seized their lands and property without shadow of claim, and drove hundreds of them homeless across the Rio Grande. They now, as they get gradually better informed, come straggling back, and often their claims give rise to litigation, usually settled by a compromise.

A friend told us, that, wishing, when he built, to square a corner of his lot, after making diligent inquiry he was unable to hear of any owner of the adjoining piece. He took the responsibility, and moved his fence over it. Not long after, he was waited upon by a Mexican woman, in a towering passion.

He carried her to a Spanish acquaintance, and explained the transaction. She was immediately appeased, told him he was welcome to the land, and has since been on the most neighborly terms, calling him always her "amigo."

Most adult Mexicans are voters by the organic law; but few take measures to make use of the right. Should they do so, they might probably, in San Antonio, have elected a government of their own. Such a step would be followed, however, by summary revolution. They are regarded by slaveholders with great contempt and suspicion, for their intimacy with slaves, and their competition with plantation labor.

Americans, in speaking of them, constantly distinguish themselves as "white folks." I once heard a new comer informing another American, that he had seen a Mexican with a revolver.

"I shouldn't think they ought to be allowed to carry fire-arms. It might be dangerous." "It would be difficult to prevent it," the other replied; "Oh, they think themselves just as good as white men."

From several counties they have been driven out altogether. At Austin, in the spring of 1853, a meeting was held, at which the citizens resolved, on the plea that Mexicans were horse-thieves, that they must quit the county. About twenty families were thus driven from their homes, and dispersed over the western counties. Deprived of their means of livelihood, and rendered furious by such wholesale injustice, it is no wonder if they should take to the very crimes with which they are charged.

A similar occurrence took place in Seguin, in 1854; and in 1855, a few families, who had returned to Austin, were again driven out.

Even at San Antonio, there had been talk of such a razzia. A Mexican, caught in an attempt to steal a horse, had been hung by a Lynching party, on the spot, for an example. His friends happened to be numerous, and were much excited, threatening violence in return. Under pretext of subduing an intended riot, the sheriff issued a call for an armed posse of 500 men, with the idea of dispersing and driving from the neighborhood a large part of the Mexican population. But the Germans, who include among them the great majority of young men suitable for such duty, did not volunteer as had been expected, and the scheme was abandoned. They were of the opinion, one of them said to me, that this was not the right and republican way. If the laws were justly and energetically administered, no other remedy would be needed. ★

SIDNEY LANIER

Sidney Lanier was once one of the most highly regarded American poets of the nineteenth century, ranked with Longfellow, Whitman, and Dickinson well into the twentieth century. Born in 1842, he was raised in Macon, Georgia, and entered Oglethorpe University at the age of fifteen. He graduated in three years, and intended to seek a PhD in Europe when the American Civil War broke out. He served in the Signal Corps of the Army of the Confederate States throughout the war, until he was captured while serving as a pilot on a British ship running the Union blockade. Lanier was imprisoned at Point Lookout in Maryland, where he contracted consumption (tuberculosis), incurable at the time.

A self-taught musician, Lanier served as a church organist and hotel orchestra flutist while simultaneously studying law, teaching school, and writing his first (and only) novel, *Tiger-Lilies* (1867). Lanier's poetry became increasingly popular during his lifetime. His health was declining, however, even at the young age of thirty. San Antonio, Texas, was advertised as a curative location for tubercular patients, so Lanier left his family to test out the climate, arriving in December 1872. While here, he played flute with the Beethoven Männerchor (founded by Simon Menger in 1847), and began composing music (one of his most famous pieces, "Blackbirds," was reportedly inspired by San Antonio's grackle population).

Lanier remained in San Antonio only a few months, having determined that his health was not improving. While he was here, he researched and wrote an "historical sketch" of San Antonio. His sketch is a fairly accurate accounting of the facts available to him from the arrival of the Spanish through the US Civil War. The final section of Lanier's sketch is one of the most evocative descriptions of San Antonio's cultural ambiance and physical environs as has ever been written. It is certainly one of the most often quoted.

Lanier's history of San Antonio was not published during his lifetime. A local bookseller, William Corner, purchased the piece from the Lanier estate and published it in his *San Antonio de Bexar: A Guide and History* (1890). A portion of it was republished as

"The Tragedy of the Alamo," which was included in *Selections from Sidney Lanier: Verse and Prose*, edited by Henry Lanier (NY: Scribner's, 1916). San Antonio historian Mary Ann Noonan Guerra republished Lanier's piece entire, together with the illustrations used in Corner's book, in *San Antonio de Bexar: Sidney Lanier's Historical Sketch.*

We include an excerpt from Lanier's history here as it provides a graphic description of the city's violent history from 1811 to the early 1820s, a period often overshadowed by the events of 1835-1836. It also provides considerable insight into the way America saw San Antonio in the late nineteenth century—a perspective that persisted almost unchanged until the late 1960s. Certainly his writing reflects an inevitable attitude of racial superiority toward Mexicans and Tejanos, but Lanier's is of the gentler sort, given his deep appreciation for the culture. He is not so kind toward Indians, and reflects the racism of his day.

Reinvigorated about his music during his stay in San Antonio, Lanier secured a position with the Peabody Orchestra in Baltimore, and was soon the first flutist. He soon became a faculty member at Johns Hopkins University, and published several books of poetry, criticism, and collections of folktales and legends for boys. Lanier died of tuberculosis in 1881. He was only thirty-nine years old.

---

from "SAN ANTONIO DE BEXAR:
AN HISTORICAL SKETCH"

. . .ON THE 8TH OF MAY, 1744, THE FIRST STONE OF the present Church of the Alamo was laid and blessed. The site of this church is nearly a quarter of a mile to the eastward of the Military plaza, where the mission to which it belonged had been located in 1722.[1] From an old record-book purporting to contain the baptisms in "the Parish of the Pueblo of San José del Alamo," it would seem that there must have been also a settlement of that name. San Antonio de Bexar, therefore—the modern city—seems to be a consolidation of the presidio of San Antonio de Bexar, the mission and pueblo (or villa) of San Antonio de Valero, and the pueblos of San Fernando and San José del Alamo.

In 1783-85 San Antonio de Valero ceased to be a Mission. For some reason it had become customary to send whatever captive Indians were brought in to the Missions below the town for Christianization. The town, however, which had been built up about the Mission buildings, remained, having a separate alcalde, and an organization politically and religiously distinct from that of San Antonio de Bexar and San Fernando for some years longer. In 1790 the population around the Alamo was increased by the addition of the people from the Presidio de los Adaes; this post was abandoned, and its inhabitants were provided with lands which had been the property of the Mission of San Antonio de Valero, lying in the neighborhood of the Alamo to the north. "The upper *labor* of the Alamo," says M. Giraud, in an interesting note which constitutes Appendix IV of Yoakum's *History of Texas*, ". . . is still commonly called by the inhabitants the *labor de los Adaesenos.*"[2] These Mission lands about the Alamo seem to have ceased to be such about this time, and to have been divided off to the Mission people, each of who received a portion, with fee-simple title. In 1793, the distinct religious organization of the Mission of San Antonio de Valero terminated, and it was aggregated to the curacy of the town of San Fernando and the presidio of San Antonio de Bexar; as appears by the following note which is found on the last page of an old Record book of baptisms in the archives of Bexar:

> On the 22d day of August, 1793, I passed this book of the Records of the pueblo of San Antonio de Valero to the archives of the curacy of the town of San Fernando and presidio of San Antonio de Bexar, by order of the most illustrious Señor Dr. Don Andres de Iylaños y Valdez, most worthy Bishop of this diocese, dated January 2d, of the same year, by reason of said pueblo having been aggregated to the curacy of Bexar; and that it may be known, I sign it.
> Fr. José; Francisco Dopez, Parroco

In the year 1800 San Antonio began to see a new sort of prisoners brought in. Instead of captive Indians, here arrived a party of eleven Americans in irons, who were the remainder of a company with which Philip Nolan, a trader between Natchez and San Antonio, had started out, and who, after a sharp fight with one hundred and fifty Spanish soldiers in which Nolan was killed, had been first induced to return to Nacogdoches, and there treacherously manacled and sent to prison at San Antonio. Again, in 1805, three Americans are brought in under guard. In this year, too, matters begin to be a little more lively in the town. Spain's neighbor on the east is not now France; for in 1803 Louisiana has been formally transferred to the United States. There is already trouble with the latter about the boundary line betwixt Louisiana and Texas. Don Antonio Cordero, the new Governor of Texas, has brought on a lot of troops through the town, and fixed his official residence here; and troops continue to march through en route to Natchitoches, where the American General Wilkinson is menacing the border. Again, in 1807, Lieutenant Zebulon M. Pike, of the United States Army, passes through town in charge of an escort. Lieutenant Pike has been sent to explore the Arkansas and Red Rivers, and to treat with the Comanches, has been apprehended by the Spanish authorities in New Mexico, carried to Santa Fe, and is now being escorted home.

At this time there are four hundred troops in San Antonio, in quarters near the Alamo. Besides these, the town has about two thousand inhabitants, mostly Spaniards and Creoles, the remainder Frenchmen, Americans, civilized Indians, and half-breeds. New settlers have come in; and what with army officers, the Governor's people, the clergy, and prominent citizens, society begins to form and to enjoy itself. The Governor, Father McGuire, Colonel Delgado, Captain Ugarte, Doctor Zerbin, dispense hospitalities and adorn social meetings. There are, in the evenings, levees at the Governor's; sometimes Mexican dances on the Plaza, at which all assist; and frequent and prolonged card parties.

But these peaceful scenes do not last long. In 1811 the passers across the San Antonio river between the Alamo and the Main Plaza behold a strange sight: it is the head of a man stuck on a pole, there, in bloody menace against rebels. This head but yesterday was on the shoulders of Colonel Delgado, a flying adherent of Hidalgo, in Mexico: Hidalgo—initiator of how long a train of Mexican revolutions!—having been also put to death in Chihuahua. It was not long before this blood was (as from of old) washed out with other blood. Bernardo Gutierrez, a fellow-rebel of the unfortunate Delgado, escaped to Natchitoches, and met young Magee, an officer of the United States army. In a short time the two had assembled a mixed force of American adventurers and rebellious Mexican republicans, had driven the Spanish troops from Nacogdoches, marched into Texas, captured the fort and supplies at La Bahia, enlisted its garrison, and sustained a siege there which the enemy was finally compelled to abandon with loss. It was in March 1813 that the Spanish besieging force set out on its retreat up the river to San Antonio. Gutierrez—Magee having committed suicide in consequence of mortification at the indignant refusal of the troops to accept a surrender he had negotiated soon after the beginning of the siege—determined to pursue. On the 28th of March he crossed the Salado, en route to San Antonio, with a force consisting of eight hundred Americans under Colonel Kemper, one hundred and eighty Mexicans led by Manchaca, under Colonel James Gaines, three hundred Lipan and Twowokana [Tonkawa] Indians, and twenty-five Cooshattie Indians. Marching along the bank of the San Antonio River, with the left flank protected by the stream, this motley army arrived within nine miles of San Antonio, when the riflemen on the right suddenly discovered the enemy ambushed in the chaparral on the side of a ridge. Here the whole force that Governor Salcedo could muster had been posted, consisting of about fifteen hundred regular troops and a thousand militia. To gain time to form, the Indians were ranged to receive the opening charge of the Spanish cavalry; the enemy meantime having immediately formed along the crest of the ridge, with twelve pieces of artillery in the centre. The Indians broke at the first shock; only the Cooshatties and a few others stood their ground. These received two other charges, in which they lost two killed and several wounded. The Americans had now made their dispositions, and proceeded to execute them with matchless coolness. They charged up the hill, stopped at thirty yards of the enemy's line, fired three rounds, loaded, then charged again, and straightway the slope towards San Antonio was dotted with Spanish fugitives, whom the Indians pursued and butchered regardless of quarter. The Spanish commander, who had pledged sword and head to Governor Salcedo that he would kill and capture the American army, could not endure the sting of his misfortune. He spurred his horse upon the American ranks, attacked Major Ross, then Colonel Kemper, and while in the act of striking the latter, was shot by private William Owen. The Spanish loss is said to have been near a thousand killed and wounded.

Next day the Americans advanced to the outskirts of San Antonio and demanded a surrender. Governor Salcedo desired to parley, to delay. A second demand was made. Governor Salcedo then marched out with his staff. He presented his sword to Captain Taylor; Taylor refused, and referred him to Colonel Kemper. Presenting to Colonel Kemper, he was in turn referred to Gutierrez. No, not to that rebel! Salcedo thrust his sword into the ground, whence Gutierrez drew it. The victors got stores, arms, and treasure. Seventeen American prisoners in the Alamo were released and armed. The troops were paid—receiving a bonus of fifteen dollars each in addition to wages—clothed and mounted out of the booty. The Indians were not forgotten in the distribution; they "were supplied," says Yoakum, "with two dollars' worth of vermilion, together with presents of the value of a hundred and thirty dollars, and sent away rejoicing."

And now flowed the blood that must answer that which dripped down the pole from poor Colonel Delgado's head. Shortly after the victory, Captain Delgado, a son of the executed rebel, falls upon his knees before Gutierrez, and demands vengeance upon the prisoner, Governor Salcedo, who apprehended and executed his father. Gutierrez arrays his army, informs them that it would be safe to send Salcedo and staff to New Orleans, and that it so happens that vessels are about to sail for that port from Matagorda Bay. The army consents (we are so fearfully and wonderfully republican in these days: the army consents) that the prisoners be sent off as proposed. Captain Delgado, with a company of Mexicans, starts in charge, ostensibly en route for Matagorda Bay. There are fifteen of the distinguished captives: Governor Salcedo, of Texas, Governor Herrera, of New Leon, Ex-Governor Cordero, whom we last saw holding levees in San Antonio, several Spanish and Mexican officers, and one citizen. Delgado gets his prisoners a mile and a half from town, halts them on the bank of the river, strips them, ties them, and cuts the throats of every man: "some of the assassins," says Colonel Navarro, whetting "their knives upon the soles of their shoes in presence of their victims."

The town of San Antonio must have been anything but a pleasant place for peaceful citizens during the next two months. Colonel Kemper, who was really the commanding officer of the American army, refused further connection with those who could be guilty of such barbarity, and left, with other American officers. Their departure left in the town an uncontrolled body of troops who feared neither God nor man; and these immediately proceeded to avail themselves of the situation by indulging in all manner of riotous and lawless pleasures. With the month of June, however, came Don Elisondo from Mexico with an army of royalists, consisting of about three thousand men, half of whom were regular troops. His advance upon San Antonio seems to have been a complete surprise, and to have been only learned by the undisciplined republican army in the town, together with the fact that he had captured their horses, which had been out grazing, and killed part of the guard which was protecting the caballada. If Elisondo had marched straight on into town, his task would probably have been an easy one. But he committed the fatal mistake of encamping a short distance from the suburbs, where he threw up two bastions with a curtain between, on a ridge near the Alazan Creek.

Meantime the republican army in the town recovered from the confusion into which they had been thrown by the first intelligence of Elisondo's proximity, and organized themselves under Gutierrez and Captain Perry. It was determined to anticipate the enemy's attack. Ingress and egress were prohibited, the sentinels doubled, and all the cannons spiked except four field-pieces. In the darkness of the night of June 4th the Americans marched quietly out of town, by file, to within hearing of the enemy's pickets, and remained there until the enemy was heard at matins. The signal to charge being given—a cheer from the right of the companies—the Americans advanced, surprised and captured the pickets in front, mounted the enemy's work, lowered his flag and hoisted their own, before they were fairly discovered through the dim dawn. The enemy struggled hard, however, and compelled the Americans to abandon the works. The latter charged again, and this time routed the enemy completely. The royalist loss is said to have been about a thousand in killed, wounded and prisoners; and that of the Americans, ninety-four killed and mortally wounded.

For some reason Gutierrez was now dismissed from the leadership of the army (we republican soldiers decapitate our commanders very quickly if they please us not!), and shortly afterwards troops and citizens went forth in grand procession to welcome Don José Alvarez Toledo, a distinguished republican Cuban who had been forwarding recruits from Louisiana to San Antonio; and having escorted him into town with much ceremony, elected him commander-in-chief of the Republican Army of the North. Toledo immediately organized a government; but the people of San Antonio enjoyed the unaccustomed blessing of civil law only a little while.

In a few days enter, from over the Mexican border, Gen. Arredondo, with the remnant of Elisondo's men and some fresh troops, about four thousand in all, en route for San Antonio. Toledo marches out to meet him with about twenty-five hundred men, one-third of whom are Americans, the balance Mexicans under Manchaca; and on the 18th of August, 1813, they come together. Arredondo decoys him into an ingenious cul de sac which he has thrown up, just south of the Medina River, and has concealed by cut bushes; and pours such a murderous fire of cannon and small arms upon him, that in spite of the gallantry of the right wing where the Americans are, the retreat which Toledo has ordered too late becomes a mere rout, and the republican army is butchered without mercy. One batch of seventy or eighty fugitives is captured by the pursuing royalists, tied, set by tens upon a log laid across a great grave, and shot!

On the 20th Arredondo enters San Antonio in great triumph, and straightway proceeds to wreak fearful vengeance upon the unhappy town for the massacre of his brother governors. Seven hundred citizens are thrown into prison. During the night of the 20th eighteen die of suffocation out of three hundred who are confined in one house. These only anticipate the remainder, who are shot, without trial, in detachments. Five hundred republican women are imprisoned in a building, derisively termed the Quinta, and compelled to make up twenty-four bushels of corn into tortillas every day for the royalist army. Having thus sent up a sweet savor of revenge to the spirits of the murdered Salcedo, Corderoi Herrera, and the others, Arredondo finally gathers their bones together and buries them. In all this blood the prosperity of San Antonio was drowned. To settlers it offered no inducements; to most of its former citizens it held out nothing but terror; and it is described as almost entirely abandoned in 1816.

In December, 1820, arrived a person in San Antonio who, though not then known as such, was really a harbinger of better times. This was Moses Austin, of Connecticut. He came to see Governor Martinez, with a view of bringing a colony to Texas. The two, with the Baron de Bastrop, put in train the preliminary application for permission to Arredondo, Commandant-General at Monterey. Austin, it is true, died soon afterwards; but he left his project to his son Stephen F., who afterwards carried it out with a patience that amounted to genius and a fortitude that was equivalent to the favor of Heaven.

On the 24th of August, 1821, Don Juan O'Donoju and Yturbide entered into the Treaty of Cordova, which substantially perfected the separation of Mexico from the mother-country. When the intelligence of this event had spread, the citizens of San Antonio returned. Moreover, about this time a tide of emigration began to set towards Texas. The Americans who had composed part of the army of Gutierrez had circulated fair reports of the country. In 1823 San Antonio is said to have had five thousand inhabitants; though the Comanches appear still to have had matters all their own way when they came into town, as they frequently did, to buy beads and other articles with skins of deer and buffalo. One would find this difficult to believe, but reasoning a priori, it is rendered probable by the fact that in the decree of the the Federal Congress of Mexico of the 24th of August, 1826, to provide for raising troops to serve in Coahuila and Texas as frontier defenders, it is ordered that out of the gross levies there shall be first preferred for military service "los vagos y mal entretenidos," vagrant and evil-disposed persons; and a posteriori, it is quite confirmed by the experience of Olmsted in San Fernando (a considerable town west of the Rio Grande) so late as 1854, where he found the Indians "lounging in and out of every house . . . with such an air as indicated they were masters of the town. They entered every door," adds Olmsted, "fell on every neck, patted the women on the check, helped themselves to whatever suited their fancy, and distributed their scowls or grunts of pleasure according to their sensations."

In the year 1824 a lot of French merchants passed through San Antonio en route to Santa Fe on a trading expedition. Some distance from town their pack-animals were all stolen by Indians; but they managed to get carts and oxen from San Antonio, and so conveyed their goods finally to Santa Fe, where they sold them at an immense profit. In 1831 the Bowie brothers, Rezin P. and James, organized in San Antonio their expedition in search of the old reputed silver mines at San Saba Mission. In the course of this unlucky venture occurred their famous Indian fight, where the two Bowies, with nine others, fought a pitched battle with one hundred and sixty-four Indians who had attacked them with arrow, with rifle, and with fire from sundown to sunset [i.e. late afternoon until dark], killing and wounding eighty-four. They then fortified their position during the night, maintained it for eight days afterwards, and finally returned to San Antonio with their horses and three wounded comrades, leaving one man killed.

It is related that in 1832 a Comanche Indian attempted to abduct a Shawnee woman in San Antonio. She escaped him, joined a party of her people who were staying some thirty-five miles from town, and informed them where the Comanches (of whom five hundred had been in town for some purpose) would probably camp. The Shawnees ambushed themselves at the spot indicated. The Comanches came on and stopped as expected: the Shawnees poured a fire into them, and repeated it as they continually rallied, until the Comanches abandoned the contest with a loss of one hundred and seventy-five dead.

Early in 1833 (or perhaps late in December 1832) arrives in San Antonio for the first time one who is to be called the father of his country. This is Sam Houston. He comes in company with the famous James Bowie, son-in-law of Vice-Governor Veramendi, and holds a consultation with the Comanche chiefs here, to arrange a meeting at Cantonment Gibson with a view to a treaty of peace. Meantime trouble is brewing. Young Texas does not get on well with his mother. What seems to hurt most is the late union of Texas with Coahuila. This we cannot stand. Stephen F. Austin goes to the City of Mexico with a memorial on the subject to the federal government. He writes from there to the municipality of San Antonio, Oct. 2d, 1833, informing the people that their request is likely to be refused, and advising them to make themselves ready for that emergency. The municipality hand this letter over to Vice-President Farias, who, already angry with Austin on an old account, arrests him on his way home and throws him in prison, back in the city of Mexico.

In October, 1834, certain people in San Antonio hold what Yoakum calls "the first strictly revolutionary meeting in Texas;" for Santa Anna has pronounced, and got to be at the head of affairs, and he refuses to separate Texas from Coahuila. So, through meetings all over the state; through conferences of citizen deputations with Col. Ugartechea, Mexican Commandant at San Antonio, for the purpose of explaining matters; through confused arguments and resolutions of the peace party and the war party; through confused rumors of the advance of Mexican General Cos with an army; through squabbling and wrangling and final fighting over the cannon that had been lent by the Post of Bexar to the people of Gonzales; through all manner of civic trouble consequent upon the imprisonment of Governor Viesca of Texas by Santa Anna, and the suspension of the progress of the civil law machine, we come to the time when the committee of San Felipe boldly cry: "Let us take Bexar and drive the Mexican soldiery out of Texas!" and presently, here, on the 28th of October, 1835, is General Cos with his army in San Antonio, fortifying for dear life, while yonder is Austin with a thousand Texans, at Mission Concepción, a mile and a half down the river below town, where Fannin and Bowie with ninety men in advance have a few hours before waged a brilliant battle with four hundred Mexicans, capturing their field-piece, killing and wounding a hundred or more, and driving the rest back to town.

General Austin believes, it seems, that Cos will surrender without a battle; and so remains at Concepción till November 2d, then marches up past the town on the east side, encamps four or five days, marches down on the west side, displays his forces on a hill side *in terrorem*, sends in a demand for surrender—and is flatly answered no. He resolves to lay siege. The days pass slowly, the enemy will not come out though allured with all manner of military enticements, and the army has no "fun," with the exception of one small skirmish, until the 26th, when "Deaf" Smith discovers a party of a hundred Mexican troops, who have been sent out to cut prairie-grass for the horses in town, and reporting them in camp, brings on what is known as the "grass fight." Colonel James Bowie attacks with a hundred mounted men; both sides are quickly reinforced, and a sharp running fight is kept up until the enemy get back to town; the Texans capturing seventy horses and killing some fifty of the enemy, with a loss of but two wounded and one missing. Meantime discontents arise. On the day before the "grass-fight," Austin resigns, having been appointed Commissioner to the United States, and Edward Burleson is elected by the army to the command. General Burleson, for some reason, seems loth to storm. Moreover, one Dr. James Grant seduces a large party with a wild project to leave San Antonio and attack Matamoras, when he declares that the whole of Mexico will rise and overwhelm Santa Anna; and on the 29th of November it is actually announced that two hundred and twenty-five men are determined to start the next morning.

But they do not start. It is whispered the town will be stormed. On the 3rd of December, Smith, Holmes, and Maverick escape from San Antonio, and give the Texan commander such information as apparently determines him to storm. Volunteers are called for to attack early next morning; all day and all night of that December 3rd the men make themselves ready, and long for the moment to advance: when here comes word from the General's quarters that the attack is put off! Chagrin and indignation prevail on all sides. On the morning of the 4th there is open disobedience of orders; whole companies refuse to parade. Finally, when on the same afternoon orders are issued to abandon camp and march for La Bahia at seven o'clock, the tumult is terrible, and it seems likely that these wild energetic souls, failing the Mexicans, will end by exterminating each other.

Midst of the confusion here arrives Mexican Lieutenant Vuavis, a deserter, and declares that the projected attack is not known (as had been assigned for reason of postponing), and that the garrison in town is in as bad order and discontent as the besiegers. At this critical moment a brave man suddenly crystallized the loose mass of discordant men and opinions into one compact force and one keen purpose. It is late in the morning, Col. Benjamin R. Milam steps forth among the men, and cries aloud: "Who will go with old Ben Milam into San Antonio?" Three hundred and one men will go.

A little before daylight on the 5th they "go," Gen. Burleson agreeing to hold his position until he hears from them. Milam marches into and along Acequia Street with his party; Johnson with his along Soledad Street. Where these debouch into the Main Plaza, Cos has thrown up breastworks and placed raking batteries. The columns march parallel along the quiet streets. Presently, as Johnson gets near the Veramendi House (which he is to occupy, while Milam is to gain De la Garza's house), a Mexican sentinel fires. Deaf Smith shoots the sentinel. The Mexicans prick up their ears, prick into their cannon-cartridges; the Plaza batteries open, the Alamo batteries join in; spade, crowbar, rifle, escopet, all are plied, and the storming of Bexar is begun.

But it would take many such papers as this to give even meagre details of all the battles that have been fought in and around San Antonio, and one must pass over the four days of this thrilling conflict with briefest mention. It is novel fighting; warfare intramural, one might say. The Texans advance inch by inch by piercing through the stone walls of the houses, pecking loop-holes with crowbars for their rifles as they gain each room, picking off the enemy from his housetops, from around his cannon, even from behind his own loopholes. On the night of the 5th with great trouble and risk the two columns succeed in opening communication with each other. On the 6th they advance a little beyond the Garza house. On the 7th brave Karnes steps forth with a crowbar and breaks into a house midway between the Garza house and the Plaza; brave Milam is stricken by a rifle ball just as he is entering the yard of the Veramendi house and falls instantly dead; and the Navarro house, one block from the Main Plaza, is gained. On the 8th they take the "Zambrano Row" of buildings, driving the enemy from it room by room; the enemy endeavor to produce a diversion with fifty men, and do, in a sense, for Burleson finds some diversion in driving them back precipitately with a six-pounder; at night those in the Zambrano Row are reinforced, and the "Priest's House" is gained amid heavy fighting.

This last is the stroke of grace. The Priest's House commands the Plaza. Early on the morning of the 9th General Cos sends a flag of truce, asking to surrender, and on the 10th agrees with Gen. Burleson upon formal and honorable articles of capitulation.

The poor citizens of San Antonio de Bexar, however, do not yet enjoy the blessings of life in quiet; these wild soldiers who have stormed the town cannot remain long without excitement. Presently Dr. Grant revives his old Matamoras project, and soon departs, carrying with him most of the troops that had been left at Bexar for its defense, together with great part of the garrison's winter supply of clothing, ammunition and provisions, and in addition "pressing" such property of the citizens as he needs, insomuch that Col. Neill, at that time in command at Bexar, writes to the Governor of Texas that the place is left destitute and defenseless. Soon afterward Col. Neill is ordered to destroy the Alamo walls and other fortifications, and bring off the artillery, since no head can be made there in the present crisis against the enemy, who is reported marching in force upon San Antonio. Having no teams, Col. Neill is unable to obey the order, and presently retires, his unpaid men having dropped off until but eighty remain, of whom Colonel Wm. B. Travis assumes command. Colonel Travis promptly calls for more troops, but gets none as yet, for the Governor and Council are at deadly quarrel, and the soldiers are all pressing towards Matamoros. Travis has brought thirty men with him; about the middle of February he is joined by Colonel Bowie with thirty others, and these, with the eighty already in garrison, constitute the defenders of San Antonio de Bexar. On the 23d of February appears General Santa Anna at the head of a well-appointed army of some four thousand men, and marches straight on into town. The Texans retire before him slowly, and finally shut themselves up in the Alamo; here straightway begins that bloodiest, smokiest, grimiest tragedy of this century. William B. Travis, James Bowie, and David Crockett, with their hundred and forty-five effective men,[3] are enclosed within a stone rectangle one hundred and ninety feet long and one hundred and twenty-two feet wide, having the old church of the Alamo in the southeast corner, in which are their quarters and magazine. They have a supply of water from the ditches that run alongside the walls, and by way of provision they have about ninety bushels of corn and thirty beef-cattle, their entire stock, all collected since the enemy came in sight. The walls are unbroken, with no angles from which to command besieging lines. They have fourteen pieces of artillery mounted, with but little ammunition.

Santa Anna demands unconditional surrender. Travis replies with a cannon shot, and the attack commences, the enemy running up a blood-red flag in town. Travis dispatches a messenger with a call to his countrymen for reinforcements, which concludes: "Though this call may be neglected, I am determined to sustain myself as long as possible, and die like a soldier who never forgets what is due to his own honor and that of his country. Victory or death!" Meantime the enemy is active. On the 25th Travis has a sharp fight to prevent him from erecting a battery raking the gate of the Alamo. At night it is erected, with another a half-mile off at the Garita, or powder-house, on a sharp eminence at the extremity of the present main street of the town. On the 26th there is skirmishing with the Mexican cavalry. In the cold—for a norther has commenced to blow and the thermometer is down to thirty-nine—the Texans make a sally successfully for wood and water, and that night they burn some old houses on the northeast that might afford cover for the enemy. So amid the enemy's constant rain of shells and balls, which miraculously hurt no one, the Texans strengthen their works and the siege goes on. On the 28th Fannin starts from Goliad with three hundred troops and four pieces of artillery, but for lack of teams and provisions quickly returns, and the little garrison is left to its fate. On the morning of the first of March there is doubtless a wild shout of welcome in the Alamo; Captain John W. Smith has managed to convey thirty-two men from Gonzales into the fort. These join the heroes, and the attack and defense go on. On the 3rd a single man, Moses Rose, escapes from the fort. His account of that day must entitle it to consecration as one of the most pathetic days of time:

About two hours before sunset on the 3rd of March, 1836, the bombardment suddenly ceased, and the enemy withdrew an unusual distance . . . . Colonel Travis paraded all his effective men in a single file, and taking his position in front of the centre, he stood for some moments apparently speechless from emotion; then nerving himself for the occasion, he addressed them substantially as follows:—

"My brave companions: stern necessity compels me to employ the few moments afforded by this probably brief cessation of conflict, in making known to you the most interesting, yet the most solemn, melancholy and unwelcome fact that humanity can realize. . . . Our fate is sealed. Within a very few days, perhaps a very few hours, we must all be in eternity! I have deceived you long by the promise of help; but I crave your pardon, hoping that after hearing my explanation you will not only regard my conduct as pardonable, but heartily sympathize with me in my extreme necessity. . . . I have continually received the strongest assurances of help from home. Every letter from the Council, and every one that I have seen from individuals at home, has teemed with assurances that our people were ready, willing and anxious to come to our relief. . . . These assurances I received as facts. . . . In the honest and simple confidence of my heart I have transmitted to you these promises of help and my confident hope of success. But the promised help has not come, and our hopes are not to be realized. I have evidently confided too much in the promises of our friends; but let us not be in haste to censure them. . . . Our friends were evidently not informed of our perilous condition in time to save us. Doubtless they would have been here by the time they expected any considerable force of the enemy. . . . My calls on Colonel Fannin remain unanswered, and my messengers have not returned. The probabilities are that his whole command has fallen into the hands of the enemy, or been cut to pieces, and that our couriers have been cut off. [So does the brave simple soul refuse to feel any bitterness in the hour of death.] Then we must die. . . . Our business is not to make a fruitless effort to save our lives, but to choose the manner of our death. But three modes are presented to us; let us choose that by which we may best serve our country. Shall we surrender and be deliberately shot without taking the life of a single enemy? Shall we try to cut our way out through the Mexican ranks and be butchered before we can kill twenty of our adversaries? I am opposed to either method. . . . Let us resolve to withstand our adversaries to the last, and at each advance to kill as many of them as possible. And when at last they shall storm our fortress, let us kill them as they come! kill them as they scale our wall! kill them as they leap within! kill them as they raise their weapons and as they use them! kill them as they kill our companions! and continue to kill them as long as one of us shall remain alive! . . . But I leave every man to his own choice. Should any man prefer to surrender . . . or to attempt an escape . . . he is at liberty to do so. My own choice is to stay in the fort and die for my country, fighting as long as breath shall remain in my body. This will I do even if you leave me alone. Do as you think best; but no man can die with me without affording me comfort in the hour of death!"

Colonel Travis then drew his sword, and with its point traced a line upon the ground extending from the right to the left of the file. Then resuming his position in front of the center, he said, "I now want every man who is determined to stay here and die with me to come across this line. Who will be the first? March!" The first respondent was Tapley Holland, who leaped the line at a bound, exclaiming, "I am ready to die for my country!" His example was instantly followed by every man in the file with the exception of Rose. . . . Every sick man that could walk, arose from his bunk and tottered across the line. Colonel Bowie, who could not leave his bed, said, "Boys, I am not able to come to you, but I wish some of you would be so kind as to remove my cot over there." Four men instantly ran to the cot, and each lifting a corner, carried it across the line. Then every sick man that could not walk made the same request, and had his bunk removed in the same way.

Rose too was deeply affected, but differently from his companions. He stood till every man but himself had crossed the line. . . . He sank upon the ground, covered his face, and yielded to his own reflections. . . . A bright idea came to his relief; he spoke the Mexican dialect very fluently, and could he once get safely out of the fort, he might easily pass for a Mexican and effect an escape. . . . He directed a searching glance at the cot of Colonel Bowie. . . . Colonel David Crockett was leaning over the cot, conversing with its occupant in an undertone. After a few seconds Bowie looked at Rose and said, "You seem not to be willing to die with us, Rose." "No," said Rose; "I am not prepared to die, and shall not do so if I can avoid it." Then Crockett also looked at him, and said, "You may as well conclude to die with us, old man, for escape is impossible." Rose made no reply, but looked at the top of the wall. "I have often done worse than to climb that wall," thought he. Suiting the action to the thought, he sprang up, seized his wallet of unwashed clothes, and ascended the wall. Standing on its top, he looked down within to take a last view of his dying friends. They were all now in motion, but what they were doing he heeded not; overpowered by his feelings, he looked away and saw them no more. . . . He threw down his wallet and leaped after it. . . . He took the road which led down the River around a bend to the ford, and through the town by the church. He waded the river at the ford and passed through the town. He saw no person . . . but the doors were all closed, and San Antonio appeared as a deserted city.

After passing through the town he turned down the River. A stillness as of death prevailed. When he had gone about a quarter of a mile below the town, his ears were saluted by the thunder of the bombardment which was then renewed. That thunder continued to remind him that his friends were true to their cause, by a continual roar with but slight intervals until a little before sunrise on the morning of the 6th, when it ceased and he heard it no more.[4]

And well may it "cease" on that morning of the 6th; for after that thrilling 3rd, the siege goes on, the enemy furious, the Texans replying calmly and slowly. Finally Santa Anna determines to storm. Some hours before daylight on the morning of the 6th, the Mexican infantry, provided with scaling ladders, and backed by the cavalry to keep them up to the work, surround the doomed fort. At daylight they advance and plant their ladders, but give back under a deadly fire from the Texans. They advance again, and again retreat. A third time—Santa Anna threatening and coaxing by turns—they plant their ladders. Now they mount the walls. The Texans are overwhelmed by sheer weight of numbers and exhaustion of continued watching and fighting. The Mexicans swarm into the fort. The Texans club their guns; one by one they fall fighting—now Travis yonder by the western wall, now Crockett here in the angle of the church-wall, now Bowie butchered and mutilated in his sick-cot, breathe quick and pass away; and presently every Texan lies dead, while there in horrid heaps are stretched five hundred and twenty-one dead Mexicans and as many more wounded! Of the human beings that were in the fort five remain alive: Mrs. Dickinson and her child, Colonel Travis' negro-servant, and two Mexican women.

The town did not long remain in the hands of the Mexicans. Events followed each other rapidly until the battle of San Jacinto, after which the dejected Santa Anna wrote his famous letter of captivity under the tree, which for a time relieved the soil of Texas from hostile footsteps. San Antonio was nevertheless not free from bloodshed, though beginning to drive a sharp trade with Mexico, and to make those approaches towards the peaceful arts which necessarily accompany trade. The Indians kept life from stagnating, and in the year 1840 occurred a bloody battle with them in the very midst of the town. Certain Comanche chiefs, pending negotiations for a treaty of peace, had promised to bring in all the captives they had; and on the 19th of March, 1840, met the Texan Commissioners in the Council House in San Antonio, to redeem their promise. Leaving twenty warriors and thirty-two women and children outside, twelve chiefs entered the council-room and presented the only captive they had brought—a little white girl—declaring that they had no others. This statement the little girl pronounced false, asserting that it was made solely for the purpose of extorting greater ransoms, and that she had but recently seen other captives in their camp. An awkward pause followed. Presently one of the chiefs inquired, How the commissioners liked it? By way of reply, the company of Captain Howard, who had been sent for, filed into the room, and the Indians were told that they would be held prisoners until they should send some of their party outside after the rest of the captives. The commissioners then rose and left the room. As they were in the act of leaving, however, one of the Indian chiefs attempted to rush through the door, and being confronted by the sentinel, stabbed him. Seeing the sentinel hurt, and Captain Howard also stabbed, the other chiefs sprang forward with knives and bows and arrows, and the fight raged until they were all killed. Meantime the warriors outside began to fight, and engaged the company of Captain Read; but, taking shelter in a stone house, were surrounded and killed. Still another detachment of the Indians managed to continue the fight until they had reached the other side of the river, when they were finally dispatched. Thirty-two Indian warriors and five Indian women and children were slain, and the rest of the women and children were made prisoners. The savages fought desperately, for seven Texans were killed and eight wounded.

The war between Texas and Mexico had now languished for some years. The project of annexation was much discussed in the United States; one great objection to it was that the United States would embroil itself with a nation with which it was at peace—Mexico—by annexing Texas, then at war. The war, however, seemed likely to die away; and to prevent the removal of the obstacle to annexation in that way, Mexico made feeble efforts to keep up such hostilities as might at least give color to the assertion that the war had not ended. Accordingly in the year 1842 a Mexican army again invested San Antonio. After a short parley Colonel Hays withdrew with his small force, and the Mexicans, numbering about seven hundred men under General Vasquez, took possession of the place and formally reorganized it as a Mexican town. They remained, however, only two days, and conducted themselves, officially, with great propriety, though the citizens are said to have lost a great deal of valuable property by unauthorized depredations of private soldiers and of Mexican citizens who accompanied the army on its departure.

Again on the 11th of September, 1842, a Mexican army of twelve hundred men under Gen. Woll, sent probably by the same policy which had dispatched the other, surprised the town of San Antonio, and, after having a few killed and wounded, took possession, the citizens having capitulated. Gen. Woll captured the entire bar of lawyers in attendance on the District Court, then in session, and held them as prisoners of war. He did not escape, however, so easily as Gen. Vasquez. The Texans gathered rapidly, and by the 17th had assembled two hundred and twenty men on the Salado, some six miles from town. Capt. Hays, with fifty men, decoyed Gen. Woll forth, and a battle ensued, from which the enemy withdrew at sunset with a loss of sixty killed and about the same number wounded, the Texans losing one killed and nine wounded. It is easy to believe that the honest citizens of San Antonio got little sleep on that night of the 17th of September, 1842. Gen. Woll was busy making preparations for retreat; and the Mexican citizens who intended to accompany him were also busy gathering up plunder right and left to take with them. At daylight they all departed. This was the last time that San Antonio de Bexar was ever in Mexican hands.

After annexation, in 1845, the town began to improve. The trade from certain portions of Mexico—Chihuahua and the neighboring States—seems always to have eagerly sought San Antonio as a point of supplies whenever peace gave it the opportunity. Presently, too, the United States Government selected San Antonio as the base for the frontier army below El Paso, and the large quantities of money expended in connection with the supply and transportation of all materiel for so long a line of forts have contributed very materially to the prosperity of the town. From a population of about 3500 in 1850, it increased to 10,000 in 1856.

Abandoning now this meagre historical sketch, and pursuing the order indicated in the enumeration of contrast and eccentricities given in the early part of this paper: one finds in San Antonio the queerest juxtaposition of civilizations, white, yellow (Mexican), red (Indian), black (negro), and all possible permutations of these significant colors. Americans, Germans, and Mexicans; besides these there are probably representatives from all European nationalities. Religious services are regularly conducted in four languages, German, Spanish, English and Polish. Perhaps the variety of the population cannot be better illustrated than by the following "commodity of good names," occurring in a slip cut from a daily paper of the town a day or two ago:

Matrimonial.—The matrimonial market for a couple of weeks past has been unusually lively, as evidenced by the following list of marriage licenses issued during that time: Cruz de la Cruz and Manuela Sauseda; Felipe Sallani and Maria del R. Lopez; G. Isabolo and Rafaela Urvana; Anto. P. Rivas and Maria Quintana; Garmel Hernandez and Seferina Rodriguez; T. B. Leighton and Franceska E. Schmidt; Rafael Diaz and Michaela Chavez: Levy Taylor and Anna Simpson, colored; Ignacio Andrada and Juliana Baltasar; August Dubiell and Philomena Muschell; James Callaghan and Mary Grenet; Albert Anz and Ida Pollock; Stephen Hoog and Mina Schneider; Wm. King and Sarah Wilson, colored; Joseph McCoy and Jesse Brown; Valentine Heck and Clara Hirsch; John F. Dunn and E. Annie Dunn.

Much interest has attached, of late years, to the climate of San Antonio, in consequence of its alleged happy influence upon consumption. One of the recognized "institutions" of the town is the consumptives, who are sent here from remote parts of the United States and from Europe, and who may be seen on fine days, in various stages of decrepitude, strolling about the streets. This present writer has the honor to be one of those strolling individuals; but he does not intend to attempt to describe the climate, for three reasons: first, because it is simply indescribable; second, if it were not so, his experience has been such as to convince him that the needs of consumptives, in point of climate, depend upon two variable elements, to wit, the stage which the patient has reached, and the peculiar temperament of each individual, and that therefore any general recommendation of any particular climate is often erroneous and sometimes fatally deceptive; and third, because he fortunately is able to present some of the facts of the climate, which may be relied upon as scientifically accurate, and from the proper study of which each intelligent consumptive can make up his mind as to the suitableness of the climate to his individual case.

San Antonio is at an altitude of 564 feet above the level of the sea,[5] in latitude 29° 28', longitude 98° 24'. It is placed just in the edge of a belt of country one hundred and fifty miles wide, reaching to the Rio Grande, and principally devoted to cattle-raising. . . . Inside, the location of the city is picturesque. Two streams, the San Antonio and San Pedro rivers, run in a direction generally parallel, though specially as far from parallelism as capricious crookedness can make itself, through the entire town. The San Antonio is about sixty feet wide; its water is usually of a lovely milky-green. The stranger, strolling on a mild sunny day through the streets, often finds himself suddenly on a bridge, and is half startled with the winding vista of sweet lawns running down to the water, of weeping willows kissing its surface, of summer houses on its banks, and of the swift yet smooth-shining stream meandering this way and that, actually combing the long sea-green locks of a trailing water-grass which sends its waving tresses down the centre of the current for hundreds of feet, and murmuring the while with a palpable Spanish lisping, which floats up among the rude noises of traffic along the street, as it were some dove-voiced Spanish nun out of the convent yonder praying heaven's mitigation of the wild battle of trade.

At the Commerce Street bridge over the San Antonio River, stands a post supporting a large sign board, upon which appears the following three legends:

Walk your horse over this bridge, or you will be fined.
Schnelles reiten über diese Brücke ist verboten.
Anda despacio con su caballo, o teme la ley.

To the meditative stroller across this bridge—and on a soft day when the Gulf breeze and the sunshine are king and queen, any stranger may be safely defied to cross this bridge without becoming meditative—there is a fine satire in the varying tone of these inscriptions—for they are by no means faithful translations of each other; a satire all the keener in that it must have been wholly unconscious. For mark: "Walk your horse, etc., or you will be fined." This is the American's warning: the alternative is a money consideration, and the appeal is solely to the pocket. But now the German is simply informed that *schnelles reiten* over this bridge *ist verboten*—is forbidden; as who should say: "So, thou quiet, law-abiding Teuton, enough for thee to know that it is forbidden simply." And lastly, the Mexican direction takes wholly a different turn from either: "Slow there with your horse, Mexicano, *o teme la ley*"—or "fear the law!"[6]

Leaving this bridge, walking down the main (Commerce) street, across the Main plaza, then past the San Fernando Cathedral, then across the Military Plaza, one comes presently to the San Pedro, a small stream ten or fifteen feet in width, up which the gazing stroller finds no romance, but mostly strict use; for there squat the Mexican women on their haunches, by their flat stones, washing the family garments, in a position the very recollection of which gives one simultaneous stitches of lumbago and sciatica, yet which they appear to maintain for hours without detriment. . . .

Crossing the San Pedro we are among the jacals [shacks] [where the] . . . more pretentious dwellings are built of adobes, or sun-dried brick. The majority of the substantial houses of the town are constructed of a whitish limestone, so soft when first quarried that it can be cut with a knife, but quickly hardening by exposure into a very durable building material. In the more pretentious two-storied dwellings there are some very good Moorish effects of projecting stone and lattice-work. A fine architectural example in the town is the San Fernando Cathedral, which presents a broad, varied and imposing façade upon the western side of the Main Plaza. . . . The curious dome, surrounded by a high wall over which its topmost slit-windows just peer—an evident relic of ancient Moorish architecture, which one finds in the rear of most of the old Spanish religious edifices in Texas—has been preserved, and still adjoins the queer priests' dormitories, which constitute the rear end of the cathedral building.

There are other notable religious edifices in town. Going back to Commerce Street, one can see a fine large church for the German Catholics (San Fernando Cathedral is Mexican Catholic). Crossing a graceful iron bridge, that turns off to the north from Commerce Street, one glances up and down the stream, which here flows between heavy and costly abutments of stone to protect the rear of the large stores whose fronts are on the Main Street, and whose rear doors open almost immediately over the water. Across the bridge in this odd nook of the stream is St. Mary's, the American Catholic Church, its rear adjoining a long three-storied stone convent building, and its yard sloping down to the water. Strolling up the river a quarter of a mile, one comes upon a long white stone building, which has evidently had much trouble to accommodate itself to the site upon which it is built, and whose line is broken into four or five abrupt angles, while its roof is varied with dormer windows and sharp projections and spires and quaint clock-faces, and its rear is mysterious with lattice-covered balconies and half-hidden corners and corridors. This is the Ursuline Convent; and standing as it does on a rocky and steep (steep for Texas plains) bank of the river, whose course its broken line follows, and down to which its long stern-looking wall descends, it is an edifice at once piquant and sombre, and one cannot resist figuring Mr. James' horseman spurring his charger up the white limestone road that winds alongside the wall, in the early twilight, when dreams come whispering down the current among the willow-sprays.

There are notable places about the town which the stranger must visit. He may ride two miles along a level road between market gardens which are vitalized by a long acequia, or ditch, fed from the river, and come presently upon the quaint gray towers of the old Mission Concepción. The old church, with its high-walled dome in the rear, is in a good state of preservation, and traces of the singular many-colored frescoing on its front are still plainly visible. Climbing a very shaky ladder, one gets upon the roof of a long stone corridor running off from the church building, and, taking good heed of the sharp-thorned cactus which abounds up there, looks over upon a quaint complication of wall-angles, nooks, and small-windowed rooms. . . .

Further down the river a couple of miles one comes to the Mission San José de Aguayo. This is more elaborate and on a larger scale than the buildings of the first Mission, and is still very beautiful. Religious services are regularly conducted here; and one can do worse things than to steal out here from town on some wonderfully calm Sunday morning, and hear a mass, and dream back the century and a half of strange, lonesome, devout, hymn-haunted and Indian-haunted years that have trailed past these walls. Five or six miles further down the river are the ruins of the Mission San Juan in much dilapidation.

Or the visitor may stroll off to the eastward, climb the hill, wander about among the graves of heroes in the large cemetery on the crest of the ridge, and please himself with the noble reaches of country east and west, and with the perfect view of the city, which from here seems "sown," like Tennyson's, "in a monstrous wrinkle of the" prairie. Or, being in search of lions, one may see the actual animal, by a stroll to the "San Pedro Springs Park," a mile or so to the northward. Here, from under a white-ledged rocky hill, burst forth three crystalline springs, which quickly unite and form the San Pedro. With spreading water-oaks, rustic pleasure buildings, promenades along smooth shaded avenues between concentric artificial lakes, a race-course, an aviary, a fine Mexican lion, a bear-pit in which are an emerald-eyed blind cinnamon bear, a large black bear, a wolf and a coyote, and other attractions, this is a very green spot indeed in the prairies. Or one may drive three miles to northward and see the romantic spot where the San Antonio River is forever being born, leaping forth from the mountain, complete, *totus*, even as Minerva from the head of Jove.

Or one may take one's stand on the Commerce Street bridge and involve oneself in the life that goes by this way and that. Yonder comes a long train of enormous blue-bodied, canvas-covered wagons, built high and square in the stern, much like a fleet of Dutch galleons, and lumbering in a ponderous way

71

that suggests cargoes of silver and gold. These are drawn by fourteen mules each, who are harnessed in four tiers, the three front tiers of four mules each, and that next the wagon of two. The "lead" mules are wee fellows, veritable mulekins; the next tier larger, and so on to the two wheel-mules, who are always as large as can be procured. Yonder fares slowly another train of wagons, drawn by great wide-horned oxen, whose evident tendency to run to hump and fore-shoulder irresistibly persuades one of their cousinship to the buffalo.

Here, now, comes somewhat that shows as if Birnam Wood had been cut into fagots and was advancing with tipsy swagger upon Dunsinane. Presently, one's gazing eye receives a sensation of hair, then of enormous ears, and then the legs appear, of the little roan-gray burros, or asses, upon whose backs that Mexican walking behind has managed to pile a mass of mesquite firewood that is simply astonishing. This mesquite is a species of acacia, whose roots and body form the principal fuel here. It yields, by exudation, a gum which is quite equal to gum Arabic, when the tannin in it is extracted. It appears to have spread over this portion of Texas within the last twenty-five years, perhaps less time. The old settlers account for its appearance by the theory that the Indians—and after them the stock-raisers—were formerly in the habit of burning off the prairie-grass annually, and that these great fires rendered it impossible for the mesquite shrub to obtain a foothold; but that now the departure of the Indians and the transfer of most of the large cattle-raising business to points further westward, have resulted in leaving the soil free for the occupation of the mesquite. It has certainly taken advantage of the opportunity. It covers the prairie thickly, in many directions as far as the eye can reach, growing to a pretty uniform height of four or five feet—though occasionally much larger—and presenting with its tough branches and innumerable formidable thorns, a singular appearance. The wood when dry is exceedingly hard and durable, and of a rich mahogany color. This recent overspread of foliage on the plains is supposed by many persons to be the cause of the quite remarkable increase of moisture in the climate of San Antonio which has been observed of late years. The phenomena—of the coincident increase of moisture and of mesquite—are unquestionable; but whether they bear the relation of cause and effect, is a question upon which the unscientific lingerers on this bridge may be permitted to hold themselves in reserve. . . .

And now as we leave the bridge in the gathering twilight and loiter down the street, we pass all manner of odd personages and "characters." Here hobbles an old Mexican who looks like old Father Time in reduced circumstances, his feet, his body, his head all swathed in rags, his face a blur of wrinkles, his beard gray-grizzled—a picture of eld such as one will rarely find. There goes a little German boy who was captured a year or two ago by Indians within three miles of San Antonio, and has just been retaken [1873] and sent home a few days ago.

Do you see that poor Mexican without any hands? A few months ago a wagon-train was captured by Indians at Howard's Wells; the teamsters, of whom he was one, were tied to the wagons and these set on fire, and this poor fellow was released by the flames burning off his hands, the rest all perishing save two. Here is a great Indian-fighter who will show you what he calls his "vouchers," being scalps of the red braves he has slain; there a gentleman who blew up his store here in '42 to keep the incoming Mexicans from benefiting by his goods, and who afterwards spent a weary imprisonment in that stern castle of Perote away down in Mexico, where the Mier prisoners (and who ever thinks nowadays of that strange, bloody Mier Expedition?) were confined; there a portly, handsome, buccaneer-looking captain who led the Texans against Cortinas in '59; there a small, intelligent-looking gentleman who at twenty was first Secretary of War of the young Texan Republic, and who is said to know the history of everything that has been done in Texas from that time to this, minutely; and so on through a perfect gauntlet of people who have odd histories, odd natures or odd appearances, we reach our hotel. . . . ★

---

1. The "original" site of Mission San Antonio de Valero, the Alamo, was a debatable proposition for many years. The original mission had at least three temporary, short-lived sites in 1718-1719. According to City Archaelologist Kay Hinds, the earliest is now presumed to have been where the Christopher Columbus Italian Society headquarters is located, beneath the parking lot of the Piazza di Colombo Park, close to San Pedro Creek, less than a mile west of the present and final location of the Alamo.
2. One labor equals about 177 acres of land.

3. Lanier's numbers—145 defenders supplemented by 32 volunteers from Gonzales on March 1—only comes to 177 defenders. The actual number, ever in dispute, is closer to 187 male defenders. At least 16 non-combatant women, children, and slaves have been surmised to have survived the battle.

4. Lanier's Note: "As transmitted by the Zuber family, whose residence was the first place at which poor Rose had dared to stop, and with whom he remained some weeks, healing the festered wounds made on his legs by the cactus-thorns during the days of his fearful journey. The account from which these extracts are taken, is contributed to the *Texas Almanac* for 1873, by W. P. Zuber, and his mother, Mary Ann Zuber." It is interesting to note how thorough was Lanier's research in that he was aware of this heretofore unknown and subsequently famous addition to the story of the Alamo even before it was published.

5. The altitude downtown is actually 624 feet, rising to 820 feet in Alamo Heights.

6. This paragraph was inserted here by Mary Ann Noonan Guerra for her 1980 edition of the history. As she wrote: "It was formerly a footnote, but has become the most oft-quoted portion of Lanier's historical sketch, and is in fact the source of the plaque on the contemporary bridge recounting this story." ★

STEVEN G. KELLMAN

A native New Yorker, Steven G. Kellman has lived in San Antonio, where he has been a professor of comparative literature at the University of Texas at San Antonio, since 1976. He is the founding president of the city's independent literary center, Gemini Ink, and a recipient of its Award for Literary Excellence as well as of the San Antonio Library Foundation's Arts and Letters Award. The twice-weekly column that Kellman wrote for the *San Antonio Light* from 1983 until the daily's demise in 1993 received the H. L. Mencken Award. A contributing writer to the *San Antonio Current* and the *Texas Observer*, he has also published in the *American Scholar, Atlantic Monthly, Bookforum, Chronicle of Higher Education, Dallas Morning News, Forward, Michigan Quarterly Review, New York Times Book Review, Georgia Review*, the *Nation, Los Angeles Times, New England Review, San Francisco Chronicle*, and *Southwest Review*, among other publications. Kellman served four terms on the board of directors of the National Book Critics Circle and received its Nona Balakian Citation for Excellence in Reviewing. His books include: *Redemption: The Life of Henry Roth* (2005), *The Translingual Imagination* (2000), *The Plague: Fiction and Resistance* (1993), *Loving Reading: Erotics of the Text* (1985), and *The Self-Begetting Novel* (1980). He is editor or coeditor of M. E. Ravage's *An American in the Making: The Life Story of an Immigrant* (2009*), Switching Languages: Translingual Writers Reflect on Their Craft* (2003), *UnderWords: Perspectives on Don DeLillo's "Underworld"* (2002), *Torpid Smoke: The Stories of Vladimir Nabokov* (2000), *Leslie Fiedler and American Culture* (1999), *Into "The Tunnel": Readings in Gass's Novel* (1998), and *Perspectives on Raging Bull* (1994).

The Yellow Rose of Texas: Decision at the Alamo

(I tell not the fall of Alamo,
Not one escaped to tell the fall of Alamo,
The hundred and fifty are dumb yet at Alamo.)
—Walt Whitman, "Song of Myself," lines 872-874

I only am escaped alone to tell thee.
—Job, I. 15

Everyone remembers the Alamo now,
but none so well as Moses, né Louis, Rose did. Rose had the superb mnemonic advantage of being present at the siege until the afternoon of March 3, 1836.[1] Convinced it was a hopeless fight, he saved his life by jumping over a wall and fleeing to safety. A veteran of Napoleonic campaigns in Italy, Spain, and Portugal, Rose was quoted as explaining his conduct during the most glorious episode in Texas history thus: "By God, I wasn't ready to die."

In 1903, the Alamo stood in more acute danger from commercial developers plotting to raze it and erect a hotel on the property than it ever did from Mexican cannon. But timely action by Clara Driscoll and Adina De Zavala, on behalf of the Daughters of the Republic of Texas, preserved the ancient mission as an historic shrine, a permanent reference point in the Texan—and American—psyche. The story of its futile resistance was celebrated in one of D.W. Griffith's early feature films, *Martyrs of the Alamo* (1915), as well as in later popular versions such as *Davy Crockett, King of the Wild Frontier* (1955), *The Last Command* (1955), and *The Alamo* (1960). Folk tradition has familiarized us with the plight of fewer than two hundred volunteers after ten days of withstanding Mexican General Antonio López de Santa Anna's five thousand soldiers. Aware that reinforcements would not be arriving and that the Texian defenders faced certain death, Colonel William Barrett Travis drew a line on the ground and grandiloquently urged all who were willing to sacrifice their lives for liberty to cross over to him. We are asked to believe that every single man—including James Bowie, who, suffering from typhoid-pneumonia, directed that his cot be carried over—crossed that line. And of course all had perished by the final onslaught three days later.

Curiously, though, none of the sixteen surviving non-combatants—women, children, and slaves who remained behind locked doors and out of touch with the fighting during the thirteen-day ordeal—had anything to say about Travis's celebrated challenge. If every witness to this scene was killed before having a chance to report it, how then in this Berkeleyan universe of silently falling trees do we know anything at all about it? Films and books which set out both to dramatize this unanimous pledge and to depict total martyrdom would seem guilty of an elementary breach of logic. They are throwing out their chili with its source.

Despite a controversy, even among scholars, to ignore or to discredit his claims, cogent evidence points to the fact that Moses Rose was the one defender who refused to cross Travis's line and who lived—until 1850—to tell about it. Nevertheless, a monument erected on the Capitol grounds in Austin in 1891 memorializes each of the defenders of the Alamo but forgets the name of Moses Rose. And as late as 1933, Amelia Williams, in the course of a thorough and informed, though flawed, study of the battle, could declare of the Rose affair: "Historians have been divided in their opinion concerning this story, the most careful students have discredited it. At best they consider it a legend, plausible perhaps but almost certainly the creation of a vivid imagination.[2] The "Alamo, Siege and Fall of" entry in Walter Prescott Webb's *The Handbook of Texas* (Austin, 1952) was also written by Amelia Williams and neglects any mention of Rose (Vol. I, pp. 22-3); however, on page 503 of Vol. II there is a separate article on Moses Rose written by R. B. Blake. DeWitt C. Reddick baldly declares in the *Encyclopedia Britannica* (Chicago, 1974, 15th ed.) that " . . . the defenders (about 187) were all killed" (Vol. 18, p. 165). And even more recently, Joe B. Frantz, in *Texas: A Bicentennial History* (New York, 1976), is both charmed by and suspicious of the Moses Rose episode, " . . . when Travis is supposed to have drawn his immortal line across the dirt floor of the Alamo and invited all who would stay and die with him to step over. . . . The symbolism of the line is as important as the veracity of the story" (p. 68). The *Encyclopedia Americana* (New York, 1975) entry on the Alamo, written by David M. Vigness, does repeat the vignette of the sword in the dust but merely attributes it to *vox populi* and never identifies the solitary dissenter: "According to a popular account, he drew a line on the ground with his sword, challenging those who wished to remain to cross the line. All but one did so" (Vol. I, p. 454). Newer travel guides revert to the myth of total martyrdom, to assertions that " . . . no male defender survived"[3] and that ". . . all the defenders were massacred."[4] Nevertheless, three book-length accounts of the fall of the Alamo—*The Alamo,* by John Myers (New York, 1948), *13 Days to Glory: The Siege of the Alamo* by Lon Tinkle (New York, 1958), and *A Time to Stand* by Walter Lord (New York, 1961)—all examine the plausibility of the Rose story and support it.

The first published version of Moses Rose's escape from the Alamo appeared in the *Texas Almanac* of 1873, fully thirty-seven years after the fact. Written by William P. Zuber, it told the story of how, fleeing eastward from the Alamo, Rose stopped to rest in Grimes County at the home of Abraham Zuber, the author's father, and of how he then recounted his extraordinary tale. William P. Zuber, as well as his mother, refined and defended this account on several other occasions.[5] However, the legend of an unmitigated massacre was apparently more appealing. And, in the absence of any testimony to corroborate that of the Zubers, the popular myth, even while assimilating the episode of the line in the dust, refused to acknowledge a dissenting figure, and skeptics even denied the very existence of Louis Moses Rose. But in 1939 R.B. Blake revealed evidence he had discovered among the official records of Nacogdoches County that demonstrated that Moses Rose was not a figment of Zuber's imagination and that he was indeed present at the Alamo.[6] Blake was unaware of documents in the French Archives that further substantiate Zuber's contentions and that provide some additional information on Rose's life before the Alamo.[7]

He was born Louis Rose in La Férée, Ardennes, on May 11, 1785. In 1806, Rose became a private in Napoleon's 101st Regiment, serving with it until 1816 and eventually attaining the rank of lieutenant. Blake repeats Zuber's assertion that Rose participated in Napoleon's disastrous Russian campaign, but this claim is not substantiated by records in the French military archives. Rose did take part in the campaigns in Naples of 1806 through 1810, in those of Portugal in 1811 and 1812, and in the Spanish campaign in 1813 (while Napoleon himself was attempting to conquer Moscow). On March 12, 1814, he was named to the Legion of Honor for his role as aide-de-camp to General Jacques de Montfort.

According to Blake and others, after Waterloo Rose became involved with clandestine schemes to restore his Emperor to power. There is, however, no record of Rose's embarcation from Livorno, along with Lallemand and a coterie of other resolute Bonapartists, or of his arrival with them in Philadelphia in December 1817. Nor is there any evidence of his participation in either of the abortive colonies attempted by unregenerate Napoleonic exiles in Champ d'Asile, Texas, and Aigleville, Alabama. Rose does surface again in 1826, in Louisiana. He was enlisted by Haden Edwards to join him in Nacogdoches, Texas, in the Fredonian Rebellion, an unsuccessful attempt to overthrow Mexican authority. He was issued Texas certificate of entry No. 580 in 1827 and stayed on in Nacogdoches after the battle. He was employed as a log-cutter and hauler for Frost Thorn's sawmill, as well as a messenger between Nacogdoches and Nachitoches, Louisiana.

Rose was apparently befriended by James Bowie, an early organizer of attempts to establish Texian independence. Rose was present at a meeting on the subject in New Orleans on October 13, 1835. County records show that, on October 24, 1835, he sold all the property he owned in Nacogdoches to one Vincente Cordova in exchange for a horse, blankets, and other supplies. He then joined a company commanded by William H. Landrum which set off for the siege of Bexar, the earlier name for San Antonio. After the surrender of General Martín Perfecto de Cos, Rose remained there several months, until massive Mexican forces under Santa Anna returned to Bexar to surround a small contingent of Texians at the Alamo mission.

On the afternoon of March 3, 1836, when the situation of the Alamo defenders had become desperate and Colonel Travis issued the celebrated challenge to his men, Moses Rose was fifty years old, twice the age of most of his comrades. Though Davy Crockett, too, was fifty and Jim Bowie forty, their commanding officer, Travis, was merely twenty-seven. Rose had probably participated in more military actions, both victories and defeats, than any of the others, and, adept at surviving, he must have felt uncomfortable with the symbolic gesture of surrendering his life and for a cause not his own and in the company of men he was separated from by a generation, a language, and a virtual continent. Travis, an impetuous and flamboyant South Carolinian, was enamored of the rhetoric of Sir Walter Scott, and Zuber quotes in detail the extensive, florid oration he delivered to his men. Travis made it clear that their prospects were hopeless but that they still had a role to play in Texas history by resisting the enemy unto death. He concluded by exhorting: "I now want every man who is determined to stay here and die with me to come across this line. Who will be first? March!"

According to the story he later told during the two to three weeks he spent with the Zubers, Rose alone remained on the other side of the line. Bowie declared: "You seem not to be willing to die with us, Rose." And he replied: "No, I am not prepared to die, and shall not do so if I can avoid it."

Travis, a lawyer who had come to Texas in 1831 fleeing an unhappy marriage, quarreled with Bowie over rank. Rose must have felt more kinship with the venerable warrior Bowie than with the impulsive young dandy. Travis assumed virtual command of the Alamo as a result of Bowie's debilitating illness, and he ignored General Sam Houston's exhortations to destroy the fortifications in Bexar and abandon the town. Convinced of the sublimity of his cause, Travis dispatched couriers with histrionic messages to the outside world, and to posterity. Here, for example, is what a proclamation he sent to potential reinforcements on February 24 declares:

> I shall never surrender or retreat. Then, I call on you in the name of Liberty, of patriotism & everything dear to the American character, to come to our aid, with all despatch—The enemy is receiving reinforcements daily & will no doubt increase to three or four thousand in four or five days. Though this call may be neglected, I am determined to sustain myself as long as possible and die like a soldier who never forgets what is due to his own honor and that of his country. Victory or death!

Travis's expansive style, his classical doctrine that *dulce et decorum est pro patria mori* might have struck Rose, a seasoned, plebeian survivor, as dangerously fatuous.

Rose vaulted a wall of the Alamo and, in order to elude Mexican soldiers, first traveled west through the town, then south for three miles along the San Antonio River, and finally east through open prairie. His swarthy complexion and black hair and the fact that he was more fluent in Spanish than English contributed to Rose's success in evading capture by Mexican forces. He fled eastward by night, through harsh, unfamiliar landscape, and the cactus thorns that lodged in his flesh resulted in lameness and chronic sores. During his escape, Rose rested for several days with a hospitable farmer to whom he told his story. When two strangers came by and heard it, they attempted to discredit Rose, alleging that he was notorious in Nacogdoches for his mendacity. The disenchanted host turned Rose out of his house, a humiliation which made Rose increasingly reluctant ever to discuss his ordeal. And his silence in turn served to discourage widespread belief in an escape from the Alamo. Revisionist accounts of the siege still encounter derision and hostility among loyal Texans.

When he reached Iola, Texas, Rose once again recounted his experiences, at the home of his friend Abraham Zuber. Zuber's black servant Maria attempted to remove Rose's garments from the pack he had thrown over the Alamo walls, in an area littered by corpses, before jumping over himself, but she found the clothing glued together with blood. Moses Rose was illiterate and always signed his name with a mark, but to compensate for an inability to read or write, it is likely that he had trained his memory to retain what he saw and heard. Despite distortions, some inevitable and some evitable, in the version of Rose's narrative that Zuber's son published decades later, it remains one of our few primary sources of what happened within the Alamo and our only authority for the story of Travis's linear bravado.

Sufficiently recuperated after two or three weeks in Iola to be able to travel again, Rose settled once more in Nacogdoches, where he opened the only butcher shop in town. It became notorious for the wretched quality of its meat, though when customers complained, Rose would respond splenetically and even violently. When a rival market opened in 1842, Rose abandoned the meat business and became a cobbler. He eventually moved to the farm of Aaron Ferguson 6.5 miles northeast of Logansport, Louisiana, where he died in 1850 and is believed buried.

During his final years in Nacogdoches, Rose was sometimes referred to as "Luesa," the Spanish feminine form of "Louis" and a way of taunting him for his presumed cowardice. Court records indicate that on April 10, 1838, a stranger named Francisco Garcia assaulted him in the street without provocation. Bleeding from a knife wound, Rose succeeded in disarming his attacker but did not press his advantage. For reasons that remain obscure, Garcia was never prosecuted.

Moses Rose never married, but a brother of his settled in Lexington, Kentucky, and raised a family. Nephew Isaac Rose's descendants, now scattered throughout the United States, have transmitted from generation to generation, and not without misgivings, the dim memory of a relative who left the Alamo. The wife of Isaac Rose's great grandson, a resident of Corpus Christi, reports that Moses Rose never received the bounty awarded all those who fought in the Texas Revolution. The State of Texas maintains that the statute of limitations on such payment expired on February 23, 1900.

The names Louis and Isaac Rose, the fact that one of Isaac's sons was named Asa, and Louis's appropriation of "Moses" as his Christian name suggest a Jewish background. Moses Rose was born in a region of France with a sizable Jewish population in the late eighteenth century, and he entered the French Army at a time when, after their legal emancipation, Jews were first being conscripted. Nacogdoches, Texas, where he resided for many years, was the home of many Jewish immigrants during the same period. Most prominent among them were Adolphus Sterne, also a participant in the Fredonian Rebellion and subsequently town alcalde, and Samuel Maas, brother-in-law of Jacques Offenbach. When Rose was called to testify as a character witness in a trial, the court transcript indicates that Juan M. Dor described Rose as "de la religion Cristiana." However, since it was illegal to testify, to own property, or to hold office in Nacogdoches unless one were declared Christian, it is quite possible that, as in the case of Adolphus Sterne, this was simply a *pro forma* avowal.

Moses Rose's Jewishness would encourage a fascinating nineteenth-century American contribution to the myth of the Wandering Jew. Rose was indeed a perpetual vagabond, a somewhat proud and pathetic alien without binding ties to any person or place. Perhaps like the modern willfully cosmopolitan Jew, he sought to create his own identity free of the determinants of race and milieu. Like Ahasuerus, who sealed himself from salvation by denying Christ, Moses Rose chose not to accept beatification through an Alamo martyrdom. Unfortunately for such archetypal Romanticism, though, a British Jew named Anthony Wolfe did choose to die at the Alamo. Moses Albert Levy, Sam Houston's surgeon-general, also took part in the earlier battle of the Alamo during the siege of Bexar in December 1935. And, remembering the Alamo, a Jew named Edward J. Johnson was killed in combat in 1836 under Fannin at Goliad, where three other Jews, Benjamin H. Mordecai, M.K. Moses, and Herman Ehrenburg, also fought for Texas. Furthermore, no living member of the Rose family, which has acquired English and Irish surnames over the past century and a half, will confirm circumstantial evidence of Jewish blood.

The romance of Moses Rose is a parable of choice—of how one man and 187 others chose to end their lives, and of how history has chosen to remember those choices. The Alamo has been preserved, physically and psychically, as a monument to a golden age when men were presumably capable of united, heroic action. To suggest that not every heart within the courtyard of a beleaguered Texas mission beat in fervent unison is to be the kind of historiographical Scrooge who insists that "it is so" about Shoeless Joe Jackson or that Thomas Jefferson spawned illegitimate black offspring. The fanciful apocryphon published by a Texas newspaper early in this century about a majestic Victor Rose who left the Alamo because of an overwhelming and exalted passion for a local woman would preserve the memory of a deserter but merely translate Roland into Tristan. And one curious film treatment of the Alamo does acknowledge an abstention from martyrdom. In *The Man from the Alamo* (1953), directed by Budd Boetticher, Glenn Ford plays the part of a North Texan named John Stroud who is delegated by the Alamo defenders to return home and care for all the fatherless families. In this astonishing Hollywood confection, Rose is transformed into a strong, silent Stroud who, unjustly persecuted as a coward, bears himself stoically and righteously.

Of course the project of debunking, of reducing historical titans to "human" dimensions, presupposes an alternative mythology of what it is to be human. Historians and valets, who sometimes turn to biography after retirement, are increasingly surly, and no man is a hero to either. Major details of the life of

Louis Moses Rose remain unknown and probably unknowable. But for an age of anxiety in which perhaps nothing that is human is not also a bit alien, this tale of a Napoleonic exile and the Texas Revolution would seem exemplary. While his Nacogdoches employer Frost Thorn remained rooted to his sawmill and his land, Rose wandered. Perhaps we need to be reminded that there are not thorns without roses. ★

1. At least that is the date Rose gave much later, when testifying before the Board of Land Commissioners of Nacogdoches County on behalf of claims filed by heirs of six Alamo victims. In "Myths and Realities of the Alamo," *The American West*, V 3 (May 1964), pp. 18-25, Walter Lord argues plausibly that March 5 is a more likely date. But Lord, who sets out to distinguish fact from fancy in stories about the Alamo, refuses to accept the legend of the line in the dust. And his failure to track down primary materials on Rose apparently leads him to say of the Alamo defenders that "…not one was a professional soldier" (p. 20).

2. "A Critical Study of the Alamo and of the Personnel of its Defenders," *Southwestern Historical Quarterly*, XXXVII, 1 (July 1933), p. 31. And Amelia Williams does not even mention Rose in her later "Notes on Alamo Survivors," *Southwestern Historical Quarterly*, XLIX (1936), pp. 634-7.

3. Harry Hansen, ed., *Texas: A Guide to the Lone Star State* (New York, new rev. ed., 1969), p. 43.

4. Beverly Hilowitz and Susan Eikov Green, eds., *Great Historic Places: An American Heritage Guide* (New York, 1980), p. 284.

5. See, for example, William P. Zuber, "My Eighty Years in Texas," *Southwestern Historical Quarterly*, V 1 (Oct. 1901), pp. 247-55.

6. R.B. Blake, "A Vindication of Rose and His Story," in *In the Shadow of History*, ed. J. Frank Dobie, Texas Folklore Society Publications XV (1939), reprinted Detroit: Folklore Associates, 1971, pp. 27-41.

7. AF IV 858, plaquette 6900, cote 91-47; and page 192 of the third volume of the records of the 101st Regiment.

PART TWO

Journalism and Political Essays

EMMA TENAYUCA

Emma Tenayuca was born in 1916 in San Antonio. The second of eleven children, Emma went to live with her grandparents at an early age. Her grandfather often took her to the Plaza de Zacate, now Milam Park, where many political figures of the early twentieth century, mostly socialists and anarchists, but especially exiles from the Mexican Revolution, gave speeches about the plight of poor workers. At sixteen, Emma became involved with the Labor Movement when she joined a picket line—and was arrested—during a strike against the Finck Cigar Company. By the age of twenty, Tenayuca had become General Secretary for ten chapters of the Workers Alliance of America.

Tenayuca was concerned about the extreme poverty and injustice suffered by Mexican American workers. Refused by both the Democratic and Republican parties, Tenayuca turned to the one party that advocated most openly for not only workers rights, but minority rights—the American Communist Party, which she joined in 1936. She married organizer Homer Bartchy in 1938. Bartchy used the alias "Homer Brooks." They were shortly elected, respectively, as the State Chairman and State Secretary of the American Communist Party in Texas.

In 1938, wages for south Texas pecan shellers (*nueceros*) were cut drastically. Cases of tuberculosis almost doubled among the workers, mostly caused by breathing pecan dust in crowded, closed rooms. Ironically, workers were used to shell pecans even though shelling machines were available, because human laborers were less expensive than the machines. Tenayuca was extremely intelligent, very well read, a powerful writer, and highly respected for both her speeches and her negotiation skills. The workers asked Tenayuca to represent them in a strike against the Southern Pecan Shelling Company. Thus, at the age of twenty-one, she led the city's twelve thousand pecan shellers in a demand for decent wages and better working conditions. At several points, well over eight thousand workers actively engaged in the strike, despite their starvation-level poverty. Company "enforcers" and local police gassed the workers, arrested, and jailed hundreds at a time.

Tenayuca was herself jailed many times and denied work because of her defense of the poor. In 1939, Tenayuca spoke at a small party meeting, held in San Antonio's Municipal Auditorium. Activist mayor and former congressman Maury Maverick Sr. had allowed use of the auditorium based on the constitutional guarantee of free speech. A mob of over five thousand Anglo-Americans stormed the auditorium, forcing Tenayuca to escape by a rear exit leading to the river.

When Tenayuca died on July 23, 1999, over a thousand people attended her funeral at San Fernando Cathedral. Tenayuca has been the inspiration for plays, corridos (ballads) and many papers, as well as a children's book written by poet Carmen Tafolla and Emma's niece, lawyer Sharyll Teneyuca, *That's Not Fair! Emma Tenayuca's Struggle for Justice*, illustrated by artist Terry Ybáñez. Tenayuca and her writing undoubtedly had an impact on San Antonio Chicana writers and activists during the *movimiento*.

Only nominally coauthored by Homer Brooks, "The Mexican Question in the Southwest" (*The Communist*, March 1939) is an example of Tenayuca's fiery political rhetoric coupled with almost prescient insight. Written in 1939, when Tenayuca was just twenty-three, the article calls for Latino-Black alliances on issues of civil rights, fully bilingual education, recognition of Anglo theft of US Latino lands, as well as coordinated international action to thwart Nazi efforts to bring fascism to the Americas. In short, before there was a Martin Luther King Jr., or a Cesar Chávez, there was Emma.

THE MEXICAN QUESTION IN THE SOUTHWEST

Emma Tenayuca and Homer Brooks
State Chairman and State Secretary, Communist Party, Texas

HISTORICAL BACKGROUND

THE WAR OF THE UNITED STATES WITH MEXICO, in 1846, following the annexation of Texas, resulted in the conquest of the territory which now makes up the states of California, New Mexico, Arizona, Colorado and part of Utah and Nevada. From the historical point of view the forcible incorporation of these areas into the United States was progressive, in that it opened up for development these territories which until then had stagnated under the inefficient, tyrannical, and semi-feudal control of Mexico. The predominant influence of the Spanish in the Southwest, particularly in California, New Mexico, Arizona, Colorado and Texas, can be seen in the names of such cities as Los Angeles, Santa Fe, San Antonio, San Diego and San Francisco.

The acquisition of these lands brought into the Union a population originally Spanish and later Mexican, whose customs, language, traditions and culture were essentially different from those of the rest of the country. In the border area of the Southwest the Mexicans have always constituted a majority, both before and after the war with Mexico.

The expansion and industrialization that followed the Civil War, lasting until a relatively late period in the Southwest, saw the importation of thousands of Mexican workers into Texas, California, Colorado and Arizona. (To a lesser degree this was true of New Mexico, for geographical reasons. Deserts and mountains bordering Mexico prevented free interrelation with old Mexico; at the same time this border region has not made for the development of large-scale capitalist farming.) Railroad companies alone were responsible for a great number of those imported. It is safe to say that most of the railroads of these five states were built by Mexican labor.

With the development of capitalist farming in these states, and particularly in California and Texas, Mexico was again a source of cheap labor. Early figures on the number of Mexicans immigrating into the United States are not available, since until a relatively late period entrance into the United States was comparatively simple. Complete figures as to the number of Mexicans in the United States are today not available, since until 1930 Mexicans living here were not classified separately.

However, between 1925 and 1929 the heaviest immigration from Mexico took place. In the course of these five years, 283,738 Mexicans entered the United States.... The 1930 census showed 1,500,000 Mexicans residing in the United States. Of these, all but 150,000 were found to be living in the states of California, Texas, New Mexico, Colorado and Arizona. However, these figures include only the foreign-born and first generation Mexicans. They exclude the large Spanish-speaking population of New Mexico, which, according to H. T. Manuel of the University of Texas, numbers over 250,000, or approximately half the state population. These figures also exclude Mexicans of the third, fourth, and fifth generations and those descendants of the early Spanish colonists of any of the other four states. Therefore, we can readily state that the Mexican population of the Southwest numbers approximately 2,000,000.

Thus, we can see that the present Mexican population in the Southwest is made up of two groups: descendants of those living in the territory at the time of annexation, and immigrant and first or second generation native-born drawn from the impoverished peasantry of Northern Mexico to work as super-exploited wage-workers in railroad and building construction and in highly developed (capitalist) agriculture in the border area. However, there is no sharp distinction between these two groups, either in their social conditions or in their treatment at the hands of the Anglo-American bourgeoisie. Assimilation among those groups which were here before the conquest of these territories by the United States has been slow, and the Spanish language remains today the language of both groups.

The distinction has been sharpened somewhat in New Mexico, since a lack of direct contact with Mexico led the majority of Mexicans to regard themselves as Spanish-Americans or Latin Americans, and consequently to regard Spain rather than Mexico as the mother country. However, this distinction is being done away with more and more by the social conditions under which the Mexicans or Spanish-Americans are suffering, which are breaking down barriers and leading to unification. The pro-Mexico sentiment among the people in New Mexico was seen when the Spanish-speaking population rallied to support Mexico during the recent oil expropriations and even raised funds to be sent to Mexico.

Those Spanish-speaking people of Texas whose ancestors were in the state prior to its annexation from Mexico today regard themselves as Mexicans. We can thus state that the Spanish-speaking population of the Southwest, both the American-born and the foreign-born, are one people.

The Mexican population of the Southwest is closely bound together by historical, political and cultural ties.

The treatment meted out to the Mexicans as a whole has, from the earliest days of the sovereignty of the United States, been that of a conquered people. From the very beginning they were robbed of their land, a process that has continued even up to the present time. In 1916, immediately following the abortive De la Rosa movement in the Texas lower Rio Grande Valley for an autonomous Mexican regime, Texas Rangers, in cooperation with land speculators, came into small Mexican villages in the border country, massacred hundreds of unarmed, peaceful Mexican villagers, and seized their lands. Sometimes the seizures were accompanied by the formality of signing bills of sale—at the point of a gun. So that, where, until 1916, virtually all the land was the property of Mexicans, today almost none of it is Mexican-owned. In many cases farmers who were well-to-do land owners today barely eke out a living employed as irregular wage workers at 60c to 75c a day on the very lands they once owned. This land-grabbing has continued under one guise or another throughout the Southwest. In New Mexico fewer than one-half of the Mexican or Spanish-American farmers retain any of their ancestral lands.

The Present Social Status of the Mexican People

With the penetration of Anglo-Americans into these states, the Mexicans have been practically segregated into colonies. This is particularly true of Colorado. Disease, low wages, discrimination, and lack of educational facilities are typical of these communities.

Mexican labor imported into the United States has uniformly received lower wages than those paid Anglo-American workers. The vast majority of the Southwest are today found doing only the most menial work, the bulk of them having been excluded from skilled crafts. In the cities, although Mexicans are found in the garment industry and laundries and as laborers in building construction, the overwhelming majority are also seasonal agricultural workers. This is true of the Mexicans in all states except the Spanish-Americans of New Mexico, where instead of being agricultural workers, the majority are small farmers, tenants or share-croppers.

. . .

Near-starvation faces thousands of Mexican agricultural workers who must live part of the year in the cities and try to get work on W.P.A. A special clause in the relief appropriation act of 1937, which excludes foreign-born workers who have not taken out citizenship papers, resulted in dismissals of thousands from W.P.A. In El Paso, for example, 600 out of 1,800 on W.P.A. were so dismissed.

The reaction of most of the Mexican W.P.A. workers to these dismissals could not lead to acquiring citizenship papers due to language, cost, and other burdensome obstacles. Their resentment was expressed by demanding the opportunity to work on all jobs, regardless of citizenship, a demand which by virtue of their historical rights in this territory is unchallengeable.

Discrimination against the Mexican people can also be seen in regard to relief appropriations. The Relief Commission of Los Angeles presents a special budget claiming that diet and living expenses are lower among the Mexicans than among other sections of the population. Since the Mexicans live in houses without electricity or natural gas, they are subject to smaller relief portions in every state of the Southwest.

The conditions of the Mexican agricultural workers can only be compared to those of the Negro sharecroppers in the South. According to the United Cannery, Agricultural, Packing and Allied Workers of America, the average wage of the Mexican beet worker in Colorado is from $100 to $200 per year. The average wage of the Texas cotton picker is considerably less; in 1938 it ranged from 35c to 75c per 100 lbs. In those places where the U.C.A.P.A.W.A. carried on struggles, the prices were raised.

In New Mexico, where the Mexicans or Spanish-Americans have been engaged in small farming, fully one half of the farmers have lost their land. Individuals such as John T. Raskob and large corporations have taken over ownership, and sharecropping is rapidly taking the place of small independent farming. Another factor which threatens the existence of the farmers of New Mexico and the agricultural workers of the Southwest has been the large migration of Anglo-American farmers from the dust bowl.

The crisis has intensified the competition for jobs; a fact that is resulting more and more in displacing Mexican workers in the cities. For example, the

Sun-Tex canneries in Texas, located in a city with an overwhelming majority of Mexicans, hires only Anglo-American workers.

The Mexicans are not only subject to wage differentials and discrimination, but a view of their political status in the five states referred to reveals conditions in many ways comparable to the political status of the Negro people in the South. Denial of voting rights to the foreign born means disfranchisement of nearly half of the adult Mexican population. Secondly, the semi-migratory character of the work of most Mexican workers disfranchises in addition many of those who are citizens. Finally, in Texas the poll tax disfranchises many of those who would otherwise be able to vote. Thus due to one or another of the three causes, in San Antonio, a city of 250,000, nearly half of whom are Mexicans, only 8,000 Mexicans were eligible to vote in 1938.

This disfranchisement has resulted in nearly complete Anglo-American domination politically in most of the communities where the Mexican people are a majority. In only two or three counties in Texas do the Mexicans hold the decisive elective positions. (In New Mexico, the situation is otherwise, since there the majority are Spanish-American, non-migratory, and no poll tax is in force.) The 800,000 Mexicans in Texas have only two representatives in the State Legislature.

Lack of representation in local or state politics and low economic standards have resulted in poor health conditions and lack of educational facilities. An example of this is Texas, where the death rate among Mexicans is decidedly higher than among Anglo-Americans, and even higher than the rate among Negroes. . . . Health conditions among Mexicans are evidently worse than among any other section of the population in the Southwest, or even in the United States. San Antonio has the highest infant mortality rate of any large city in the United States. It likewise has a higher rate of deaths from tuberculosis than any other city in the country.

The unequal treatment that the Mexican people suffer is manifested in all phases of life. The practice of excluding Mexicans from hotels and restaurants is prevalent in all these five states. A few years ago an international incident took place in Victoria, Texas, when an official delegation of students from Mexico was excluded from a restaurant. Signs bar Mexicans from dance halls in

Los Angeles. In Colorado small town restaurants display signs: "White Trade Only."

Segregation of Mexican children in small town public schools in Texas is a common practice. Several years ago a group of Mexican taxpayers in San Antonio, by threatening to withhold the payment of school taxes, successfully fought this issue. A few months ago, Dr. Juan Del Rio, a resident of San Marcos, had to bring suit against the school board of that city to win the right of his children to attend the school established for Anglo-American children.

The suppression of the Spanish language, of the native culture of the Mexicans, is one of the reasons for the high rate of illiteracy. The most important reason is, of course, the semi-migratory life of the agricultural worker, which forces the children out of school at an early age, and makes school attendance irregular for many. . . .

To summarize, the Mexican people of the Southwest have a common historical background and are bound by a common culture, language, and communal life. It should be noted, however, that the Mexican communities exist side by side with Anglo-American communities within a territory where the populated districts are separated by large but thinly populated mountainous and arid regions.

Should the conclusion, therefore, be drawn that the Mexican people in the Southwest constitute a nation—or that they form a segment of the Mexican nation (South of the Rio Grande)? Our view is no. Historically, the Mexican people in the Southwest have evolved in a series of bordering, though separated, communities, their economic life inextricably connecting them, not only with one another, but with the Anglo-American population in each of these separated Mexican communities. Therefore, their economic (and hence, their political) interests are welded to those of the Anglo-American people of the Southwest.

We must accordingly regard the Mexican people in the Southwest as part of the American nation, who, however, have not been so accepted heretofore by the American bourgeoisie; the latter has continued to hinder the process of national unification of the American people by treating the Mexican and Spanish-Americans as a conquered people.

Comrade Stalin's classic definition of a nation states: *"A nation is a histori-cally evolved, stable community of language, territory, economic life, and psycholog-ical make-up manifested in a community of culture."*[1] We see, therefore, that the Mexicans in the United States lack two of the important characteristics of a nation, namely, territorial and economic community.

THE SIMILARITY BETWEEN MEXICAN AND NEGRO CONDITIONS

The status of the Mexican people as an oppressed national group may be compared in a number of aspects with that of the Negro people in the South today. The policy of a wage differential, based upon the super-exploitation of the Negroes, has been carried over from the South and applied to the Mexican population of the Southwest. The treatment accorded the Mexicans is also a carryover to the United States of Wall Street's imperialistic exploitation of Latin America.

The degree of oppression can also be compared to that suffered by the Negro people. Every effort of the Mexican people to organize has been met by repression, as in the case of the San Antonio pecan workers. The threat of deportation has been an important weapon used by the reactionary forces to break strikes and keep the workers from organizing.

Likewise, we might compare the social forms of discrimination of the Mexicans, previously cited, with those of the Negro people.

SOCIAL AND POLITICAL DEMANDS IN RECENT STRUGGLES

During the first series of demonstrations among the unemployed in San Antonio, the Border Patrolmen were used against the Mexicans. Scores were herded before the United States Immigration office and threatened with deportation merely for membership in the Workers Alliance. On one occasion a number were beaten, including several American-born Mexicans.

The demand for the right to organize into unions without interference from the immigration authorities was immediately raised. As a result of the struggle by the Mexicans around this issue, the Border Patrolmen of San Antonio have not been used again as a strike-breaking agency.

Upon the formation of locals of the U.C.A.P.A.W.A. in the Rio Grande

Valley in Texas, the Mexican workers raised the demand for school conducted in Spanish. At the Brownsville (Texas) district convention of the U.C.A.P.A.W.A., a resolution calling for the establishment of schools to be conducted in both English and Spanish in all towns where Mexicans were a majority was unanimously adopted.

A year ago the announcement by the Workers Alliance of San Antonio of a campaign to combat illiteracy brought 250 Mexicans who registered for classes. However, the Mexicans would only attend classes providing they were taught in Spanish, a demand to which the W.P.A. acceded.

The tendency of the Mexican people toward solidarity was clearly manifested during the pecan strike in San Antonio a year ago. Scores of small Mexican merchants signed petitions demanding of Mayor Quinn the right of the strikers peacefully to picket the factories without interference from the police.

The recent struggles of Mexicans in New Mexico are significant. Liga Obrera, an organization of small farmers, has not only fought evictions successfully, but has also taken up the struggle against all kinds of discrimination and for W.P.A. jobs. Thus Liga Obrera and the U.C.A.P.A.W.A. unions in Texas and Colorado have not only taken up the economic demands of the workers, but have entered the struggle for social, cultural and political demands.

WHAT PATH TO FOLLOW

Until now the various struggles of the Mexican people in the Southwest have been limited in the main to isolated instances enjoying only partial or purely local support. Strike struggles by the Mexican workers in all Southwestern states; struggles to hold the land in New Mexico; large demonstrations against discrimination in relief in most centers of Mexican population, particularly in San Antonio; and, finally, occasional struggles by various middle-class organizations, especially the League of United Latin American Citizens (L.U.L.A.C.) against discrimination and segregation, is the record of recent years.

The struggles of the last few years signalize the awakening of the Mexicans and Spanish-Americans in the Southwest. *The task is now to build the democratic front among the Mexican masses through unifying them on the basis of specific needs and in support of the social and economic measures of the New Deal.*

A significant beginning in this direction is the forthcoming First Congress of the Mexican and Spanish-American people, to be held in Albuquerque, New Mexico. . . . The preparations for the Congress are a direct outgrowth of the mass struggles in San Antonio and New Mexico. It is sponsored by labor, fraternal and religious organizations among the Mexican people, as well as by Anglo-American political and community leaders in Southwestern states.

The desire of the Mexican people for unification is indicated, not only by the present preparations for this Congress, but also by two conferences held recently in Texas, initiated independently of the Congress movement but which now have joined in its sponsorship. We refer here to the Dallas national conference of the Camara de Trabajadores Mexicanos of the United States, a national group of loosely federated workers' clubs, and the Port Arthur State Conference of Mexican Societies, initiated by a number of Mexican fraternal societies with consular support.

In California, a thoroughly representative State Congress of the Mexican people has been held in preparation for the national gathering. Similar steps are under way in New Mexico, Colorado and Arizona.

Upon what is this movement for Mexican unification based? What are its main objectives?

It is a people's movement, uniting the interest of large and important sections of the population, over two million strong, who, in alliance with the country's democratic forces, in the Southwest and nationally, can free themselves from the special oppression and discrimination in all its phases that have existed for almost a century.

The struggle is directed:

1. Against economic discrimination—extra low wages; expropriation of small land holders; discrimination in the right to work in all trades and crafts, particularly skilled trades; discrimination against professional and white collar workers; discrimination in relief and right to employment in W.P.A.

2. For educational and cultural equality—equal educational facilities for

the Mexican population; no discrimination against children of Mexican parentage; a special system of schooling to meet the needs of migratory families; the study of the Spanish language and the use of Spanish as well as English in the public schools and universities in communities where Mexicans are a majority; the granting of equal status to the Spanish language, as has been done in New Mexico and in those counties and states where the Mexican people form a large part of the total population.

3. Against social oppression—for laws making illegal the various forms of Jim-Crowism, segregation in living quarters, schools, parks, hotels, restaurants, etc. This struggle must be linked with that of the Negro people.

4. Against political repression. The struggle for the right to vote is divided into two phases:

(a) The majority of the Mexicans are American-born. The problem is, therefore, one of enforcing their citizenship rights. This means demanding that all legal and extra-legal restrictions to the free exercise of the ballot be removed. These include residence qualifications, difficult for semi-migratory workers to meet; and in Texas, the elimination of the poll tax.

(b) Those who are foreign born must join with all of the immigrant groups in the United States to secure the democratization of the federal regulations pertaining to the length of time, cost, and language conditions required for citizenship; the aim being to simplify the process whereby all who intend to remain permanent residents of the United States—and this includes nearly all the Mexicans—and who express a desire for naturalization, can become citizens.

In some states, as in Texas, it may become feasible to restore, at least until federal requirements for becoming citizens become less onerous, the provisions in the Texas state constitution which, until 1921, granted voting rights to all Mexicans and other foreign born, citizens and non-citizens, providing they met residence requirements and declared their desire for American citizenship.[2]

In this general movement the leading role will undoubtedly be played by the proletarian base of the Mexican population, its overwhelming majority. This is already evident from the impetus given the movement for Mexican rights by the large strike struggles in Texas, California and Colorado. The surest guarantee for the full and successful development of the people's movement will be in further trade union organization among the Mexican workers; in the first place, in the A.C.A.P.A.W.A., affiliated with the C.I.O.

It would, of course, be the greatest mistake to give a purely *labor* aspect to this broad people's movement. But to be most effective, this movement must bring about the closest relationship with the labor and democratic forces in the Anglo-American population of the Southwest.

That the Anglo-Americans will respond to any initiative taken by Mexican people in seeking a closer relationship and mutual benefits is evident from such examples as that in Colorado, where the Mexican beet workers (U.C.A.P.A.W.A.) have an agreement with the Anglo-American farmers for joint action against the beet-sugar interests that exploit them both.

In San Antonio, last year's strike of 12,000 pecan workers could not have been successful without the important support it received from national and state councils of the C.I.O. and from progressive Anglo-American political leaders, such as Maury Maverick, in defense of civil rights. In the Texas Rio Grande Valley, unity between the small Anglo-American farmers and the Mexican agricultural workers will be the key to improving the conditions of both.

STERILE PATHS

One of the oldest organizations among the Mexican people is the League of United Latin American Citizens (L.U.L.A.C.) with branches in most of the Southwestern states. In the past, its viewpoint was colored by the outlook of petty-bourgeois native-born, who seek escape from the general oppression that has been the lot of the Mexican people as a whole. It meant an attempt to achieve Americanization, while barring the still un-naturalized foreign-born from membership.

It resulted in the glorification of the English language and Anglo-American culture to the extent of prohibiting Spanish within the local societies. And, finally, it ignored the need for labor organization among the masses of super-exploited workers. This program of the L.U.L.A.C. resulted almost from the beginning in its isolation from the Mexican masses, who felt that it would lead them nowhere except to a possible split between the native and foreign-born. The extreme to which this policy led the L.U.L.A.C. was shown in Colorado a few years ago, when, at the height of the depression, a Republican governor proposed to deport 50,000 Mexican workers who were on relief, and the L.U.L.A.C. in Denver endorsed this proposal.

Recently, this splitting policy of the L.U.L.A.C. has undergone significant changes. An amendment to its constitution recognizes Mexico as the cultural motherland. In several cities in Texas and in New Mexico, the L.U.L.A.C. has entered into cooperative relationship with other Mexican groups, including labor organizations. In Texas they have led successful struggles against segregation in public schools, parks, etc., not only in behalf of American citizens, but of all Mexicans. With this change in the orientation of L.U.L.A.C., which is welcomed by all friends of the people's unification, it can be confidently expected that this important organization of the Mexican middle class will play an increasing role in the general movement for Mexican rights.

Among the proposed solutions to the Mexican question is the idea of repatriation. By this proposal, the 2,000,000 Mexican and Spanish-American people in the Southwest can be transported to Mexico. It is easy to see that this plan is fantastic, if only because, as we have shown, the 2,000,000 people under consideration are bound to the American soil by historical roots, cultural peculiarities, due to intermingling through several generations with the Anglo-Americans, who hold that either repatriation or some other means of exodus—at least from the larger cities—is an economic necessity, on the assumption that (as, for example, in San Antonio) "there is such a large population of unskilled common labor that the problem of their reemployment can never be solved." To these people we must say that the solution lies:

1. In removing the barriers to employment of Mexicans in all categories of skilled, white collar and professional work.
2. In facilitating the cultural development of the Mexican people,

which will help eliminate the conditions responsible for their status as unskilled workers.

The attitude of the American bourgeoisie to the Mexican question in the Southwest is not uniform. That section which derives super-profits from the exploitation of Mexican wage labor is content with the status quo. Another section is anxious now that capitalist expansion and construction in the Southwest have passed their peak to get rid of the relief burden of the unemployed masses, by deportation to Mexico, à la Hitler. A third section still clings to the former program of the L.U.L.A.C.—Americanization by assimilation.

It is only recently, with the growth of the labor movement among the Mexican people, that a correct program has developed, calling for abolition of all restrictions—economic, political and cultural—and for due recognition of the historic rights of the Mexican people in this territory.

THE SIGNIFICANCE OF THE MEXICAN RIGHTS MOVEMENT

"No people oppressing other people can be free," wrote Engels[3] in 1874. The correctness of Engels's statement is validated in the low wages, and generally low social status of the majority of the Anglo-American workers who live in the areas where the Mexican people form a large portion of the population. The status of the Mexican people in those areas has, further, tended to make them easy prey to corrupt and reactionary political machines—a consequence that affects the vital interests of the Anglo-American population in the Southwest.

The rise of the Mexican people's movement is therefore of crucial importance to the general democratic and progressive movement of the Anglo-American people in the Southwest, which is already developing under the leadership of such men as Maury Maverick in Texas and Olson in California.

It is likewise significant in relation to the movement for Negro rights in the South. For, the special exploitation of the Mexican people in the Southwest is, in many respects, simply a continuation of the special exploitation and oppression to which the Negro people in the South have been subjected. A blow against the oppression of one will be a blow for the freedom of both.

Internationally, the Mexican and Spanish-American people's movement in the United States has an important bearing on the relationship between the United States and Latin America, especially Mexico. Unless the "Good Neighbor" policy begins at home, with respect to the treatment of the Mexican people, it will be difficult to convince Latin Americans of the sincerity of this policy.

It is interesting to note that a fascist publication in Mexico City, *Novedades*, a vehicle for Nazi influence, and therefore an opponent of the efforts made in Lima to organize the Western Hemisphere against fascist penetration, seized upon the fate of the 2,000,000 Mexicans in the Southwest—whose condition is described as being worse than that of the Jews in Germany—as an argument: (1) against the Mexican people concerning themselves with Jewish persecutions in Germany; (2) for a struggle against "Jewish-dominated capitalists" of the United States, who "hold the Mexican population of the Southwest in bondage." The winning of the people in the Southwest for an anti-fascist peace policy and for continental solidarity of the Western Hemisphere, therefore, means winning them to a realization of the need for granting recognition to the historical rights of the Mexican people in the Southwest.

Due to their proximity to Mexico, it is important to the democratic people's front movement in that country that the Mexican people of the United States be organized, united and brought into progressive alignment with the democratic forces of the United States, as a barrier to the efforts of the Nazi-financed Mexican fascists to win a base among the Mexicans in the border states in order to further their aims in Mexico itself.

The Mexican people's movement in the Southwest will constitute one more important and powerful link in the growing movement for the democratic front in the United States. The achievement of its objectives will be a decisive step forward toward the national unification of the American people.[4] ★

---

1. Joseph Stalin, *Marxism and the National and Colonial Question,* p. 8, International Publishers, New York.

2. The special status due to historic conditions that the Mexican people occupied prior to the migration of Anglo-Americans into the Southwestern states can be seen from the following two factors: First, only six months' residence but not citizenship was the requirement for voting among Mexicans in Texas until 1921, when the state constitution was amended. Secondly, the Spanish language has, from the earliest days, been an official language alongside of English in New Mexico. However, this does not mean that the Mexicans during this time were not subject to discrimination, Jim-Crowism, and unequal wages.

3. *Volksstaat*, 1874, No. 69.

4. "Only through the medium of *an alliance of peoples conducting a self-sacrificing struggle for the cause of peace* is it possible to frustrate the criminal plans of the instigators of war. A defense cordon of armed peoples who have joined their forces with the great Soviet people will doom fascism to impotence and hasten on its defeat and its inevitable ruin."
— *Manifesto of the Executive Committee of the Communist International*, Nov. 7, 1938

Jan Jarboe Russell

Born in Beaumont, Texas, Jan Jarboe Russell graduated from the University of Texas at Austin in 1972 and became a political reporter for the *San Antonio Light*. In 1976, she joined the Hearst Bureau in Washington, DC. Later, she was a columnist for the *San Antonio Express-News*. After a year as a Nieman Fellow at Harvard in 1984, she began to pursue long-form journalism and joined *Texas Monthly* magazine as a senior editor. Her 1989 story, "Adoption: The Woes of Wednesday's Child," about the need for reform of adoption practices in Texas, was selected the best magazine story of the year by the Headliner's Club in Austin. In 1993, she won that award again for a story entitled "Why me?" about the family of the Rev. Jimmy Allen, who lost three members to AIDS. She is currently a contributing editor to *Texas Monthly*. She is the author of *Lady Bird: A Biography of Mrs. Johnson* (Scribner's, 1999), named by the *Washington Post* as one of the best books of the year. In 2015, Scribner's published *The Train To Crystal City*, a *New York Times* bestseller. The book exposes the little-known story of a family internment camp located in Crystal City, Texas, during World War II. *The Train To Crystal City* won the 2016 Carr P. Collins Award for Best Book of Nonfiction, given by the Texas Institute of Letters. Jan lives in San Antonio with her husband, Dr. Lewis F. Russell Jr.

Letter from San Antonio
No Retreat! No Surrender!

Besieged by critics on all sides, the Daughters of the Republic of Texas have once again vowed to fight to the death. But is it finally time for the defenders of the Alamo to raise the white flag?

At about noon on June 13, 2010, the feast day of Saint Anthony, four actors carried an eight-foot statue of San Antonio's namesake and brought it to rest in front of the Alamo. They were under the direction of Rolando Briseño, a

58-year-old artist and impresario with closely cropped dark hair and inquisitive, darting eyes. Briseño's forehead was beaded with sweat, and he wore a crisp, short-sleeved guayabera and a triumphant smile as he led a procession of more than two hundred revelers in the staging of a fiesta designed to, in his words, "reconceptualize the Alamo as a space for celebrating the confluences of cultures—Native American, African, Mexican, and Anglo—rather than a shrine to Anglo dominance."

On Briseño's mark, the bearers flipped the statue upside down. "In Catholic tradition, people pray to saints for help," he said earnestly. "The statue of Saint Anthony is turned upside down when praying for favors. Many of us have asked for years that Mexican Americans, heirs of the builders and descendants of the original people of this city, share in the Alamo legacy."

Soon the fiesta began. A Native American shaman blessed Briseño and the crowd of mostly Mexican American scholars, artists, and writers, waving a seashell filled with incense as halos of sweet-smelling sage floated through the air. Finally Briseño declared the event a success. For a day at least, Hispanics had participated in the story of the Alamo. With another swift flip, Saint Anthony stood right side up against the backdrop of the mute and immobile facade of the mission. Everyone cheered, including the usual herd of tourists who had gathered in the plaza.

Less than a week later, when the news broke that the state's attorney general had launched an investigation into the Daughters of the Republic of Texas for failing to fix the cracked and leaky roof in the nearly three-hundred-year-old chapel, some in San Antonio speculated that the public spell cast by Briseño may have supernaturally contributed to the DRT's troubles. In addition to finding themselves under official scrutiny by Greg Abbott, the powerful matriarchs, who have been the custodians of the Alamo since 1905, were also at loggerheads with Governor Rick Perry for attempting to acquire a federal trademark on the words "The Alamo."

But that is only one front in the battle for control of what most people revere as the shrine of Texas liberty. As the stewardship of the starchy old guard of the DRT is being threatened, many aspects of the myth of the Alamo are crumbling under the weight of rapid cultural change. And just as in the original battle, no one is backing down. The DRT won't give an inch. Modern-day secessionists routinely hold rallies in front of the Alamo. Petitions are circulated in support of Arizona's anti-immigration laws. And activists such as Briseño and Rosie Castro, the mother of San Antonio mayor Julián Castro, have fired back. Complaining of the mythologizing of Anglo heroes at the battle of 1836 and the disparaging of Mexicans, Rosie was quoted last May in the *New York Times Magazine* as saying this of the Alamo: "I can truly say that I hate that place and everything it stands for."

The tension has been building for generations. Indeed, from the moment the DRT took control in 1905 there was infighting among the organization. A divide emerged between two women: Adina Emilia de Zavala, whose grandfather Lorenzo De Zavala served as the first vice president of the Republic of Texas, and Clara Driscoll, a daughter of a wealthy railroad and ranching tycoon. Clara had the upper hand as she had paid $5,000 for a thirty-day option on the Alamo and advanced another $17,812 as down payment for the state to purchase the Alamo. When the twenty-ninth Texas Legislature voted to appropriate $65,000 to purchase the Alamo on January 26, 1905, they transferred the Alamo to Clara's chapter of the DRT (formally known as the Alamo Mission Chapter) not to Adina's chapter (known as the De Zavala Chapter). The two women were at odds over the long barracks property on the Alamo grounds. Clara believed that the long barracks were immaterial to history and wanted them torn down and the space converted to a park. Adina, a teacher and historian, was convinced that the barracks were the site of the major portion of the historic battle of 1836 and should be saved. Lawsuits were filed. On February 13, Adina barricaded herself within the long barracks for three days and refused water or food. The impassioned sit-in made headlines across the country but was not successful. In the end, Clara's faction won the battle—the two-story stonewalls of the barracks were demolished. While the fight was centered on the long barracks, a subtext of the fight revolved around Adina's mixed ethnic ancestry: she was Mexican and Irish heritage on her father's side while Clara was not only rich but a clear representation of Anglo dominance.

Many years later, on October 24, 1960, John Wayne's *The Alamo* premiered at San Antonio's Woodlawn Theatre. As Davy Crockett, Wayne personified the rugged ideal of Texans as an independent breed. Wayne swaggers and says in the film, "'Republic.' I like the sound of the word. Means people can live free, talk free, go or come, buy or sell. Some words give you a feeling. 'Republic' is one of those words that makes me tight in the throat." For many, Wayne's speech describes not only the dream of the Alamo but the dream of Texas itself.

"I was in elementary school when the movie premiered," said Virginia Van Cleave, the chairwoman of the Alamo Committee of the DRT. "It was a huge event for the city. John Wayne came, and the celebration lasted for days." In 2010, to commemorate the anniversary of the noble lost battle, the cash-strapped Daughters have planned a fund-raising gala on the stone plaza in front of the Alamo. Wayne's daughter and granddaughter were on hand to accept the Daughters' first Spirit of the Alamo award, which was posthumously given to the actor. Once again, the legend of Crockett, dying as Wayne did in the movie, surrounded by an army of Mexicans led by a tyrant, will be celebrated. Whether the story of the battle is told *ranchera* style, over robust bowls of chili, by dry-eyed historians, or by Walt Disney, we find the seeds not only of independence but our historic ethnic unease.

On a bright, sunny morning Van Cleave was at work in the DRT's inner sanctum, which is located behind the gardens of the Alamo. Her desk was stacked high with papers, architectural drawings, and photos of cracks in the roof of what the DRT calls "the shrine." Van Cleave is a large, softly shaped woman with a sweet, distinctly Southern disposition. She wore a gold necklace strung with charms of San Antonio's five Spanish missions. As she leaned forward, the Alamo charm dangled directly over her heart. Since the Alamo has lost two directors and a marketing director—all professionals with deep résumés—in less than two years, Van Cleave, a volunteer, now runs the day-to-day operations. "The DRT is doing its work," said Van Cleave wearily. "We are under scrutiny, but we believe our good work at maintaining the Alamo for one hundred and five years at no cost to the state speaks for itself. We will protect the Alamo."

The DRT's 2010 battle with the state began with infighting at the organization, whose 6,700 members all meet this requirement: They are lineal descendants of a man or a woman who served the Republic of Texas prior to annexation, in 1846. The dispute centers on money. In 2006, faced with a costly list of preservation repairs, the DRT launched an unprecedented $60 million fund-raising campaign. Erin Bowman, a tall, attractive sixty-year-old blonde with a track record of raising significant money for other causes in San Antonio, was named chairman. Though Bowman was herself a Daughter, she did not play by the DRT's rules. Traditionally most of the DRT's money has been raised through the sale of tourist trinkets in the Alamo gift shop and through the sale of "Native Texan" license plates. Bowman had other ideas. She chose to meet with potential donors on her own but refused to share her list of contacts with the group.

Madge Roberts, the DRT's president general at the time, and the other 23 members of the governing committee were infuriated. A wise move might have been to retreat and let Bowman, who had quickly raised $1 million, continue to collect the cash. But as everyone knows, retreat at the Alamo is not an option. In May 2008 Bowman was fired. Undeterred, she and Dianne MacDiarmid, another well-connected Daughter, started the Alamo Endowment to raise money for preservation. Seven months later, the two women were summoned to a hearing at the exclusive Barton Creek Resort and Spa, in Austin. Both were expelled. "It didn't bother me," said Bowman, who continues to raise money for the Alamo through her organization. "The women in charge don't know anything at all about business. They are living in the dark ages. My blood makes me a Daughter, not them."

Troubles deepened last September when the *San Antonio Express-News* reported that of the $213,452.30 the DRT had spent from the sale of "Native Texan" license plates from 2005 through 2008, only a little more than $37,000—or 17 percent—had gone to support the Alamo. State officials, from the governor on down, immediately sounded the alarm. State senator Leticia Van de Putte, whose district included the Alamo, was particularly miffed when she learned that the DRT had spent $50,000 of the money on the French Legation Museum, an 1841 house it maintains in Austin. "That was a defining moment for me," said Van de Putte. "I don't understand how the Daughters justify spending so little for the Alamo, which attracts two and a half million visitors a year and is in desperate need of repair."

On a muggy morning, Sarah Reveley, a 65-year-old renegade member of the DRT, sat on the couch in her cozy bungalow in Alamo Heights, an affluent neighborhood north of downtown San Antonio. She was dressed in jeans and a "Don't Mess With Texas" T-shirt. "I think the DRT is toast," she said with a vintage Texas good-ol'-girl accent. "Nobody—not the governor, the attorney general, nor the Legislature—can ignore their mismanagement of the most revered historic site in Texas."

A few months earlier, Reveley hunkered down with her computer in her study. Surrounded by books, financial documents, and minutes from DRT committee meetings, Reveley slowly compiled research. On February 1, 2010 she did the unthinkable: She formally requested that the DRT be removed as custodian. She filed a two-page official complaint with the attorney general's office, with 34 documents attached, accusing the DRT of failing to preserve the Alamo. She went back through thirty years of master plans to outline the lack of follow-through on preservation efforts. Most damaging, she reported that the DRT had failed to act when a 2007 report identified leaks and cracks within the vaulted roof of the chapel. A few days later, small bits of plaster fell from the roof, and barricades were erected to protect tourists. "I may appear to be wacko," said Reveley, a sixth-generation Texan of German descent, "but believe me, I am studious, and like my ancestors, I do not give up a fight."

Van Cleave insists that the DRT has not neglected the roof. In July a new engineer's report identified rainwater seepage into the chapel as the primary threat to the roof, not the cracks, and suggested that the 73-year-old copper, lead-coated exterior be replaced. "The roof has been and is now our number one priority," said Van Cleave. "We have the money to fix it, and we'll get it done."

But it didn't take long for the DRT to push back against Reveley. She received an official notice in late August that she too faced expulsion. Reveley decided not to fight her removal, which would bring the total number of women expelled from the DRT during its entire history to four—three of them casualties of the current battle. It was similar to the DRT's 1905 battle with Reveley playing the role of Adina De Zavala as the outcast.

The modern-day line in the sand over who controls the Alamo was drawn in April 2010, when state officials learned that the DRT had applied for a federal trademark to register the words "The Alamo." From the isolation of the fortress within the Alamo's compound, the idea made perfect sense. The Daughters weren't trying to prevent the use of the words "The Alamo" for any of the thousands of businesses that utilize the name, from Alamo Fire Works to Alamo Cafe. The DRT wanted to trademark the words "The Alamo" so it could sell official T-shirts and merchandise. In late July lawyers for the state filed a brief with the US Patent and Trademark Office formally opposing the DRT's application. In essence, Governor Perry and his lawyers said, the Alamo belongs to Texas, not the DRT.

Though bills were routinely filed in the Legislature during the 1990s to remove the DRT as custodian on the grounds that its interpretation of the Alamo's history was racist, the culture wars hadn't yet heated up and the group's power was impenetrable. The iron grip of the DRT has weakened thanks to the latest round of controversies. "We must protect the Alamo," said Van de Putte. "I no longer have full confidence in the DRT's ability to ensure the shrine's structural integrity."

In 2011, the Texas Legislature was fed up with the DRT. Members passed two bills transferring management from the DRT to the state's Land Office. In March 2012, Land Commissioner George P. Bush took control of the Alamo and formally rescinded the DRT's custodial powers. A few months later the DRT was officially evicted from the premises.

For many in San Antonio it is difficult to imagine a future without the DRT. Many Texans have always viewed the Alamo through the organization's lens or have projected onto it Wayne's interpretation that it is a worldwide symbol of freedom over tyranny. Year after year, those who live in San Antonio see the Alamo as a combination of holy shrine, battle site, tourist attraction, and political carnival. They see the martyrdom of Bowie, Crockett, and Travis, as well as the Alamo's shadowy side: the relentless pitting of Anglos against Mexican Americans, the obsession with blood lineage, and the confusion between sentimentality and realism.

In time perhaps the two sides of the myth may at long last be resolved. What many Hispanics want is not a simple, one-sided story of Mexicans versus Texans but a more complete history. In 2001 independent filmmaker Jim Mendiola, a San Antonio native, and Rubén Ortiz-Torres, a contemporary artist from Mexico City, created an art installation that included two hologram prints of the iconic facade of the Alamo. As the viewer approached, the building slowly disappeared, as if it were an illusion. In many ways, the Alamo functions as a Rorschach test for Texans: What you see depends entirely on who you are.

Van de Putte, for example, is eligible by blood to be a Daughter herself. Like most Hispanics, she believed the John Wayne version of the Alamo's story for most of her life. "It wasn't until I was in college that I learned that Susanna Dickinson wasn't the only woman who survived the battle," said Van de Putte. "Eleven Tejano women and eight children also survived. Their history has been erased."

How would someone like Lionel Sosa, an advertising guru who has designed political advertising campaigns aimed at Hispanic voters for every Republican presidential candidate since Ronald Reagan, explain the Alamo story? "Healing with Latinos is definitely possible but only when the full story is told," said Sosa, a trim, elegant man with a gentle, soft-spoken demeanor. "The Mexicans were trying to get back the land they lost when the immigrant Texans reneged on their deal with Mexico. They were given the land in exchange for populating Texas, then decided it was theirs. Does that make them heroes? Most people who visit the Alamo today go home with the impression that the Mexicans were the bad guys and the defenders of the Alamo the good guys. There are no good guys or bad guys here, only the two sides defending their territories." It was as though Sosa was speaking for the ghost of Adina De Zavala.

Early one summer morning, two hundred noisy teenagers, many with earbuds dangling from iPods, wandered around Alamo Plaza. They were from nearby YMCA camps, and about half were Anglo and the other half Hispanic. In other words, the group represented the population of Texas in the near future.

"It sure is small," said one.

"Not much to see here," said another.

Whatever the Alamo is or is not, it remains the central symbol of Texas, one of the places that define us. In the end, the current battle is about not only how the Alamo will be remembered but whether more than half of Texans will remember it at all. The fight—in 1836 and now—is for the future of Texas. ★

RICARDO SÁNCHEZ

Ricardo Sánchez (1941-1995) burst upon the San Antonio scene in 1983 when he opened a bookstore, Paperbacks y Más, which rapidly became a creative space for readings and performances. For three years, 1985-1988, he wrote a weekly column for the *San Antonio Express-News*, in which he recounted in his inimitable intellectual *caló* his discoveries as he wandered the city, marveling at its "majestic concatenation of possibilities." He wrote of himself: "I am a poet who needs to question all intents and purposes—that is quite simply the only way my eyes can see." He was simultaneously contentious and celebratory, a figure who could spin spontaneous poetry at a bar for hours, creating a cadre of friends and fans who remained fiercely loyal long after he had left the city.

Born in 1941 in El Paso, the youngest of thirteen children, he had an adventurous life that began with growing up as a young pachuco in the Barrio del Diablo. Stints in the US Army and the prison systems of both California and Texas were matched by a passion for writing and education. In 1971, his book *Canto y Grito Mi Liberación* was published by Míctla Publications, which Sánchez created to publish Chicano writers whose works were ignored by mainstream presses. *Canto y Grito Mi Liberación: The Liberation of a Chicano Mind* was republished in 1973 by Anchor Books (Doubleday), and it became a mainstay of the Chicano literary *movimiento*. Sponsored by a Ford Foundation grant, Sánchez earned a PhD in American Studies from the Union Institute & University in Cincinnati, Ohio.

This column appeared in the *San Antonio Express-News*, May 29, 1988.

THE MEANING OF CHICANO

ALL PEOPLES ARE RESILIENT AND SENTIENT, and culture is their shaping and honing element. Everyone carries a sense of one's people, and the name that evolves through a people's cultural history is a precious and sacred symbolic talisman. Chicanos are no different from other groups that impress their nomenclatures upon time and space.

Rubén Salazar, a broadcast and print reporter in California, wrote about the human and social condition(s) of Chicanos. He wrote of a people that had become veritable "strangers in their own land," yet he stressed that *Chicano* meant looking at oneself through one's "own" eyes and not through Anglo bifocals.

Those words were a godsend to many of us, for those words of simplicity and rationality were spiritually and intellectually liberating.

Salazar was killed by the Los Angeles Police Department, and the speculation persists that he was assassinated for his stands on behalf of a voiceless people.

Others say it was accident.

Others claim that it was an accident on Aug. 29, 1970, when the Chicano Moratorium Against the Vietnam War caused to be unleashed a police department bent on subjugating a much-maligned and oppressed community. Salazar's words still find a hospitable space among those who cherish Chicano culture and arts.

Though many former proponents of Chicanismo have retreated from the notion of a people having the right and responsibility to name its "real" world, there still remain those who savor the name Chicano as an authentic expression evolving from a history of struggle and creativity. Like the phoenix arising from its ashes, the term has resurfaced in the arts.

A group of San Antonio artists has an exhibition at the Art Cellar . . . that speaks to that notion—Ondas Chicanas. "Onda is like our bag, our thing," artist Jim Valdez said. "It means our way of seeing and saying our way of life."

According to Jesús "Chista" Cantú, an artist-activist since the 1960s, Chicano is the expression that truly speaks to those who are from this land, yet excluded from complete participation in the social arena.

Chicano, by its very definition, is a politically charged name, but all names are so. It is a word created in the cultural foundry of a people who believe in their right to name themselves. Other names are labels that are superficial at best.

Hispanic means someone who is Spanish or of Peninsular culture, but Chicanos are mestizos whose bloodlines are much more índio than español.

Arnoldo Carlos Vento, professor of Spanish and Chicano cultural studies at UT-Austin as well as a creative writer, speaks to the importance of people naming their own world. "Too many of our incoming Chicano students have been kept from a real knowledge of their history and culture," Vento said, and upon studying their cultural history, some of these students express anger and a willingness to probe into our culture. "Chicano is a valid, historic term, and not some media creation nor a government-imposed definition. In teaching Mexican-Chicano literary thought, I want students to know and understand history."

The word is both modern and pre-Hispanic, and comes from the Maya Quiché, coined during nearly prehistoric times.

"It was not a pejorative term. It meant a person who emigrates for a better life. . . . Another era which also saw the word gain popular usage was during and after the 1910 Revolution, and it was a concept attacked by middle-class Mexican-Americans, perhaps due to fear of repression. . . . A third period of popularization was the advent of the Chicano Movement, and it was hailed as a positive consciousness-raising world view."

In his recent novel *La Cueva de Naltzatlan*, published by Fondo de Cultura Económica in Mexico City, Vento speaks out to that nomenclature.

Reimundo "Tigre" Pérez, a poet-activist originally from Laredo, wrote during the first Canto al Pueblo about authenticity's being a primary value and responsibility for poets and artists; that people as a group or as individuals should care about their personal and collective vision(s).

"Pueblo/cultiva lo tuyo/y defiende/lo tuyo," Tigre wrote, lovingly asking people to cultivate what is theirs and also to defend it.

Those notions of defining one's world while seeking creative means to impress one's name and legacy upon the fabric of human cultural history are important.

I marvel at the creativity of all people, for there is much to celebrate in every culture, language and people. The nuances of value we share undergird us as we struggle from day to day. It is that sparkle that emanates from realizing the humanity in and of one's people and culture. It is the force and empowerment of Chicano poetry and literature celebrating a people and the world at large.

The word Chicano sings to the right of all beings to define their world and in so doing learn to respect and appreciate our wonderful and life-giving differences.

Qué viva la raza humana in all our human hues and nuances! ★

Cary Clack

Cary Clack grew up on the near East side of San Antonio, when that part of the city was dominated by the huge Alamo Iron Works. Where the Alamodome now stands, once there was a mammoth industrial complex, surrounded by sedate and historic neighborhoods, rich in history and culture—history and culture that few have documented so lovingly or so well as did Clack in his newspaper columns that ran in the *San Antonio Express-News* from 1994 to 2011.

In 1998 he became the first African American to join the *Express-News* Editorial Board. For six years in a row, Clack won the *San Antonio Current*'s reader's choice poll for Best Columnist in the city; three times he was selected Best Columnist by *San Antonio Magazine*'s Editors' and Readers' Choice Poll. Other awards included the Press Club of Dallas's Katie Award. In 2008, he received the Friends of the San Antonio Public Library's Arts and Letters Award for writing. In 2009, Trinity University Press published a collection of his columns, *Clowns and Rats Scare Me*.

After Clack graduated from St. Mary's University in 1985, he had been a Scholar-Intern at the Martin Luther King Jr. Center for Nonviolent Social Change in Atlanta, where he wrote CNN commentaries for Coretta Scott King. In 2011, a unique opportunity arose, and he resigned his position at the *Express-News* to become communications director for the congressional campaign of Joaquin Castro. Upon Castro's election Clack became his district director. In 2014, Clack became communications director for San Antonio's first African American mayor, Ivy Taylor. He now writes columns for the *Express-News* and editorials for the *Houston Chronicle*.

Bridging Cultures

San Antonio Express-News, February 29, 2004

THE TWO LONGEST STREETS, BOTH STRETCHING more than six miles, that connect the historically Mexican American West Side to the historically African American East side are Commerce Street and a street with four names.

Beginning as Buena Vista on the west, it crests on a bridge before becoming Dolorosa and Market streets downtown, and ending as Montana on the east.

As a native San Antonian, I've crossed the Buena Vista Street Bridge hundreds of times. As an African American living in a city that is predominantly Mexican American, I've crossed the bridge between African American culture and Mexican American culture all of my life, naturally and without thought that it was anything other than normal.

Growing up as a member of an ethnic group that was small in number and dwarfed by two other groups, I felt like the stepchild not invited to the ball. I felt an aching irrelevancy. Yet even those feelings couldn't dampen my love for this city and its diversity. I was raised to appreciate all people and cultures. If I'd been born and raised in Milwaukee, I'm sure I would have a special affinity for Polish culture.

But I was born and raised in San Antonio, and other than my own African American heritage, there are no other cultures that I embrace, or feel more comfortable in, than Mexican American and Latin American. In both, there are a soul and passion absolutely necessary to my being.

Most of my neighbors on the East Side were black, but Latinos also lived among us. It was a neighborhood of both the middle class and the poor, of beautiful houses and some that were run down. It was far from a slum or ghetto, but it says a lot about the mentality of my friends and me that, as children, we would feel sorry for the rare white family that would move into our neighborhood. We believed that no white family, if they could afford to do otherwise, would choose to live near us, those who were black and brown. That had to mean a huge fall from the paradise we imagined all white people lived in. But they never stayed long, moving, we assumed, to someplace better.

On Saturday afternoons, I could stand outside and hear both R&B and Tejano music. One block down the street was the neighborhood convenience store that was owned by a Mexican American named Joe, who lived in the back with his family. But the first tamales I ate were bought three blocks down from the black-owned icehouse on the corner of South Pine and East Commerce, across from the Friedrich Building. They'd complement the Mexican food my grandmother cooked every two weeks.

Except for first grade, all of my education came in integrated schools.

My oldest friend from those years is Charlie Puente, from second grade. As a child, my exposure to the home lives of people who weren't black came from my Mexican American friends, like Charlie, who invited me over to spend Saturdays with them and to sleepovers. I learned that their home life wasn't that different from mine. I didn't relate to them as Mexican Americans, or them to me as African American. We were just kids with interesting stories to tell in different accents.

Today, there are, at times, unspoken tensions between Mexican Americans and African Americans that I worry will erupt. One reason is because blacks and browns can be just as prejudiced as whites. Bigotry is colorblind. Another factor, perhaps larger, is that members of both groups sometimes make the mistake of fighting over small pieces of the economic and political pies, instead of working together to create more and bigger pies. Then there is the recent argument over the "status" of who is the country's largest minority.

My family is extraordinarily diverse and includes a Mexican American aunt; two cousins who are black and Mexican American; and a niece whose mother is Puerto Rican. Because of my family, I live my life as if there are no walls separating me from people who have a heritage and history different from my own. I have much to learn from others, and they from me. I believe that's how a free and open child of the world should live, crossing the bridges into other cultures.

For it's in the crossing and re-crossing of these bridges that we keep them from crumbling.

Losing the Ice House
San Antonio Express-News, February 27, 2002

IN MONDAY'S TWILIGHT, AS A MAN driving by watched, a small boy wandered around a pile of fresh rubble on the corner of East Commerce and South Pine. If the boy noticed the man, he wouldn't have understood why he stared so hard at the rubble. But the day will come, years from now, when the child will understand. It will be a day when pieces of his past, a place that was a landmark of his childhood, lie in ruins and he looks upon them with the same nostalgic gaze.

The bulldozing of the debilitated and abandoned structure, across the street from the Friedrich Building, was overdue. It had been dead for years but wasn't buried until Monday. In the prime of its life it had been an ice house; the most convenient and happening ice house in Denver Heights on the city's East Side.

If many of the patrons knew its name, they never used it. In the '60s, '70s and '80s it was simply "the ice house," as in "I'm going to go get a beer at the ice house," or "There's a card game over at the ice house," or "Meet me at the ice house on the corner of Commerce and Pine," or "Momma, bring me something back from the ice house."

At the ice house, besides candy, chips, soda and beer, you could get some delicious tamales. For many of the children in the neighborhood their introduction to tamales was through the ice house. They also sold sausage there that was good, but not nearly as good as the sausage you could get over at Johnny Johnson's on Montana and South Olive.

After picking up some tamales or sausage, you could go two stores down on Commerce and get some moon cookies at the largest mom-and-pop store in the neighborhood.

In the ice house, you could sit outside or in a small room where you could eat and drink or play cards or dominoes while the jukebox played the best of Motown and Stax as well as James Brown, Sly and the Family Stone, Aretha Franklin, Al Green, B.B. King, Gladys Knight and the Pips, and Bobby "Blue" Bland. The music may have been loud and the lyrics sometimes suggestive, but parents didn't have to cover up their children's ears because of any vulgarities.

When the 5 o'clock whistle at Alamo Iron Works sounded, everyone in the neighborhood knew workers there as well as some of the people from Friedrich would gather at the ice house to down a few. To be sure, there were some who spent too much time at the ice house, ignoring their families while blowing their money and wasting their lives on drink. Sometimes there were fights and sometimes the police had to be called, but mostly the ice house was where people went to have a good time, especially if they didn't have money or transportation to go anywhere else.

The ice house even got a little national attention in the late 1980s when it was mentioned in a *New York Times* story that proclaimed San Antonio the ice house capital of the world. But the world and neighborhoods change. In 1993, the ice house closed. On Monday it was demolished.

The boy walked away from the rubble.

The man drove away from his past. ★

PART THREE

Poetry and Prose Poems

Angela de Hoyos

If anyone has ever been truly "larger than life," it was Angela De Hoyos (1924-2009). A bit shy of four-eight, she was, as Rudolfo Anaya puts it, "one of our giants." She was a walking contradiction in many senses. She was older than even the oldest of the activist writers who created the Chicano literary movement in the 1960s and 1970s— Rudolfo Anaya, Tomás Rivera, and Rolando Hinojosa. Yet De Hoyos always seemed part of a younger generation. Such was her passion. She surrounded herself with younger writers, especially when her press, M&A Editions, began turning out the first works of young Chicanas like Carmen Tafolla, Evangelina Vigil, and Inés Hernández. M&A Editions was the very definition of "small press." De Hoyos edited and designed the books in her home studio, and her husband, Moises Sandoval, printed them in their garage.

The Chicano political movement did not begin in one place or another, but the Chicano literary movement was essentially proclaimed at the 1969 Chicano Youth Conference in Denver. Two poems defined it: Corky Gonzales's "Yo Soy Joaquin" and Alurista's "El Plan Espiritual de Aztlán." The *movimiento* was very male dominated. Then along came Angela De Hoyos. She often chided "the guys"—meaning Corky and Alurista, among others—for being blind to half of the workers for the revolution. Within a very short time, De Hoyos's first two chapbooks, *Arise, Chicano: and Other Poems* and *Chicano Poems for the Barrio* (both 1975) were being used interchangeably as literary works and political documents. Importantly, they constituted the very first Chicana feminist statements.

Selected Poems/Selecciones, her third book, was first published as *Selecciones* (Cuadernos del Caballo Verde, Universidad Veracruzana, Xalapa, Mexico, 1976), then issued in a facing-page bilingual edition the next year. This transitional book established a dialectic between personal poems and narrative ones, between past and present, between, as Spanish critic Chazarra Montiel put it, "the instinctual desires for life and death." Angela's last published book, *Woman, Woman* (Arte Público, 1985), was also her largest and most complex. Rolando Hinojosa wrote in his introduction, "Beware! You are in the hands of a poet. You're meant to read slowly, to ponder, to reread. . . ."

De Hoyos was a coeditor, with Bryce and Mary Guerrero Milligan, of two ground-breaking anthologies of Latina literature: *Daughters of the Fifth Sun: A Collection of Latina Fiction and Poetry* (Putnam/ Riverhead, 1995) and *¡Floricanto Sí! A Collection of Latina Poetry* (Penguin, 1998).

As Carmen Tafolla once wrote, "Angela carried the art of poetry to its highest standard, opened doors for young writers, documented the struggle of the Chicano Literary Movement, and shouldered the weight of so many social issues which she confronted in an activist and artful craft."

Arise, Chicano!

In your migrant's world of hand-to-mouth days,
your children go smileless to a cold bed;
the bare walls rockaby the same wry song,
a ragged dirge, thin as the air . . .

I have seen you go down
under the shrewd heel of exploit—
your long suns of brutal sweat
with ignoble pittance crowned.

Trapped in the never-ending fields
where you stoop, dreaming of sweeter dawns,
while the mocking whip of slavehood
confiscates your moment of reverie.

Or beneath the stars—offended
by your rude songs of rebellion—
. . . when, at last, you shroud your dreams
and with them, your hymn of hope.

Thus a bitterness in your life:
wherever you turn for solace
there is an embargo.
How to express your anguish

when not even your burning words
are yours, they are borrowed
from the festering barrios of poverty,
and the sadness in your eyes
only reflects the mute pain of your people.

Arise, Chicano! —that divine spark within you
surely says— Wash your wounds
and swathe your agonies.
There is no one to succor you.
You must be your own messiah.

Hermano

"Remember the Alamo"
. . . and my Spanish ancestors
who had the sense to build it.

I was born too late
in a land
that no longer belongs to me
(so it says, right here in this Texas History).

Ay, mi San Antonio de Bexar
ciudad-reina de la frontera,
the long hand of greed
was destined to seize you!

. . . Qué nadie te oyó cuando caíste,
cuando esos hombres rudos te hurtaron? . . .
Blind-folded they led you
to a marriage of means
while your Spanish blood
smouldered within you.

Tu cielo
ya no me pertenece.
Ni el Alamo, ni la Villita,
ni el río que a capricho
por tu mero centro corre.
Ni las misiones

— joyas de tu pasado —
    San Juan Capistrano
    Concepción
    San José
    La Espada
: They belong to a pilgrim
who arrived here only yesterday
whose racist tongue says to me: I hate
Meskins. You're a Meskin. Why don't you
go back to where you came from?
Yes, amigo . . . ! Why don't I? Why don't I
resurrect the Pinta, the Niña and the Santa María
—and you can scare up your little 'Flor de Mayo'—
so we can all sail back
to where we came from: the motherland womb.

I was born too late
or perhaps I was born too soon:
It is not yet my time;
this is not yet my home.

I must wait for the conquering barbarian
to learn the Spanish word for love:
HERMANO

A Lesson in Semantics

Men, she said
sometimes in order to
say it
it is
necessary
to spit
the word. ★

CARMEN TAFOLLA

Carmen Tafolla is a native of the west side barrios of San Antonio and the author of more than twenty books. Tafolla has been recognized by the National Association for Chicana and Chicano Studies for work that "gives voice to the peoples and cultures of this land" and has received numerous recognitions, including: the St. Mary's University Art of Peace Award for "work which contributes to peace, justice, and human understanding"; the City of San Antonio's Distinction in the Arts award; the Charlotte Zolotow Award for best children's picture book writing (the first Latina to be so honored); the Américas Award, presented at the Library of Congress; two Tomás Rivera Book Awards; two ALA Notable Books; and two international Latino Book Awards. The 2018 president of the Texas Institute of Letters, she is currently Writer-in-Residence and professor of Children's, Youth & Transformative Literature at the University of Texas San Antonio.

In 2012, Tafolla was named the first-ever Poet Laureate of San Antonio. She was also the 2015 Poet Laureate for the state of Texas.

She is the author of *Curandera* (M&A Editions, 1983) which was reissued in a thirtieth anniversary edition by Wings Press. *Curandera* has the distinction of being included on the list of books banned by the Arizona legislature. Elsewhere, it is a beloved classic volume of poetry, and is considered a core document among scholars of code switching in poetry. Tafolla's nonfiction, illustrated children's book, *That's Not Fair! Emma Tenayuca's Struggle for Justice / No Es Justo: La Lucha de Emma Tenayuca por la Justicia* (Wings Press, 2008) was named by *Criticas* magazine as one of the Best Children's Books of 2008. Her collection of ekphrastic poems, *Rebozos* (Wings Press, 2012) won the International Latino Book Award in three different categories—Best Book of Bilingual Poetry, Best Illustrated Book, and Best Gift Book. Her collection of short fiction, *The Holy Tortilla and a Pot of Beans: A Feast of Short Fiction* (Wings Press, 2008) received the 2009 Tomás Rivera Book Award for Young Adult Mexican-American Literature. Tafolla is the author of *Sonnets and Salsa*, a collection of poems—including many unconventional sonnets—that "thematically cross cultures and move into questions of human survival on this earth" (Dr. Wolfgang Karrer). It was this collection that prompted Ana Castillo to call Tafolla a "pioneer of Chicana literature and a unique Southwestern voice." Her most recent collection is *This River Here: Poems of San Antonio* (Wings Press, 2014).

A website—http://carmen.salsa.net/—is devoted to the life and work of Carmen Tafolla, and provides extensive educational resources.

This River Here

This river here
is full of me and mine.
This river here
is full of you and yours.

Right here
(or maybe a little farther down)
my great-grandmother washed the dirt
out of her family's clothes,
soaking them, scrubbing them,
bringing them up
clean.

Right here
(or maybe a little farther down)
my grampa washed the sins
out of his congregation's souls,
baptizing them, scrubbing them,
bringing them up
clean.

Right here
(or maybe a little farther down)

my great-great grandma froze with fear
as she glimpsed,
between the lean, dark trees,
a lean, dark Indian peering at her.

She ran home screaming, "¡Ay, los Indios!
Aí vienen los I-i-indios!!"
as he threw pebbles at her,
laughing.
Till one day she got mad
and stayed
and threw pebbles
right back at him!

After they got married,
they built their house right here
(or maybe a little farther down.)

Right here,
my father gathered
mesquite beans and wild berries
working with a passion
during the Depression.
His eager sweat poured off
and mixed so easily
with the water of this river here.

Right here,
my mother cried in silence,
so far from her home,
sitting with her one brown suitcase,
a traveled trunk packed full with blessings,
and rolling tears of loneliness and longing
which mixed (again so easily)
with the currents of this river here.
Right here we'd pour out picnics,
and childhood's blood from
dirty scrapes on dirty knees,
and every generation's first-hand stories
of the weeping lady La Llorona
haunting the river every night,
crying "Ayyy, mis hi-i-i-ijos!"—
(It happened right here!)

The fear dripped off our skin
and the blood dripped off our scrapes
and they mixed with the river water,
right here.

Right here,
the stories and the stillness
of those gone before us
haunt us still,
now grown, our scrapes in different places,
the voices of those now dead
quieter,
but not too far away . . .

Right here we were married,
you and I,
and the music filled the air,
danced in,
dipped in,
mixed in
with the river water
. . . dirt and sins,
    fear and anger,
    sweat and tears,
    love and music,
    blood.
And memories . . .
It was right here!

And right here we stand,
washing clean our memories,
baptizing our hearts,
gathering past and present,
dancing to the flow
we find
right here
or maybe—
a little farther
down.

San Antonio is a young Yanaguana woman

all spirit, strength and spark
her skin a cinnamon summer, an autumn pecan
her eyes steady stars in October's dark sky
arms graceful as weeping willow branches
she unravels her hair

that long dark wave of a river
winding, winding right through our hearts
pouring clear through our dreams
that's when she sings
in ancient rhythms of her native tongue
unconquered tunes twirled like mesquite bark
gnarled like the centuries of river oak
shaping the gentleness of buffalo grass
the wildness of wind
a melody trickling cool as river water

San Antonio is a
young strong
Yanaguana woman
who learned Spanish
and then English
and then Tex-Mex
or German, Vietnamese, Czech, Greek, Karén
and a hundred other flowing tongues
to lull the child to sleep

San Antonio is a
young strong smart
Yanaguana woman
who sings chants calls declaims exalts
in all the languages
of her embroidered rebozo bordado
of colors and cultures
but never once forgets
the hum and the rumble
of her still-growing
reaching
river
roots

Right in one language

"Write in one language," they say
and agents sit and glare hairy brows
over foreign words, and almost trying hope,
say, "It's not French, is it?"

But it isn't.

Nor is my mind
when I try tight, clean lines
manicured to be like Leave
it to Beaver's house
        straight sidewalk
        so square hedges
        and if there's one on
this   side there's also one on   that
Equally paced
    placed
    spaced
    controlled

"You seem to lose control of the line
in this one," he says, "it all explodes."
    I see bilingüe-beautiful
    explosions —
    two worlds collide
    two tongues dance
    inside the cheek
    together
Por aquí, poquito   and a dash allá también
    salsa—chacha—disco polka

Rock that Texan cumbia
in a molcajete mezcla!
But restrain yourself —
the Man pleads sanity —
Trim the excess —
just enough and nothing more
Think Shaker room and lots of light —
two windows, Puritan-clean floor, and chairs
up on clean simple pegs—three —
y
    las
        palabritas
            mías
                    are straining at the yoke

two-headed sunflowers
    peeking through St. Moderatius grass
      waiting for familias grandes
garden growing wild
      with Mexican hierbitas, spices, rosas,
      baby trees nurtured así, muy natural
      —no one knows yet
      if they're two years old
      and should be weaned
          or pruned
              or toilet trained
      but they are given only
      agua y cariñitos,
      shade and sun and compañía

City Inspection Crew,
House and Gardens Crew,

Publications Crew agree
the lack of discipline
lack of Puritan
purity
pior y tí.

Chaucer must have felt like this,
        the old Pachuco playing his TexMex onto the page
and even then the critics said,
        "Write
        in one language."
But he looked at all that cleanness, so controlled,
        forms halved, and just could not deny
his own familia, primos from both sides,
        weeds that liked to crawl
        over sidewalks, pa' juntarse,
        visit, stretch out comfy,
        natural and lusty
        hybrid wealth,
and told them it was just because
he was undisciplined
    unpolished
            and did not know
                        how to make love
                        with just
                        one
                        person
                        in the room
                        or
                        on the page

And he, like me,
did what he wanted anyway

But
You, like they,
want Shaker hallways
and I grow Mexican gardens and backyards.
There are 2 many colors in the marketplace
to play modest, when Mexico and
Gloria Rodíguez say,
"¡Estos gringos con su Match-Match,
y a mí me gusta Mix-Mix!"

There are 2 many cariños to be
                    created
to stay within the lines,
2 many times
when I want to tell you:
There is room
    here
    for two
    tongues
    inside this
    kiss. ★

EVANGELINA VIGIL

Evangelina Vigil was born in San Antonio in 1949. She grew up on the west side, which she often celebrates in her poetry, reveling in the neighborhood's natural code-switching between English and Spanish. She learned the stories of her family's journey from Parras de la Fuente, Coahuila, Mexico, from her maternal grandmother and great uncle. Her mother instilled a love of reading. Her father, whose Tejano family roots are in Seguin, inspired her musical pursuits. With an ear always turned to the radio, Vigil began writing poetry at a very young age, inspired by American songbook and pop music lyrics and melodies.

A scholarship to Prairie View A&M University in 1968 led to a major in English at the University of Houston. She returned to San Antonio in 1976 and became involved in the local *movimiento*. Her first chapbook, *Nade y Nade,* was published by Angela De Hoyos's M&A Editions in 1978. *Thirty an' Seen a Lot*, (Arte Público Press, 1982), with its iconic cover photo of Vigil in front of the Bar America, was awarded the American Book Award. She edited one of the first, if not *the* first all-Latina anthologies, *Woman of Her Word: Hispanic Women Write* (Arte Público, 1983). She is the author of one other collection of poetry, *The Computer is Down* (Arte Público, 1987) and a children's book, *Marina's Muumuu/El muumuu de Marina* (Arte Público, 2001). Vigil also translated Tomás Rivera's novel … *Y No Se lo Tragó la Tierra (… And the Earth Did Not Devour Him).*

Vigil teaches Mexican American and US Hispanic literature at the University of Houston. In addition to composing poetry and spoken word pieces, she performs original songs and Latin classics with LJazz. She served as the longtime host of *Viva Houston* and producer of public affairs programs with the local ABC-TV network. Currently, she holds the post of Public Information Officer with the City of Houston Department of Neighborhoods.

como embrujada

How strange
to have this compelling urge
to write to ghost readers.

I spill my whole life on you
and don't even know who you are.

I don't understand it.
I've always been taught
to be very careful who you trust.

Qué confianza, verdad?

was fun running 'round descalza

barefoot is how I always used to be
running barefoot
like on that hot summer
in the San Juan Projects
they spray-painted all the buildings
pastel pink, blue, green, pale yellow, gray
and in cauldrons tar bubbling, steaming
(time to repair the roofs)
its white steam filling summer air with aromas of nostalgia
for the future
and you, barefoot,
tender feet jumping with precision
careful not to land on nest of burrs and stickers
careful not to tread too long on sidewalks

converted by the scorching sun into comales
"¡hasta se puede freír un huevo en esas banquetas!"
exclamaba la gente
este verano tan caliente
no sooner than had the building wall/canvasses been painted clean
did barrio kids take to carving new inspirations
and chuco hieroglyphics
and new figure drawings of naked women
and their parts
and messages for all
"la Diana es puta"
"el Lalo es joto"
y que "la Chelo se deja"
decorated by hearts and crosses
and war communications
among rivaling gangs
El Circle
La India
pretty soon kids took to just plain peeling plastic pastel paint
to unveil historical murals
of immediate past well-remembered
más monas encueradas
and "Lupe loves Tony"
"always and forever"
"Con Safos"
y "Sin Safos"
y que "el Chuy es relaje"
and other innocent desmadres de la juventud
secret fear in every child
que su nombre apareciera allí
y la música de los radios
animando

"Do you wanna dance under the moonlight?
Kiss me Baby, all through the night.
Oh, baby, do you wanna dance?"

was fun running 'round descalza
playing hopscotch
correr sin pisar las líneas—
te vas con el diablo

was fun running 'round descalza
shiny brown legs leaping with precision
to avoid nido de cadillos crowned with tiny blossoms pink
to tread but ever so lightly on scorching cement
to cut across streets glistening with freshly laid tar
its steam creating a horizon of mirages
rubber thongs sticking, smelting
to land on cool dark clover carpet green
in your child's joyful mind
"got to get to la tiendita, buy us
some popsicles and Momma's Tuesday *Light!*"

was fun running 'round descalza ★

NAOMI SHIHAB NYE

Naomi Shihab Nye was born in St. Louis, Missouri, in 1952. Her father, journalist Aziz Shihab, had emigrated from Palestine and married an American. When Naomi was fifteen, the family returned to the Shihab hometown of Ramallah, in Palestine, and she attended an Armenian school in the Old City in Jerusalem. The family returned to the US shortly before the Six-Day War began. They settled in San Antonio, where Naomi attended high school and later earned a BA in English and World Religions from Trinity University, where she also studied creative writing with Robert Flynn.

Nye published her first poem when she was seven years old, and she has been prolific ever since. Her first collection of poems, *Different Ways to Pray: Poems* (1980), explored the theme of similarities and differences between cultures, which would become one of her lifelong areas of focus. *Hugging the Jukebox* (1982), won the Texas Institute of Letters' Voertman Poetry Prize, the first of many honors. It too focuses on the varying perspectives of diverse peoples around the globe. It was this that attracted the attention of the US Information Agency, which provided Nye with the opportunity to travel across Asia and the Middle East as a poetry ambassador.

Her ability to connect with audiences and readers literally all over the planet is curiously fused with her intimate descriptions of life in San Antonio's most colorful neighborhoods. During the 1970s and 1980s she worked in artist-in-the-schools programs all around the city, and it is—even now—not unusual to meet writers and teachers who will say without hesitation that Nye's visit to their classroom was among the most important moments of their lives. As William Stafford once wrote, Nye is "a champion of the literature of encouragement and heart. Reading her work enhances life."

Nye's other books include the poetry collections *19 Varieties of Gazelle: Poems of the Middle East; A Maze Me: Poems for Girls; Red Suitcase; Yellow Glove; Fuel: Poems; Transfer*, and *You & Yours* (2005), which received the Isabella Gardner Poetry Prize. She is also the author of a collection of essays entitled *Never in a Hurry: Essays on*

People and Places; young-adult novels *Habibi* (a semi-autobiographical story of an Arab-American teenager who moves to Jerusalem in the 1990s) and *The Turtle of Oman*.

Nye has edited many anthologies of poems, including *This Same Sky: A Collection of Poems from around the World*, which contains translated work by 129 poets from 68 different countries, and *Is This Forever, Or What?: Poems & Paintings from Texas*.

Nye has won many awards and fellowships, among them four Pushcart Prizes, the Jane Addams Children's Book Award, the Paterson Poetry Prize, and many notable book and best book citations from the American Library Association. In 2009, Nye was elected a chancellor of the Academy of American Poets. In 2013, she was awarded the NSK Neustadt Prize for Children's Literature.

Will You Hold My Bullet Please?

In those days there were many things we did not want.

Our father drove us to Mexico because the dentist was cheaper.

We never said the word "poor." *How much did the gas cost, Dad?* Gas was cheap then.

There were no interesting towns between San Antonio and Nuevo Laredo, only scrub brush and cactus, then the irritating wait at the border.

So I was happy on our second visit when the Mexican dentist tripped on a mat, stabbing me in the knee with a metal pick.

The wound bled generously. Our father would never take us there again.

He found an affordable dentist in a San Antonio building called Collins Garden. Yesterday I saw it being wrecked by bulldozers—dusty mountain of concrete, smoked glass simmering in heat. Goodbye Monopoly delusions. . . .

Lyman the new dentist appeared to have little interest in dentistry.

While "cleaning our teeth" with bleaching potion, (no brushing, flossing or scraping), he spoke of Mexican music, land deals in south Texas, the pleasures of rural living. Later we visited Lyman at his home, a run-down stucco hacienda in a field of scrub brush and cactus. We waited five hours for a fish to be grilled in a pit. Our father began calling him, "My friend!" and went to lunch with him. Lyman wanted us all to call him by his first name, which made me wonder if he were really a dentist.

My teeth did not feel clean.

Soon our father bought land from Lyman. Though we never seemed to have any extra money, apparently Dad and the dentist made some sort of deal and the land was going to become more valuable in six months, which of course it never did.

The land was tucked away on a rutted road near the Polish settlement of Panna Maria. For two months we spent time looking for it. My father carried a map drawn on a napkin from a Mexican café where he and Lyman had sealed the deal.

It was the ugliest land ever. Even the mesquites were twisted—the shade from their gnarled branches felt ominous. Holes where snakes lived, mysterious ditches, heaps of rotten wood. Our father stared at us. "Someday this will all be yours."

One evening he took a deep breath. "I have bad news. Our friend Lyman has been arrested."

"What?"

"A week ago. I just heard about it. He wants me to visit him at the jail."

"For selling ugly land or for being a bad dentist? For what, Dad?"

"Cocaine."

"Cocaine?" I had never heard my father say the word before. It did not seem right in his vocabulary—like *matador* or *toreador*. "What was he doing with it? Using or selling it?"

"Perhaps being a repository—storing it for others. He may not have known what he had."

"Sure, that sounds likely."

I had never smoked pot or taken an aspirin. Cocaine seemed like a ticket to the underworld for all I knew. My dad asked me to go to the jail with him. "Why, Dad? I don't LIKE Lyman. I'm sure he has no desire to see me."

"Well, do it for me. I need your support."

So we drove to the jail. Lyman could only have one visitor at a time.

"I'll just wait on the sidewalk, Dad. Or take a walk." Prisoners shouted through the grillwork. "Baby, bring me a burger!"

I could not imagine Lyman cooped up in such an environment. Despite his eccentricities, he was an optimist with geraniums growing in clay pots.

My father paused. He wore his blue *guayabera* shirt, tucked pockets and pearly buttons. "Honey, I need you to hold this for me while I go in. I'm shocked, really. I just reached for my I.D. at the security desk. Glad they didn't notice...."

My father handed me a bullet.

He shrugged. "I'm not sure what this is."

"Dad? Are you serious? You want me to sit in front of the jail, a raggedy teenager, HOLDING A BULLET? Dad, why do you HAVE a bullet? Do you have a gun?"

"Not on me," he said.

"BUT YOU HAVE ONE?"

It stunned me that my gentle father, who once cried when he caught a mouse in a mousetrap, ("I didn't realize it would *kill them*") could think of owning one. What was he doing with it?

Wild dogs. Those nuts who phoned Mom to say they had Dad tied up. Burglars. He never mentioned what surely was the real reason he owned a gun—he got a good deal on one. Possibly Lyman had sold it to him. Maybe it was the bonus for owning that hideous land. One day you would wake up and need to commit suicide. I said, "Dad, this is weird."

He shrugged again, sheepish. He knew something was a little "off" in the scene. And I strode down the block with a bullet in my pocket, through the baked streets of that San Antonio summer, past the 24 Hour Bail office, the sagging Cactus Hotel sign, the store for checkered western wear, the greasy Cadillac Bar. Not yet the bearer of a driver's license, I felt the weight of undesirable things I would be forced to carry as an adult—tax receipts, mortgages, other people's artillery accessories, etc. I weighed a thousand pounds. Lyman would be in jail a long time, then get out and die. The land he had sold us would become a smudge in a history of shaky transactions. My father would die. No gun of any kind would be found among his pitiful possessions at the time of his death. Even the building called Collins Garden would be crushed into rubble decades later during a sudden rainstorm, as diners at La Fonda up the block raced from patio tables into the restaurant proper, holding menus over their heads against the surprise.

West Side

In certain neighborhoods
the air is paved with names.
Domingo, Monico, Francisco,
shining rivulets of sound.
Names opening wet circles inside the mouth,
sprinkling bright vowels
across the deserts of
Bill, Bob, John.

The names are worn
on silver linked chains.
María lives in Pablo Alley,
Esperanza rides the Santiago bus!
They click together like charms.
O save us from the boarded-up windows,
the pistol crack in a dark backyard,
save us from the leaky roof,
the rattled textbook which never smiles.
Let the names be verses
in a city that sings!

The Rider

A boy told me
if he roller-skated fast enough
his loneliness couldn't catch up to him,

the best reason I ever heard
for trying to be a champion.

What I wonder tonight
pedaling hard down King William Street
is if it translates to bicycles.

A victory! To leave your loneliness
panting behind you on some street corner
while you float free into a cloud of sudden azaleas,
pink petals that have never felt loneliness,
no matter how slowly they fell.

Because of Libraries We Can Say These Things

She is holding the book close to her body,
carrying it home on the cracked sidewalk,
down the tangled hill.
If a dog runs at her again, she will use the book as a shield.

She looked hard among the long lines
of books to find this one.
When they start talking about money,
when the day contains such long and hot places
she will go inside.

An orange bed is waiting.
Story without corners.
She will have two families.
They will eat at different hours.

She is carrying a book past the fire station
and the five-and-dime.
What this town has not given her
the book will provide: a sheep,
a wilderness of new solutions.
The book has already lived through its troubles.
The book has a calm cover, a straight spine.

When the step returns to itself
as the best place for sitting,
and the old men up and down the street
are latching their clippers,

she will not be alone.
She will have a book to open
and open and open.
Her life starts here.

Frankly

No one has time for the dying.
And they don't have time for us either.
Our lunch dates and appointments,
their fitful sleeps and crusted eyes.

Students circling in a parking lot
down the road certainly don't have time.
First period coming too soon will scatter
clumps of flirtation.

Moms in fitness garb
with grocery lists and car pool numbers
stuck to refrigerators,
have too many of the living to pick up, drop off.

At the end we bore the dying,
our teary smiles, pitiful offerings.
Frank said, "If I could only get back
to my desk, back to work,"

and closed his eyes. Last line.
What a surprise to learn
the greatest pleasure of life was
all that daily labor. ★

ROBERT BONAZZI

Critic Robert Peters praised Robert Bonazzi's first book of poetry, *Living the Borrowed Life* (New Rivers, 1974), for the poet's "consummate style" and poems "sophisticated in their patterns and designs." *Fictive Music* (Wings Press, 1979) was cited in *The Prose Poem: An International Anthology*, and praised by *Publishers Weekly, Choice* and *Library Journal*. Paul Christensen, writing of Bonazzi's *Maestro of Solitude: New Poems & Poetics* (Wings, 2007), said "Bonazzi has taken poetry to its limits of subtlety, where sense nearly but not quite gives out into silence and awe." His latest works include *The Scribbling Cure: Poems & Prose Poems* (Pecan Grove, 2012); a collection of essays and reviews, *Beyond the Margins: Literary Commentaries* (Wings Press 2015); and a collection of short fiction, *Awakened by Surprise (*Lamar University Literary Press, 2016).

Bonazzi is the author of the critically acclaimed *Man in the Mirror: John Howard Griffin and the Story of Black Like Me* (New York: Orbis Books, 1997). He recently completed the authorized biography of John Howard Griffin, entitled *Reluctant Activist (*TCU Press, 2017). Bonazzi has written introductions or afterwards to Griffin's *Black Like Me; Scattered Shadows: A Memoir of Blindness and Vision; Street of the Seven Angels; Follow the Ecstasy: The Hermitage Years of Thomas Merton;* and *Available Light: Exile in Mexico.* His work has appeared in hundreds of publications—in France, Germany, the UK, Japan, Canada, Mexico, Peru, and the US.

Born in New York City in 1942, Bonazzi has also lived in San Francisco, Mexico City, Florida, and several Texas cities. From 1966 until 2000, he edited and published over one hundred titles under his Latitudes Press imprint.

Secret Missions of San Antonio

Studio A

Mockingbirds tutor this parrot in
the outlandish art of imitation—infinite
birdsong inhabited by echoes.

Cacti exalt with upraised leaves—chewed
to near symmetry by anonymous insects.

II

No matter how pots are re-arranged,
light breaks in. Praise its palette,
subtly bathing the verandah.

Painted clouds shift unnoticed above
our stupendous fall from grace.

III

Confident cat Dino knows his name,
goes out the door. Bookmark tail
extends beyond vocabulary.

Alley tom scratches to enter,
brief black grunt, counterpointing
long white purr of street thesaurus.

Silent felinity prowls beneath
a steep flight of stairs.

Studio B

"For the sake of argument," Lorenzo said,
"there are no straight lines in nature."
My father was a precise carpenter,
who did elegant finish-work, yet
never claimed perfection.

II

Old cat Dino moves with purpose,
a tattered suitcase set down slowly.

Refusing nostalgic projection—suddenly
he leaps upon the birdbath to drink.

III

Exiled to grief when loved ones die—
old ego hangs on, living gracelessly.

Irony smiles as a last refuge of cynicism—
reaching sarcasm, we're halfway there.

Sober, I secretly hid the key.
Stoned, I cannot find it.

IV

I fly across a blank page
(wrapped in a cloudy idea)
words crawl or question
 & then a line breaks off—

V

Never saw it coming, random theft by caitiffs.
Fat money clip replaced by a lump of coal.

Up in flames & your body made of paper!

Around in a rolling chair,
I rearrange fallen stars.

Once In A Blue Moon
> The trouble with *The School of Hard Knocks* is that
> you keep taking the same courses over and over.
> —Daniel L. Robertson

Once

Parents snoring in their wedding bed,
as I walk the primal hall of memory.

There is a Bonazzi Street, only a block long,
between a treatment plant and a cemetery.
Lorenzo attested to it, when the street
raised its unpronounceable sign!

Baseball an unconscious metaphor,
our first rough draft. Odd choices for
boyhood heroes, you pointed out, since
I never hit lefty for power like the late Duke
and you never ran bases like the Say Hey Kid.

When to strike the balance between not
being old, yet not trying to act young?
Alert eye spies beautiful women;
other stares beyond notice.

Twice

Lost islands loom beyond discovery.
Unfathomable undertow near beaches,
bringing ashore inimitable long-haired
Comanche crown I knelt to praise,
adoring silver in her raven hair.

One eye bore a childhood scar—
early wisdom, a bloody back-story.
The other blinks beyond innocence.
Beautiful petite soul opens a vision.
We came together in a dry season.

Thrice

Old cat Dino mauled by stray dogs for sport.
(Could not save him from hard-wired pack.)
He rests beneath a statue of Saint Francis.

All disclaimers make claims.
Each point rings silent counterpoints.

High on insomnia, nothingness streams
along the dark hairs of these arms.
What are the blue tributaries crossing
known territory, quaintly called the
backs of our hands?

Next

To wish, to wish to live,
to wish to relive existence.
To wish for a different life.

Wrote heroic tales in youth,
loved winter—awake all night!
Now meditations embrace sunsets.

How to reinvent beginnings,
drink from eternal springs,
to be what must change?

Intermezzi

> *Everything changes;*
> *everything is connected.*
> *Pay attention.*
>   *—Jane Hirshfield*

I

From the writing studio
I amble over backyard pavers,
up deck stairs into the house.

II

Returning between blue *intermezzi*
across a wilted green oasis, never
count steps or words.

III

Stopping to rearrange potted plants,
I wonder at suggestive clouds,
an unexpected cold wind.

IV

Far away, our brother died today.
Leaves turn yellow and red.
Crisp brown ones fall. ★

BRYCE MILLIGAN

Born in Dallas in 1953, Bryce Milligan has lived in the King William historical district of San Antonio since 1977. He is married to librarian and writer Mary Guerrero Milligan, with whom he has edited two anthologies, *Daughters of the Fifth Sun: A Collection of Latina Fiction and Poetry* (Riverhead, 1995)—the first all-Latina anthology to be published by a major American publishing house—and *Floricanto Sí: A Collection of Latina Poetry* (Penguin, 1998). He has edited several other anthologies, including *Literary San Antonio.*

Milligan was the book columnist for the *San Antonio Express-News* and the *San Antonio Light* during the 1980s and early 1990s. His articles and reviews have appeared in numerous publications from the *New York Times* to the *Los Angeles Times.* He was the editor of two literary journals, *Pax: A Journal for Peace through Culture* (1983-1987) and (with Robert Bonazzi) *Vortex: A Critical Review* (1986-1990). He directed the Guadalupe Cultural Arts Center's literature program and its Texas Small Press Book Fair, San Antonio Inter-American Book Fair, and Latina Letters conferences. Milligan has been the publisher of Wings Press since 1995. Ramón Renteria, *El Paso Times* Book Editor, wrote that, "Without publishers like Milligan's Wing Press, Latino and Chicano literature would remain in a deep well in America."

Milligan is the author of four historical novels and short story collections for young adults. *With the Wind, Kevin Dolan* (1987) received the Texas Library Association's Lone Star Book Award. One of his children's books, *Brigid's Cloak,* was a 2002 "Best of the Year" pick by both the Bank Street College and *Publishers Weekly.* Some of his gallery theater pieces have run continuously at the Witte Museum for more than thirty years. Milligan is also the author of eight collections of poetry, the most recent being *Take to the Highway: Arabesques for Travelers* (West End Press, 2016.) A luthier and a singer/songwriter, he has also taught creative writing workshops from California to Prague.

Milligan is a recipient of the San Antonio Public Library's Arts and Letters Award and its "Library Champion" award, Gemini Ink's "Award for Literary Excellence," the St. Mary's University President's Peace Commission's "Art of Peace Award" for "creating work that enhances human understanding through the arts," the Notable Writers Book Prize, and the Writers League of Texas poetry prize, among other honors.

Eós and the Train Horns

I.

Dawning memory is tangled in its tellings, fractured into multiple perspectives, more than one of which could have been yours, so you remain unsure of exactly how far away the red and yellow Santa Fe Chief was when your grandfather yanked you off the tracks in front of his yellow and brown depot in White Deer, Texas. A few yards, a quarter mile? They tell you that you were two years old (there's most of the problem: whose memories are you remembering?) but you *know* you remember specifically placing two buffalo nickels on the hot iron track, to be flattened by the Chief. Or was it the Santa Fe El Capitán? Or are the crushed nickels later memories layered upon an earlier one? You remember the vibrations, the sun's glare on the silvered steel, the heat of the cinder bed and other . . . things that appear too closely observed: the rattlesnake dozing in the shade beneath the wooden loading platform, the twisted brown faces in the rust etching the cast iron wheels of a baggage cart with its curved oak handles worn smooth as glass, the tap-tap-tappeting of your grandfather's telegraph key, the rhythmic squeak of the speckled blue porcelain-on-metal Western Union sign swinging in the endless Panhandle wind, the painting of a Navaho bead maker on a fading Santa Fe calendar on the depot wall, the echo of your father's warbled whistling of an Edith Piaf song—things too richly enshrined in the telling to have been true of the moment but which were certainly true of the time. And thus unravels your first living memory, leaving you to re-weave the tapestry of who you really are.

II.

Fifty years on and you awake as Eós tints the San Antonio sky; you awake to a concert of train horns, surrounded, embraced in your bed by the encircling sweep of familiar rumbling freights, locomotives of shadow and steel crossing the still-dark streets with their soft Spanish names—Guadalupe, Frio, Flores, Presa—past the ghosts of long-gone stations that saw armies off to war and welcomed generations of refugees from the wars across the Rio Grande, pulling a hundred gondolas and tank cars and box cars, some of them empty, open to the wind, singing their own great hollow songs as they pound out a low echoing grumble from downtown's last wooden trestle, when there enters another strain: the one remaining passenger train rounding the center of the city. Sharp braking squeals punctuate Amtrak's Air Chimes, feathered by their engineer into a sweet tenor above the mellow baritone chords of Burlington Northern's old Nathan and Leslie horns, instruments half a century old, all supported by the thrumming mellifluous Primes of the Union Pacific and Santa Fe freights. No rules of harmonization apply to this chorale as mockingbirds and mourning doves join in the hymn to the dawn. Swinging left at Carolina Street, headed north with their increasing beat toward Sunset Station, locomotives serenade the heart of the city, set the day in motion with lullabies and alarms, lonesome moans and howls of joy—all rising with the memory of that first train horn, bearing down on you, flying west across the Panhandle plains, singing its warning song to the station master in a tiny cattle town where you could have been crushed like buffalo nickels beneath steel wheels, a brilliant but brief smear of blood on the tracks.

III.

On a moonless night, a dark, dark night, running a steady 70 miles an hour along the banks of the Mississippi with city lights dancing on the black waters, you stand between the cars of the former Panama Limited, newly re-christened as the only briefly discontinued City of New Orleans, tossing cigarettes into the night and singing "The Train They Call the City of New Orleans" with a blue-suited, brass-buttoned conductor, while the old E-8-A's and newer Pooch engines thrum down the rails from Chicago to the Gulf. Closer to dawn, you bring hot chocolate to your son, destined to stare at the sky for the rest of his life, and together you struggle to see stars through the murky dome of the observation car. The University of Chicago's gargoyles fall away as a once-and-future place as you try to hold this moment, freeze it, fix it even as you feel its edges fray, watch its colors fade like a Polaroid left in the sun, until only the train songs and the stars remain.

San Antonio Nights

Away from the literate river
where I can still hear Lanier's flute
and his rattling cough,
where Crane leapt
to save a pretty face and sprained
both pride and an ankle,
and O. Henry watched
the tuberculars dying
along with the frontier.
Away from the literate river
where Frost mourned and Kerouac drank.
Away from the Alamo where heroic ashes
still burn the nostrils,
where history has a meaning
but time does not.

Away from all the charms
of the sleepy green stream,
I am caught by a moment
in the long dark rain
when my heart catches

at a child's cry —stills
to listen, to identify
to search my own house.
The cry summons me away
from the safety of fire and book,
calls me into the streets
to seek
a face
to match
the pain.

Trusting Steel

Here in the flux of flood and drought
that is south Texas, my Decembers
are wheelbarrows of freshly split oak.

Here, where I have the luxury of abhorring
the evening-splitting rasp and growl
of the chainsaw, I allow myself
to trust a simpler tool.

It is best when the streets have gone silent
and the heavy stroke of steel on oak resounds
house to house—
                here, deep in this city.

The chunk and thud assumes
a natural meter and again I hear Frost
rasping out memories of all his
maple and birch woods.

And here is Hall
tucking up the leaves
against the house at Eagle Pond,
banking the cold fragile flames
that await the deeper insulation
of the silencing snow.

With each fall of my red axe their lines
rear up like the faces
of forgotten friends
and I hear a cautious halting pace
in frozen woods
I shall never call
my own.

A thousand miles to the west, Ortiz
cuts piñon, loosing a wilder smell,
preparing a different spell,
                    but aching
with the same ritual.

Here I cut the green oak into lengths
then let it lie a single summer.
A San Antonio August will almost
split it for you, so that
it leaps apart at the touch
of December's blade. ★

ROSEMARY CATACALOS

Although both sides of her family have lived in San Antonio, Texas, since 1910, Rosemary Catacalos was born in St. Petersburg, Florida. She recovered from this accident of birth with alacrity and spent her childhood on the east side of San Antonio. Of Greek and Mexican heritage, Catacalos is known for blending the history, folklore, and mythologies of those cultures into her carefully crafted poems, which often feature closely observed San Antonio settings. Catacalos is featured in the award-winning book and documentary, *The Children of the Revolución* (Sosa & Sosa, 2013).

In the 1960s, Catacalos was a reporter and arts columnist for the *San Antonio Light*. Her first book, a letterpress chapbook, *As Long As It Takes* (St. Louis: Iguana Press), was published in 1984, as was her first full-length collection, *Again for the First Time* (Santa Fe: Tooth of Time Books), which was awarded the Texas Institute of Letters Poetry Prize. A thirtieth anniversary edition of *Again for the First Time* was published by Wings Press. Her poetry has appeared in numerous literary magazines, including *Southwest Review, The Progressive,* and *Parnassus: Poetry in Review.* She has received several Pushcart Prize nominations and a Special Mention in *Pushcart Prize IX: Best of the Small Presses.* Her work has twice been collected in *Best American Poetry* (NY: Scribner, 1996 and 2003).

Catacalos was awarded the Dobie-Paisano Fellowship (Texas Institute of Letters and the University of Texas) in 1985, as well as a National Endowment for the Arts creative writing fellowship. She directed the literature program at the Guadalupe Cultural Arts Center (1986-1989), where she expanded the Annual Texas Small Press Book Fair into the San Antonio Inter-American Book Fair. Catacalos spent 1989 to 2003 in California, where she was first a Stegner Creative Writing Fellow at Stanford University, then executive director of The Poetry Center/American Poetry Archives at San Francisco State University (1991-1996). She was a visiting scholar at the Institute for Research on Women and Gender at Stanford until she returned to San Antonio in 2003 to become the executive director of Gemini Ink, a literary arts center. She retired from Gemini Ink in 2012. In 2008 Catacalos received the Macondo Foundation's 2008 Elvira Cordero Cisneros Award. A fine press chapbook, *Begin Here* (Wings Press), honored her selection as the Poet Laureate of Texas for 2013.

La Casa

The house by the *acequia*,
its front porch dark and
cool with begonias,
an old house, always there,
always of the same adobe,
always full of the same lessons.
We would like to stop.
We know we belonged there once.
Our mothers are inside.
All the mothers are inside,
lighting candles, swaying
back and forth on their knees,
begging the Virgin's forgiveness
for having reeled us out
on such very weak string.
They are afraid for us.
They know we will not stop.
We will only wave as we pass by.
They will go on praying
that we might be simple again.

David Talamántez on the Last Day of Second Grade
San Antonio, Texas 1988

David Talamántez, whose mother is at work, leaves his mark
    everywhere in the schoolyard,
tosses pages from a thick sheaf of lined paper high in the air one
    by one, watches them

catch on the teachers' car bumpers, drift into the chalky narrow shade
    of the water fountain,
One last batch, stapled together, he rolls tight into a makeshift horn
    through which he shouts

David! and *David, yes!* before hurling it away hard and darting across
    Brazos Street against
the light, the little sag of head and shoulders when, safe on the other
    side, he kicks a can

in the gutter and wanders toward home. David Talamántez believes
    birds are warm blooded,
the way they are quick in the air and give out long strings of
    complicated music, different

all the time, not like cats and dogs. For this he was marked down in
    Science, and for putting
his name in the wrong place, on the right with the date, *not* on
    the left with Science

Questions, and for not skipping a line between his heading
    and his answers. The X's for wrong
things are big, much bigger than David Talamántez's tiny writing.
    Write larger, his teacher says

in red ink across the tops of many pages. *Messy!* she says on others
    where he has erased
and started over, erased and started over. Spelling, Language

    Expression, Sentences Using
the Following Words. *Neck. I have a neck name. No!* 20's, 30's. *Think
    again!* He's good
in Art, though, makes 70 on Reading Station Artist's Corner, where
    he's traced and colored

an illustration from *Henny Penny.* A goose with red-and-white striped
    shirt, a hen in a turquoise
dress. Points off for the birds, cloud and butterfly he's drawn in
    freehand. *Not in the original*

picture! Twenty-five points off for writing nothing in the blank after
    This is my favorite scene
in the book because.... There's a page called Rules. *Listen! Always
    working! Stay in your seat!*

Raise your hand before you speak! No fighting! Be quiet! Rules copied
    from the board, no grade,
only a giant red checkmark. Later there is a test on Rules. *Listen! Alay
    ercng! Sast in ao snet!*

Rars aone bfo your spek! No finagn! Be cayt! He gets 70 on Rules, 10 on
    Spelling. An old man
stoops to pick up a crumpled drawing of a large family crowded
    around a table, an apartment

with bars on the windows in Alazán Courts, a huge sun in one corner
    saying, *Too mush noys!*
The grade is 90. *Nice details!* And there's

another mark, on this paper

and all the others, the one in the doorway of La Rosa Beauty Shop,
    the one that blew under

the pool table at La Tenampa, the ones older kids have wadded up
    like big spit balls, the ones run

over by cars. On every single page David Talamántez has crossed out
    the teacher's red numbers
and written in huge letters, blue ink, *Yes! David, yes!* ★

Swallow Wings

for Maya Angelou, with profound respect and gratitude

I been to church, folks.
I'm an East Side Meskin Greek and
I been to church. I'm here to say
I grew up hearin' folks sing over hard
times in the key of, *Uh, uh, girl. It ain't nothin'*
'bout lettin' go a this life.
I grew up in a 'hood where every day at noon
black girls at Ralph Waldo Emerson Junior High School
made a sacred drum of the corner mailbox, beatin'
on it to raise the dead. And make them dance.
I grew up readin' in the George Washington Carver
Library, and marvelin' at the white
lightnin' gloves that Top Ladies of Distinction
use for church. I grew up where grits is *indeed*
groceries, and a hale mountain of a woman passed
my house daily, always sayin' the same thing:
Your name Rosemary? My name Rosemary, too.

I grew up, folks, and I been down 'til I couldn't
get no more down in me. And now a preacher lady
come to town and caused me to paint my face and
put on some good clothes and go to church.
And I'm here to say I have a right
to take this tone, 'cause it ain't nothin'
'bout lettin' go a this life.
Swallows keep makin' their wings
out to be commas on the sky.
World keep sayin' and, and, and, and,
and.

Listen, Querido, They're Playing Our Song
Or, Summer Ritual with a Poet Friend

You arrive every year with the worst heat,
always on one of those killer days when dogs
won't come out from under cars
after nine in the morning
and even the neighborhood madman leaves off
his battle with the gods
and stands mostly in the thin shade
of a phone pole with his arms folded
and staring straight ahead.
Always on one of those consuming afternoons
when every nerve is uncovered
and it burns the insides to breathe
and the *chicharras* keep saying
over and over how much
has been lost or forgotten or left unsaid
and the only thing for it is to drink
beer after beer in Salinas' air-conditioned bar

and play pool with strangers
and make the best of it.
But I digress.
I was saying how you always show up in flames,
a sheaf of poems hanging from your elbow,
and how you ask your same few questions
and how your eyes always look away
before the answers have a chance
to stir up even a little breeze.
Always nervous. Always a little fearful.

As though the heat might want
to make an example of us
for our attempts to master the spaces
between feeling as well as feeling itself.

As though we had not had years of practice
with holding our hearts in the fire
and at the last minute snatching them back. ★

WENDY BARKER

Born in New Jersey, Wendy Barker grew up in Arizona. She spent much of the 1960s and early 1970s teaching public school in Berkeley, California, next door to the headquarters of the Black Panthers. In 1981 she earned her PhD at the University of California at Davis. Flying in for her job interview at the University of Texas at San Antonio in 1982, looking down at the land, Barker "fell in love and has never fallen out of love with our region's landscape." She is now Poet-in-Residence and the Pearl LeWinn Professor of Creative Writing at UTSA. Barker is married to the critic and biographer Steven G. Kellman.

Barker's sixth full-length collection of poems is *One Blackbird at a Time*, winner of the John Ciardi Prize (BkMk Press, 2015). Her novel in prose poems, *Nothing Between Us: The Berkeley Years* (runner-up for the Del Sol Prize) was released by Del Sol Press in 2009. Earlier full-length collections of poetry include *Poems from Paradise* (WordTech, 2005), *Way of Whiteness* (Wings Press, 2000), *Let the Ice Speak* (Ithaca House, 1991), and *Winter Chickens* (Corona Publishing Co., 1990). Wendy has also published four chapbooks, *From the Moon, Earth is Blue* (Wings Press, 2015), *Things of the Weather* (Pudding House Press, 2009), *Between Frames* (Pecan Grove Press, 2006), and *Eve Remembers* (Aark Arts, 1996). A selection of poems accompanied by autobiographical essays, *Poems' Progress* (Absey & Co.), appeared in 2002, and a collection of translations (with Saranindranath Tagore) from the Bengali of India's Nobel Prize-winning poet, *Rabindranath Tagore: Final Poems* (George Braziller, 2001), received the Sourette Diehl Fraser Award from the Texas Institute of Letters. Wendy's poems, essays, and translations have appeared in many journals and anthologies, including *The Best American Poetry*. She has read her poetry at dozens of universities, bookstores, festivals, and conferences throughout the US, Europe, and India. As a scholar, she is the author of *Lunacy of Light: Emily Dickinson and the Experience of Metaphor* (Southern Illinois University Press, 1987) as well as coeditor (with Sandra M. Gilbert) of *The House Is Made of Poetry: The Art of Ruth Stone* (Southern Illinois University Press, 1996). She coedited, with Dave Parsons, the anthology, *Far Out: Poems of the '60s* (Wings Press, 2016).

Recipient of an NEA fellowship, a Rockefeller residency fellowship at Bellagio, as well as other awards in poetry, including the Writers' League of Texas Book Award (which she has received twice) and the Mary Elinore Smith Poetry Prize from *The American Scholar,* she has also been a Fulbright senior lecturer in Bulgaria. Her work has been translated into Hindi, Chinese, Japanese, Russian, and Bulgarian.

High Sky

The sky has slipped its stitches,
the feathered cirrus, wool of cumulus,
gauze shreds of layered stratus
gone with the unexpected guests
who left this morning
after a night of pelted rain.
Now the sun flashes and shears
the few seams left
till bare skin bursts through
and we're down to ourselves,
two loose threads, the knot undone.

Inheritance

After my father died, my mother talked of a tree
she had seen at the edge of a field in fall:
a great tree as if on fire, she said, and she wanted
the rest of her life to be like that, one blaze
before the leaves fell, before it all was gone.
Now in the entry near her front door hangs a print
of a winter tree, rounded, heavy, white with snow.

Late winter, you and I have walked this way so often.
I thought I knew what to expect, oaks dropping
their brittle leaves, pushed off by their own buds.
Juniper, scrub. Grasses bent, shadowed with mold.

There is never a way to describe the things that rise
before you. A flush of white straight ahead, a breath
lifting. We turn from the path we'd been following,
into the mud of an abandoned road, to face this scent
of blossom, these circling bees, this bursting:
an old pear, gone back to its wild, original rootstock,
blooming over its intricate branches, a perfect oval.

Trash

"Trash," he said, as we walked the line
between our almost-country properties.
Again I pointed, trees and shrubs
whose names I didn't know, but "trash,"
he said again. Anything not oak.

That neighbor knew three kinds of trees:
live, pin, and Spanish oak. The rest should go.
And now I've lived here twenty years
I know how chainsaws take out everything
that isn't oak, not just the junipers

that choke the other plants nearby, but also
Texas buckeyes, magenta blooming in
the spring, redbuds, huisachillo, sweet acacia.
Mexican persimmon's bark blends velvet
grays and silky browns, its rounded leaves

bright yellow-green before the purple fruit
draws birds that nest on into June—
buntings and the wrens above the grasses,
gramas and the bluestems. November,
the seed heads in waves of burgundy, of red.

Our city council said they'd leave the trees
when clearing for the city hall. But like
that neighbor years ago, they meant
the oaks. Now they've called a meeting.
Oak wilt has hit the neighborhood, and

oaks are what we're left with. Too much
construction, trimming of the trees, their
wounds not treated. The virus travels
through the maze of connecting roots.
And once a tree's infected, it's trash. ★

Mariana Aitches

Mariana Aitches is a native of San Antonio, Texas, where she grew up in Victoria Courts, one of the country's oldest subsidized public housing projects. She graduated from San Antonio Community College before going on to receive her PhD from the University of North Texas in 1990.

An award-winning professor, she was a senior lecturer in the department of History at the University of Texas at San Antonio, focusing on American Indian studies, as well as race, ethnicity, gender, and class. Her poems have appeared in various journals, including *Borderlands*, the *Texas Observer*, and the *Café Review*, as well as anthologies, including *Beloved on the Earth* (Holy Cow Press, 2009). She is the author of *Fishing for Light* (Wings Press, 2009) and *Ours is a Flower* (Pecan Grove Press, 2010).

A Mother's October

Now is the time of year
when wind-pushed gold leaves
on chrysanthemum feet moved her
like a boat on a river; she laughed
at life like the dream she wanted
to have before that long-ago

fall when the blunt Texas sky she loved
rushed into their year like a dream
that pushes you cloud-like and leaves
you panting, hard as a child
who has raked all day and moved
piles of pecan leaves into one heap.

Moving slowly now, she remembers
that fall—that day, blue—no one
dreamed it would change forever,
tilt her world askew. Leaves
swirled in wind like eddies in a river,
fell in drifts. The pecan tree sang

to the child who peered down
from the roof, full of flying
dreams—the youngest, the wild one
they all loved the most. Shouting up,
they cautiously moved close to the edge

of the shed. *Careful, don't fall*,
she called, but the child said, *leave me
alone. I'll fly into that pile of leaves,*

land like a bird. She would always
remember that—how reckless

dreams can be. Before the next fall,
she took them all to a treeless place—
desert nights piled within walls
a child could fall safely into. Where
dangerous dreams moved inside.

Winter Solstice

A narrow river. Shallow.
Not fast or slow. Not warm.
Not cold. Clear enough to see

light-colored rocks lining
the sandy bottom. In my
dream I am not running

or even picking a way through
stones not jagged or smooth,
sharp on bare feet from time

to time, navigable
in the even flow. No, in this dream
I am standing

motionless on one long leg,
right foot braced
against left knee.

Like the white heron
at the lily-thick edge
of the San Antonio River,

poised to find minnows
in opaque water.
Like my grandma Ida

in her resting position,

strong brown arm
casting a cane pole
into the muddy waters
of the Guadalupe, head

thrown back laughing
at the crazy blessing:
moonlight in a place
warm enough to fish.

Fishing for Light

*The present life of man on earth is like
the swift flight of a single sparrow through
the banqueting hall. . . .*
   —Venerable Bede (673-735)

No. We want something more about joy,
more moments loving the light inside
before dark calls the monster into the hall.

One by one, birds fly through the wide hall—
 shadows on fire-lit walls
 brighter than the night outside.
A swallow soars in by the south door,
traces high rafters. Open sky.
The time it takes to pass through the north door,
span of a life.

I am in love with the kinglet lost from its migrating flock
   who spins an airy path,
      pecan tree to reflecting glass, manic tap of a beak,
      red-feathered head flashing November sun.
This morning, still, at my bedroom window—
the cat stretches on the sill
watching a small bird looking   for itself.

Dia de Los Muertos at Mission Park Cemetery—
   Mama and I speak with Grandma in her grave—
   San Antonio light spikes across waxwings
      roosting in cedars, trees of the dead.
1896–1986. Symmetry in numbers, balance of a life—
ridiculous chrysanthemums in a pock-marked urn.
Mama cries. I rise like a note.
Dash on a headstone,
   space between the birth of light
   and the night when a spirit flew.
Standing here, who will know the stories?
The grandmother, who lived like a hummingbird—
drunk in a hot pink ocean of penta flowers.

November in Texas: mockingbirds shove
   between branches of persimmon trees—
      snatching the orange globes.
Outside, beyond the acrid noise of pecans
on metal roofs, a flat cerulean sky, the unbroken
blue. This cannot last.

A station wagon packed with kids—southside—
    rag-quilts for naps under trees—fried chicken,
    sugared cookies shaped like marks on a deck of cards—
    food we don't know we won't eat when we're old.
Laughing in late fall, we chase doves on a leafy bank
of the river where grandmother wades
in afternoon light looking for fish.

The day you died, a white bird
    drifted in my kitchen, circled, swept away
    into night; my bones wept for a whispered *come with me*
    but the spirit sang *stay. I am here with you.*
We will drink red wine under turning trees, remember
leaning back-to-back on October porches, laughing,
dreaming of being beautifully old, faces lit—
chrysanthemum explosions on the west wall. ★

DEBORAH PARÉDEZ

Deborah Parédez was born and raised in San Antonio where her family has lived since the 1730s. This particular Tejana/o history informs her dedication to troubling the traditional borders of genre, nation, language, and culture. She is the author of the poetry collection, *This Side of Skin* (Wings Press, 2002), and of the award-winning critical study, *Selenidad: Selena, Latinos, and the Performance of Memory* (Duke University Press, 2009). Her poetry and essays have appeared in the *New York Times, Los Angeles Review of Books, Poetry, Callaloo, Feminist Studies,* and elsewhere. She has lived on both coasts, endured a handful of Chicago winters, and taught American poetry in Paris, but through it all, she has remained rooted by her San Antonio love of *raspas*, sincerity, and the Spurs. Parédez earned a PhD in Interdisciplinary Theatre and Dance from Northwestern University. She has taught at Vassar, the Sorbonne Nouvelle, and the University of Texas at Austin, where she was Associate Director and Interim Director of the Center for Mexican American Studies. She now lives in New York City, where she is a professor of creative writing and ethnic studies at Columbia University.

Crape Myrtle, 1943

Not much use for school—
all those bells marking the time.

Mornings on my way
I'd stall outside Miss Tina's—

Mama warning about her type—
hair teased high and charcoal eyes

Revlon lips painted to a sneer—
the first real *Pachuca* on our block.

I'd let go my satchel of books
wrapped in sacks like market fish

like something dead.
I'd linger near her flushed

crape myrtle bush—the branches
dressed in their pink crinolines.

When you're standing that close
you notice things—like how to force

the bloom—how to break open
a bud between your finger and thumb—

the fuscia unfolding from its hull
like a blush across a girl's face.

That spring the white sailors docked—
set out to kill every *zoot* they saw.

Our boys beaten bloody in the street
stripped of their shark skin suits

still managing somehow to stand upright
when the cops came with clubs and cuffs.

Everywhere that year these small
explosions blossoming from our fists.

St. Joske's

Since before the war there was always work.
In '38, Papa sweating all day
for the WPA, Mrs. Wright
hiring Mama and her sisters to mind
the children and the wash—plenty to watch
after in white folks' homes, too much to name.

Took my diploma when they called my name.
Droughton's Business College trained us for work
that spun our rough hands to silk. My wristwatch
wound mornings to keep time with the workday,
shorthand scrawl etched and sprawling in my mind.
I learned to type and file and smile and write

a message in clear script, to get it right
the first time, not forget the fancy names
of men in suits, to keep it all in mind.
Guarantee Shoe Company, where I worked
first, had me stamping bills, but busy days
I made sales, rang the register and watched

ladies with delicate feet and watches
sparkling with jewel-light from their thin wrists write
checks in their husband's names. But come Friday
I thought only of the check with my name
on it. Treated myself after work
to a *Joske's* fountain soda, my mind's

burdens lifting like bubbles, wallet mined
for jukebox dimes. I'd sit a while to watch
the shoppers and the clerks on break from work

bent over pie at the counter, a rite
shared by the weary no matter their names,
Formica hewn like a pew on Sunday.

Joske's was a fancy store in its day.
Perfumed aisles and Persian rugs—had to mind
your manners, not give our folks a bad name—
fourth-floor Fantasyland's Santa on watch.
St. Joseph's Church next store keeping folks right
with God, refused to sell when *Joske's* worked
up its expansion plans. Still came the day
they worked their dozers, dollar signs in mind.
We watched that store exert its divine right.

Bustillo Drive Grocery

On the corner of Bustillo Drive
in the years before the campaign
to widen the street so cars veered off
Roosevelt Avenue right into mailboxes
right into stray dogs and second cousins,
in the years before we found the cockroach
floating inside a bottle of R.C. Cola
and swore off sodas forever
our righteous boycotts lasting
only halfway through Lent,
in the years before the thieves
tore through the screen doors and cracked
open the cash registers and *Abuelito's* head
with the butts of their guns, in the years
before I turned sour as *chamoy*
coarse and tough as stale *chicharón*,

I was in charge of *los dulces.*
In those years, *Abuelita* harnessed
me with my first job, setting me on a stool
behind the counter, setting me
like chocolate poured—quick—into the
candy mold before it hardens.
In the afternoons I fulfilled my duties
with a reverence for the expansive variations,
the countless shapes of sweetness:
aligning cylinders of Life Savers by flavor,
the Milky Ways near the 3 Musketeers,
the dainty swirled straws of Pixy Sticks near
the prized plastic heads of Pez dispensers,
the packets of Pop Rocks in grape, cherry, and orange.
I sat tall on my stool, a big girl, I was in charge
of *los dulces.* In the shelves above my reach
jars of Spanish olives, bottles of Bayer aspirin,
rolls of Charmin stood at attention,
awaiting their orders, but I could not be bothered
by the weight of such practical inventory.
I cared only for saccharine indulgence
so when on Friday nights the regular crowd
of relatives arrived for the gossip and the gambling,
I descended from my *dulce* throne
leaned coyly against the domino table
until Uncle Louis finished off his Falstaff
slapped his last domino down and with the same
triumphant hand, grabbed hold of me, swooped me up,
the fringes of my crocheted *poncho* fanning out in radiant plume.
He would lower me into the cavernous
depths of the old-time soda water cooler
that ran the length of the front wall, the length of a coffin
and twice as deep, my body plunged head first

into the cool humming darkness, arms outstretched,
hands grabbing hold of a slender bottleneck
and just then—catch complete—my plumed body
in pelican dive—I went soaring again—
Uncle Louis pulling me out from the depths,
poncho fringes fluttering, giggles spouting
from my mouth, syrupy bubbles erupting
from the opened bottle of my shaken Orange Crush.
In those years, my unwavering devotion to *los dulces,*
my faith in the choreography of return spurred
every harrowing descent, brought me back
every time—flushed and dizzy and eager for more.

Poem for the King William Dancers

San Antonio summer night
shadows set free from late afternoon's spell

        begin to move
    muevete muevete ¡aye!

spinning across the floor of that cantina
on the corner just off highway 281
our *cumbias* slippery dark
like the Shiner Bock that slides
down our throats slippery dark
like the pools of eyes that reflect
our movements from the bar—
we could drown there—
so we don't bother with these men
with the plot lines that spin
in their slippery dark minds

let them stare and lean
as dogged flowers toward the sun
we're here for the
slide—kick—gallop
of the *cumbia*

we're as complicated as Cuba
refined as table sugar
wrecking our stockings
when we bothered to wear them—
the wreckage so complete by winter
they had to shut that place down ★

JIM LaVILLA-HAVELIN

Jim LaVilla-Havelin is a San Antonio poet, educator, critic, and community arts organizer. Originally from upstate New York, LaVilla-Havelin founded the poetry series "Poetry Central" in Rochester in the early 1970s, edited the *Poetry Central Newsletter*, and hosted a weekly radio program, *Parnassus of the Air*, on WXXI, the Rochester PBS affiliate. He has worked in museum education most of his life, in Rochester, New York, Cleveland, Ohio, and San Antonio. Since retiring from seventeen years as the Young Artist Programs Director at the Southwest School of Art, LaVilla-Havelin has devoted his attention to teaching for Gemini Ink's incarcerated youth programs, the Golden Program of Bihl Haus Arts, The McNay Museum, and with workshops, teacher trainings, and consultancies. He is the coordinator and cofounder of San Antonio's National Poetry Month celebrations and community-wide calendar. He has been the poetry editor at the *San Antonio Express-News* for several years. Lavilla-Havelin is the author of five books of poetry, including *What the Diamond Does Is Hold It All In* (White Pine Press, 1978), *Rites of Passage* (Charon Books, 1969), *Simon's Masterpiece* (White Pine Press, 1983), *Counting* (Pecan Grove Press, 2010), and *West: poems of a place* (Wings Press, 2017).

Earl Abel's

french toast, cheese omelet, hash browns
a rasher of bacon
        every city has one
         a venerated favorite
all deco curves
            fifties Chevy
    an aging wait staff
    who would get to know you

with names like marge, louise, walter
    ready to get you "the usual"
chipped china, old patterns, nowhere to get
                replacements
mashed potatoes, gravy, fried chicken —
    in the south no one feels the need
    to call it "southern fried"
pie
    pies with a reputation
open all night
but inside you could never tell
    light level so muted and no windows
    it could be three in the morning
    air conditioning so cold you could
    almost see your breath
    like sucking in after eating a mint
as if the cold, the dark, and the quiet were one
pickled beets
    juices black in the semi-darkness
if you hear no real warmth from me
    I didn't grow up here

iced tea
refilling your coffee cup
regulars
    who have outlived styles, argyle, madras,
    the sixties
iceberg lettuce, ranch dressing
tuna
memory connected to taste.
    color, sound, and shape
    less vivid than present
sleekness

after the prom
special meals, if not fancy ones
meat loaf, American cheese, white bread
    with curving crust
    like the Alamo
    the curves of simple rising
everything sliced, everything curved
    as easy as drawl
    Americana on a
    plate

In the Courtyard

In the McNay's courtyard
aflourish with plants, almost tropical,
I could have stepped into a Rousseau.
But then the tiles—maybe Matisse —
patterns, borders, color accents
in corners
            across sun-splashed surfaces
a world of warm and easy curves.

And the staircase
          each riser's tiles different

                   a riot of

shapes and colors
          decorative and, step by

                step,

narrative
    at the same time.

The world is alive with stories, even in those places
where we are at rest.

from *Some Trees*
  for Carlos Cortez

    Carlos built a tree for us
            steel girders
            mesh
                   and concrete

    worked the concrete
    with forks and spoons
    with pigments (a secret mix)

    to make believable bark

                 to the eye and to the hand
    a family art form
    passed down
    he hadn't been sure
    for a long time
    if he wanted to learn

    now, sure-handed he transforms
    concrete—
              a forest
             alchemist

    metalworkers
    built a staircase that spiraled

around the trunk
        up to a nest
        to watch from

at the roots—
        a cave-like space
        a place to sit and read stories
        with no cookie elves

and if you look closely
in that half-dark
with your eyes and with your hands

scraped into the surfaces of this hidden spot—

his children's names—
nice ★

CAROL COFFEE REPOSA

Carol Coffee Reposa was born in 1943 and has lived in San Antonio most of her life. After earning her MA from the University of Texas in Austin, she moved to San Antonio in 1969. She taught English literature and creative writing at San Antonio College for over thirty years, and has been a vital member of San Antonio literary community. She was named the 2018 Poet Laureate of Texas.

Her poems have appeared in numerous journals. She is the author of three books of poetry: *At the Border: Winter Lights* (Pecan Grove Press, 1992); *Facts of Life* (Browder Springs Press, 2002); and *Underground Musicians (*Lamar University Press, 2013*)*. She is also the author of a chapbook, *The Green Room* (Pecan Grove Press, 1998). Twice nominated for the Pushcart Prize, she also has received two Fulbright/Hays Fellowships, the first for study in Russia (1995) and a second for research in Peru and Ecuador (1999). Her writings about San Antonio reflect a deep understanding of the city's past and present and its cultural importance, its peaceful demeanor.

Cicadas

They come here every August
Butternut armies
Camping in the sycamores
Breaking up the stillness
With their drum rolls
Throbbing in the dust
And dead-end heat,
Their brief maneuvers
Carried out in clattering waves
And overlapping tides,

A corps of offbeat castanets
Not quite in sync
Until September
When their cadences
Grow fainter
Slow almost
To a crawl.

Later we will find
Abandoned instruments,
Their ragged traps
On flowers, fences, leaves.
We look for sound.

Great Horned Owl

He swooped into our yard at dusk
Heavy with the smell of coming rain
Settling on the topmost branch
Of a decaying tree
Still studded with pecans.
The dogs went wild
Pawed at the trunk
Howled like Furies.

I watched for magic light
Reflections of lost places
Glowing in his eyes
But he did nothing, stayed above us
Calm as a marble bust
While darkness gathered in his wings,
A silhouette in charcoal

One shade deeper than the night.
Almost fused with evening
He started to unfurl
In secret, languid ritual
The way someone might raise a flag
When no one else could see,
Stiff fabric flapping several times
In lumbering majesty
Before he lofted slowly into stars.

Alamo Plaza at Night

Even now, tourists come
To gaze up at the chipped façade,
Weathered double doors,
Oaks twisted into dark, floodlights
Trained along their branches.
Cameras flash against white limestone
Pocked with centuries
And gunshots long ago.

Within the walls
And Roman arches
Heavy with their bars
Are tidy gardens:
Boston ferns droop languidly
Toward fresh-cut grass
And copper plants.
Goldfish wallow in their quiet ponds.

Outside people talk about the mission,

Where to go, what to eat.
Visitors brood over maps
And time-lapse shots. Children peer
At plaques, words lost
Within a diesel's whine, the clop-clop
Of a horse's hooves, wind rising
In dark trees, voices gathered
Finally
Into the stones. ★

Jacinto Jesús Cardona

Jacinto Jesús Cardona, a.k.a. Jesse, is the author *At The Wheel Of A Blue Chevrolet* (Amapola Press, 1993) and *Pan Dulce* (Chili Verde Press, 1998). He is not a prolific poet, but several of his poems have become iconic pieces of San Antonio literature, especially when delivered in Cardona's richly rolling baritone. As he puts it in one of his signature phrases, "My writing celebrates my Tex Mex experience. I celebrate the x in Tex and the x in Mex and the humble x my mother used to make."

Cardona has read his poetry on "Latin File" on National Public Radio and on PBS television stations. He has also appeared in two documentaries: *Voices From Texas*, by independent filmmaker, Ray Santisteban, and in *The Mexican-Americans*, by New York Public Television. Cardona is a two-time champion of *La Voz de San Antonio*, a spoken word poetry contest. In 2015 his poem "Bato Con Khakis" was selected for performance by Symphony Space in New York.

Cardona's poem "Full Moon" was selected for VIA/San Antonio Transit's "Poetry on the Move" as part of National Poetry Month. In 2012 he was a finalist for the William Stafford Prize sponsored by *Rosebud Magazine*.

He grew up in Alice, the "Hub of South Texas," but has lived and taught in San Antonio since 1974. Cardona currently teaches English at Incarnate Word High School and at Trinity University for the Upward Bound Program. In 1999 he was awarded the Trinity Prize for Teaching Excellence. He is also the recipient of the Imagineer Award from the Learning About Learning Foundation, and the Ford Salute to Education's Award for the Arts.

Bar America

Where "Ladies Are Always Welcome"
and Jimmy Edwards and the Latin Breed

battle it out with Timi Yuro on the jukebox.
John F. Kennedy en paz descansa
in a plastic frame next to the packets
of dry shrimp and fried pork skins.

Un chaparrito in his blue seersucker suit
se despide de sus compas,
including la mujer sola in the red booth

who confides to Lola
that her cigarette lighter
leaks in her purse
while I jot down a title:
The Idea of Fraternity in America

Chicharras

In 1614 the archbishop of Lima, Perú, mandated the burning
of all musical instruments: pan pipes, flutes, whistles, rattles, bells,
and trumpets made of pottery, shell, bone, and wood.

Chi-charrrrrr-as,
in 90-plus Tonatiuh degrees, you keep buzzing love songs,
sucking root juice until you tumble to the ground and sing no more,
disappearing with dog day afternoons.

Chi-charrrrrr-as,
I knew you when I was into caliche streets
baking under snake-slithering heat waves,
my bare feet oblivious of Timber Creek
where your reedy monotones charmed Walt Whitman's bones
recovering from a paralytic stroke.

In 90-plus Tonatiuh degrees, I celebrate your shell-shape drumhead
and how you compress your digestive apparatus into very little space
because you are more into resonating your musical membrane
with the colors of the rainbow, like la Raza Cósmica
dancing cumbia crazy all over Aztlántejas USA.

Chi-charrrrrr-as
Texas Hill Country chicharras,
chicharras from West Texas,
chicharras from the Hub of South Texas
and the visiting chicharras from Chicago.

Pan Dulce

I remember riding my fenderless bike
to la panadería del pueblo.
Sometimes I would go alone,
sometimes I would dream I took abuelo by the hand.

I remember pan dulce tasting even sweeter
after confessing my sins at St. Joseph Catholic Church.
Nothing like dulcified bread
for crucified bones.

I remember standing in front of the glass displays,
telling el panadero, "I'll take one of these,
and one of those, and one of these."
Unlike the cool pachuco who came in
asking for pan de polvo, un regalo
y un hueso azucarado to go,
I had not mastered the names of pan dulce.

So imagine my thrill,
imagine the authority in my chavalón bones
when I returned asking for dos huesos azucarados,
two sugared bones to go.

Yes, I remember pan dulce,
la Virgen de Guadalupe bordered by blue neon lights
and how the smell of canela
reminded me of abuelito's piloncillo skin.

Avocado Avenue

I don't live on Avocado Avenue,
and I've never been in the vicinity
of avocado trees, but I must confess
de vez en cuando I would rather be
un vagabundo hawking velvet avocados
por los barrios de Aztlántejas USA.
Yes, I must confess
I am an avocado aficionado.
I will vouch for any avocado.

You see, avocados are not vociferous.
They are content to be versant
with philosophical window sills.
Who would vilify an avocado?
Visualize two avocados,
two summer syllables on a window sill
ripening under Tonatiuh's vocabulario,
and you visualize world peace:
paz paz paz.

Avocados are not equivocados;
they are not into hate, do not equivocate.
Aguacates are not into voodoo economics.
They just want a place on your Mexican plate.
But what must aguacates think?
Mexican food is chic;
it's made the New York celebrity list;
it's Gucci bags next to guacamole bowls.

No, there are no revolutions on Guadalupe Street,
only the blooming rosebushes by Rudy's transmission. ★

Celeste Guzmán Mendoza

Celeste Guzmán Mendoza is a native of San Antonio. Her poems and essays have appeared in *Poet Lore, Borderlands, Salamander,* and other journals. She has also had essays and poems appear in the following anthologies: *This Promiscuous Light: Young Women Poets of San Antonio* (Wings Press, 1996); *Floricanto Si!: A Collection of Latina Poetry* (Penguin, 1998); *Red Boots and Attitude: The Spirit of Texas Women Writers* (Eakin Press, 2003); *Telling Tongues: A Latin@ Anthology on Language Experience* (Calaca Press, 2007); *Her Texas: Story, Image, Poem & Song* (Wings Press, 2015); and *Entre Guadalupe y Malinche: Tejanas in Literature and Art* (University of Texas Press, 2015). Her chapbook of poetry, *Cande, te estoy llamando,* won the 1999 Poesía Tejana Prize from Wings Press. Her most recent collection is *Beneath the Halo* (Wings, 2013).

Mendoza graduated from Barnard College and holds a MFA in poetry from Bennington Writing Seminars and a Certificate in Spanish from the Universidad Nacional Autónoma de México. She is currently completing a PhD at the University of Texas at Austin. She is a cofounder of CantoMundo, a master workshop for Latina/o poets.

Mendoza is also a playwright. Her plays have been produced by the Guadalupe Cultural Arts Center and Teatro Vivo. *Burnt Sienna* won the 1996 American College Theater Festival's Ten Minute Play Award.

Mendoza lives with her husband in Austin, Texas. She currently works as the associate director of development at the Teresa Lozano Long Institute for Latin American Studies of the University of Texas at Austin.

Tío Chucho would have you believe

that Tía Chavela was named for Port
Isabel not a saint.

He says this each time we drive
toward the bay, seagulls cutting
into his, *Pos sí, es cierto. ¿No me creen?*

How could we believe a story like that?
Port Isabel with its bikinied, bosomy,
bottom-heavy ladies, and beer joints

filled with young white boys in swimming
chones and chanclas, and t-shirt shop
after t-shirt shop—has nothing to do

with Tía Chavela's horn-rimmed trifocals,
SAS shoes, casita with furniture covered
in plastic, and altar with stained photos

of her mother. In one she holds a bunny
and a palm-sized statue of el sagrado
corazón. No. Nada que ver. But el Tío.

Maybe he remembers Tía's youth
before their six children suckled
her breasts dry. Or maybe he wants

us to laugh with him. Share something.
Our English a wound so deep
between us. Los pochos and him—

viejito always thinking of his Mexico
lindo. We could ask Tía to set him straight
but why bother. Every year, once a year

he gets to say it, resolved that it could be
true and that would make them as American
as us. Just as good. Maybe so good
that next year he could bring Tía Chavela
in their own car, stay in their own hotel,
and pretend together that this is the better

life,
worth the leaving,
worth the remembering.

About faith

I prayed ever since I could speak,
before I could read.

I confessed every Saturday
before Sunday communion,
fasted every Friday, walked
the Stations of the Cross on Thursdays.

Every day was for God. If it hadn't been
who would I be?

A girl with long hair and buck teeth,
who made a home altar out of cardboard,
sat her Malibu Barbie next to her Baby Jesus
swaddled in blue, prayed Hail Marys in Spanish,
sometimes forgetting a verse, and yet

I still felt holy.
No one screamed at me. Or touched me.

I was alone.

Believing in the one thing
far enough away to not hurt me.

Crooked pinky

Lisa jutted her hands up to my face, *I'm a Rodríguez too.*
Got grandma's pinkies. All us Rodríguez women are crooked
little-finger ladies. We're buried with beaded rosaries wrapped
snuggly around our clasped palms, crucifixes dangling below
the crook in our pinkies. Lisa feels connected to us. She is
and isn't. Half-Canadian so she's a pale-skinned, blue-eyed,
dirty blonde and didn't grow up eating tacos; at 22
she can't hold one without the stuffing dangling or falling
out. But the pinky is her proof that she is from this line
of hard, dark-skinned Mexican women, rock candy ladies
that take espinas from nopales with our teeth when a knife
isn't handy. We are known for starting fights with other women
and even our husbands could (but never would) confess to receiving
a cracked bone or two from a Rodríguez woman's clenched fist.
The crocheted doilies we make are coasters for our beer. We knit

for our husbands so they'll know our hands are agile with sharp
objects. Lisa doesn't know this history, can't name our abuela's
hand cream, doesn't know great tia's secret handshake. But
she has the crooked pinky every Rodríguez woman carries
as we live our lives any way but straight. ★

AMALIA ORTIZ

Originally from La Feria, Texas, Amalia Ortiz grew up in San Antonio. She studied Creative Writing at the University of Texas-Rio Grande Valley and splits her time between San Antonio and Harlingen, Texas. During a Hedgebrook fellowship, she wrote her poetry musical, *Carmen de la Calle.* In 2014, she completed an IC3 residency at the National Hispanic Cultural Center in Albuquerque. She is also a recipient of the Alfredo Cisneros Del Moral Fellowship.

Ortiz is widely known as a Tejana actor/writer/activist. She was featured on three seasons of *Russell Simmons presents Def Poetry* on HBO, and on the NAACP Image Awards program on FOX. She is the creator of "Otra Esa on the Public Transit," a powerful one-woman stage show about destination and destiny, which she performed at San Antonio's Guadalupe Theater and Talento Bilingüe de Houston. She also stars in the award-winning independent film *Speeder Kills,* which was broadcast on SiTV and PBS. As a member of Chicano Messengers of Spoken Word, she cowrote and performed the poetry/theater piece, "Fear of a Brown Planet," in San Francisco, Miami, Denver, and Houston. *Latina Magazine* honored Amalia for her role in founding, cowriting, directing, and performing in "Women of ILL Repute: Refute!" which was presented at a number of festivals and conferences in Texas and at many universities.

Amalia Ortiz was the first Latina poet to reach the final round at the National Poetry Slam, where her team took second place. She is a San Antonio Puro Slam three-time champion; an Open Slam Champion and Tag Team Champion (with Gary Mex Glazner) at the Taos Poetry Circus; and winner of the inaugural Ultimate Poetry Boxing Championship.

Ortiz's poetry is included on the spoken word compilations PoetCD.com, Sampler Vol. I, *NYC Urbana: the Very Best of 2003* and *The Chicano Messengers of Spoken Word.* She participated in the Slam America National Bus Tour and is featured on the tour documentary *A Busload of Poets.* She is the author of *Rant. Chant. Chisme.* (Wings Press 2015), selected by NBC News as one of the ten best Latino/a books of 2015 and winner of the Writers League of Texas Discovery Prize.

Girl Strolls Down Nogalitos Street

for Jacquie on Taft

Girl must be walking to a beat in her head
'cause her metronome hips make music
Abuelitas frown as she passes
waist playin' bass as her heels drum the pavement
Can't really blame her though
Girl can't help it
This city just sings through her

the night Ram died

Ramiro 'Ram' Ayala, whose iconic bar Taco Land became an institu-
tion for underground music for more than three decades, was shot to
death early Friday in a possible robbery attempt, police said.
— John Tedesco, Jim Beal, and Mary Moreno,
San Antonio Express-News, online (06/25/2005)

the city burned hot and humid
in sticky, sweaty celebration
the night that Ram died

the night Ram died
1,000,000 lungs
exhaled whoops and
howls-at-the-moon
into the San Anto skyline

downtown, a traffic jam honked a horn concerto
heard all the way to Alamo Heights
the beat of bass bumped bumper-to-bumper

in gridlock automobile standstill
amid 1,000,000 patas on the pavement
parading in puro pinche pachanga parranda
in true San Antonio style

the night Ram died
San Anto was drunk on another Spurs championship
intoxication stumbling stranger into embracing stranger
violating public drunkenness, open container, liquor laws
and creating uncontrolled crowd dangers
while wheelie poppin' motorcycle cops looked the other way
the night that Ram died
was like some Tejano holiday
raza invented
like wrapping New Year's inside Cinco de Mayo
and sprinkling two weeks of Fiesta on top

but Ram
a crusty old loud-talkin' man
wasn't one of those 1,000,000 fans
Fuck the Spurs!
Ram of beer and barflies
Ram of pool hustlers and punk rockers

Ram was behind the helm of Taco Land
and Taco Land was a dive bar
on the river near old factories and warehouses
no touristy river walk pretension there
only the cinder block shell
of a no frills ice house
wallpapered three layers thick with rock iconography
graffiti, flyers, and band bumper-stickers
a few busted vinyl booths, a pool table

and a kickass jukebox full of records
as old as the backed up plumbing
in the ladies room where every gal
sprawled in a shaky spider stance
over the clogged toilet

and, oh lord!
it's hard to pee when the walls won't stop moving
uncountable nights spent spewing
vomitous into the river

at Taco Land
on any given night
Ram peddled dollar Lone Stars
and sucked swigs off his mystery hooch two liter
opening his stage
to guitars growling
alcohol attitudes
and ass-whipping elbows thrown to the furious beat
of rock and roll rebellion
fueled by Ram's belligerent rants of
    Don't be a pussy!

on nights thick with dope smoke
overheated kids hung on the patio
praying for a breeze to blow
from the muddy river banks down below
there hobo river rats
rested serene on cardboard pallets
or sometimes waited to sleep under a picnic bench on the patio
once last call was hollered and the party moved elsewhere

'cause this was a home away from home

to many homeless and boozers
to the rockers and losers
freaks and fans
shady hookers and bands
on any given night at Taco Land

the night Ram died
the streets were alive with 1,000,000 joyous cries
but as San Anto partied
the music died   with a gunshot

petty thieves killed the man behind the bar

but not the legend

the Dead Milkmen immortalized
the local music scene canonized

the shrine of over thirty years of South Texas punk rock history

the night Ram died
you might as well have buried the pyramid with the man
or set him aflame atop his building
a pyre burning on the river
their ashes as inseparable as their legacy
untimely extinguished
like a cigarette butt savagely crushed beneath a biker boot

the night Ram died,
1,000,000 souls
shouted to the heavens in unison
where one can imagine his soul joined the celebration
of 1,000,000 voices victorious

these hands which have never picked cotton

my father unexpectedly pulled the car to the side of the interstate
and ordered his four children out into the cotton field
confused, we set down our video games
and flipped off the headphones
following reluctantly

he said, you've never picked cotton
you have no idea what it's like
it looks so soft, but it has thorns
which cut at the fingers even through gloves

we mortified teens reached down
with sideways glances embarrassed by the passing cars
plucked tiny clouds while rolling eyes
swallow a hand full of humble
but the real lesson would not be digested until years later

they say the first generation sacrifices
so that the second generation can achieve
only for the third generation to squander
and these third generation hands
these hands have never picked cotton

these hands, which have never picked cotton
softer than father's or grandfather's
these hands have never felt the prick of burrs
scrape deep, draw blood

these fruitless hands, which have never plucked grapes from the vine
are strangers to orange groves and grapefruit rows
these fragile knuckles have never scraped over washboards

or scrubbed floors for money
but have been caressed by abuela who did so in my place
these hands, which have spent more hours pushing buttons
than planting
with these fingertips
tender as abuelo's whispers
uncalloused as the fulfillment of grandmother's wishes

tender as this back, which has never ached in labor
never felt the sun baked flesh stretched beyond endurance
never known struggle as synonymous with sunrise
this body may not know, but must never forget

these hands, which have never worked leather
hammered heels, yanked soles, repaired saddles
sanded and polished shoes
grampa did, so that I may not

they say the first generation sacrifices
the second generation achieves
for the third generation to squander
and these third generation hands need to find purpose
these empty hands hold so much promise
these hands, which have never picked cotton

this body
the bones, muscle, youth not yet sacrificed to feed children
this body understands struggle builds character
but is still searching for what these hands will build

these selfish hands
these lazy, delicate hands
assimilated american made

these idle devil's playthings
play dead as if incapable of growing, crafting sculpting
a new america with these hands

these hands, which have never loaded weapons
these eyes, which have never stared war and death in the face
spared by dad's tour of duty
claim all these things I've never done
the softness of this body feels dad's scars
etched someplace on the skin of my soul

these legs, which have never hiked foreign jungles
are these legs so untested
that they will be the first generation not able to support their
    own weight?
will they buckle only to lay around and lounge?
was that abuelo's goal
moving to this land of 3rd, 4th, 5th generations
where what comes easily goes unesteemed
as these hands cover the ignorantly bored yawn of privilege

these hands, which have never picked cotton
become more american at rest
softer, dumber
their long-term memory loss bashing that next
    generation of immigrants
who dare aspire to my luxury of laziness

resting on
these feet, which have never walked factory floors
spent more time marching in protest than harvesting produce
these clumsy hands
more hours in libraries than in labor

in classrooms than cleaning public bathrooms

more toys than tools
more theory than action

these grateful hands write words of hope
of remembering and being remembered
give back this gift
scratch feeble offerings
to those who came before

these hands
these reverent hands grapple to fold together the past and the present
like hands folding in prayer
in the tradition of my abuela, bisabuela, tatarabuela
pray to their same god my modern concerns
to remember and be remembered

these feet stand on shoulders
reach down not to pick cotton
but to pull up the next generation
these words are for you
to remember and be remembered
to give and receive opportunity

these hands, which have never picked cotton, are ready
to park the car at the side of the road
snap the children out of their stupor
and into the fields
to appreciate the art of craft
of digging in the earth as creators

if struggle breeds character and sloth a deadly sin
then I am either the harvest my ancestors cultivated
or their sacrifices sinfully squandered
they say the first generation sacrifices
the second achieves
for the third to squander
and these third generation hands which have never picked cotton
these obligated hands are not my own ★

LAURIE ANN GUERRERO

Laurie Ann Guerrero was born and raised in the Southside of San Antonio. Guerrero holds a BA in English from Smith College and an MFA in poetry from Drew University. Her first publication, *Babies under the Skin* (2007), won the Panhandler Chapbook Award, chosen by Naomi Shihab Nye.

Her next book, *A Tongue in the Mouth of the Dying* (2013), won the Montoya Poetry Prize and was published by the University of Notre Dame Press. It was listed as one of fourteen "must-read works of Chicano literature" by Rigoberto González and received an International Latino Book Award. Guerrero's latest collection is *A Crown for Gumecindo* (Aztlan Libre Press, 2015). Guerrero's poetry and critical work have appeared or are forthcoming in *Poetry, Indiana Review, Luna Luna, Huizache, Texas Monthly, Bellevue Review, Borderlands: Texas Poetry Review, Women's Studies Quarterly, Texas Observer, Chicana/Latina Studies, Feminist Studies,* and others.

Guerrero succeeded Carmen Tafolla as Poet Laureate of the city of San Antonio in 2014, and she was appointed the 2016 Poet Laureate of Texas. While she was poet laureate of San Antonio, one of her initiatives was to establish the San Antonio Poetry Archives at Palo Alto College. Other honors include grants from the Artist Foundation of San Antonio and the Alfredo Cisneros del Moral Foundation.

She recently became the Writer in Residence at Texas A&M University in San Antonio.

Sundays After Breakfast:
A Lesson in Cotton Picking

South Texas, 1943

In grandpa's memory, I hide in the shadows, I suture mesquite

trees, cactus plants, cotton weigh scales to my spine, thick
and necessary as skin. I memorize the dance: feet shuffling
in the dust, fluttering hands like birds nest-building, the blood

that stains brown birds red. They stuff cotton sacks, handstitched by my great-great grandmother, twelve feet long:

Mexican polkas, segregated picture shows,
shifty-eyed big-brothers listening for the rolling

tongue of laziness or spunk. *¡Cállate, prieto!*
says my fifteen-year-old grandfather to a fearless friend

who chats up a blonde in the white-only section—
her skin brighter than the August sun. Grandpa passes

in his good sombrero, hair slicked like he hasn't been in a field
all day. I watch him pick my grandma by the color

of her dress and of her eyes, and because she's lucky,
not by how much cotton she can pick.

Esperanza Tells Her Friends
The Story Of La Llorona

She killed her babies in the river over there by the Bill Miller
Barbecue place, you know, by the Holy Mother Church. She was
friends with my grandma; they played bingo together, I think.

Oh, yeah, why did she kill 'em?

Sundays After Breakfast:
A Lesson In Speech

There were no names for men like that—gringos
who stitched up their rules, their white garb, laced snug
the issues of the day: *Lord didn't make us to mix*

with them folk, said hoods. But God's got nothing to do
with the black boys dumped still alive into a restless river.
God's got nothing to do with having to tell their mamas.

That bloody water ran through each dark vein across Texas,
fed the Gulf, all its brown-skinned people. This, grandpa could name:
los cuerpos—bodies swaying above the cotton like sheets hanging
     on a line.

No importaba que no eras negro, pero que no eras gringo.
No, it didn't matter that you weren't black, grandpa says
pushing himself from the table, but that you weren't white.

He lived his life this way: silent, like every man after him:
opening his mouth only to eat, holding his head above the cotton,
between white men and black boys. ★

JENNY BROWNE

Jenny Browne is the author of three collections of poems, *At Once (2003)* and *The Second Reason (2007)*, both from the University of Tampa Press, and *Dear Stranger* (University of Texas Press, 2013). Her poems and essays have appeared in *American Poetry Review*, *Gulf Coast*, *Pleiades*, the *New York Times*, *Tin House*, and *Threepenny Review*. Writing in *The Believer*, Stephen Burt said, "Her poems retain the unpredictability not of a roulette wheel or a supernova, but of a quirky, wise friend in another city, one whose reactions surprise us even once we know her enough to trust her well." Browne has written that good poetry expresses "how it feels to be a human moving through both the physical and imagined world."

Her work has been featured on buses in Austin, Texas, in the "Modern Love" column of the *New York Times*, and onstage at the Dallas Museum of Art. She was selected by the University of Iowa International Writers Program and the US State Department in 2011 to teach poetry in the Dadaab Refugee Camp in Kenya.

A former James Michener Fellow at the University of Texas in Austin, she has received grants from the San Antonio Artist Foundation, the Texas Writers League, and the National Endowment for the Arts. Currently she is an Associate Professor of English at Trinity University. She was the 2016-2017 Poet Laureate of San Antonio, and the 2017 Poet Laureate of Texas. She lives with her husband, photographer Scott Martin, and their two daughters in downtown San Antonio.

The Man Who Gives Bad Directions
In Downtown San Antonio

The first time I realized that I had said *keep going*
through three lights not two I tried to catch
the couple with out of state plates but they were

already turning left from the middle lane without
signaling, slowly making their way towards my mistake.
I imagined them passing the wax museum, steering
towards where the sky widens with the white silence
of egrets this time of year and the silver fish shadow
deeper with their secrets. I used to tell myself
if two rights make an L and three a U, one wrong makes
an accident. But a hundred wrongs, that's a life.
I'm not a bad man but I met my wife trying to talk
to her sister. I still can't dance. But that first night
when I turned her the wrong way, we crashed
and she caught her breath in my arms. *Where's the Alamo?*
That's one kind of mission. This is another.
Truth is you're already lost when you find me. Listen closely,
there are mesquite bricks breathing beneath this road.
The turns it takes followed cows not rulers. And smothered
beneath the exit where you got off the highway was once
a place called Jimmy Woo's where the counter divided
by color but the Mexicans in the kitchen served them all
the same grey chow mien. See, you're leaning out
your window now, nodding without ever taking
your eyes from my face.

There's a Slow Green River
I've Been Living By

1.
If I were forced to begin in the midst of the hardest
movement it is starless and the dark
painted wood

of the kitchen floor lines my forehead as inside

a womb grinds her houseful of stones
into dust. A woman's voice
repeating *you are close. You have a whole boneyard of*
contractions behind you. She said boneyard.
She said behind me.

2.
Were the winter mornings when
my body was still only one body

and I ran past The Mug Club
and the crumbling bricks

of the Russian Orthodox Church, past
an aged German Shepherd turning

manic circles in the dirt and the purple
ceramic eagle bolted to the roof

of the high school, past Andy's
Taco House that used to be Bob's

Barbeque that used to be Praise the Lord
Fried Chicken just as every green shatter

of glass I stepped around used to be
whole and quenching

to where the river begins because
back then I could still pretend

there were beginnings and ends,
a being with boundaries.

3.
I have tried to be a good river fore-
    seeable and faithful
to the innate knowing what
    is bank, what is flow.
Above the red evening
    light skids off
the slopes of abandoned
    grain silos, rows of steel
breasts aimed skyward.
    They've been turned
into studios for sculptors,
    people who know the material
creates the form.

4.

A single cactus flat flung into loose dirt multiplies, peacocks out like
shallow rooted fireworks and works its thousand hands over the windows, behind the gutters and under the fence reaching and reaching
like the pictures I've seen of refugees until it is all I can see and I hold
the heavy red fruit in my gloved palm and slice it lengthwise with the
sharpest knife then scoop the magenta pulp into a bowl and it is sunrise and it is open-heart surgery and it is placental, clotted and full of
black seeds and it stains my teeth.

5.
There's a photograph
tacked to the wall above
this desk. I am seven months
full, a pale and swollen moon floating
the sea at Vieques. The Marines called it
Green Beach. The locals, Punta Arenas, point
of sand, where the smallest part names the whole.

222

If the camera turned its back and followed the road
up into the hills it would see how even though the
soldiers haven't been gone long the green is already swallowing everything, moving over
the empty weapons caches, imagining
them into burial mounds or ripe
bellies, swelling multiple
selves, growing bigger
the closer we come

6.
And then.

I have always slept better next to rivers

and loved the low grind of coal barges, slow floating
	mountain ranges

that make the turn wide then wider.

And I have watched the spaces between
the scales of a garden snake expand

as animal moves through animal.

I have squinted at the sky
and seen the sun move through a pinhole

and birth is still not like
anything.

7.
I make another list

of all I have ever loved and twist it
into the open end of a bottle and leave it

more open.

8.
If the one thing I will never know is the only thing
I know it is green and it keeps moving.

In one version of this story the cypress tree bends down
and reties her own shoes but you know how that goes.

Everyone is still learning, pausing, reaching low
for the place where another kind of breathing takes hold

and grows wild and deeper. I'd like to tell you about it
but that would mean I'm talking again, using words

like contraction, dilate and divisible by
instead of following anything down and down.

See how the squirrels chew with their mouths open, scattering
green pecan pieces on our big ideas.

See how they stare back without blinking.

9.
I am trying to keep something alive.
It is a slippery thing. It is re-learning
how to breathe. It is screaming.
Say New
    Orleans.
Say black

coffee.
Say the night
    watchman all love

the three-legged dog who walks
his owner to the news stand.
And the news, who does it love?

Eyes, hands, some newborn sun
shattering its own face back
in the pattern of broken glass?

10.
Spring and our new dog leans into the screen door. Her vulva swollen and dripping leaf shaped rusty smears on the porch steps. Soon
we will fix this but today we cannot contain her season. We cannot
change that blood is the sister of green or that despite the word season, meaning certain conditions into which a year is traditionally
divided, every-thing still seems to happen at once. Pass the frenzied
barking on both sides of the street.

11.
This could be the world. An air-
conditioned green room you've seen

before. Inside, a young man repeats
exactly what you want then misspells

your name on a recycled paper cup.
I dream a counter where you can
order your teeth any size you like.
See we can choose our coffee

but we can't choose our monsters.
This fall the earth turns itself

into a sway-backed animal,
all claws and fleas fox-trotting

round the damp stinking anus.
A single blind destructive eye.

On TV, circling red with
yellow rings and yellow

with red rings and
none of them our green.

12.
Note found inside a bottle:

I have seen several Septembers in search
of a new name. I have heard *do not rest*
and *do not forget.* I have asked why
all the parades are followed by women
with brooms. I have answered
pour the unhappiness out. I strap
my child to my back and walk
towards a river. It is the same river.

13.
The water under the bridge is filled with tiny
black fish, a school of commas. They clarify
that once I waited, grew larger, multiplied
and became two. I divided, stood and walked

on a river of selves. No remainder.
The fish swallow the o's we throw whole.

The wall echoes any word we shout. Even stop.
Even this hot. Impossible, the popsicle.

14.
If a root swallows the corner of the path, if green, if nothing
lasts, not even a child's name written with a sharp rock

on the buckled sidewalk then we must hide
the rock beneath a low blooming rosemary bush.

It will be our secret. You can find it again, each
morning like a mind, a surprise. Or a sky. ★

PART FOUR

Drama

THEATER IN SAN ANTONIO

Requirements of size necessitate limiting the number of dramatic pieces we can include in this anthology. However, something should be said about the role of the theater in San Antonio. Of course, that history began *sans* stage and curtains. The first dramatic productions were glorified mystery plays, arranged by the Spanish padres for the edification of their indigenous flocks. These evolved into the neighborhood *posadas* and *pastorelas*, performed to this day, every Christmas season.

The most elaborate of these is *Los Pastores*, which has been performed for the most part by the same families for the last hundred years. The current version of this "shepherd's play" came together in San Antonio early in the twentieth century when several westside families began to combine their versions of the play. Doroteo Domínguez memorized the play as he had heard it in San Luis Potosí and hired someone to write it down as he recited it; Sacramento Grimaldo wrote it down from his memories of performances he heard as a child; Santos Esparza wrote down a version of it from memory when a cousin absconded with the family manuscript; "Old Salvador" retained a manuscript he had copied down as a boy from the parish script in Irapuato, Mexico. Our Lady of Guadalupe Catholic Church, in 1949, sponsored the publication of the text, edited by Rev. Carmelo Tranchese, S.J., with musical notation by Carmela Montalvo, O.S.B. As Julia Nott Waugh wrote in her *The Silver Cradle: Las Posadas, Los Pastores and Other Mexican American Traditions* (University of Texas Press, 1955): "Thus it comes about every year that a group of Mexican laboring folk, sometimes several groups, produces in this Texas town a mystery play that was old when Joan of Arc was burned in the Rouen market place."

From the late nineteenth century through the 1940s, *carpas*—traveling tent theaters—provided theatrical entertainments that included vaudeville acts, musical performances, comedic sketches (many of them highly political), dancers, even circus acts on trapeze and high wire. The most famous company was La Carpa García, founded in San Antonio in 1914 by members of the extended García family, managed by Manuel V. García until the company disbanded in 1947.

Numerous Mexican touring companies made San Antonio their northernmost stop, beginning as early as the 1880s. As the political situation in Mexico became more intense, at least one of these companies—the Concepción Hernández-Villalongín company—settled here permanently. They would be the opening performance at the San Antonio Opera House in 1900.

One of the first large theaters to open in San Antonio was Beethoven Hall, located opposite La Villita on South Alamo Street, which was built in 1895 by the members of the Beethoven Männerchor. This German men's choir was founded 1847 as the Männergesang-Verein by Johann Nicholaus Simon Menger, the city's most prominent hotelier. The group was renamed in 1867 by by August Thielepape, the mayor of San Antonio at the time. Beethoven Hall burned down in 1913 and was rebuilt the following year, but was sold to the city in 1921. It remains an active performance space, which now houses the Magik Theater, a very popular children's theater directed by Richard Rosen. The Männerchor, by 1921 a German heritage society as well as a choir, purchased a home at 422 Pereida Street that year in what is now the King William (think Kaiser Wilhelm) historical district and turned it into the Beethoven Männerchor Halle und Bier Garten—still a great place to sing, dance, and drink German beer at its century-old bar.

Sicilian boot makers Sam and Joseph Lucchese settled in San Antonio in 1882 and were extremely successful. The Lucchese family founded six different theaters between 1900 and 1950, including Teatro Zaragosa, Teatro Nacional, Teatro Guadalupe, Teatro Progresso, and the Alameda.

Teatro Nacional opened at the corner of Commerce and Santa Rosa streets in 1919 and operated there until 1970. It was a huge theater when it opened, with 1,200 seats. Opera diva María del Carmen Martínez's production of *Malvaloca* was the opening show. Her company stayed on for several months, playing an extensive repertoire of Spanish drama. Another international star to perform early on at Teatro Nacional was Carmen Cassaude de León. In his *A History of Hispanic Theatre in the United States: Origins to 1940* (University of Texas Press, 1990), Nicolás Kanellos writes: "In the middle of her run there [at the Nacional] she was regaled with an original poem in her honor written by Oswaldo Sánchez of San Antonio. The six-stanza poem, published in *La Prensa* on July 18, 1919, not only praised the crystalline voice of the Spanish singer but made her a symbol of solidarity of the Hispanic people." Alas, we know little else about this poet.

The Alameda opened in 1949, billing itself as the "largest Spanish language theater in the United States." It hosted both films and theatrical performances, drawing
some of the greatest talents of Latin America, such as Cantinflas, "La Chata" Noloesca,
and Pedro Gonzalez Gonzalez, as well as Spanish opera, visiting writers, and Cuban
stage bands. Large historical murals, lit with black lights, graced its walls and entrance.

It should be stressed that Mexicans and Mexican Americans of this period expected "good" theater to be a learning experience, reinforcing moral lessons, improving language, and exemplifying the best in artistic and cultural traditions. That this was not
always the case is shown in articles by high-minded critics who occasionally scoffed at
the fare being offered, although such opinions could have been confusing the offerings
of the carpas with those of the more formal teatros.

Large downtown theaters began to appear in the early twentieth century. The
Plaza Theater opened on Alamo Plaza in 1912. It hosted touring plays, operas, and
symphonic performances as well as movies. The theater was razed in 1938 to accommodate an expansion of the Joske's department store. The Aztec Theater was built in
1926 and is one of the only surviving examples of the Mayan Revival style of theater
architecture in the nation. The Majestic Theater opened in 1929 as the second largest
movie theater in the country, with seating for 3,700 patrons. It also hosted major dramatic and musical performances. The interior was a blend of Spanish styles, with towers and balconies, a night-sky ceiling, lobby aquariums, and exotic statuary. It remains
a sight to be seen.

On a smaller scale but with a very rich history was the Westside's Guadalupe Theater,
built in 1942, and the Eastside's Cameo Theater, built in 1940. Louis Armstrong, B. B.
King, and Fats Domino were among the early performers who performed there. The
Cameo was one of the few theaters to actively seek out the work of local playwrights,
including Sterling Houston, whose work is included here. The Guadalupe Theater
closed in 1965, but reopened as the centerpiece of the Guadalupe Cultural Arts Center
in 1983. The Guadalupe, with its own theater company and youth acting group, produced numerous Chicano plays throughout the 1980s and '90s. It also continues to
produce the country's longest-running Latino film festival, CineFestival.

The San Antonio Little Theater was founded in 1912 by Sarah Barton Bindley,
an outlet for her dramatic club, which had been meeting at the St. Anthony Hotel.
Movers and shakers all, they succeeded in getting the city of San Antonio to build

the first city-owned theater in the country, an elegant Greek Revivial building which opened in San Pedro Park in 1929. (In 1939, the city built another theater—the outdoor Arneson River Theater, just across the river from La Villita.) San Antonio Little Theater, now The Playhouse, also supported the work of local playwrights.

In short, there has been plenty of access to theatrical space in San Antonio for a very long time. This has not, however, produced an overwhelming number of native playwrights. Turn-of-the-century Spanish-language playwrights included A. López Manzano and Rafael Téllez Girón (about whom we know almost nothing other than that they received rave reviews in the local press). Josephina Niggli practically grew up in the San Antonio Little Theater, but she wrote almost all of her plays and films while living outside of Texas.

Some contemporary playwrights include Gregg Barrios, Severo Pérez, William Jack Sibley, and others. Barrios, a native of Victoria, Texas, has lived and worked in and around San Antonio off and on since 1969, excepting a decade-long stint as a book critic for the *Los Angeles Times*. He also worked for a time as the books editor for the *San Antonio Express-News*. An Annenberg Getty Fellow and a board member of the National Book Critics Circle, he is primarily a playwright. His first plays—in the style of *teatro campesino*—were written while teaching in Crystal City in the 1970s. Some of his best work includes "Ship of Fools: An Alibiography," about Katherine Anne Porter, and "Rancho Pancho," about Tennessee Williams. Severo Pérez grew up in a working class neighborhood in Westside San Antonio and graduated from the University of Texas, Austin. For over forty years, as an award-winning filmmaker, playwright, and writer, he has produced works for PBS, network and cable television, corporate sponsors, and the educational market. His feature film adaptation of the novel … *And the Earth Did Not Swallow Him* (1994) by Tomás Rivera won eleven international awards, including one for Best Director and five for Best Picture. He cowrote "Soldierboy" with his wife, Judith Schiffer Perez. The play premiered in 1982 and was directed by Luis Valdez, Creative Director of *El Teatro Campesino*. Subsequently, "Soldierboy" has been performed throughout the US. William Jack Sibley is the author of over a dozen plays and screenplays and three novels. His first play, *Governor's Mansion*, won the Southwest Regional Playwright's Competition and was produced at Center Stage in Austin. His play *Mortally Fine* was produced off-Broadway at The Actors Outlet in 1985.

STERLING HOUSTON

Sterling Houston (1945-2006) grew up on the east side of San Antonio and was a life-long student of Black history and culture in San Antonio. He was a performer, a writer, and a prolific and innovative avant-garde playwright. During his lifetime, he wrote thirty plays and three short novels, including *Le Griffon: A True Tale of Supernatural Love* (Pecan Grove Press, 1999). Twenty-four of his plays were first produced by Jump-Start Performance Company in San Antonio, from 1988 to 2006. Venues included the Blue Star Arts Complex (Jump-Start Theater), the Carver Cultural Center, and St. Philip's College in San Antonio. His plays were also produced in other parts of the country, including New York, Cleveland, Chicago, and San Francisco. Houston's plays were published in three collections, *Four Plays by Sterling Houston* (Urban Communication, Inc., 1998), *Myth, Magic, and Farce: Four Multicultural Plays by Sterling Houston* (University of North Texas Press, 2005), and *High Yello Rose and Other Texas Plays*, (Wings Press, 2011), all edited by Dr. Sandra M. Mayo. Houston edited a collection of performance pieces, *Jump-Start Play Works* (Wings Press, 2004).

Houston worked with some of the greatest practitioners of modern American theater from 1964 to 1981, including Charles Ludlum, Sam Shepard, and George C. Wolfe. Houston returned to San Antonio in 1981 and shortly afterward joined the Jump-Start Performance Co. He served as writer-in-residence and artistic director for the company from 1989 until his death in November 2006. Houston's personal papers are archived in the University of Texas at San Antonio's permanent San Antonio Authors Collection.

Houston was known for his biting social commentary, his taste for burlesque humor, and his mastery of multiple genres. His work almost always focused on the intersection of history, myth, and folklore. His was a versatile theatricality that combined domestic drama, farce, docudrama, and musical theatre, and employed a variety of postmodern special effects.

Driving Wheel is mainly set in San Antonio in the mid 1960s. The main character, Joe Jr., has returned home to confront his demons, especially his conflicted relationship with his father, now deceased. Maya Angelou encouraged Houston to write this play after he had discussed his own history. *Driving Wheel* was first produced by the JumpStart Performance Co. in 1992, at the Carver Cultural Center in San Antonio.

Driving Wheel
a memory play

Characters

Clarice Ferguson	A 50-ish widow
Joe Ferguson Jr.	A failed poet, Clarice's son; 30s
Joe Ferguson Sr.	The ghost of a father and husband
Maude Esther	Friend and neighbor; 40-ish
Charles Harold	Maude Esther's brother
Veronica	Maude Esther's 12-year-old daughter

Setting:

San Antonio, Texas. In the side yard and porches of two modest frame houses; mid-1960s.

ACT ONE

Scene 1
(At center in the middle of a side yard between two houses is an old American car with the hood open. Downstage right is MAUDE E.'s back stoop, and upstage left is the side-porch of the FERGUSON house. JOE JR. is bent over the car engine, tinkering with a wrench. VERONICA is jumping rope DS, MAUDE is in her kitchen area dialing wall phone. Music up.)

CLARICE: Hello? Reverend? How do? This is Mrs. Ferguson. Clarice
Ferguson, that's right. I joined your congregation about a year ago, right
after I buried my husband . . . well, Greater Mount Calvary is such a big
church now; it's hard to remember everybody, I would think. Yes that's
right, I work for the Board of Education, same as your wife, I work in the
cafeteria at Douglass, where she's assistant principal. Yes, it sure is a small
world, isn't it . . . *(shouts out door)* Turn it down please, Junior; I'm on the
phone! *(JR. turns down the car radio.)*

VERONICA: *(Rhyme-singing as she jumps rope)*
Oh Mary Mack, Mack, Mack.
All dressed in Black, Black, Black.
With forty-four buttons, buttons, buttons;
all down her back, back, back.

CLARICE: Beg pardon? Well, yes, I imagine you must be very busy and all,
but I was wondering if you had a little time to see me soon, in private. Oh
no; it ain't about me! I'm healthy and in my right mind, for the time being
anyway. It's my son. My boy, Joseph Ferguson, Jr. I'm worried about him.
No, he isn't sick, he's . . . he just doesn't have no get-up-and-go about him.
Not that he's a trifling kind of person, not at all. Keeps his room neat as
a pin, doesn't stay out all night worrying me to death like some boys do.
But ever since my husband passed, Junior's been grieving worse than me,
though he doesn't think I see it . . .

VERONICA: *(Rhyme-singing)* . . .
She jumped so high, high, high;
she touched the sky, sky, sky;
and she didn't come back, back, back;
'til the fourth of July, ly, ly!

CLARICE: How's that Reverend? Oh, indeed? From who did you hear this?
Oh, well, it doesn't really matter about that kind of talk anyway. It doesn't

matter to me who he loves so long as he can love somebody. Crosses were sure enough made to bear, that's right. But that's not why I'm concerned about him, no, you see, he's gone and bought himself this old junk car, and my boy don't know nothing about cars. Nothing. I just can't understand it. It's odd when I think about it; his daddy drove a truck for forty years, but he would never teach that child to drive . . .

VERONICA: *(Rhyme-singing)*
I asked my Mamma; for fifteen cents;
to see the elephant jump the fence;
he jumped so high; he touched the sky;
he didn't come back 'til the Fourth of July . . . !

(She crosses to c. and watches JR.) What you doin'?

JOE JR.: Nothing. What you doin'?

MAUDE: *(Leans out her door)* Veronica! Leave that man alone and come in here and eat, girl!

VERONICA: O.K. Bye Junior. *(She goes into her house. M.E. comes down to JR.)*

MAUDE: You fixin' it all up, huh?

JR.: Trying to.

MAUDE: Guess it's too late to get your money back . . .

JR.: I'm keeping it. I know it can go again. Sure has a good radio.

MAUDE: You know, Joe Jr., you never did strike me as real, what you call, mechanically inclined, more the artistic type. Don't get me wrong now, ain't nothing wrong with that. Where's your mamma?

JR.: She's in the house. On the phone, I think.

MAUDE: *(Calling out)* CLARICE! *(To JR.)* Now my older brother, Charles Harold, he was always real mechanical; could fix damn near anything. *(Calling)* Oh CLARICE! *(To JR.)* He's coming over after while to play bid whist with us.

JR.: Charles Harold?

MAUDE: Unh huh. You want me to ask him to look at it for you?

JR.: O.K., sure.

MAUDE: 'Course, he ain't been inclined to do much of anything since his wife passed.

CLARICE: *(Comes out her door)* Maude Esther; hi girl. I thought that must be you hollering my name out. I was talking on the phone.

MAUDE: What you got smelling so good, chile?

CLARICE: Mustard greens.

MAUDE: Sister, them greens be sho' nuff talking up the neighborhood.

CLARICE: They're about ready. You want some?

MAUDE: No honey, I came to see if I could borrow your card table. You still got that old card table don't you?

CLARICE: Yeah, sure you can. Come on in. *(MAUDE goes past CLARICE into door.)* There it is, right there 'side the Frigidaire. Junior, don't you want some of these good old greens?

JR.: Yeah, sure; thanks Mamma. I just want to try one more thing here.

CLARICE: Do you know what you're doing in there, son?

JR.: No. But I just might get lucky, you know. Can't have bad luck all the time. It's mathematically impossible.

CLARICE: Lord . . . ! I'll bring some on out to you. I know you must be hungry.

MAUDE: *(Enters carrying card table)* Thanks, sugar pie. See you about eight o'clock then.

CLARICE: Oh, I'll be there.

MAUDE: Don't forget what I said, now. Wear something cute. Bye Jr. Don't work too hard.

JR.: Bye Maude Esther. *(MAUDE goes into her house.)* What's she talking about; 'Wear something cute'? *(Scrapes his hand in engine)* Oww! Shit. Maybe I ought to take a little break.

CLARICE: Be right back. I'll bring you some greens and corncakes. *(She goes in.)*

JR.: Sounds delightful. Lunch al fresco! *(He crosses DR to water hose, turns it on and rinses his hands.)*

CAR RADIO: Folks, don't forget next Saturday night the Eastwood Country Club will present the fabulous Little Junior Parker, for two dynamic shows at nine and twelve midnight, and cats and kitties, you might want to get there early, 'cause when Junior Parker's in town the crowds do come 'round. He'll be singing all his hits backed by a twelve piece orchestra turning it every which-a-way but loose. So get on out to Eastwood, this Saturday, people and check out the one and only Little Junior Parker. It'll make you say "Oh, Yeah!" *(Music: "Foxy Devil")*

JR.: *(Shouts.)* Bring me a beer, too, would you please!

CLARICE: *(Brings out a tray with two steaming bowls)* Sometimes food tastes better when you eat it outside. Why is that you think?

JR.: *(Takes food and beer)* I don't know. Probably reminds us of when we lived in the jungle.

CLARICE: I knew you'd have a answer. Is there anything my child don't know?

JR.: Good greens! *(He gulps food and beer.)* Ain't nothing like this in New York.

CLARICE: They got greens in New York; I know better. Drinking beer in the afternoon, is that a New York thing?

JR.: Don't worry about it. I can deal. What did you do woman, stick your big toe in these?

CLARICE: Quit now! You remind me of your daddy when you talk like that. He used to say I put my whole foot in them. Ha!

JR.: You really miss him, huh.

CLARICE: Like an arm yanked out of its socket. Dreamed about him, again last night.

JR.: Did you?

CLARICE: It was a funny dream. He was all dressed up in a sandy colored lawn suit, spectator shoes, diamond tie pin. He always was a natural sport. For the longest time, he just stared at me, his eyes kinda turned down at the sides, like he was about to cry. Then he reached in his pocket, pulled something out and handed it to me in my hand. It was a little white baby shoe, kinda worn, scuffed on the sides. It felt real heavy in my hand, and when I turned it over, emptying it into other hand, out poured a shiny little pile of diamonds. It was the funniest thing. Been dead and gone for more than a year, and the man can't rest right for worrying about me. Poor thing.

JR.: You got me to worry about you now.

CLARICE: I know. That's what worries me. I mean, I'm worried about you.

JR.: Me? Don't worry about me.

CLARICE: But what you gonna do? Don't you want to go back to New York?

JR.: No, Mamma. New York has changed, and I have too, boy have I.

CLARICE: You don't have to tell me if you don't want to. I just wish your daddy had lived to . . . I don't mean to talk about him all the time. I hate it when women talk about their dead husbands like they were the weather, or something everybody cared about.

JR.: I like when you talk about him. Seem like I hardly got to know him.

CLARICE: *(Suddenly angry)* That's because both of you were so damn hard-headed! *(Calm)* You were his heart, you know. His hope. Know what he said when he first laid eyes on you?

JR.: What?

CLARICE: He said 'Oh, here's my little Cadillac driver!' The mid-wife, old Mrs. Flores, had given you a little bath and was holding you up in her arms when he busted into the room, right off the road, truck motor still running he was so excited. Took one look at you and said 'Oh! Oh! Here's my little Cadillac driver! Gonna drive me all the way to California!'

JR.: What did he mean by that? California, huh?

CLARICE: It's the truth from here to heaven.

JR.: Then what happened?

CLARICE: Then you started to laugh. Yes! Laugh out loud. I don't mean no little baby grin, but a pure-dee laugh out loud. Sound like an old man.

JR.: Musta scared ya'll half to death.

CLARICE: Old Miz Flores had been a mid-wife since horse and buggy days, you know, and she swore up and down she'd never heard no new-born baby laugh like that. Cry yes; but LAUGH? Want some more greens? There's plenty. Help yourself. I've got to git, if I'm gonna make it to the beauty shop on time.

JR.: Getting your hair fixed just to play cards with Maude Esther 'nem? What's she cooking up for you tonight, some kind of blind date?

CLARICE: Nothing formal as that, I guarantee you. I'll be back in a little bit. *(She exits. Music up.)*

JR.: *(Returns to open hood, tinkers for a minute, gives up and takes a swig of his beer)* So I'm hardheaded? Was that it, Daddy? What kept you from giving me anything of yourself? You promised so much—then withheld fulfillment. Did you even try to understand? I'm a poet. Images and emotions run in my veins instead of blood. All you saw was softness, weakness. When I went to New York, you put barbed wire on top of the wall that had already grown between us. Maybe I am a fool. But I'm true to my foolishness. I'm sorry you were disappointed in me. But I'm not sorry for myself. Suffering is to the poet like high-octane fuel, allowing him to get to far away places with great speed and efficiency. *(He drains beer can, opens front door of car and lies down. DRIVING WHEEL music up. JR. sleeps as lights change to evening. Light inside car pops on as JOE SR. rises from backseat. He gets out of car and smiles at JR. as lights and music fade to OUT.)*

Scene 2

(Sound of insects and birds singing. Lights up on JR. tinkering with engine as before. JOE SR. stands near him. The light is dreamy and rich with shafts of sun colors.)

JOE SR.: Well, oh well! Went and bought yourself an automobile did you!

JOE JR.: That's right.

JOE SR.: That's good, that's good. A man without an automobile is a piss poor fella, and that's for damn sure. How much she cost you?

JR.: Hundred dollars. As is.

SR.: Hundred dollars cash? Where'd you get that kind of money, son.

JR.: Wasn't that hard really. Cutting grass, throwing the paper . . . whatever. I gave half to Mamma and saved the other half, till I had enough. No big thing.

SR.: Well ain't you something. Yessir, a fella without a car ain't about much of nothing. Couldn't be. It's a matter of time and distance. If you're walking, you see, you spend all your time getting where you going, and once you get there, if it turns out to be someplace you don't really want to be, you got to wait for the bus driver, or some other driver to drive you, before you can get the hell on out.

JR.: I guess you're right.

SR.: And Shoot! In this town, folks waiting at the bus stop can die of frost-bite in the wintertime and sunstroke in the summer. God bless the child that's got his own car! Is it running?

JR.: I drove it over here yesterday, but when I tried to start it up again, nothing happened.

SR.: You mean it wouldn't turn over?

JR.: It wouldn't do nothing, not even click.

SR.: Get in and crank it up.

JR.: *(Gets in car and tries the ignition.)* See? Nothing. And the battery was just recharged. I recharged it myself.

SR.: No, it ain't your battery.

JR.: *(After a pause)* So what do you think it is? The starter?

SR.: *(Slides under car. He gets back up, dusting off his hands.)* What you have here, son, is a solenoid problem.

JR.: A solenoid problem. You mind telling me what the hell a solenoid is?

SR.: A solenoid, you see, is this little whatchamadoo that fits into the starter. If the solenoid goes out, then the starter don't start, and there you sit.

JR.: So here I sit; so what can I do? Can I fix it?

SR.: It can't be fixed; it's got to be replaced. Don't suppose you got a spare one around here.

JR.: Right.

SR.: Got a little screwdriver? A little one?

JR.: Yeah. *(Gets tool from trunk.)* What's up?

SR.: I think I can make you a temporary adjustment. Till you can get it replaced. *(He slides under car.)* You know Junior, ain't nothing to taking care of no car. Just simple easy things'll add five or ten years to the life of any automobile. Even this old tank.

JR.: Simple like what?

SR.: Well the main thing is to always check your fluid levels. 'Specially your oil. Change it more often than you're supposed to. I'm serious. If you pull out that dipstick and the fluid that drips off looks more like black-strap molasses than cane syrup, then it's time for an oil change. *(He gets back up.)* Get in and try it now.

JR.: *(Car cranks without turning over)* Sounds like it wants to start.

SR.: It sure wants to, don't it. Try it again. It wouldn't hurt to have these cables replaced. They split in a few places. Means big trouble down the line. . . . What it really comes down to is: pretty much you take care of it; it'll take care of you, whether it's a horse, an automobile, or a child for that matter.

JR.: What do you mean by that exactly?

SR.: Don't exactly mean anything by it other than just saying it cause it's true.

JR.: Truth has many faces.

SR.: More like different expressions on the same face. Know what I mean?

JR.: It's too late for all that. Why did you come back to haunt me? It's over. I don't need you.

SR.: Yeah. But maybe I need you. You don't seem real surprised to see me.

JR.: The last time you surprised me was when I was fifteen, and one of your friends told you I was 'like that'; and you realized that I was one of them, that I was 'funny' as you called it, not daring to say the word 'gay.' You slapped me across the face with the back of your hand, remember? As though my queerness was somehow an insult to your fatherhood. That you were the injured party, not me.

SR.: I didn't come back to argue all that up again. I can't change who I am anymore than you can. But now that I'm dead, I found my voice at last. Do you hear me? Do you hear what I'm trying to say to you?

JR.: I'm trying to hear. I'm starting to hear.

SR.: Good. Got any gasoline?

JR.: Half a can in the trunk.

SR.: Bring it here and let me show you something. Now, take a little of that gas and drip it right down the middle of that carburetor, there; not too much, now. Yeah. Alright, go on try to start it now.

JR.: *(Cranks engine and car starts. He guns the motor.)* Alright!

SR.: Ha ha! Come on then let's take it for a drive around the block. There's a couple'a'more things I got to tell you.

(They drive off as lights fade to out. Music up.)

Scene 3

(Music up. Lights up on MAUDE, in her window on telephone.)

MAUDE: . . . Yes girl, you know I got to go out to Eastwood and see Little Jr. Parker. Us married women got to take our thrills when we can get 'em. What you mean 'your husband won't let you.' Don't tell him. You gonna be with me, how much trouble can you get into? What? No. I do not think Little Junior Parker is ugly; even if that nose is kinda spread all across his face. Girl, with a voice like that, he can come over here and be ugly on me any time! What you say! Ha! Well, if you can't go, you just CANT, that's that. Maybe I can get my neighbor to go with me. Clarice. You know Clarice. Used to be Clarice Hawkins. Went to Wheatley with us long years ago. That's the one! Married Joe Ferguson, had a son that went off to New York and got into the Life. What you mean 'What life?' The Gay Life, girl. I swear, sometimes you are so country. He's a sweet boy, but he got a hard way to go. His daddy was so hard on him when he was coming up. You know the kind . . .

(Lights crossfade to Ferguson area—flashback to the past)

CLARICE: Don't be so hard on him Joe; he didn't mean nothing! Please!

SR.: Get out of my way! *(JOE SR. pushes JR. and he falls.)*

CLARICE: He's sick. Can't you see he's sick?

SR.: Sick hell! He's drunk! You got the nerve to come in here falling down drunk, as hard as I work to get some respect for this family, and you come disgracing yourself!

JR.: I didn't mean . . . I . . . !

SR.: You had a wreck, didn't you! After I told you not to drive . . . You and that boy Buddy driving around in his Daddy's car like a couple of common hoods. You still not too big for me to take my belt off to your ass!

CLARICE: Joseph don't! You got all the neighbors looking out their windows!

SR.: Let 'em look! You think they didn't see the police car pull up and bring this no account to my front door?

JR.: I don't care let 'em see . . . let 'em see everything . . . !

CLARICE: You only got another month till graduation! You can do what you want! Don't mess it up now, come on in the house and wash your face, son.

JR.: *(After a pause JR. becomes nauseous, holds his mouth and runs inside.)*

CLARICE: JUNIOR! *(She follows him in.)*

SR.: *(Unfastens his belt, pulling it off during following.)* Don't you vomit on that floor! Goddammit, I'm gone make you lick it up! *(He goes in. Lights crossfade to MAUDE.)*

(Return to present)

MAUDE: . . . Yeah, girl; I don't know why people make problems out of little things that just keep life from being boring. Let me get off this phone, I got company coming directly, and haven't started cleaning this place. See you later, alligator.

Scene 4

(Music up as lights crossfade to CLARICE getting her hair done.)

CLARICE: I met Joseph Ferguson when I was twenty years old, and we were married within a year. But Joseph wasn't my first husband, no indeed. When we met, I had been the widow Hawkins for two years, having married old Rev. Hawkins when I wasn't nothing but seventeen. He had a heart attack about a year later, during an exceptionally vigorous usher board meeting. People tried to say I caused his heart attack, you know how people talk, but I wasn't nowhere near him when it happened. Then Joseph Ferguson began to court me, as gently as you please.

   We both sang in the choir, which was one of the only things I liked about Rev. Hawkins's church. Joe took me out on my first date. We went dancing at the Avalon Grill, to a real live band and everything. We got married at the court house, and Junior was born nine months later to the day. Joseph was a good provider. Made a pretty good wage for a colored man back then. Worked for the same people, Larkins Furniture Co, driving a truck for almost thirty years. He was a man who actually liked grocery shopping; knew where all the bargains were. Funny the things you think about. He never cared too much for white folks, his dislike made bitter by fear. 'That's how they are,' he'd say, after reading about some devilishness done to the colored by the white. 'That's just how they are!' Like he could bear their cruelty if it was natural, and not inhuman like it always seems. He wasn't in favor of integration and all that. Him and Junior just argued about it all the time. *(Lights crossfade to DS)*

(Return to past)

SR.: Aw you don't know nothing about white people, nothing! None of you young ones know anything about nothing, but you think you know everything there is to know.

JR.: You all the time worrying about white folks. The hell with them.

SR.: To hell with them? It's fine to talk about to hell with them when hell is where they would like to see us all.

JR.: There's good ones and bad, just like colored.

SR.: But good or bad, he owns the whole pie! How you come talking about getting your piece of the pie, when he owns the whole pie; hell, the whole bakery. White man's only use for the nigger is just that; to use him. Take what you got and give you nothing to show for it. My grandmama was born a slave over in Guadalupe county; it's on the record at the court-house. Not her birth, mind you; but the fact that she was her master's property.

JR.: Slavery was a long time ago, Daddy. We got Mr. Thurgood Marshall now. Brown versus Board of Education.

SR.: You think if he lets you in his schools, he'll let you in his world? All you gonna do is lose your own Negro schools. Colleges. Look at Commerce Street down by the S.R Station. We got blocks of colored business,

251

restaurants, hotels, tailor shops, barbershops, a picture show; it'll all get wiped out; all we worked for, fighting up hill every step, is just gonna get washed away in a wave of "brotherhood"!

JR.: That's why I can't wait to get out of this town! Progress don't mean nothing around here.

SR.: I'll tell you what means something to me. Having you respect what I say to you as much as you do those white teachers at that white school!

(Lights crossfade to CLARICE in the present)

CLARICE: *(She is dressing to go out.)* He had a bad temper. But worse than his fussing was his silence. Days might go by and you wouldn't know what had made him mad; just that his mouth was all stuck out again about something. I learned to deal with it, but Junior would take it personally.

(Crossfade to past)

JR.: What? What did I do? I can't say I'm sorry, if I don't know what I did.

SR.: *(After a pause)* . . . Stay away from that boy Buddy, he's no good and I don't want him coming over here no more. You hear me?

JR.: Why? What did he do to you?

SR.: Don't get smart. You know what you need to know.

JR.: *(Sighs in frustration as SR. exits.) (Lights cross fade to card game area)*

(Return to present)

CLARICE: We lived a pretty good life, the three of us. Always paid the rent, kept food in the house. Then Joe Jr. quit college and ran off to New York to find himself, as he put it. Then Joseph took sick and after a few years, died on me; just like Reverend Hawkins had done so many years before. Except I never loved Reverend Hawkins, and I didn't have to watch him die, day by day. Joe was eaten alive by cancer and regret, until the pain of both combined can't even be killed by dope. Then death comes like a mercy. But death isn't really the end of anything; is it? Not the end of anything at all.

MAUDE: *(After a pause)* Come on, Clarice! It's your play, girl.

CLARICE: Oh, excuse me; I kinda drifted off didn't I. *(She plays a card.)*

MAUDE: No, sugar; clubs is trumps. Ain't you got no hearts?

CLARICE: I'm sorry. You'd think I never played cards before.

CHARLES HAROLD: That's alright partner; we can still whup 'em.

VERONICA: How come I have to play cards? *(No reply)* How come Mama?

MAUDE: Because your daddy ticked me off royally, so I had to tell him about himself. He left out of here bookin' knowing that I had invited company to play cards, and went off somewhere in the streets to suck his thumb, I expect.

VERONICA: I still don't see why I have to.

MAUDE: Because I said so. Now be still and play girl. I don't want to have to wear you out in front of company. *(To CLARICE)* Just getting to be so FAST. You lucky you never had no little girl.

VERONICA: I got to be fast to keep up with my 1965 CLASS!

MAUDE: Girl, I'm going to knock the naps out of your big head, if you don't quit.

CHARLES: Maybe we shouldn't play cards right now, Maude Esther . . .

MAUDE: No indeed! I invited Clarice over here to play cards, and we are going to play!

CLARICE: It's O.K. by me, whatever we do. It's nice to get out of my house, even if it is just next door.

MAUDE: Next Saturday night is Little Junior Parker at Eastwood. Come on go with us, Clarice. All you do is work and go to church. Don't you think that'd be what's happening? You come too, brother-mine . . .

CHARLES: Yeah, if Clarice would be kind enough . . .

CLARICE: Why not? I haven't been out to Eastwood since Junior was little.

VERONICA: Junior is a punk.

MAUDE: Girl, I'm gonna have to kill you. *(Raises her hand as if to strike; VERONICA gets up to dodge her.)*

VERONICA: Junior is a sissy punk! Junior is a sissy punk! *(VERONICA runs off as MAUDE rises.)*

MAUDE: Veronica! Lord, I swear, I don't know where she gets it. Veronica! Girl, you better answer me when I call you. Ya'll excuse me, please. *(Exits)*

CLARICE: *(After a pause)* You have any children, Charles Harold?

CHARLES: Me? Oh yes. Four girls. All married and moved. I've got nine grandbabies. Believe that? A young fella like me?

CLARICE: That's nice.

CHARLES: And you?

CLARICE: What? Oh; just the one. Son. Still not married. He's home with me.

CHARLES. Well, shoot! I got enough grand kids to spare you a couple, till he comes through.

CLARICE: That's mighty nice of you. You seem such a kind person.

CHARLES: Kind enough, when folks let me. But I'm going to have to fuss at my sister, for keeping you a secret for so long . . .

CLARICE: You wouldn't be trying to flirt with me now, would you sir?

CHARLES: I'm surprised I still remember how. It doesn't offend you does it? I know how it is with that grief situation. My wife passed two years ago this April. Sugar diabetes. Suffered with it a long time, you know how it is.

CLARICE: I'm sorry to say I do.

CHARLES: But that grief situation, that mourning thing, it's on-going, everyday. Some days it'll hit you hard, but most times it's like a low humming noise in the background. It doesn't ever really go away.

CLARICE: I like the way you put that. You have a nice way with words. My son is a poet. Had his poems printed in a book when he was up in New York. I'll show it to you sometime.

CHARLES: I'd like that. We have some mighty great Negro poets in this country, you know. Countee Cullen, Langston Hughes . . . Do you like poetry?

CLARICE: I don't know much about it. But I like Junior's. Even if I don't always understand it. When he was in high school, he would stay in his room for hours writing and reading. Come home, eat, and then I might not see him till the next morning. You know, when a child is gifted he's often misunderstood. He'd always be getting his feelings hurt, by some teacher or some jealous classmate. And him and his daddy didn't get along. So he just felt safer in that room with the door closed, playing the radio and writing his poems, long after his daddy and I had gone to bed.

(Crossfade to JR. in the past sitting at desk. Music up. JR. is typing the last section of a poem into a portable typewriter. A cigarette curls up from the ash-tray. He pulls paper from typewriter, and begins to read.)

Searching for Bethlehem in the stormy desert
I stumbled upon Mecca in the form of a smooth black tower.
It vibrates at my touch
Reproducing the deep brown cello music
Of my mother's voice.
I bless myself for being blessed in the twisted metal face
Of hope shattered like headlights in head-on crashes.
I declare myself to be a thing as complete as an idea in the mind
Of some unique and cunning ancient god,
Containing all things essential for a journey in this world
Of multiple realities
Of sacred laughter and
Profane tears.

(Return to present. Lights crossfade to card game area. VERONICA and MAUDE enter.)

MAUDE: Veronica has something to tell ya'll. Go on, now.

VERONICA: I apologize for being so rude and sassy . . .

MAUDE: And what else . . . I

VERONICA: . . . And I promise not to do it no more.

MAUDE: ANY more.

VERONICA: Anymore.

MAUDE: That's fine. Now you may be excused to do your homework, young lady. *(VERONICA exits.)* Lord, I don't know what I'm going to do with that girl.

CLARICE: I know she doesn't mean any harm. She's just a child.

MAUDE: I am so sorry this evening turned out this way. I wanted everything to be so nice . . .

CHARLES: Plans can be like that sister; don't be worrying about it too much. I got to meet this nice lady, didn't I? And we going to Eastwood Saturday night ain't we?

CLARICE: Sure, we going; a real date, that's right.

CHARLES: Say! How 'bout if I drive us all up to the Dairy Queen for a malted milk! Huh? What do you say?

VERONICA: *(Shouts from off-stage.)* Bring me a chocolate!

MAUDE: You better get that lesson. Don't make me come back in there.

CHARLES: How about it, Clarice? Wouldn't a nice malted milk hit the spot?

CLARICE: That would cool me down a bit. So warm this evening.

MAUDE: But we don't want you to cool off too much, do we Brother?

CHARLES: Well no; I reckon we don't.

Scene 5

(Current time—mid-1960s. Music Up. Lights up as car comes to center. JR. and SR. are driving through the neighborhood.)

SR.: Look out! Did you see that Jackass! *(Shaking his fist.)* Asshole! Ya see, that's one of many benefits of driving around in traffic; you get to chastise transgressors on the spot.

JR.: I don't think they heard you. I hope not.

SR.: That light's getting ready to change. Get ready to stop now . . .

JR.: Wow, Dad, are you psychic too? Is that one of the side-effects of being dead?

SR.: Shoot! That's nothing, minor stuff. I could fly if I took the notion to do so. Take off and fly right through the air. But I wouldn't want to scare you. You might lose control.

JR.: Thanks. And try not to burst into flames, if you can help it.

SR.: Son, it just wouldn't be right if I didn't tell you something else, something that's not easy for me to say . . .

JR.: Uh oh. Maybe I should pull over.

SR.: There's a price. A price you pay for driving. And the price is always going up. Not down.

JR.: I guess that's fair. Balance in all things, they say.

SR.: For some, having a car is nothing short of a continuous heartache. Just keeping it running right is a constant challenge. No sooner you get your brakes done, buy a new set of tires, then the water pump goes out and the transmission ain't acting right.

JR.: I suppose any old car would be . . .

SR.: That's just it! Not just old ones; the new ones too. And all of them burn gas and eat up insurance money. It's the price you pay, you understand; the PRICE!

JR.: Yeah, I hear what you're saying. A car is like a family: great to have around when you need 'em, but always needing something you don't want to give.

SR.: Let me tell you something; there's worse things than being needed. Even by a machine. Look out! Don't you see that stop sign? Don't trust the other driver to see you.

JR.: I see the stop sign. It's a four-way stop sign.

SR.: See, *(Looking out window)* that's just what I'm talking about. That was a white lady driving, and white ladies don't necessarily believe that stop signs apply to them.

JR.: So, how you handling the white folks on the other side? Don't tell me you got integrated at last!

SR.: It ain't nothing like that. Ain't no white folks over there.

JR.: What?

SR.: No black folks either; not exactly, you see . . . it's kinda hard to explain. Plus, I ain't exactly been over to the other side, not all the way over. Not yet.

JR.: Wow, I hope I remember this when I wake up.

SR.: Turn right here, and we'll be right back home.

JR.: This IS my dream, isn't it? Not yours?

SR.: All of it's a dream, Joseph, yours, mine, and all the rest of it. That's what makes it so funny. *(Starts to laugh)* So damn funny.

JR.: What's funny?

SR.: All of it! People crying at funerals! Ha! HA! Saying, 'I'll love you forever!' HA! HA! HA! Talking about 'Peace On Earth!!' Peace in the valley! *(calming down)* Peace in the valley, some day. *(Lights crossfade)* Home, home again. That's enough driving for me for a while. Enough sightseeing, too . . . Things change so fast. Too fast.

JR.: Has it really changed that much?

SR.: I almost didn't recognize it. Commerce Street used to be so alive! I guess I was too, long years ago.

JR.: How did I do? Driving pretty good huh?

SR.: You did alright, for a beginner.

JR.: It's hard for you to give me a compliment, isn't it? Why you always have to be the hard one?

SR.: Ha! You think I'm hard? Now, my papa, Old man Wilson, he was a sonofabitch. Always angry about something; with his mouth all stuck out. Couldn't please him if you saved his life. But I forgave him his licks and hurtful words. Even the way he talked to my mamma; I forgave him.

JR.: You want me to say I forgive you?

SR.: Listen, son. The most important thing about driving a car, the one thing above all else, you must always do. Look out for the other fella.

JR.: Look both ways at a stop sign?

SR.: Promise me you will. Every time.

JR.: O.K. I promise.

SR.: 'Cause sure as you're born, no matter how fine your driving is, how razor sharp your responses are, here comes some sucker late for work, or drunk, runs a stop sign and hits you broadside. Next thing you know, you waiting for the bus again.

JR.: Why are you telling me all this now? For ten years you hardly had anything to say to me.

SR.: I wanted to. I wanted to talk. Told myself I'd wait till I saw you again. Wait till you came home. But when I finally did see you again, I couldn't concentrate on anything but my pain. There you were. My fine boy. Standing by my hospital bed. If I could have made a sound I wouldn't have known what to say. And when I looked in your eyes, all I could see looking back at me was my own sick pain, magnified by yours. Cancer had been feasting on my insides for months, like every day was Thanksgiving. But it wasn't till I saw you again that I knew I was really going to die.

JR.: I never hated you.

SR.: You didn't even come to my funeral.

JR.: I couldn't bring myself to go. I heard the undertaker stuffed cotton in your cheeks to make you look more natural. I couldn't bear to see it.

SR.: Old Franklin Brothers did a hell of a nice job. Very artistic! You should'a seen it.

JR.: Maybe I should have.

SR.: *(Rooster crows)* Look, I can't be hanging around here much longer. It's good you stayed around here to help your mamma some; but you got to start thinking about yourself. I know you want to be moving on someday soon.

JR.: I did go to the graveyard though, and I watched them lower you into the ground. Watched the yellow chrysanthemum petals fall onto your coffin lid. Ashes and dust. I wanted to scream. Scream in frustration and rage.

But mamma saw it building up in my throat. She grabbed me by the arm, saying: 'No, not here. Don't embarrass us. Be strong. Scream later.' But later never came, and neither have the tears.

SR.: *(Pulls stickpin from his tie.)* Here. I want you to have this old horseshoe pin. Ain't but one of the diamonds real. I forget which one. You take it now. It was pretty lucky for me, when all's said and done. Go on, take it. Luck to me now is like water to a drowning man.

JR.: I can't take that. It's part of you. Besides, you already gave me something of yourself. *(He pats car.)*

SR.: I'm glad about that, son; and you've given me a way to get on over *(SR. vanishes as dogs bark. Lights out.)*

Scene 6

(Current time, present, mid-1960s.) (Lights up. JR. is sleeping inside car with his feet out the open car door. It is late evening. Crickets and distant music. VERONICA comes out carrying garbage.)

VERONICA: Here Kitty-Kitty-Kitty. *(She notices JR's feet out car window and goes to investigate. She touches his foot. He wakes.)* Mamma! Miss Clarice! Junior done passed out drunk!

(CLARICE comes out followed by MAUDE and CHARLES)

CLARICE: Junior?! What in the world? You'll catch your death of cold out here in this night air.

JR.: What . . . ? I'm not cold.

MAUDE: *(Picks up beer can)* Man, you got your head that bad on one can of beer? Well, you know your daddy couldn't hold his liquor neither.

CLARICE: Maude Esther! Don't speak ill of the dead.

JR.: I don't remember falling asleep.

VERONICA: Take me for a ride when you get sober; if this old thing can run.

CHARLES: Is this the old car you wanted me to look at?

MAUDE: Yes! Junior, this is my brother Charles Harold. You believe he paid a hundred dollars for this pile of junk.

CHARLES: How you doin'? *(Looks under car hood)* Let me take a look. It don't look that bad to me. Give it a crank. *(Car engine starts; motor guns.)* Ain't nothing wrong with that motor.

CLARICE: You fixed it!

JR.: Yeah, how 'bout that? *(Gets out of car.)*

VERONICA: Take us for a ride right now, Junior! *(VERONICA gets in car and bounces on front seat.)* Ouch! Something bit me! Oh look! it's an old pin. Finders keepers, losers weepers! *(She gets out of car and runs around.)*

CLARICE: Let me see that! *(VERONICA gives pin to her.)* That's what I thought; a diamond horseshoe!

CHARLES: Must have been left by a previous driver.

CLARICE: It belongs to Junior now. Doesn't it belong to you now, Junior?

JR.: By rights, I guess it does. *(Lights dim to out)*

Scene 7

Epilogue

(A few weeks later. JR. is polishing car. MAUDE attends grill, as VERONICA sets paper plates.)

VERONICA: When we gonna eat, Mamma? I'm hungry.

MAUDE: Soon as Charles Harold and Clarice get here. Go get yourself some potato salad out of the ice box if you're hungry. *(VERONICA goes in.)* I wonder what's keeping those two?

JR.: It's good to see them getting along so well; Mamma needs to get out more.

MAUDE: YOU the one needs to get out. How come you didn't go to Eastwood with us? It was fun.

JR.: Mamma said she had a good time.

MAUDE: Honey, yes! Got right into the swing. You know that Little Junior Parker really puts on a show. Had sweat soaking clean through his silver shark-skin suit! Ha! All the women just hollering, and Clarice was right there hollering with 'em!

JR.: Alright!

MAUDE: Hey! I heard you got accepted at college! University of California hey, hey! I hear they a pretty fast bunch out there.

JR.: I can deal with it. I got to.

MAUDE: They really gave you a scholarship for making up poems?

JR.: Somebody must think they're pretty good.

MAUDE: I know Clarice is proud. She's sure gonna be lonesome with you gone.

(CLARICE and CHARLES enter)

CHARLES: Hope ya'll saved us some barbecue.

MAUDE: Hey! We been waiting for you.

CLARICE: We lost track of the time walking around downtown.

MAUDE: Veronica, bring out the potato salad and Kool Aid.

JR.: What's happening downtown?

CLARICE: We just window shopped. I like looking in Joske's windows at all those nice clothes I can't afford. *(VERONICA comes out with salad, etc.)*

CHARLES: But that's just a temporary situation. Junior's going off to be a famous writer, get rich, and bring it all back home to you. Ain't that right?

JR.: I don't know. Not many poets get rich, Charles.

VERONICA: You gonna drive that old car all the way to California?

JR.: Uh huh. New tires, tuned-up and ready to hit the road . . .

MAUDE: That car ain't no older than you, miss smartness; both of ya'll got a few good years left.

CLARICE: Junior, you won't try to drive all night, will you? Pull over side the road and sleep when you get tired. Promise me.

JR.: Oh yeah; I intend to take my time.

CLARICE: Your Daddy would be so proud of you; going off on your own. He knew you were born to drive yourself to whatever life holds for you. I knew too; ever since you were little, that day at Playland Park . . .

JR.: I almost forgot about that. Fourth of July, wasn't it?

CLARICE: That's right! Junior wasn't nothing but five or six. Well, bless his heart, he heard this announcement on the radio, where the radio man had said they here having this big old celebration over at Playland Park for the Fourth of July, which it was that day, with fireworks and the army band and all, and everybody was welcome. He stressed that word: EVERYBODY. Now, who was I to tell this child he wasn't somebody? He was bound and determined to go to Playland Park to watch the fireworks along with everybody else who was welcomed that day. Now, remember this was in the late forties. Folks around here still lived pretty much the way they had since emancipation. Still had 'Colored only' or 'Whites only' signs on everything from restaurants to toilets. Yeah, toilets! Like their shit was too good to go down with ours. Yes Lord, Jim Crow was in full flight, and not too many of us were acting up about it in those days—lynching was not unheard of. So for us to go to Playland Park on a day we were not welcome was more than a notion. But there was no denying that boy. So sure of himself; nothing would do him but to go. So I took a deep breath, talked to God a minute, and we went on over there. It was about a half an hour away on the bus-line. He just couldn't stop talking all the way over; he was so excited, and me trying to think who I'd call if we got arrested. We got to the entrance, and I paid the admission. The girl took my money and didn't say anything. We went through the turnstile, and I started to think; maybe Junior was right. Fourth of July. Everybody welcome. Well that boy took off running right over to this merry-go-round of little cars and plopped himself down in the red one. He started jerking the little steering wheel back and forth and smiled up at me. 'Look Mamma, I'm drivin'!' But he never got to go 'round. I looked and saw some other little children pulling to get into the kiddie-cars, but their parents, seeing the dark child in the red car, held them back. Then I heard someone shout at me. 'Hey you!' I turned and saw this white fella grinning at me. 'What's the matter with you, gal?' he said; This ain't no Juneteenth!' He gave me my money back. Take that kid and go, before you run off all my business.' Junior sat very still in that little car watching us. I went over and pulled him out of the car; he said 'We not gonna ride today, Mamma?' 'No, baby,' I said, 'not today. We'll come back another time.'

We sat at that bus stop for what seemed like years, watching the little white children come and go with their folks, laughing and carrying balloons and cotton-candy like they didn't have a care in the world. The bus finally got there just as the fireworks began to light up the sky. He looked out the bus window at them till we turned the corner and we couldn't see them anymore. Junior looked at me, real serious like and said, 'Don't cry Mamma'; do you remember? 'Don't cry. We gonna drive one day. One day we gonna drive, for real.'

(JR. and CLARICE embrace, as lights go to OUT.)

THE END ★

PART FIVE

FICTION

A. T. Myrthe
(Fr. Anthony Ganilh)

A. T. Myrthe was a pseudonym for, we believe, a French Catholic missionary priest, Father Anthony Ganilh. Born in France, Fr. Ganilh was ordained in Kentucky in 1817. He is known to have been the parish priest in Mobile, Alabama, in 1826, and to have visited New Orleans on several occasions. It is presumed that he came to Texas in 1828 and stayed for a decade, reappearing at St. Joseph's College in Kentucky in 1838. He is the author of the (so he claimed) first novel to be written in Texas. The author's knowledge of South Texas shows that he must have spent a good deal of time observing both the culture and physical environs about which he writes. We cannot say for certain, but it seems very likely that a portion of his novel was written in San Antonio.

Not surprisingly, given the anti-Catholic tone of his novel, Ganilh left the priesthood in 1841. *Mexico versus Texas, a Descriptive Novel, most of the Characters of which consist of Living Persons,* was published anonymously (by "a Texian") in Philadelphia in 1838. The novel must have been at least moderately successful, as it was republished in 1841, this time in New York, under the title *Ambrosia de Letinez, or The First Texian Novel, embracing A Description of the Countries Bordering on the Rio Bravo, with Incidents of the War of Independence.*

The novel begins with the birth of "our hero," Ambrosio de Letinez, in Durango, Mexico. His Spanish-Mexican mother, who dies in childbirth, makes her American protestant husband promise to raise Ambrosio as a Catholic. The father leaves Ambrosio to be raised by priests, then decamps back to the United States. By the age of eighteen, Ambrosio is a cavalry commander under General Urrea, fighting in the Texas revolution. The novel carries on a religious debate throughout, while the young Ambrosio, handsome to a fault, is captured after the Battle of San Jacinto, escapes, rescues a young American girl (who turns out to be a cousin, "impossible to behold without admiration") from a shipwreck—of course, they fall in love—and escapes again. Several somewhat picaresque adventures follow, including this brief midnight visit to San Pedro Springs and an encounter with a band of unusually friendly Comanches. Captain Ambrosio de Letinez and his guide, a freed "quarteroon" slave named Flambeau, are seeking to escape Texas and reach the safety of Mexico.

---

from *Ambrosio de Letinez, or, The First Texian Novel*

THE COUNTRY ABOUT THE GUADALUPE RIVER is the most fertile it is possible to imagine; but being somewhat swampy, it is inferior in point of salubrity, to the district of Bexar, and the river San Anton, which may be considered as destined to become the paradise of North America. To the most salubrious climate, it unites the most enchanting scenery, consisting of an elegant mixture of hill and dale, watered by large springs, which furnish abundant supplies for irrigation. The temperature is such, that winters are hardly felt, and two yearly crops of Indian corn are the regular tribute of husbandry. . . . To all these advantages, is to be added the facility of raising cattle, the wild grass being so excellent and abundant that they multiply without any care on the part of the owner. And then the fruits! From the orange and cherimoya, of southern climes, to the apple and pear of northern regions; the immense variety of Pomona's gifts embellishes this land, and enriches the husbandman. The most delightful districts of the south of France, with all the wealth and refinement which ages of civilization have accumulated, do not deserve to be compared with this blessed spot. . . .

At last, the time appointed for the continuation of their journey arrived, but, before leaving their encampment, they held a consultation about the route which it was most prudent to pursue. Should they incline too much to the south, they were in danger of meeting with parties of Texians, either of those that had accompanied Filisola's army in their retreat, or others, who might be prowling about the country in the direction of Bexar. Should they incline too much to the north, they might fall into the hands of straggling parties of Comanches, or other Indians scarcely less formidable than the Texians. Their perplexity was great, but, after long debates, they thought that steering a middle way would be most prudent. In consequence, they took a northwest course towards the Rio Bravo—calculating upon leaving San Antonio somewhat on their left. The Captain had heard so much about the large mountain springs, which form the river San Anton, that he would be no means pass by without seeing them, and Flambeau was obliged to indulge him with the sight, but he conducted him to the spot during the night, in order to incur less danger of exposure. There, a vast body of water gushes out of four large pools, of unfathomable depth, and as clear as crystal, giving rise to a stream that would be navigable, were it not for the rapidity of its course. As our hero was lost in amaze, at the beauty of the scene, the quarteroon exclaimed, "Here is a place marked out by nature for one of the great cities of the globe. Water power enough to work as much machinery as Manchester boasts, a level road, from hence to the sea, the most fertile land, for hundreds of miles around, the most healthy and pleasant climate in North America, and the neighborhood of some rich mines of silver, all contributes to render this locality of paramount importance."

After satisfying their curiosity, they resumed their journey and soon crossed the river Medina. Having, now as they supposed, passed the most exposed places, they bent their course toward the south, intending to strike the Rio Bravo, between Presidio del Rio Grande and Laredo. But notwithstanding the prudence with which they shaped their route, they had the misfortune of encountering a party of Comanches, whom they especially dreaded. They were just emerging from a thick *nopalera*, when they descried two Indians, on horseback, coming towards them. It appeared that the latter had no design upon our travellers, for, as soon as they perceived them, they gave a loud whoop, in sign of surprise, and disappeared from the back of the animals on which they were mounted. The horses fled, retaking the way by which they had come, whilst there remained no vestige of the riders—nor could the poor quarteroon imagine by what legerdemain they had vanished. From the first moment he descried them, he had incessantly kept his eyes on them and he was sure they could not have alighted and fled, on foot, without being perceived, yet it seemed their horses were, now, running off without their riders.

The captain diverted himself, for a while, in seeing him so much puzzled, but, at last, explained to him that the Comanches are the best riders of any people, ancient or modern, that it is a very ordinary thing with them, in a flight, to lie in a horizontal position, on the side of their horse less exposed to the arrows of the enemy, and that they are enabled to continue a considerable time, in such a difficult posture, by putting one leg through a loop, depending from the saddle-bow, and provided for the purpose; while they hold, by the horse's mane, with *one hand*, and find means to manage their shield, with the other.

"I have no doubt," continued he, "it is precisely the way in which these fellows are now effecting their retreat; but I am afraid they are not the only ones of their nation in this vicinity, and I wish we may not fall into the hand of some larger party. This neighborhood is one of their haunts, and the two who have just fled from us with so much precipitation are, probably, spies, sent about to make discoveries."

"And what if we should encounter them?" said Flambeau.

"It is not a thing to be trifled with," replied the Mexican. "They are irreconcilable enemies to my countrymen. But I have the facility of passing myself for an American. Should we encounter them, beware making any resistance, and let me manage everything by myself. I have heard a great deal about their ways and customs, and am more likely to succeed than you in soothing them, or winning their favor."

The captain's forebodings proved but too true. They had hardly proceeded a league, when they saw themselves invested by a large party, consisting, at least, of two hundred men on horseback, many of whom were armed with lances, some with rifles, but none of whom was without a bow and arrows. Instead of manifesting any fear, Señor de Lentinez, on the contrary, drew toward the nearest group, with an air of confidence, bearing a buffalo robe, spread on high, which, according to the notions of those tribes, answers the purposes of a flag of truce; and the Indians manifested their respect for this sign of peace, by stopping short. The captain was no sooner within speaking distance, than he began to harangue the Comanches, in English, for he supposed that, in so large a number, there would be some one acquainted with the language of the Americans, and able to translate the substance of his address, for the information of the others. He told them that he and his companion were Texians, sent as spies toward the Rio Grande, and that a considerable army of their country-men was on its way, to lay waste all the towns on the banks of that river, after which the country would be abandoned to the Indians, its ancient and lawful possessors. He added that he was commissioned to propose an alliance between his people and the Comanches, in order to direct their simultaneous efforts against the Mexicans.

His expectations proved true. Several Indians understood English suffi-ciently well to seize the meaning of his address, the various items of which were translated by them and commented upon, for the information of their fellow citizens or, rather companions in arms, whilst our hero waved his buffalo robe to and fro, with a gentle motion, and indicated by many accompanying gestures that he was a messenger of peace. ★

O. HENRY

O. Henry (William Sydney Porter) arrived in Texas from North Carolina in 1882. He was twenty years old. He worked on a ranch for a couple of years before taking a job in Austin at the Texas Land Office. In 1887, he sold his first story to a magazine, and in 1894, he bought a weekly newspaper and renamed it the *Rolling Stone*. Soon circulation expanded to include San Antonio, and O. Henry met Henry Ryder-Taylor, a former editor at the *San Antonio Daily News* and city editor of the *San Antonio Daily Light*. The friends set up an office in a two-room house at 903 S. Presa Street (now a parking lot).

The O. Henry house, as it is now known, was moved in 1968 to the grounds of the old Lone Star Brewery as part of several renewal projects associated with HemisFair. Thirty years later it was relocated to the corner of Laredo and Dolorosa, adjacent to the site of the old Bella Union Theater. (This is supposedly one of the "theaters" mentioned in his story "A Fog in Santone.") O. Henry was known to frequent the theaters and saloons of the area termed "Little Mexico." The *Rolling Stone* was a vehicle both for O. Henry's wit and his political views. In 1895 the *Rolling Stone* printed a broadside lampooning then-mayor Bryan Callaghan. Callaghan won his election and turned his ire on the paper. Up in Austin, the *Rolling Stone* was being boycotted by Texas Germans, who also had been insulted by the paper. Within months the paper folded and O. Henry headed to Houston.

It should be noted that *all* of O. Henry's stories partake generously of the racist stereotypes rampant in his day. Many contemporary editors would be tempted to omit such stories, but they were beloved for generations, and until the dawn of the 1960s, they painted San Antonio's cultural milieu in not only an acceptable light, but in one considered charming by many Americans. Since no one in this Tricentennial year of our city would claim that we have completely overcome this flaw, it is of considerable educational value to examine it with an unflinching eye. All that being said, O. Henry's "The Enchanted Kiss" is likely the funniest story ever set in the city, full of ironic asides, non sequitur responses, Spanish malapropisms, and outrageously outlandish situations.

San Antonio provided O. Henry with a great deal of grist for his creative mill. The city is the setting for a half dozen short stories, and is mentioned in others (twenty-four are set in Texas). One enjoyable aspect of his San Antonio stories is that the contemporary reader can often still follow O. Henry's characters through the streets, visiting many of the same locations.

In "The Enchanted Kiss," for example, the young overly romantic protagonist, Samuel Tansey, finds himself enveloped in an absinthe fog (ah, that "green-eyed fairy"!), coming to rest on the steps of the "convent of Santa Mercedes," which is clearly recognizable as the old Ursuline Convent (later Ursuline Academy), now the Southwest School of Art. Poor Tansey. For the rest of the story, although he never physically leaves the steps, he hallucinates himself wandering a very strange landscape—perhaps even time-traveling "on some new plane of understanding." Eventually he finds himself as the Quixote-like savior of his beloved Miss Peek—who is about to be sold by her father to be consumed by a 403-year-old cannibal masquerading as a Spanish grandee masquerading as an Alamo Plaza chili merchant. Nothing written under the influence of LSD has anything on O. Henry's description of this absinthe evening!

The Enchanted Kiss

But a clerk in the Cut-rate Drug Store was Samuel Tansey, yet his slender frame was a pad that enfolded the passion of Romeo, the gloom of Laura, the romance of D'Artagnan, and the desperate inspiration of Melnotte. Pity, then, that he had been denied expression, that he was doomed to the burden of utter timidity and diffidence, that Fate had set him tongue-tied and scarlet before the muslin-clad angels whom he adored and vainly longed to rescue, clasp, comfort, and subdue.

The clock's hands were pointing close upon the hour of ten while Tansey was playing billiards with a number of his friends. On alternate evenings he was released from duty at the store after seven o'clock. Even among his fellow men, Tansey was timorous and constrained. In his imagination he had done valiant deeds and performed acts of distinguished gallantry; but in fact he was a sallow youth of twenty-three, with an over-modest demeanor and scant vocabulary.

When the clock struck ten, Tansey hastily laid down his cue and struck sharply upon the show-case with a coin for the attendant to come and receive the pay for his score.

"What's your hurry, Tansey?" called one. "Got another engagement?"

"Tansey got an engagement!" echoed another. "Not on your life. Tansey's got to get home at Motten by her Peek's orders."

"It's no such thing," chimed in a pale youth, taking a large cigar from his mouth; "Tansey's afraid to be late because Miss Katie might come down stairs to unlock the door, and kiss him in the hall."

This last delicate piece of raillery sent a fiery tingle into Tansey's blood, for the indictment was true—barring the kiss. That was a thing to dream of; to wildly hope for; but too remote and sacred a thing to think of lightly.

Casting a cold and contemptuous look at the speaker—a punishment commensurate with his own diffident spirit—Tansey left the room, descending the stairs into the street.

For two years he had silently adored Miss Peek, worshipping her from a spiritual distance through which her attractions took on stellar brightness and mystery. Mrs. Peek kept a few choice boarders, among whom was Tansey. The other young men romped with Katie, chased her with crickets in their fingers, and "jollied" her with an irreverent freedom that turned Tansey's heart into cold lead in his bosom. The signs of his adoration were few—a tremulous "Good morning," stealthy glances at her during meals, and occasionally (Oh, rapture!) a blushing, delirious game of cribbage with her in the parlour on some rare evening when a miraculous lack of engagement kept her at home. Kiss him in the hall! Aye, he feared it, but it was an ecstatic fear such as Elijah must have felt when the chariot lifted him into the unknown.

But to-night the gibes of his associates had stung him to a feeling of forward, lawless mutiny; a defiant, challenging, atavistic recklessness. Spirit of corsair, adventurer, lover, poet, bohemian, possessed him. The stars he saw above him seemed no more unattainable, no less high, than the favor of Miss Peek or the fearsome sweetness of her delectable lips. His fate seemed to him strangely dramatic and pathetic, and to call for a solace consonant with its extremity. A saloon was near by, and to this he flitted, calling for absinthe—beyond doubt the drink most adequate to his mood—the tipple of the roue, the abandoned, the vainly sighing lover.

Once he drank of it, and again, and then again until he felt a strange, exalted sense of non-participation in worldly affairs pervade him. Tansey was no drinker; his consumption of three absinthe anisettes within almost as few minutes proclaimed his unproficiency in the art; Tansey was merely flooding with unproven liquor his sorrows; which record and tradition alleged to be drownable.

Coming out upon the sidewalk, he snapped his fingers defiantly in the direction of the Peek homestead, turned the other way, and voyaged, Columbus-like into the wilds of an enchanted street. Nor is the figure exorbitant, for, beyond his store the foot of Tansey had scarcely been set for years—store and boarding-house; between these ports he was charted to run, and contrary currents had rarely deflected his prow.

Tansey aimlessly protracted his walk, and, whether it was his unfamiliarity with the district, his recent accession of audacious errantry, or the sophistical whisper of a certain green-eyed fairy, he came at last to tread a shuttered, blank, and echoing thoroughfare, dark and unpeopled. And, suddenly, this way came to an end (as many streets do in the Spanish-built, archaic town of San Antone), butting its head against an imminent, high, brick wall. No—the street still lived! To the right and to the left it breathed through slender tubes of exit—narrow, somnolent ravines, cobble paved and unlighted. Accommodating a rise in the street to the right was reared a phantom flight of five luminous steps of limestone, flanked by a wall of the same height and of the same material.

Upon one of these steps Tansey seated himself and bethought him of his love, and how she might never know she was his love. And of Mother Peek, fat, vigilant and kind; not unpleased, Tansey thought, that he and Katie should play cribbage in the parlor together. For the Cut-rate had not cut his salary, which, sordidly speaking, ranked him star boarder at the Peek's. And he thought of Captain Peek, Katie's father, a man he dreaded and abhorred; a genteel loafer and spendthrift, battening upon the labor of his women-folk; a very queer fish, and, according to repute, not of the freshest.

The night had turned chill and foggy. The heart of the town, with its noises, was left behind. Reflected from the high vapors, its distant lights were manifest in quivering, cone-shaped streamers, in questionable blushes of unnamed colors, in unstable, ghostly waves of far, electric flashes. Now that the darkness was become more friendly, the wall against which the street splintered developed a stone coping topped with an armature of spikes. Beyond it loomed what appeared to be the acute angles of mountain peaks, pierced here and there by little lambent parallelograms. Considering this vista, Tansey at length persuaded himself that the seeming mountains were, in fact, the convent of Santa Mercedes, with which ancient and bulky pile he was better familiar from different coins of view. A pleasant note of singing in his ears reinforced his opinion. High, sweet, holy caroling, far and harmonious and uprising, as of sanctified nuns at their responses. At what hour did the Sisters sing? He tried to think—was it six, eight, twelve? Tansey leaned his back against the limestone wall and wondered. Strange things followed. The air was full of white, fluttering pigeons that circled about, and settled upon the convent wall. The wall blossomed with a quantity of shining green eyes that blinked and peered at him from the solid masonry. A pink, classic nymph came from an excavation in the cavernous road and danced, barefoot and airy, upon the ragged flints. The sky was traversed by a company of beribboned cats, marching in stupendous, aerial procession. The noise of singing grew louder; an illumination of unseasonable fireflies danced past, and strange whispers came out of the dark without meaning or excuse.

Without amazement Tansey took note of these phenomena. He was on some new plane of understanding, though his mind seemed to him clear and, indeed, happily tranquil.

A desire for movement and exploration seized him: he rose and turned into the black gash of street to his right. For a time the high wall formed one of its boundaries; but further on, two rows of black-windowed houses closed it in.

Here was the city's quarter once given over to the Spaniard. Here were still his forbidding abodes of concrete and adobe, standing cold and indomitable against the century. From the murky fissure, the eye saw, flung against the sky, the tangled filigree of his Moorish balconies. Through stone archways breaths of dead, vault-chilled air coughed upon him; his feet struck jingling iron rings in staples stone-buried for half a cycle. Along these paltry avenues had swaggered the arrogant Don, had caracoled and serenaded and blustered while the tomahawk and the pioneer's rifle were already uplifted to expel him from a continent. And Tansey, stumbling through this old-world dust, looked up, dark as it was, and saw Andalusian beauties glimmering on the balconies. Some of them were laughing and listening to the goblin music that still followed; others harked fearfully through the night, trying to catch the hoof beats of caballeros whose last echoes from those stones had died away a century ago. Those women were silent, but Tansey heard the jangle of horseless bridle-bits, the whirr of riderless rowels, and, now and then, a muttered malediction in a foreign tongue. But he was not frightened. Shadows, nor shadows of sounds could not daunt him. Afraid? No. Afraid of Mother Peek? Afraid to face the girl of his heart? Afraid of tipsy Captain Peek? Nay! nor of these apparitions, nor of that spectral singing that always pursued him. Singing! He would show them! He lifted up a strong and untuneful voice: "When you hear them bells go tingalingling," serving notice upon those mysterious agencies that if it should come to a face-to-face encounter:

"There'll be a hot time
In the old town
To-night!"

How long Tansey consumed in treading this haunted byway was not clear to him, but in time he emerged into a more commodious avenue. When within a few yards of the corner he perceived, through a window, that a small confectionary of mean appearance was set in the angle. His same glance that estimated its meager equipment, its cheap soda-water fountain and stock of tobacco and sweets, took cognizance of Captain Peek within lighting a cigar at a swinging gaslight.

As Tansey rounded the corner Captain Peek came out, and they met vis-a-vis. An exultant joy filled Tansey when he found himself sustaining the encounter with implicit courage. Peek, indeed! He raised his hand, and snapped his fingers loudly.

It was Peek himself who quailed guiltily before the valiant mien of the drug clerk. Sharp surprise and a palpable fear bourgeoned upon the Captain's face. And, verily, that face was one to rather call up such expressions on the faces of others. The face of a libidinous heathen idol, small eyed, with carven folds in the heavy jowls, and a consuming, pagan license in its expression. In the gutter just beyond the store Tansey saw a closed carriage standing with its back toward him and a motionless driver perched in his place.

"Why, it's Tansey!" exclaimed Captain Peek. "How are you, Tansey? H-have a cigar, Tansey?"

"Why, it's Peek!" cried Tansey, jubilant at his own temerity. "What deviltry are you up to now, Peek? Back streets and a closed carriage! Fie! Peek!"

"There's no one in the carriage," said the Captain, smoothly.

"Everybody out of it is in luck," continued Tansey, aggressively. "I'd love for you to know, Peek, that I'm not stuck on you. You're a bottle-nosed scoundrel."

"Why, the little rat's drunk!" cried the Captain, joyfully; "only drunk, and I thought he was on! Go home, Tansey, and quit bothering grown persons on the street."

But just then a white-clad figure sprang out of the carriage, and a shrill voice—Katie's voice—sliced the air: "Sam! Sam!—help me, Sam!"

Tansey sprung toward her, but Captain Peek interposed his bulky form. Wonder of wonders! the whilom spiritless youth struck out with his right, and the hulking Captain went over in a swearing heap. Tansey flew to Katie, and took her in his arms like a conquering knight. She raised her face, and he kissed her—violets! electricity! caramels! champagne! Here was the attainment of a dream that brought no disenchantment.

"Oh, Sam," cried Katie, when she could, "I knew you would come to rescue me. What do you suppose the mean things they were going to do with me?"

"Have your picture taken," said Tansey, wondering at the foolishness of his remark.

"No, they were going to eat me. I heard them talking about it."

"Eat you!" said Tansey, after pondering a moment. "That can't be; there's no plates."

But a sudden noise warned him to turn. Down upon him were bearing the Captain and a monstrous long-bearded dwarf in a spangled cloak and red trunk-hose. The dwarf leaped twenty feet and clutched them. The Captain seized Katie and hurled her, shrieking, back into the carriage, himself followed, and the vehicle dashed away. The dwarf lifted Tansey high above his head and ran with him into the store. Holding him with one hand, he raised the lid of an enormous chest half filled with cakes of ice, flung Tansey inside, and closed down the cover.

The force of the fall must have been great, for Tansey lost consciousness. When his faculties revived his first sensation was one of severe cold along his back and limbs. Opening his eyes, he found himself to be seated upon the limestone steps still facing the wall and convent of Santa Mercedes. His first thought was of the ecstatic kiss from Katie. The outrageous villainy of Captain Peek, the unnatural mystery of the situation, his preposterous conflict with the improbable dwarf—these things roused and angered him, but left no impression of the unreal.

"I'll go back there to-morrow," he grumbled aloud, "and knock the head off that comic-opera squab. Running out and picking up perfect strangers, and shoving them into cold storage!"

But the kiss remained uppermost in his mind. "I might have done that long ago," he mused. "She liked it, too. She called me 'Sam' four times. I'll not go up that street again. Too much scrapping. Guess I'll move down the other way. Wonder what she meant by saying they were going to eat her!"

Tansey began to feel sleepy, but after a while he decided to move along again. This time he ventured into the street to his left. It ran level for a distance, and then dipped gently downward, opening into a vast, dim, barren space—the old Military Plaza. To his left, some hundred yards distant, he saw a cluster of flickering lights along the Plaza's border. He knew the locality at once.

Huddled within narrow confines were the remnants of the once-famous purveyors of the celebrated Mexican national cookery. A few years before, their nightly encampments upon the historic Alamo Plaza, in the heart of the city, had been a carnival, a saturnalia that was renowned throughout the land. Then the caterers numbered hundreds; the patrons thousands. Drawn by the coquettish *señoritas*, the music of the weird Spanish minstrels, and the strange piquant Mexican dishes served at a hundred competing tables, crowds thronged the Alamo Plaza all night. Travellers, rancheros, family parties, gay gasconading rounders, sightseers and prowlers of polyglot, owlish San Antone mingled there at the centre of the city's fun and frolic. The popping of corks, pistols, and questions; the glitter of eyes, jewels and daggers; the ring of laughter and coin—these were the order of the night.

But now no longer. To some half-dozen tents, fires, and tables had dwindled the picturesque festival, and these had been relegated to an ancient disused plaza.

Often had Tansey strolled down to these stands at night to partake of the delectable *chili-con-carne*, a dish evolved by the genius of Mexico, composed of delicate meats minced with aromatic herbs and the poignant *chili Colorado*—a compound full of singular flavor and a fiery zest delightful to the Southron's palate.

The titillating odour of this concoction came now, on the breeze, to the nostrils of Tansey, awakening in him hunger for it. As he turned in that direction he saw a carriage dash up to the Mexicans' tents out of the gloom of the Plaza. Some figures moved back and forward in the uncertain light of the lanterns, and then the carriage was driven swiftly away.

Tansey approached, and sat at one of the tables covered with gaudy oilcloth. Traffic was dull at the moment. A few half-grown boys noisily fared at another table; the Mexicans hung listless and phlegmatic about their wares. And it was still. The night hum of the city crowded to the wall of dark buildings surrounding the Plaza, and subsided to an indefinite buzz through which sharply perforated the crackle of the languid fires and the rattle of fork and spoon. A sedative wind blew from the southeast. The starless firmament pressed down upon the earth like a leaden cover.

In all that quiet Tansey turned his head suddenly, and saw, without disquietude, a troop of spectral horsemen deploy into the Plaza and charge a luminous line of infantry that advanced to sustain the shock. He saw the fierce flame of cannon and small arms, but heard no sound. The careless victualers lounged vacantly, not deigning to view the conflict. Tansey mildly wondered to what nations these mute combatants might belong; turned his back to them and ordered his chili and coffee from the Mexican woman who advanced to serve him. This woman was old and careworn; her face was lined like the rind of a cantaloupe. She fetched the viands from a vessel set by the smoldering fire, and then retired to a tent, dark within, that stood near by.

Presently Tansey heard a turmoil in the tent; a wailing, broken-hearted pleading in the harmonious Spanish tongue, and then two figures tumbled out into the light of the lanterns. One was the old woman; the other was a man clothed with a sumptuous and flashing splendor. The woman seemed to clutch and beseech from him something against his will. The man broke from her and struck her brutally back into the tent, where she lay, whimpering and invisible. Observing Tansey, he walked rapidly to the table where he sat. Tansey recognized him to be Ramon Torres, a Mexican, the proprietor of the stand he was patronizing.

Torres was a handsome, nearly full-blooded descendant of the Spanish, seemingly about thirty years of age, and of a haughty, but extremely courteous demeanor. To-night he was dressed with signal magnificence. His costume was that of a triumphant *matador*, made of purple velvet almost hidden by jeweled embroidery. Diamonds of enormous size flashed upon his garb and his hands. He reached for a chair, and, seating himself at the opposite side of the table, began to roll a finical cigarette.

"Ah, Meester Tansee," he said, with a sultry fire in his silky, black eyes, "I give myself pleasure to see you this evening. Meester Tansee, you have many times come to eat at my table. I theenk you a safe man—a verree good friend. How much would it please you to leeve forever?"

"Not come back any more?" inquired Tansey.

"No; not leave—*leeve*; the not-to-die."

"I would call that," said Tansey, "a snap."

Torres leaned his elbows upon the table, swallowed a mouthful of smoke, and spake—each word being projected in a little puff of gray.

"How old do you theenk I am, Meester Tansee?"

"Oh, twenty-eight or thirty."

"Thees day," said the Mexican, "ees my birthday. I am four hundred and three years of old to-day."

"Another proof," said Tansey, airily, "of the healthfulness of our climate."

"Eet is not the air. I am to relate to you a secret of verree fine value. Listen me, Meester Tansee. At the age of twenty-three I arrive in Mexico from Spain. When? In the year fifteen hundred nineteen, with the *soldados* of Hernando Cortez. I come to thees country seventeen fifteen. I saw your Alamo reduced. It was like yesterday to me. Three hundred ninety-six year ago I learn the secret always to leeve. Look at these clothes I war—at these *diamantes*. Do you theenk I buy them with the money I make with selling the *chili-con-carne*, Meester Tansee?"

"I should think not," said Tansey, promptly. Torres laughed loudly.

"*Valgame Dios!* but I do. But it not the kind you eating now. I make a deef-erent kind, the eating of which makes men to always leeve. What do you think! One thousand people I supply—*diez pesos* each one pays me the month. You see! ten thousand *pesos* everee month! *Que diable!* how not I wear the fine *ropa!* You see that old woman try to hold me back a little while ago? That ees my wife. When I marry her she is young—seventeen year—*bonita*. Like the rest she ees become old and—what you say!—tough? I am the same—young all the time. To-night I resolve to dress myself and find another wife befitting my age. This old woman try to scr-r-ratch my face. Ha! ha! Meester Tansee—same way they do *entre los Americanos*."

"And this health-food you spoke of?" said Tansey.

"Hear me," said Torres, leaning over the table until he lay flat upon it; "eet is the *chili-con-carne* made not from the beef or the chicken, but from the flesh of the *señorita*—young and tender. That ees the secret. Everee month you must eat of it, having care to do so before the moon is full, and you will not die any times. See how I trust you, friend Tansee! To-night I have bought one young lade—verree pretty—so *fina, gorda, blandita!* To-morrow the *chili* will be ready. *Ahora si!* One thousand dollars I pay for thees young ladee. From an *Americano* I have bought—a verree tip-top man—*el Capitan Peek—que es, Señor?*"

For Tansey had sprung to his feet, upsetting the chair. The words of Katie reverberated in his ears: "They're going to eat me, Sam." This, then, was the monstrous fate to which she had been delivered by her unnatural parent. The carriage he had seen drive up from the Plaza was Captain Peek's. Where was Katie? Perhaps already—

Before he could decide what to do a loud scream came from the tent. The old Mexican woman ran out, a flashing knife in her hand. "I have released her," she cried. "You shall kill no more. They will hang you—*ingrato—encatador!*"

Torres, with a hissing exclamation, sprang at her.

"Ramoncito!" she shrieked; "once you loved me."

The Mexican's arm raised and descended. "You are old," he cried; and she fell and lay motionless.

Another scream; the flaps of the tent were flung aside, and there stood Katie, white with fear, her wrists still bound with a cruel cord.

"Sam!" she cried, "save me again!"

Tansey rounded the table, and flung himself, with superb nerve, upon the Mexican. Just then a clangour began; the clocks of the city were tolling the midnight hour. Tansey clutched at Torres, and, for a moment, felt in his grasp the crunch of velvet and the cold facets of the glittering gems. The next instant, the bedecked caballero turned in his hands to a shrunken, leather-visaged, white-bearded, old, old, screaming mummy, sandaled, ragged, and four hundred and three. The Mexican woman was crawling to her feet, and laughing. She shook her brown hand in the face of the whining *viejo*.

"Go, now," she cried, "and seek your *señorita*. It was I, Ramoncito, who brought you to this. Within each moon you eat of the life-giving *chili*. It was I that kept the wrong time for you. You should have eaten *yesterday* instead of *to-morrow*. It is too late. Off with you, *hombre!* You are too old for me!"

"This," decided Tansey, releasing his hold of the gray-beard, "is a private family matter concerning age, and no business of mine."

With one of the table knives he hastened to saw asunder the fetters of the fair captive; and then, for the second time that night he kissed Katie Peek—tasted again the sweetness, the wonder, the thrill of it, attained once more the maximum of his incessant dreams.

The next instant an icy blade was driven deep between his shoulders; he felt his blood slowly congeal; heard the senile cackle of the perennial Spaniard; saw the Plaza rise and reel till the zenith crashed into the horizon—and knew no more.

When Tansey opened his eyes again he was sitting upon those self-same steps gazing upon the dark bulk of the sleeping convent. In the middle of his back was still the acute, chilling pain. How had he been conveyed back there again? He got stiffly to his feet and stretched his cramped limbs. Supporting himself against the stonework he revolved in his mind the extravagant adventures that had befallen him each time he had strayed from the steps that night. In reviewing them certain features strained his credulity. Had he really met Captain Peek or Katie or the unparalleled Mexican in his wanders—had he really encountered them under commonplace conditions and his over-stimulated brain had supplied the incongruities? However that might be, a sudden, elating thought caused him an intense joy. Nearly all of us have, at some point in our lives—either to excuse our own stupidity or to placate our consciences—promulgated some theory of fatalism. We have set up an intelligent Fate that works by codes and signals. Tansey had done likewise; and now he read, through the night's incidents, the finger-prints of destiny. Each excursion that he had made had led to the one paramount finale—to Katie and that kiss, which survived and grew strong and intoxicating in his memory. Clearly, Fate was holding up to him the mirror that night, calling him to observe what awaited him at the end of whichever road he might take. He immediately turned, and hurried homeward.

Clothed in an elaborate, pale blue wrapper, cut to fit, Miss Katie Peek reclined in an armchair before a waning fire in her room. Her little, bare feet were thrust into house-shoes rimmed with swan's down. By the light of a small lamp she was attacking the society news of the latest Sunday paper. Some happy substance, seemingly indestructible, was being rhythmically crushed between her small white teeth. Miss Katie read of functions and furbelows, but she kept a vigilant ear for outside sounds and a frequent eye upon the clock over the mantel. At every footstep upon the asphalt sidewalk her smooth, round chin would cease for a moment its regular rise and fall, and a frown of listening would pucker her pretty brows.

At last she heard the latch of the iron gate click. She sprang up, tripped softly to the mirror, where she made a few of those feminine, flickering passes at her front hair and throat which are warranted to hypnotize the approaching guest.

The door-bell rang. Miss Katie, in her haste, turned the blaze of the lamp lower instead of higher, and hastened noiselessly down stairs into the hall. She turned the key, the door opened, and Mr. Tansey side-stepped in.

"Why, the i-de-a!" exclaimed Miss Katie, "is this you, Mr. Tansey? It's after midnight. Aren't you ashamed to wake me up at such an hour to let you in? You're just *awful*!"

"I was late," said Tansey, brilliantly.

"I should think you were! Ma was awfully worried about you. When you weren't in by ten, that hateful Tom McGill said you were out calling on another—said you were out calling on some young lady. I just despise Mr. McGill. Well, I'm not going to scold you any more, Mr. Tansey, if it *is* a little late—Oh! I turned it the wrong way!"

Miss Katie gave a little scream. Absent-mindedly she had turned the blaze of the lamp entirely out instead of higher. It was very dark.

Tansey heard a musical, soft giggle, and breathed an entrancing odor of heliotrope. A groping light hand touched his arm."

"How awkward I was! Can you find your way—Sam?"

"I—I think I have a match, Miss K-Katie."

A scratching sound; a flame; a glow of light held at arm's length by the recreant follower of Destiny illuminating a tableau which shall end the ignominious chronicle—a maid with unkissed, curling, contemptuous lips slowly lifting the lamp chimney and allowing the wick to ignite; then waving a scornful and abjuring hand toward the staircase—the unhappy Tansey, erstwhile champion in the prophetic lists of fortune, ingloriously ascending to his just and certain doom, while (let us imagine) half within the wings stands the imminent figure of Fate jerking wildly at the wrong strings, and mixing things up in her usual able manner.

O. HENRY AND THE BRIDGE AT THE HEART OF THE CITY

Bridges are curiously important for literary visitors to San Antonio, whether iron or wood or concrete, and have figured prominently in both nonfiction and fiction since the founding of the city. Understandably, much has been written about the great bridges of the world, so why the Commerce Street bridge in San Antonio has been so fascinating to writers for so long is something of a mystery. It is, after all, a small bridge over a small river. Nevertheless, the charm of this bridge at the heart of the city has proven to be exceedingly enduring.

The first time a bridge is mentioned in the literature of San Antonio was in a report of an incident in 1736. A Franciscan padre tried to close the one bridge across the river to protest the demands of the new governor. The governor threatened to tie the priest to a mule and send him back to Mexico City. That bridge was where Commerce Street now crosses the San Antonio River, and it is mentioned in several documents throughout the eighteenth century. Of course, the bridge was important in both the 1835 siege of Bexar and the 1836 battle at the Alamo, and figures in every novel written about those events.

In 1852, Frederick Law Olmsted, the famous landscape architect who would later design Central Park in New York, described the Commerce Street bridge as a place where one might "lean for hours over the bridge rail" watching the river, "rich blue and pure as crystal, flowing rapidly but noiselessly over pebbles and between reedy banks." Two decades later, in 1873, Sidney Lanier wrote that "any stranger may be safely defied to cross this bridge without becoming meditative." In March 1895, Stephen Crane reportedly leapt from the Commerce Street bridge to save a young woman from drowning. Apparently, she was merely washing clothes and Crane's reward for his bravery consisted solely of a sprained ankle.

The 1890s saw a flurry of bridge building in San Antonio as eight new iron bridges were laid. Ornate, brightly painted, with metal lattice pedestrian walkways and decorative spires, each was a work of art. (Today, the bridge that most resembles its original appearance is the Augusta Street Bridge, near the

Southwest School of Art. It was constructed in Connecticut and laid in 1890.) These were the bridges that so fascinated O. Henry that he mentioned them in five of the six stories he set in San Antonio.

In "The Higher Abdication," O. Henry's character Curly "stood a few moments in the narrow, mesquite-paved street. The winding, doubling streets, leading nowhere, bewildered him. And then there was a little river, crooked as a pothook, that crawled through the middle of town, crossed by a hundred bridges so nearly alike that they got on Curly's nerves." The number of bridges is more accurate in "A Fog in Santone," where the tubercular hero finds himself on "a little iron bridge, one of the score or more in the heart of the city, under which the small tortuous river flows."

O. Henry was closely associated with the most famous bridge in the city, the Commerce Street bridge, a one-of-a-kind creation that featured four lighted twelve-foot-tall "church steeples" along with Indian-head drinking fountains. The Commerce Street bridge was renamed in honor of O. Henry by the city fathers (and so labeled with a brass plaque) after the writer became famous, but before his death on June 5, 1910, in New York. We have no indication of what he thought of the honor.

By 1914, Commerce Street had a new bridge—the present one. The old iron span was moved downstream to Johnson Street in the King William neighborhood, where it would remain—minus its Indian-head drinking fountains and one of its corner spires, eventually even losing the plaque bearing O. Henry's name—until 1967. That year, the San Antonio River Authority decided to widen the river in preparation for HemisFair, which would open the following year. The O. Henry / Johnson Street Bridge and the bridge at Guenther Street (one block over) were both dismantled and laid in piles beside the river. The Conservation Society had obtained a written promise from the River Authority that the bridge would be restored to its former glory, but, alas, 90 percent of it was melted down for scrap before the error was noticed. Only a few parts from two of the original corner spires and some of the brass handrails remained.

The Conservation Society was adamant that the bridge be rebuilt, so bids were taken. All were rejected as too high. After a decade or so, the parties agreed to build a replica, incorporating what was left of the original. On July 7, 1983, a "little iron bridge," painted red and green with brass trim, was lowered into place at the Johnson Street site. This pedestrian bridge is longer than the original, but neither so wide nor so tall as the original. One spire was created from the left-over iron parts of the original, and three more spires were cast in aluminum.

No historical designation exists at the site. One small additional problem for die-hard O. Henry fans is that no one marked which of the spires is the original before they were painted. If one wishes to lean upon the original spire, perhaps in the manner of a man who died with nine empty whiskey bottles under his bed, one must tap on all four and listen for the difference between aluminum and iron. ★

Josephina Niggli

Josephina (aka Josefina) María Niggli (1910-1983) was an author, playwright, actor, teacher, and photographer. Born in Monterrey, she came to San Antonio during the Mexican Revolution and became a part of the city's lively arts scene during the Depression. She began her writing career when her father financed the printing of her first book, a collection of poems, *Mexican Silhouettes* (Monterrey, Mexico, 1928).

Niggli went on to become a popular playwright and novelist. She began publishing poems and short stories in magazines such as *Mexican Life* and *Ladies Home Journal*. She relates that one of the nuns at Incarnate Word College, Sister Mary Clement, locked her in a room and would not let her come out until she had finished a short story for the *Ladies Home Journal* annual contest, for which she won second prize. Niggli was an early San Antonio radio personality, writing and producing for KTSA Radio. She began to experiment with drama at the San Antonio Little Theatre and, in 1935, joined the Carolina Playmakers at the University of North Carolina at Chapel Hill. She completed her MA degree with *Singing Valley*, produced by the Carolina Playmakers in 1938.

Niggli was particularly adept at writing plays about Mexico: *The Fair God*, *The Cry of Dolores*, *Azteca*, and her powerful feminist play about the women of the Revolution, *Soldadera*. Just prior to the outbreak of World War II, she worked at the Universidad Autónoma de Mexico with theater director Rodolfo Usigli, who had written a preface to Niggli's *Mexican Folk Plays* (University of North Carolina Press, 1938). She spent the last two years of the war in San Antonio, writing and occasionally working at Rosengren's Books. Niggli's first novel of interconnected stories, *Mexican Village* (University of North Carolina Press, 1945), was followed closely by *Step Down Elder Brother* (Rinehart, 1947). *Mexican Village* was made into a movie, *Sombrero*, a musical (of all things) starring Ricardo Montalban and Pier Angeli. Niggli worked briefly in Hollywood for 20th Century Fox. In 1950 she was awarded a fellowship to work in the Abbey Theatre in Dublin. In 1956 she was hired to teach English and drama at Western Carolina University, where she remained until her retirement in 1975, and where a theater is named in her honor. Her third and final novel was *A Miracle for Mexico* (New York Graphic Society, 1964). San Antonio was always "home," and Mexico was always her inspiration, but according to scholar and collector Bill Fisher, Niggli was somewhat miffed at being so stereotyped. The story included here is evidence of her efforts to expand her horizons. Her own family's history extended to pre-Civil War years, when her (paternal) Castroville ancestors "decamped to Eagle Pass," near the location of this story.

Although not a Latina by blood, she was adopted by the Chicana literary community after critic Gloria Anzaldúa praised her as a cultural interpreter in Anzaldúa's seminal 1987 work, *Borderlands/La Frontera*.

Saint's Day

Captain Avila ran his hand over his bearded cheek and looked at the tower beam from which dangled the bells. He could read the three names carved inside each rim: Santa Cecilia, Santa María, Santo Tomás. In the peaceful days before these terrible months in 1863, every sunrise and sunset the little bell on the left would sing, sweet and high, "San-ta Ce-cee-li-a."

He smiled and thought of his girl Cecilia, far to the southeast in Laredo. Her body swayed from side to side when she walked—as swayed the bell rope. His hand stretched toward the rope.

"Leave it alone," said Major Williams, emerging from the stair hole.

"Only a little tinkle. Who could hear it?"

Williams shook his head. He was a lean, big-nosed man, ten years older than young Avila. "Everything is too damned quiet."

He wondered if Williams was remembering how quiet it had been just before the Yanks swarmed into Yellow River and took the town. But that was three months ago, and this was June. He said lightly, "Today is my girl's saint's day."

Williams grinned at him. "Hell, I'm Protestant. I don't know the saints."

Tom Avila twisted the bell-rope around his hand. "Cecilia, the same as the little bell's. Surely a bell should ring on its own saint's day."

Williams moved over to the low wall that enclosed the tower and gazed across the meadows to the grove of live oak trees. "Orders are to hold this tower 'without unnecessary display of strength.'" His deep voice held a note of puzzlement as he propped his arms on the wall and rested his weight on them.

"Now we're stuck here," Avila said mournfully, "in this church on this deserted ranch. I want to go where the fighting is. . . ."

"Where the medals are," Williams said dryly.

Avila blazed with anger, then laughed ruefully. "I've got a girl in Laredo. She likes medals . . . and brave men."

Williams' eyes were somber. "Poor little hero." And then, sharply, "What's that kid doing?" He leaned far out over the parapet, turning his face upwards. "Hey, bub, what you doing?"

Avila leaned out also. A small Mexican boy, his chin still smooth, was perched on one of the tower's outer spires. He smiled impishly down at them, said in Spanish, "I've just relieved the tower sentry, my major."

Williams, who had grown up on border speech, snapped, "Get back to your post, Cleto."

The boy's face worked in puzzlement. "The sergeant said the top of the tower, my major."

Williams' voice gentled. "The sergeant meant the flat platform above the bells, not the spire. Can you climb back? No! Don't move. I'll have a soldier throw a rope to you." He clattered down the stairs.

Avila, still bending across the parapet, could see fear come into the boy. "The major will bring you to safety, Cletito."

The boy's stomach contracted, and he pushed his backbone closer against the spire. "It's the first time I've relieved the sentry." He looked at Avila with liquid black eyes, solemnly admiring him for being grown and a captain. "I thought I was doing right."

Far below, Avila could hear men running about, barking orders. To keep the boy from height-fear, he asked, "Do you see anything?"

Cleto had a baby's round face. "There are the ranch houses, the roofs tumbled in. Has there been a great battle here, my captain?"

"A long time ago," said Avila, "when Texas was still a part of Mexico, Indians came and destroyed the ranch, killed all the people who did not escape to the fort. The ones who lived came back and restored the church with wood." He was talking rapidly to keep the boy's mind occupied. This is the worst of war, he thought. Children turn into men before they are children.

"Why did the Indians leave this tower, my captain?"

Men were scrambling up the outer ladder. Only a few minutes more. He thought quickly, invented, "Why, they were afraid to disturb the bells. The bells are very powerful."

"Yes," said Cleto, "The Devil is afraid of the bells. He cannot steal the souls of good Christians when he hears the bells."

Avila was relieved to see a rope swirl out and catch on the spire. A hoarse voice shouted for the boy to slip his foot in the noose. The twilight glow etched the boy's body as he swung to safety.

In a moment Williams slid over the parapet, then stood silently watching the rescue squad descend to the ground. When he lit a cigarette, his hands trembled. "I gave the sergeant hell, but he said it was the young'un's turn, and I reckon he was right. Once you accept them as soldiers, you can't treat them like babies." He added with a little snort, "He's thirteen."

"I was thirteen," Avila said seriously, "when I first entered the Military College in Mexico City."

"That was a hell of a lot different."

Avila knew it was different. Son of a retired Mexican general, he had been reared in the military tradition, and did not walk into the College with a captured gun and proof of having killed five Comanches.

He repressed a slight shudder and sat down on the cold stone floor. "Cecilia thinks I go to battle every morning at ten. She thinks I keep office hours in battle."

Williams said nothing. He puffed at a cigarette, his face blank. Avila thought, he is counting the men. But no matter how often he counts, we are only twenty. One major, one captain, one sergeant, two corporals, and fifteen soldiers.

He thought of the original company that had started from Laredo. There had been fifty, including four lieutenants, all of them, except Major Williams, Tex-Mex, proud of Texas and their Confederate grays. But they had been ambushed by Comanches, and now there were twenty, and no lieutenants.

He looked down at his own dirty uniform and grinned. It had lost its elegance and was just a modest covering for a tired, unwashed body.

"I had a letter from my cousin Jim," Williams said. "He's with the Fourth Texas near Richmond."

Avila sighed enviously, "It must be very fine, with all the balls and the pretty girls. I was in Richmond once. They've got awfully pretty girls."

Williams suddenly laughed much too loud, caught the laughter and deepened it to a chuckle. "My cousin Jim says he feels sorry for us, swinging in our hammocks and drinking out of clean glasses. He don't know how we're standing the hardships of war."

"Drinking," sighed Avila. "Cognac is a good drink."

Williams wrinkled his big nose. "Who has brandy in this forsaken hole?"

"My orderly says the sergeant knows where one of the corporals has a bottle hidden. He got it from a dead lieutenant after the Indian attack."

The major pulled his hand across his mouth. "Goodbye, brandy."

Avila rolled over on one elbow. "As long as the *mescal* holds out, the men wouldn't touch the cognac. They like liquor that tears out the throat."

The dusk was deepening, but it was still light enough for them to see each other's faces. Williams winked, Avila nodded, went to the stair-hole and kneeling, called his orderly. When the man thrust his body through the hole, he held the cognac in one hand. "After so much excitement, my captain."

Avila clutched the bottle and grinned. "Remind me to recommend you for a sergeant."

The man's laughter thrust two deep dimples into his brown cheeks. "As you say, my captain." He laughed again and went down the steps. Avila rubbed his hands over the bottle in awe.

"French. It must have belonged to Valdés. The other three wouldn't have had sense enough ..."

Williams said heavily, "Stop talking and pass the bottle."

Avila found his knife and began prying out the cork. "This is a Saint Cecilia miracle. She loves my girl, and my girl loves me. Sweet Cecilia could do nothing less than send me a bottle of French brandy. Drink some miracle, you Protestant."

The liquor gurgled pleasantly down Williams' throat. The captain snatched at the bottle and tilted in his turn. They were on rigidly rationed food, and the warmth felt good in their stomachs. The darkness was cozy now.

Williams said, "If we draped a blanket around a lamp we could play two-handed stud . . ."

His voice was chopped off by the zing of a bullet. From above came the terrified screech of the boy. "Yankees! In the tree grove. Yankees!"

There came the sound of sliding. They saw the boy's body falling past their level. It turned like a leaf before it struck the ground.

Avila started toward the parapet, but a barked order sent him pounding down the stairs after Williams. The men were running to their positions, crouching with rifles behind a lately built breastwork. As Avila examined the few boxes of ammunition, he knew that the danger was from superior Federal equipment and the possibility of a Union-Texan in command. "Saint Cecilia," he prayed silently, "make that Yankee commander a Massachusetts boy."

The moon was rising behind the line of trees, its silver spraying over the meadow's lush grass. They could see the Federals spread in a thin, straight line, "Battle formation," Avila muttered.

The sergeant said jeeringly, "Obviously a very northern general."

One of the soldiers, who had been fond of little Cleto, stood up and shouted defiance. The answering bullet took him in the throat. The other men were well protected behind the breastwork. Avila stayed with the ammunition, but Williams—knowing his child-like Mexicans—ran up and down behind the men, patting them on the shoulder, murmuring encouragingly to them. He had grabbed up a rifle, and now and then he took a shot at the oncoming Federals. Above the powder fumes rose the sharp smell of sweat. Moonlight made sighting difficult, and still the Federals advanced. Williams shouted, "Into the church!"

They swung the huge doors shut. The men, twenty no longer but eighteen, crouched at previously plotted positions. There was a dull plunk against one plank wall, and then a crackle as the dry timber caught fire. There were other plunks, and now the whole wall was aflame. The sergeant shouted, "A Texan with brains."

Williams muttered through set lips, "Fire arrows—a damned Comanche trick." But he had prepared for this, too, when he first saw the wooden church hooked to the stone tower. Buckets of water were in their proper places. The two officers sluiced the thatched roof that was now beginning to smoulder. Not enough. Smoke thickened the air. A corporal gurgled, "They don't know you made us break an opening through to the tower, my major."

"Saint Cecilia," Avila prayed, "you worked the miracle of the cognac. Work a bigger one now. If you love my girl, sweet saint, remember that my girl loves me."

Then he was too busy dashing water on flames to pray any more. An enemy bullet found his orderly. Twenty, he thought, nineteen, seventeen. We retrogress.

The red glow turned the smoke to orange. He could feel it curling through his nostrils and mouth, choking his lungs. He was coughing so violently, Williams' order to retreat up the winding stairs, slippery with age, slid into his mind without sound. In the stone tower, heat from the flaming church seared his tortured chest.

Williams stared down at the fanned out Federals. "They probably think they've got a hundred of us trapped here."

Avila crawled to him, tugged at his boot. "We're . . ." he smothered a cough, turned it into a laugh. "If we don't surrender, we'll be roasted."

Williams looked at him somberly. "Want to rot in a Yankee prison?"

Avila shrugged. "Medals are for heroes. And my girl damn well likes medals."

The sergeant joined them, his hat pushed to the back of his head, his face oily from the heat. "The boy piled some hay at the foot of the outside ladder. He liked to jump in it."

An explosion tumbled them floorwards. The three men said in once voice, "Cannon!"

"If they get our range," Williams muttered, "We won't have to worry about roasting."

They stumbled to the ladder side, saw its bullet-splintered frame broken too high up for escape. But the hay was piled deep at the base, protected by the stone tower from fire.

"The bell ropes," gasped the sergeant. One of the soldiers dropped his gun and sprang to the rope of Santo Tomás.

"No!" Avila shouted. "Use the rope of Santa Cecilia. She won't fail us—not today—not on the ninth of June."

The second cannon ball exploded forty yards away, concussion sucking the wind out of them. Williams gulped for air, then grinned, flung back his head, and howled the wildcat rebel yell.

The rope of Santa Cecilia uncurled over the tower side, its heavy knotted end just missing the top of the hay pile. The men slid down, dropped into the hay, rolled free and dashed for the safety of the woods that led to the mountains. The moon was already setting.

They were all down now but Avila and Williams. The Federals had discovered the exit and were lacing the side wall with bullets. The two friends shook hands. "When I open my house in Hell treat it as your own," Avila said, and swung from the parapet. The rope burned his palms as he slid downwards, and he was grateful for the fragrant hay that engulfed him. The sergeant had waited for him. "Good brother," Avila said, and then, glancing upwards, "Here comes the major. Rapid fire to cover him." The rifle barked, but a Federal bullet snapped the rope, and Williams plummeted downwards, bounced in the hay as in a net.

Avila and the sergeant pounded toward the woods, Williams at their heels. And then they were safe in the darkness. Low whistles brought the men to them.

"Count off," Williams whispered. Including themselves, there were twelve, with two wounded. Fifty, to twenty, to twelve, thought Avila. They moved silently through the trees.

Avila whispered, "What made that old stone tower so important?"

"How the hell should I know? Here, have a drink." Williams took the cognac bottle from his blouse and pressed it into Avila's hand.

The young captain sighed. "You are a very polite Protestant, treating a saint's gift with proper respect, especially on her saint's day."

"You talk too much," Williams growled, but the warm liquid, flowing down his throat, mollified him. ★

Jay Brandon

Jay Brandon is a successful attorney and a prolific, award-winning mystery novelist. A native of San Antonio, he holds a MA in writing from Johns Hopkins University and a law degree from the University of Houston. All but one of Brandon's numerous novels are set in San Antonio and South Texas, and they are rich with local detail and voices. His extensive experience working in the District Attorney's office in Bexar County and with the Fourth Court of Appeals has provided him plenty of insights into the workings of the legal system, and how what is "accepted history" is often a long way from the "real history."

Brandon is the author of seventeen novels and one book of nonfiction, as well as a number of short stories published in anthologies. His novels include classics like *Fade the Heat* (1990), which was short-listed for the Edgar Award, *Rules of Evidence* (1992), *Loose Among the Lambs* (1993), as well as an international thriller, *Shadow Knight's Mate* (Wings Press, 2015). He once wrote a novel that was serialized over the course of two years in the *San Antonio Express-News*. Eventually that book was published as *Milagro Lane* (Wings Press, 2009).

"A Jury of His Peers" is based on an historical event: the September 1842 invasion of Texas by Mexican forces under General Woll, during which San Antonio was surrounded by 1,600 Mexican troops. A brief engagement was fought during a heavy morning fog, resulting in several casualties. A Mr. Corasco negotiated the city's immediate surrender once the size of Woll's army became evident. It is assumed that Santa Anna, still the president of Mexico, had intended the invasion to disrupt civil government in Texas, to punish Texans for their raid on Santa Fe the year before, and to make a show of force against the United States, where the annexation of Texas was becoming a popular cause. Woll's invasion happened to occur when the district court was in session, which meant that most of the lawyers in South Texas were in San Antonio at the time. Woll demanded as prisoners "all male Anglo citizens." Among the fifty-five taken were the presiding District Court Judge Anderson Hutchinson and several prominent Texas attorneys and politicians such as Sam Maverick and William Early Jones. As it happened, all members but one of the San Antonio Bar were taken prisoner. Woll marched them to Perote Prison near Vera Cruz. Some were released in a few months, some held as long as two years, and many died either en route or in prison.

A Jury of His Peers

The attorneys taken hostage by an arm of the Mexican Army three days hence have not reappeared. The town is much perturbed, and there is some talk of mounting a rescue effort.
—*San Antonio (TX) Gazette*, September 14, 1842

They straggled back to San Antonio in ones and twos and small groups as they were released from Perote Prison. Some traveled overland, some by boat across the Gulf of Mexico. But each arrived bedraggled, thinner, and with watchful eyes. Some of the men had families to greet their returns, most had friends, all had practices. But it was hard to resume their lives. Nothing they could lay their hands to seemed as worthwhile as just the fact of being free.

For a while, it wasn't clear everyone was coming back. The Mexicans might well kill a few of their number as an example or because they didn't have family to ransom them. While the released men woke every morning overjoyed to find light coming through windows, a part of them remained in prison with their friends.

One of the last of the lawyers to return to San Antonio was William "Bill" Harcourt. He had spent more than a year in prison in Mexico, and his home-town appeared very changed; both larger—as he approached from the south on horseback, the buildings appeared a vast intrusion on the landscape—and smaller; when he got to the heart of the city, the buildings were neither as many nor as impressive as he remembered. He stayed at home for five days and nights, he and his wife reliving their meeting, courtship, and honeymoon, accelerated by past knowledge. For that long, not even the nearest neighbors saw them, and it was as if Mrs. Harcourt had vanished along with her husband, rather than that he had returned.

But pleasant as it was to catch up on events and become reacquainted with his wife, staying in the house was too strong a reminder of confinement, so on the sixth day, Bill strolled downtown to his law office. It was a bright day in February, and the walk cheered him. Being surrounded by people and buildings and commerce made him feel safe. But as soon as he stepped into the gloom of the offices, he thought, *Why do people choose to imprison themselves like this?*

Harcourt was not an imposing man. Of average size when he was taken hostage, he was now slender to the point of emaciation. Well under six feet tall, he still felt the whitewashed ceiling of the offices as a constant presence only inches above his head. His brown hair had grown thicker and longer and he hadn't yet cut it back, so he had the look of a frontiersman though he wore his best suit, one that had stayed safely in his closet all this time, with gray pants and a black frock coat with tails.

Harcourt broke into his first smile of the day when greeted by the clerk, Henry, a lad of barely twenty, who studied law in the offices while performing the clerk's duties: copying documents, running to the courthouse to peruse deeds, looking up statutes, emptying spittoons.

"Henry!" Harcourt cried, clapping the young man's shoulders. "Still clerking here?" It seemed a wonder to him that life had gone on as usual in his absence. Besides, what clerkly duties had he performed with all the lawyers in town vanished?

"Actually, I'm an attorney now, sir. I took my examinations six months ago."

"Good for you! Well, nature hates a vacuum. I guess the town needed to grow more lawyers while we were gone. Have you been busy?"

Henry looked embarrassed. Harcourt noticed the other people in the room.

At the time of the lawyers' abrupt departure from town on September 11, 1842, these offices had been shared by five lawyers. The entry room in which Harcourt and Henry now stood had served as a reception area, law library, and common room, with each lawyer having a small private office for receiving clients. Men were emerging from those offices now, two with smiles of greeting, one with a more interesting expression. A year and a half in captivity, learning the personalities and moods of the different guards, watching for signs of a beating or possible chance for ingratiation, had made Bill Harcourt a quick study of countenances, and he saw in these faces more than their owners intended. Even the smiles of his old partners had traces of apprehension. While they were glad to see him, they saw the possibility of imminent conflict. The stranger, who held a quill pen in his right hand, looked openly puzzled and anxious.

The next moment, there was a tumult of welcome, but Harcourt didn't forget his first impression. What conflict was hidden here?

Greeting him most effusively and openly was Samuel Maverick. Maverick was one of the leading lawyers in town, and though relatively new to Texas, one of the foremost citizens of San Antonio. He had been trying a case in court on September 11th when the invading Mexican forces captured the courthouse and every lawyer in town. Maverick had also been one of the first three prisoners released, but he had still spent six months in Perote Prison, so he and Harcourt were colleagues in more than the practice of law.

"You've been back almost a year," Harcourt said, "so I assume you've stolen all the legal business. Just like those cattle you refuse to brand, any client without another lawyer's name on him must belong to Maverick."

"I haven't had to steal them," Maverick said genially. "They've pressed themselves on me like fallen flowers when the tavern is empty."

"And express themselves just as satisfied with your services, I'm sure," Harcourt answered. The men laughed.

But raised voices from the last office gradually intruded on their reunion. Both men were even more sensitive to loud voices than Harcourt was to the flicker of an eyelid, because during their months of captivity, shouting had nearly always preceded a beating, or worse. These voices were only directed against each other, but they still drew the men's attention. Harcourt glanced inquiringly at Maverick, who rolled his eyes.

Harcourt recognized one of the voices, and a small smile shaped his thin lips. In Perote Prison, the lawyers had been chained together two by two. Being joined in that fashion creates either enduring friendship or such sensitivity that the other man's breathing becomes an irritant. One night, Maverick had gotten into a fist fight with his chain mate. But Bill Harcourt and one of the men now shouting in the adjoining office, John Lawrence, had become fast friends—and confidants in more ways than one.

John had shared these offices with Harcourt for more than two years, but they had only been acquaintances. Now, after a year spent chained together, they were strange twins, their minds running along the same tracks. Somewhat. Bill knew the plans John had shared and some secrets he hadn't meant to share, such as the names he murmured in his sleep at night.

John had been a prematurely middle-aged, thirty-year-old man with a small pot belly, a shy wife of five years, a hearty laugh, but thoughtful moods. Like the other captives, though, he was changed now. Bill stepped into John's office and saw him pushing a younger man away from the desk. The young man appeared a dandy in tight white trousers, a gray vest with a gold watch chain across it, and a blue coat with a flower in its lapel. Where had he gotten a rosebud in February? It was a small mystery Harcourt's mind brushed aside while taking in the man's even features, lively blue eyes, and trace of a smile even as he was being pushed backward by a man made lean and pale.

A woman in a small bonnet stood between them: Madelyn, John's wife; thin and delicately-featured, with light brown hair. One of her hands reached toward her husband, importuning. The other hand, Bill saw at a quick glance, was on the younger man's arm, just before she removed it.

"Come, sir!" the young man said. "There's no thievery here. I made an arrangement, first with your clerk, then with your wife—whom some thought your widow. Without me, your practice would have died completely."

John recovered himself. Perhaps he saw his old friend out of the corner of his eye, or sensed the others clustering in the doorway. "Thank you," he said, in the tone of a gentleman thanking a groom for having kept his horse exercised. "But now, as you see, I've returned. You can find accommodations elsewhere or go back to Austin."

"Oh, I like it here," the young man said. It was strange how his handsome face nonetheless seemed to find a sneer its most natural expression. "Truth to tell, people like me, too. Some of your clients will not be so delighted with your return. You don't own them, you know."

"And they don't know you," John snapped. "When they do—"

The young man raised his voice, his eyes suddenly lit from within. "It's not only your clients who prefer me. I'm not trying to take over your life, Mr. Lawrence. But I think I can perform it better. I've sat in your chair, I've read your pleadings. I can do better. And not only there. You know, don't you? She must have told—"

Bill Harcourt was whipping across the room and over the desk without conscious thought. Harcourt's forearm was across the young man's throat and his fist in his stomach. When the man began choking, Harcourt recovered himself. He brushed off the younger man's jacket and spoke in his best court-room voice. "Sorry for the strange introduction. I thought I saw a dangerous insect. Perhaps a scorpion. I am William Harcourt. You seem to have met my old friend, John Lawrence, whose office we're standing in. Hello, Madelyn. You look lovelier than ever."

To the young man's credit, he was not slow-witted or lacking grace. He removed his hand from his throat and nodded his head politely. By this time, he was aware of the crowded nature of the offices, and perhaps regretted the indiscretion he had been about to perform. It would not have done him much credit, not here. "My pleasure," he murmured. "You two must have a great deal to discuss after your adventure together."

Harcourt, who had mastered his anger completely, smiled. "Oh, John and I have had many months to discuss every topic."

The young man—Harcourt was beginning to think it a good idea to learn his name—gave him a frank look before regaining his smile. Then he turned it on John, who stood shuddering with fists clenched. He didn't have his friend Harcourt's composure. Like many mild men, he was not used to his own anger and couldn't master it quickly.

"You and I still have much to discuss," the young man said as he left the office, greeting the other lawyers affably on his way out. He didn't glance back at Madelyn, whose hand had removed itself from his arm in an instant when Bill had appeared.

"William," she said graciously, extending her hand to him.

So the three of them stood and chatted, as if nothing had just happened. Bill chatted amiably with Madelyn, but noticed that her other hand never

extended to her husband's arm. John and Bill had been released from confinement at the same time, but obviously, John had needed less time to reacquaint
himself with his wife and had been out in the world sooner.

Speaking of the last few days, Harcourt said to his former chain mate, "I
felt like an amputee, with only my own two legs to account for. I had forgotten
how to walk alone." John laughed, and laughter came from the doorway, too.
The three lawyers there knew exactly what he meant.

After a minute John took up his office, and his wife left alone.

* * *

Henry, the former clerk, had taken over William Harcourt's old office.
Harcourt glanced into it, but showed no inclination to enter. "No, don't bother,
Henry. You keep the desk. Let's wait to see whether I need it or another."

The other attorneys went off to the courthouse, but Harcourt demurred.
In their absences, he owned the offices. He wandered into John's, or the office
that had been John Lawrence's, wondering how it was changed. On the desk,
he found a ledger book. John had always been very careful in his accounts.
Harcourt leafed through it, noting columns of income and brief notations of
services performed. Then the writing changed, though still recording similar
transactions. Obviously, the young Austin lawyer had taken over John's account
book, along with other parts of his life. Harcourt leafed through the book to the
blank pages at the end, then sat musing.

As he had said, nature hates a vacuum and rushes to fill it. But nature has
even stricter rules against two bodies occupying the same space.

The Texas Republic was short-lived (1836-1845), but no one living in it
knew it would be. For all they knew, they had founded an enduring nation.
Mexico, on the other hand, never acknowledged the sovereignty of the new
country, still considering it a rebel province of its own. Its army continued
to make raids into Texas, designed to humiliate more than to conquer. The
Mexican President, Santa Anna, hated Texas, and no part of it more than San
Antonio, the scene of his triumph at the Alamo, but which had shrugged off
that tragedy to become the largest, most thriving city in Texas. The Alamo was

in fact already a tourist destination, the shrine of Texas liberty. Two Mexican raids into San Antonio had wreaked havoc, and the second had accomplished its strange goal. Mexican soldiers had captured the courthouse and every lawyer in town, marching them deep into Mexico and captivity in the castle of Perote.

In Mexico, the imprisoned lawyers had often speculated on the nature of life in their absence. "I think people will be more civil to each other," one man had ventured. "They'll have to be, won't they, without courts to resolve their disputes?"

Samuel Maverick had shaken his shaggy head. "They'll kill each other," he'd intoned in his slow, gloomy voice, so suited to a courtroom. "The town will devolve back to the frontier. The law is what protects us from chaos, and none of us is very far removed from chaos."

In the darkness of the dungeon, Harcourt's voice had come slyly, like one of the vermin that crept through their sleeping straw. "I'm glad you didn't tell me until now that we were upholding civilization, like Atlas. I couldn't have borne up under the strain."

John Lawrence's laugh had been the first, followed by general hilarity, which they cut off quickly at the sound of an outer door. The Mexicans hated nothing so much as laughter from their captives.

Back in town now, on his second day home, Bill Harcourt wondered which of their speculations had been true. He dropped in on his friend the general store keeper, a one-time ranch hand who was smarter than his lot in life and had seen the need for mercantilism. His store prospered in dry goods, hardware, and feed. Prospered enough that he could sit on the porch and tell an old friend what life had been like in his absence.

"Oh, there was a mite more killing than usual, that's true, but hardly any that didn't need it. And we still had police, of course. There was no breakdown in law—no more than ordinary. A few folks had to sit in jail longer than they would have, I suppose, but no one had much sympathy for them. Two or three had their hangings delayed for want of a trial, but they seemed satisfied to wait."

"But the ordinary civil disputes," Bill questioned, "what did people do when they could no longer cry, 'I'll see you in court'?"

The shopkeeper shrugged. "They fought, of course. Sometimes right here on this street. Unless the dispute was between women, then they went at each other in slyer and more crippling ways. But mostly, men settled their differences the time-honored way."

"Trial by combat," Bill mused. He could see it taking place as if in front of him. "Older than law. And a good fist fight is much quicker and more satisfying than a trial, for both the participants and the spectators."

"Yup," the shopkeeper said complacently.

For the rest of the day and the next, Bill stayed away from his old friend John, and from the courthouse. In the last year and a half, his comradely desire to spend time with his colleagues had been more than satisfied. Instead, he walked around the town, re-familiarizing himself with the houses and buildings and trying to ignore the insubstantial quality they seemed to have now. He resumed acquaintances with his children and had long, quiet talks with his wife. In his absence, his wife had acquired more cattle and hired a man to plant more acres. She had done more than get by, enough so that he could wander about like a kept man for another week or more, and Bill didn't mind a bit. His wife's resourcefulness meant he didn't have to return immediately to the practice of law, and he felt no desire to do so. The old forms seemed strange to him, empty rituals. He picked up a deed in his old office and found its language ridiculous.

William Harcourt might never have tried a case again if not for the murder.

In the days of the Texas Republic, adventurers and settlers created a nation from their imaginations and faulty memories. Squatting in buildings that had housed the governments under Spain and then Mexico, they made institutions out of a traveler's fever dream of history. Their court system borrowed from England and stole from Spain, with bits of French thrown in for flavor. The beauty of this system was that a hometown lawyer could always claim he was working in one tradition or another, while the arcana of the law discouraged new competition.

But with all the hometown lawyers gone for so many months, inevitably a few others had moved in, down from Austin or over from Nacogdoches. Common sense would say that these were not the brightest lights of their local bars. No one would leave a thriving practice to move into a town whose own lawyers might return any day. On the other hand, San Antonio was a booming town and needed legal transactions. A few out-of-town lawyers took the gamble, including the young dandy whom Bill had attacked in John's office. The young fellow turned out to have a name, Luke Enright. They would put it on a cheap tombstone if his body turned up.

Two days after his fight with John Lawrence, Enright's horse came in riderless, blood on its saddle. People knew the horse, and they knew Enright's last dispute.

The lawyers were all in the courthouse, an ostentatiously named one-story building on Main Street. Most lawyers spent most days in the courthouse, trying a case or observing a trial or researching land or water titles. Or gossiping, as they were doing at four o'clock of the afternoon when the chief of police came in. He might have been seeking a warrant, but finding the object of his search in the courtroom, he proposed to take him into custody that minute. "John Lawrence, you're under arrest for the murder of Luke Enright."

"Who?" asked one of the lawyers.

"The little bastard who took over my practice," John said. A good attorney would have shut his mouth before he could finish the thought aloud, but he had no attorney.

"He took over more than that," the chief said portentously. "While you were gone, he and your—well, he was a lodger in your house."

"My wife needed an income," John said, sounding sullen and unconvincing to everyone.

There were several rejoinders to that, referring to Mrs. Lawrence's needs, but no one spoke them aloud.

"And your wife is gone, too," the chief announced as if it proved his point. "Did you kill them both at once?"

"No," another man said quickly. "I saw Mrs. Lawrence riding out myself, with luggage in her carriage."

"Which direction?"

"North. The Austin road."

"Horrified by what you'd done," the chief of police said to John, moving toward him.

John shook his head. "Just going to visit her sister for a while."

"You can explain to a jury," the chief said, reaching for John.

As he did so, the courtroom door opened, and everyone looked toward it. There was a certain apprehension in some of those gazes. One of the last times some of them had seen that door open, Mexican troops had come through it. But this late afternoon, the lowering sun only cast the shadow of one man. William Harcourt had returned to the courthouse.

He seemed to be well-informed of what was happening. "What do you propose to do with the prisoner, chief?" he asked briskly.

"Put him in jail, wait for—well, the circuit judge, I suppose."

"What about bail? He's entitled to indictment by a grand jury, as well. But we have neither magistrate to set bond nor district judge to call a grand jury."

The only district judge in the region had been captured along with the rest of the lawyers. One of the first three released, he had immediately returned to his home state of Mississippi, declaring it was unsafe to practice law in Texas. No one had yet been appointed or elected to take his place.

Judge was a position of distinction and honor, but it did not pay very well in the days of the Republic and offered no retirement pension. Lawyers took turns at the position, serving for a term or perhaps two out of a sense of duty, but always returning to more lucrative private practice. There were two men in the room who could claim the lifelong title of "Judge," but no current holder of the office.

"He'll just have to wait," the police chief declared. Everyone in the room murmured at that. The lawyers didn't like to think of their colleague sitting in jail with no legal recourse.

"I believe the Constitution entitles him to speedy trial if he demands it," another lawyer observed. Harcourt was glad he no longer had to do all the proposing. "That's right," another one said, "and a grand jury to determine whether there's cause to hold him."

"Well, we just don't have those things," the police chief said, beginning to sound sulky. He was usually comfortable in his authority, but being the only non-lawyer in a room full of attorneys made a man want to stand with his back to a wall.

"We can have," Harcourt said quietly.

The room went quiet. The nearly two dozen lawyers in the room looked around at each other. Most of them had served on a jury at one time or another, being readily available when a call for jurors went out. They were in a court-room where hundreds of trials had been conducted. If any other group had thought of conducting an inquiry, they would have been a kangaroo court or a lynch mob, but this group could make it official.

"I don't want to sit in jail," John said. He hadn't moved from his chair.

"Would you rather be hanged tomorrow?" Sam Maverick said, stalking to the center of the room. "That's what we're talking about. There wouldn't be any appeal. This is real, John."

"Yes," the prisoner said. "I'd prefer that, if a jury of my peers thinks it just."

He sounded resigned and yet eager. Men looked at each other, wondering if they were ready to assume this responsibility. It was a moment before they realized that Bill Harcourt was speaking.

"Sam Maverick is one of the largest landholders in this county," he drawled as if telling a story. Bill stood by the jury box, leaning against its rail. "And we know he has large herds of cattle, some of them taken in fees. But he refuses to brand them. They roam free, so he can claim any unbranded cow is his."

"I've never—" Maverick began, but Bill waved him silent.

"Well, we are all mavericks now. Unbranded rogues, who answer to no one. That was the lesson of Perote. The lesson the Mexican general intended to teach us when he kidnapped us from this room. Our institutions are hollow, except as we give them form. There are only rules because we submit ourselves to the rule of law. Otherwise, this is a frontier. This building is a sham, unless we fill it with justice."

The men began to assemble themselves, some moving toward the jury box. Quickly, a lawyer named Early Jones was suggested and chosen as judge. Without much formality, the district clerk swore him in, with an oath to uphold the laws of the republic of Texas.

"We need a prosecutor and the accused needs a defender," the new judge said.

Several lawyers moved toward John. Only Bill stepped toward the clerk. "I'll prosecute."

The silence was puzzled. Bill and John were known to be friends. And they all knew Bill as a tenacious and thorough trial lawyer who had sent more than one man to prison while serving as a special prosecutor. Several lawyers, including John himself, looking up in surprise, wondered if Bill bore some secret grudge against the man with whom he'd been chained for more than a year.

"Unless there are any objections?" Bill asked, looking around.

No one said a thing. A few shook their heads.

"You need to take the oath," the clerk said.

Bill hesitated. "To do what?"

"Uphold the laws—" someone began, but another who had served one term as district attorney interrupted.

"The prosecutor is sworn to do justice."

"I'll take that oath," Bill said, and did so.

Samuel Maverick looked at the new prosecutor, then went to stand beside the accused. "I'll defend. If John will have me."

The defendant shook his hand, sealing the agreement.

A dozen men were sworn in as jurors. Others took seats inside the bar. They were all part of this. Without a consensus of opinion, there could be no resolution. Judge Jones assumed the bench and a more formal air. "Call your first witness."

Bill said, "Chief, come forward and give your evidence."

The chief of police walked slowly and suspiciously into their midst. No one cared about his suspicions. They knew this proceeding to be as legal as they could make it, whether they waited for a duly appointed judge or not. They would take their responsibilities seriously. No one seemed to feel this more strongly than Bill Harcourt, who looked sternly at the witness, ignoring the defendant's troubled stare.

"Well, there's the horse," the chief of police began slowly. "It's Enright's horse, all right. No one saw him ride out. The horse returned with blood on his saddle. Mr. Lawrence has no alibi for the whole morning. He's known not to be living with his wife since shortly after his return. Mrs. Lawrence is gone too, as if she knows—"

"Object to speculation," Maverick said quickly.

"There are Comanches still about, aren't there, Chief? Why would you not think young Mr. Enright merely the victim of an Indian attack?"

"No red man would let a horse go," the chief said positively. Men nodded at that. "Besides, there are also the quarrels. Besides the one some of you gentlemen saw, Mr. Lawrence and Enright exchanged words and almost came to blows two other times, one of them just yesterday afternoon. Now, Enright may have taken clients from several of you in your absence, but only Mr. Lawrence suffered so personal a loss."

They all turned to look at John, including the new judge. The accused tried to look composed.

"And this afternoon, John Lawrence returned to his office, cleared young Mr. Enright's things out, and resumed his practice as if he knew the matter was settled."

The accusation had been pretty speculative until then, but the chief's last words made good sense to everyone. "Your witness," Harcourt said.

Maverick had few questions, only establishing that the chief of police had no more evidence of Enright's demise or current whereabouts. "Do you think that's enough to condemn a man?" he asked, which was really aimed at his opponent.

"I haven't rested my case," Bill Harcourt said. "I suggest we adjourn this proceeding to John Lawrence's office."

The suggestion was unorthodox, but so was this entire proceeding. The law offices were just across the street. Within ten minutes, the offices were crowded. The jurors stood together against one wall of John's own office. "I'll call Henry Reynolds," Bill said, and the young clerk, now lawyer, came forward shyly.

Harcourt quickly established that the presumed deceased had used this office in John Lawrence's absence and had continued to do so even after his return. Disputes between the two men over possession of the office had grown more heated.

"And did you ever overhear any exchanges between *Mrs.* Lawrence and either of the two men? Come, Henry, you're sworn to give testimony."

A very mature look shot out of Henry's boyish face, turning his eyes much older for a moment. Only Bill caught the expression. "No, sir," Henry said staunchly. "They kept personal matters private."

"Not enough so," Bill remarked. He picked up a book from the desk, the same one he had handled two days earlier. "Do you recognize this?"

Henry nodded. "Mr. Lawrence's ledger book."

Bill held it up to an open page. "Like this office, not entirely his own anymore. Note the change in handwriting in the later pages. Please note also," he said to the jury, "that the income figures show a prospering practice. More so than when John kept it. I'll offer Republic's Exhibit One."

The book was admitted, and Maverick leafed through it, conferring quietly with his client.

Bill opened a drawer of the desk. His hand rummaged among the contents, and he drew out a pocket watch. "Do you recognize this?"

Several men did, from their expressions. "It looks like Mr. Enright's, sir. He told me once he'd inherited it from his grandfather. It was one of his most prized possessions."

Bill dropped it on the desk. "Yet here it sits. Does a man leave town and leave behind his most favored possession, as well as a thriving practice? The Republic rests. Gentlemen," he said to the jury, "even if this case remains open, I doubt there will be any more evidence one way or the other unless Enright's body turns up, and even that wouldn't tell us much. This matter can be settled tonight."

Samuel Maverick said, "The defense calls Martin Stenberg." After it was established that he was the man who had said earlier he'd seen Mrs. Lawrence riding out of town in her carriage, Maverick asked, "Which direction was she going, Martin?"

"I think I said. North, toward Austin."

"And she was traveling alone, with luggage?"

"Yes, sir."

"No more questions."

Bill just shrugged.

"The defense will call John Lawrence."

Defendants were not normally allowed to testify in their own defense, since it was presumed their testimony would be untrustworthy. Bill pointed this out.

"I'm calling him for a limited purpose, not to deny his guilt," Maverick said, and Bill let the legal point go.

"John," Maverick said sternly. "Where was your wife going?"

"We'd separated," John Lawrence said quietly. "You all seem to know that. She was going to stay with her sister."

"And where does her sister live?"

"Philadelphia."

"When she's gone to visit her sister in the past, how did she go?"

"To Galveston," the accused said quietly. "To take a ship."

Men, including jurors, nodded. The answer made sense. And Galveston was not north of them. It was south and east. "The defense rests," Maverick said abruptly.

Bill Harcourt made a brief summation. "Luke Enright may not have been well-liked by the men in this room, but he deserves justice. He had increasingly violent quarrels with the defendant, then his horse turns up showing blood. Outside the courthouse, no more evidence than that would be needed. The young man had everything he wanted here. Why would he leave so abruptly? No, men, the chief of police is right. I ask for your guilty verdict."

Samuel Maverick had been looking over the two exhibits. When his turn came, he stood with both in his hands. Walking toward the jury box, he leafed through the ledger book. After the last page Harcourt had displayed, there were two dozen blank pages. But at the back, the new handwriting began again, with different names and figures. "Mr. Enright was apparently keeping track of more than his profits. These pages seem to be in a cipher. What did he want to hide? Which raises the question, what do we know about him? What did he leave behind, in Austin or elsewhere? When a man changes cities of residence, it's usually to escape something. I suggest, gentlemen, when a man writes different figures in a different place in the book, he's recording something other than what's recorded in the front. Could it be debts? Look at these numbers. They far outweigh the meager earnings in front. Could it be that the people to whom Enright owed these debts had caught up to him, or were about to do so? *There's a reason for a man to light out in a hurry.*

"And this was a lawyer. An angry young man who bore a grudge. There's no use to run if you're still pursued. Much better to make your creditors think you're dead. And if young Enright was going to fake his death, what better sweetness than to have his revenge at the same time? Initiate another quarrel with the man he hated, *then* flee."

Maverick surveyed the jurors, hardheaded lawyers who looked skeptical. And flee without his horse? they were clearly thinking.

"And leave with his lover. Yes. I hate to suggest scandal, but look at the facts. Mrs. Lawrence rode north. Not the direction she would normally take, but the direction from which young Enright came. They met, he cut himself and dripped blood on the saddle, and they rode away, Enright laughing to himself."

These jurors were lawyers, and not used to sitting silent in a courtroom. One said, "That's a fanciful picture, Maverick," and his neighbor added, "What about the watch he left behind? His most treasured possession. He wouldn't have run off without it."

The watch in question dangled from Maverick's hand. "This watch? The one he inherited from his grandfather? Look at the inside of the case, gentlemen. This watch has a manufacturer's date of 1838. It's very young for a treasured family heirloom."

He handed it across, and the jurors inspected it eagerly. Some looked at the defendant with new expressions, while others narrowed their eyes.

Bill Harcourt declined rebuttal argument. The verdict was swift. The jurors didn't even leave their box, only huddled together, then one stood to say, "Your Honor, we find the defendant not guilty."

The chief of police sputtered, but the new judge assured him that the verdict was as legal as a poll tax. The room surged around John with congratulations. It was important that nearly every lawyer in town had participated. They would spread the word. There might be speculation that the attorneys had protected one of their own, but not the kind of presumed guilt that would have dogged John Lawrence without this proceeding.

Besides, in the Republic of Texas there were rumors much more damaging to reputation than that one had killed a man. That suspicion added a touch of stature.

The men gradually cleared out of the offices. John declined offers of celebration until, with glances, the men understood that Bill Harcourt was lingering, too. The men had a friendship to repair.

When the men were alone, John still sitting on his rickety wooden chair, Bill leaning back against the desk, Bill said simply, "Forgive me?"

John laughed. "I thought no one might volunteer to prosecute me, then there'd have been no trial and no exoneration. I owe you more—"

"Well, you know my passion for justice," Bill said archly.

"I do, actually."

Bill gave his friend a sidelong glance. "Stealing a man's livelihood, and his wife, and not being content with that, wanting to take his reputation as well, I call that worse than rustling. And"—his voice rose a little—"to do it while we were rotting in that hole. If you *had* killed him I'd call it just."

"When we were marched out of the courthouse on September 11th . . ." John began.

It was a date that would speak an entire narrative for the rest of their lives.

"—we were told we'd be released at the border. Then we wondered whether we'd be murdered. Just coming back here seemed a dream of paradise. But I didn't have waiting for me what many of you had."

The childless marriage between John and his wife was, at least to the public eye, a cool one. And the names he had murmured in his sleep in Perote Prison had not been women's names. Bill wondered if young Henry knew the truth. If he did, he would keep it to himself. To Bill, a man's personal life and preferences were his own business, but here on the western frontier, a suggestion of unmanliness could ruin a man.

"After our year on the brink of death," he said, "other things seemed like small considerations."

John fingered the only exhibits from the hasty trial. "You introduced the only evidence in the trial," he said slowly. "This ledger. The first pages are in my writing, true, but then there are some pages torn out."

"Are there? Perhaps Enright wanted to put some space between your accounts and his."

John went on, in his quiet, lawyerly way. "The entries in the back are in the same handwriting, true, but no one has compared that writing to some of the pleadings Enright filed. The way you handled things, there wasn't time for that kind of investigation." Harcourt didn't answer. "And as for that watch, who knows whether that's the same one Enright carried or where it came from?"

"You're right. Perhaps Enright planted it there to implicate you, because he couldn't bear to leave behind the real one."

John gave him a look rather than an answer. "My point is that there wasn't time tonight to—to place this evidence here. It must have been done before I was accused. Even before I . . ."

Bill didn't want to hear a confession. "Maybe I was protecting myself," he said. "He trifled with more than one practice, and maybe with more than one wife. Or maybe I just took the opportunity while the rest of you went about your legal business to give the young man a stern lecture and run him out of here. Then made sure there'd be no accusations over his absence that could be sustained."

These would have been interesting speculations, between two other men. But these two knew the truth. John finally stood and walked close to his friend. "I know how fierce a litigator you are. It must have hurt you," he said, "to lose this trial."

"Lose?" Bill looked genuinely surprised. "You forget. The oath I took was to see justice done. I consider this trial one of my most significant victories."

They went out together, into a new town.

William Harcourt—Bill—was induced to serve one term as judge, which he performed to universal respect, but declined reappointment. The end of his tenure coincided with the end of the Texas Republic. In the Mexican War that followed, he and his wife did well in cotton for uniforms. He was a colonel in the War Between the States, which touched Texas but lightly. He lived through turmoil and transformation and rebirth, and closed out his life toward the end of the century he had made his own, to great local renown, never having resumed the practice of law.

Nor did he and his old friend John Lawrence ever tell anyone each other's secrets. ★

STEPHEN HARRIGAN

J. Frank Dobie claimed that "every Texan has two hometowns, his own and San Antonio." That is certainly true of Stephen Harrigan—born in Oklahoma, raised in Abilene and Corpus Christi, and long a resident of Austin. His *The Gates of the Alamo* (2000) has been celebrated as the best novel about the Alamo *ever*—and there have been many, many contenders for that title. *The Gates of the Alamo* was a *New York Times* bestseller and Notable Book, and received a host of national awards. Harrigan himself has been honored with the Texas Book Festival's Texas Writers Award, the Lon Tinkle Award for lifetime achievement (Texas Institute of Letters), and induction into the Texas Literary Hall of Fame. The author of ten books of fiction and nonfiction, and several television movies, Harrigan is a faculty fellow at the James A. Michener Center for Writers (University of Texas) and a writer-at-large for *Texas Monthly*.

Harrigan's novel *Remember Ben Clayton* (2011) won the James Fenimore Cooper Prize (Society of American Historians) for the best work of historical fiction. An absolutely masterful novel, it focuses on sculptor Francis "Gil" Gilheaney, a New York sculptor who has settled into a kind of artistic exile in San Antonio. His daughter Maureen is an equally talented sculptor. Gil is immersed in creating a memorial statue to honor the son of Lamar Clayton, a classically reclusive Texas rancher. The son, Ben Clayton, was a casualty in World War I, only recently concluded.

In this excerpt from *Remember Ben Clayton*, Harrigan's description of an evening walk through the city is almost a prose poem, rife with beloved landmarks, many of them only memories now. Knowing readers will find several historical character parallels here: Francis Gilheaney bears a certain resemblance to Pompeo Coppini, the sculptor of the Alamo Cenotaph (though the monument described here bears no resemblance to the actual cenotaph); Maureen resembles Coppini's assistant and "adopted" daughter, the Texas-born sculptor Waldine Tauch (who sculpted the "First Inhabitant" statue on the Commerce Street bridge); and Maureen's beau, Vance Martindale, is a thinly veiled portrait of J. Frank Dobie.

from *Remember Ben Clayton*

Months earlier, in secret, Maureen had entered
the competition for a city sculpture commission. The piece was to be placed on
the Commerce Street bridge and called "The Spirit of the Waters" in homage
to the San Antonio River, which passed below. It had seemed natural not to
tell her father, though it had been difficult to locate a space in which to model
the piece and sometimes awkward to invent excuses to leave the house for the
extended periods of work required.

In the end, she had been able to commandeer the studio of a friend who
taught art at the Ursuline Academy. The studio was vacant only on Saturdays,
but so far it had suited her schedule, and the bulk of the work was now finished
and would be ready for the judging competition next week. Her father would
not begin the Clayton piece in earnest for another few weeks or so, and her
presence in his studio was not yet in demand. She had told him this morning
that she was going out to spend the day with Vance Martindale, which was not
rigorously true but not false either, since Vance had written that he would be
in San Antonio over the weekend and wanted to see her.

She had decided to hide her participation in the competition from her
father because she knew she would not have been able to abide his enthusiasm.
The congratulations, expressions of confidence, and unsought suggestions that
would emerge from his interest would, she knew, quickly subsume her own
uncertain ambition. She would be not just his daughter but his blood-bound
protégé, a role to which her own authentic worth as a sculptor would forever
be hostage.

It was a sense of that authentic worth that she was trying to recapture now.
Back in New York, she had come close to achieving some sort of independent
success. She had steadily applied for commissions, sometimes using a false
name, carefully testing the waters to see if she would be taken seriously in her
own right and not just politely accommodated as the daughter of a well-known
sculptor. None of the commissions had come her way, but she had not really
expected them to. She was a woman, which would have made rising to the top
of the list unlikely in the first place, and she was young, with no reputation. But

there had been enough encouraging comments on her work to make her believe she was being noticed and that with time and patience she might advance into a career.

But her rising confidence had coincided with her father's deepening frustration at the direction his own career was heading in New York and his abrupt decision to move the family to San Antonio to take advantage of the new Texas commissions that kept falling into his lap after the success of his Alamo piece. Maureen could have refused to move, of course. She had even gently aired the possibility to her father, who had responded with reasonable words but with such a hurt and betrayed expression in his eyes that she was astonished at how strongly it was in her power to wound him. And she could not really leave her mother to face the Texas wilderness—as she imagined San Antonio to be—without a daughter's support. If she had been in love it might have made a difference; she might have had the cruelty to remain in New York and abandon her parents to the edge of the known world. But she had not been in love, only mired in an indifferent half-courtship with a young newspaperman who, as it turned out, was interested in women only for propriety's sake. Breaking up with him had involved no heartbreak at all—just more dispiriting evidence that her lifelong fear of being undesired was rooted in some sort of objective truth.

On a Sunday afternoon last summer Maureen had taken a solo San Antonio bicycling excursion, following the course of the river past the old missions, sketching all the way, trying to conjure up something for the "Spirit of the Waters" piece besides the sprites and maidens and various genii that she knew would be the starting point of most of the other contestants. She wanted to depict the river rather than to airily personify it, and as she studied the almost-finished clay model now, she thought she just might have succeeded.

She had created four tablets, one for each side of a short column, that re-created in relief the things she had observed from her bicycle: noble cypress trunks, moldering Spanish aqueducts, swooping herons, and perching kingfishers. As a New Yorker who had lived in San Antonio for only six years, she believed she had rendered these elements with an outsider's reverence. The coziness of the little river, its spring-fed clarity, its exotic history of Indians and Spanish explorers and filibusters had unexpectedly stirred her. As she stared at the panels, she began to realize she had been drawn to something else as well: not just to the generative idea of "the Spirit of the Waters" but to the fetid over-abundance of the foliage, to the spectral menace of the cypress knees rising from the water and the loops of grapevine hanging from the trees like snares. Beneath the celebratory business was something darker, an homage to a mysterious and unwelcoming place, the place where her own compliant exile had begun and where her mother's life had come to its end.

She heard bootsteps echoing in the empty hallway outside: Vance Martindale was here. She glanced at her reflection in the window glass and quickly began covering the four panels with a moistened cloth.

"Caught you," he said when he swept into the room. "It must be something scandalous or you wouldn't be covering it up."

"It's something you may not have an opinion about until it's finished," she said. "And maybe not even then."

He took the crooked pipe out of his mouth with one hand and lifted his hat with the other as he stood there grinning at her. For all his natural bluster and confidence he was oddly shy with her, and she still did not quite know how to read him.

"I need to buy a new suit," he said.

"You certainly do." He was wearing a rumpled out-of-season white suit, the side pockets where he kept his pipe and keys and change bulging carelessly. The brim of his hat was floppy with abuse, and he needed a haircut. He was an inch shorter than she was, bowlegged from a boyhood of ranch work in South Texas, and had a proud hayseed grin, which Maureen suspected was a conscious foil for his brilliant mind.

The studied carelessness of his appearance had appealed to her from the first. It was maybe a little put on, but she didn't mind. They had been con-spicuously at ease around each other ever since they were introduced at the unveiling of her father's memorial to the defenders of the Alamo, a piece for which Vance had written a robust appreciation in the *Southwestern Historical Quarterly*. Since Vance lived in Austin and she in San Antonio, their relation-ship had existed mostly as a fitful flirtation. But he was coming to San Antonio more and more lately, always on the excuse of some bit of academic business or other. If it was true—as she hoped it was—that the real purpose of these visits was to see her, he had not yet brought himself to admit it.

"I'm serious," he said as she gathered up her things and locked her friend's studio. "I'm going to Joske's to buy a new suit and I need you to consult. I've decided to give those Philistines in the English Department an opportunity to take me seriously. But if I'm going to look my dashing best I need a woman's opinion."

They walked along the river, following it downtown. Vance said he was in town to interview a Mexican boy healer for a book he was writing on Texas folklore. His scholarly enthusiasms were rooted in the culture and history of his own state, which made him a low-paid eccentric in the English Department of the University of Texas. The donnish professors there, believing the youth of the state should be taught their Shakespeare and Gibbon, had no great affection for someone who insisted on teaching them cowboy songs or tall tales of the open range.

He was extremely interested to hear about Maureen's visit to Lamar Clayton's ranch, and kept pumping her for answers about things she had not thought to notice—how much acreage he had, what variety of cattle he ran, whether he employed any Mexican vaqueros as hands, what his brand looked like.

"I could write a whole book on brands alone," he said as they stepped down from the streetcar onto Alamo Plaza. "Cortés, for instance, right after the conquest wasted no time in branding his cattle with Latin crosses. Of course, you could go all the way back to the pharaohs if you wanted to—"

"But I don't really want to," Maureen chided.

He laughed and offered his arm as they crossed the plaza and it felt good to take it, to adopt the pose of a normal woman strolling with a winningly eccentric man, a man who might this very day finally kiss her, who might someday declare he loved her.

Cars were parked up and down the streets and around the perimeter of the little plaza in front of the Alamo. There were palm trees everywhere, a sight that had always been more alien to her than the strange revered ruin itself. In front of the open door of the old mission, a family was posing for a snapshot, the young children squirming and protesting as their perfectionist father stalked about with his camera, searching for the best angle. Other families were lined up behind them, waiting for their chance to record their presence at this great inexplicable shrine.

"Would it embarrass you if I tipped my hat?" Vance said as they walked past the ancient church.

"Yes, very much."

He tipped his hat to the Alamo anyway, to annoy her.

At the edge of the plaza they passed her father's monument to the heroes of the Alamo, four bronze figures crouched behind a palisade wall, Davy Crockett in the foreground urgently priming the pan of his flintlock rifle. The piece had taken three contentious years to complete. At first her father had to counter the charges that an Alamo statue could not be entrusted to anyone but a native Texan, and then he had to convince the city fathers that his conception—a dynamic tableau of frightened men in a desperate fight—would be far more memorable than the stolid portraiture they had originally envisioned. Then of course there had been the all-consuming work itself. Maureen had spent almost a year in research, gathering rifles and powder horns and haversacks from the attics of old pioneer families, consulting with historians about the structure of the palisade wall that Crockett and his men were said to have defended, examining moth-eaten frock coats and beaver hats from the period in order to present her father with authentic options for the clothing the figures would wear.

She paused now in their walk to stand before the statue for a moment, pretending to Vance to be concerned about a shiny spot on one of the defenders' knees where the patina was starting to rub off, but really to admire the feeling and skill that her father had brought to the work. Crockett was depicted as the middle-aged man he had been. There was a fatalistic resolution in his face as he stared down at his rifle. But one of the defenders next to him, the figure Rusty Holloway had posed for, was only a boy, and though his face was proportionately correct it seemed to be elongated with terror, almost as if the sculptor who prided himself on realism had found it necessary to make a concession to the modernist distortion he distrusted. It was the face of a young man who knew with certainty he was about to die, and in staring at it now Maureen could not help but think of Ben Clayton, and wonder if his last moments had been this fearful and frenetic.

"Strong work," Vance said. "Maybe a little too sincere for the twentieth century."

"My father has no use for artistic fashions."

"Nor do I. I write about cowboy songs, remember? Shall we get my suit?"

Joske's department store was at the end of the block. She accompanied Vance as he clomped rapidly on his booted feet through the women's department, past autumn suits and coats, the new blouses of georgette crepe. The end of the war had brought forth a flowering of goods everywhere, and nowhere more abundantly than on the display tables of the department stores. In passing, she fingered the material of a light-blue poplin suit, coveting it despite the certainty that it would not come close to draping as elegantly on her full figure as it did on the slender mannequin.

Vance was not so slender himself, but he was immune to that sort of self-consciousness. She stood there listening as he described exactly what he wanted to a sales clerk in the men's ready-to-wear department. Then he sought her opinion on various gray or plaid or brown worsteds that the clerk brought forth for him to try on.

Together they decided on a suitably rustic brown check—he said it reminded him of the color of a Nueces River cutbank—and while the tailor marked it for alterations Maureen wandered idly through the busy store, surveying the new belted men's suits, the wider lapels, the straw hats that were back in fashion after the war. She remembered the moment last year when she had been shopping with her mother and a somber bell had rung at noon and everyone—the customers, floorwalkers, elevator boys, cash girls with their hands full of bills—had stopped in mid-action. "May we all take a silent moment," the manager had proclaimed from the top of the stairs, "to pray for victory, and for our young men far away in France and on the seas."

The memory came back to her now with chastening force. During the war she had done volunteer work for the Lone Star Hospitality Service, serving doughnuts and passing out magazines at the train station to anxious, high-spirited soldiers being shipped overseas. Along with the rest of the customers that day in Joske's she had inclined her head and mumbled her prayers for the boys' safekeeping. But somehow the emotional gravity of the war itself had bypassed her. After that moment of silence, she had returned to the concerns of her daily life, fretting about her future, worrying about her mother's unhappiness in San Antonio, calculating her own odds for ever escaping into something resembling her own life.

When had that been? September? October? Could it have been the very day when Ben Clayton was killed in France?

In any case, it had not been long after that day when the city sirens finally wailed in honor of the armistice, when Maureen and her family had joined the rally in front of the Alamo, thinking that not just the war was over but the influenza crisis as well. And it had been that next morning that her mother had woken with a fever.

"I've got the rest of the day to kill," Vance said when he tracked her down. He was wearing his old suit and his proudly abused hat. "What shall we do?"

She was irritated at his assumption that she was perfectly free for the rest of the day as well, free to serve as his companion and verbal sparring partner. But she was not irritated enough to deny herself the rare pleasure of spending the day with a man of her own age, a man whose blustery sense of himself she rather liked. She dared not hope too aggressively that he was really interested in her, that he had something more in mind than a lively, bantering friendship. It was up to him to reveal himself.

She took his arm again as they walked out of the store and into the sunlight. She was still obscurely stirred up, still thinking about the war and the way its effects were coming to rest in her soul.

"Tell me about France," she said to Vance. "What was it like for you?"

"No tales of valor, I'm afraid. I might have had some to tell if our boat had been a little faster, but as it was we got there just before the armistice. All that training, and I didn't have the honor of firing even one volley at the evil Hun. But I very much admired the landscape—those hedges in Breton—and there were times when the battery was doing horse maneuvers and I was galloping up and down the column shouting orders that I felt like some exalted version of myself."

"So it was fun?"

"My shameful little secret. And thanks to the beneficence of the AEF I was able to stay on in Paris for three months studying at the Sorbonne. The finest time of my life. You should see Paris, Maureen."

She would very much like to see Paris, to live there as her father had when he was young, but she left this obvious fact unexpressed.

They went to the pictures. Vance found her a seat and then went out to the popcorn wagon in front of the theater, leaving her to read the deflating introductory title card on her own. "To these Women, and their pitiful hours of waiting for the love that never comes, we dedicate our story."

The picture was called *True Heart Susie*. It billed itself as the story of a "plain girl." But Lillian Gish wasn't plain, not in the way Maureen understood the word. She was a woman you would certainly notice on the street. Her figure was slim, her small face was soft in profile but radiant and beseeching when she looked straight at the camera or into the face of the smug and oblivious boyfriend whose college education she had financed by selling her family's cow.

It was a ridiculous story, of course, as so many of them were. Vance whispered wisecracks into her ear all the way through it. Maureen smiled at his wit, but she couldn't deny that every once in a while Lillian Gish's simpering emoting brushed against a chord of real feeling. Here was Susie in the pew, watching as the love of her life married another; saying nothing of her disappointment to anyone, just collapsing afterward all alone in theatrical sobs. Maureen recognized that element of uncomplaining muteness in herself. It was not pride, as it seemed to be with True Heart Susie—it was just a deflated acceptance, something she had had to fight against all her life.

It was night when they walked out. He suggested dinner. They strolled along Commerce Street all the way past the cathedral and on to Haymarket Plaza, where the Chili Queens had their booths and long picnic tables set up, and where the music from the mariachis blasted forth into the still night air. It was warm, like a summer night back home in New York. The plaza was filled with Mexican families and with Anglo visitors like themselves drawn by the easeful, exotic atmosphere of a more ancient Texas.

"I hear Rosa has the best enchiladas," Vance said, guiding her to one of the rude wooden tables. The trumpets of the mariachis sounded with such piercing force that it seemed to her that the colored lanterns overhead swayed in reaction to the notes muscling their way through the air. Vance had to shout over the music to give their order to Rosa, a sharp-featured, good-humored woman with an entrepreneurial demeanor.

As they ate their enchiladas, Maureen told Vance all about the Pawnee Scout and her father's fruitless expedition to Omaha to save it.

"What a horrifying ordeal," he said. She appreciated the way he could swerve from irony to full-hearted warmth and sincerity. "To lose something like that, something you've given your soul to. I can't think of a similar case, a statue lost before the sculptor's eyes. How is he managing?"

"He was in his studio when I left this morning. When he's in his studio he's usually happy enough."

"I admire your father," Vance said. "In fact, being a poor cowhand turned professor, I'm in awe of the very idea of being able to capture someone's likeness in sculpture."

"You needn't necessarily be in awe," she said. "A lot of it is just technical."

"I don't believe it."

"It's true. On a normal human body, the legs are half of the overall height. The average human figure is eight heads tall. The ear is just behind the midline of the vertical axis of the head, and so on. You can get a long way with just basic knowledge like that."

"But not all the way."

"No," she said.

"I'd be in awe of your work too if you wouldn't cover it up when you hear me coming."

"I have to. You're a natural critic."

"Not of you, Miss Gilheaney."

He looked at her across the picnic table, the paper lanterns swaying above them, the music swelling as the mariachis headed in their direction. If this were a picture like *True Heart Susie* it would be the moment he moved the greasy dinner plates out of the way and leaned across the table to kiss her. He wanted to, she could tell that. He held her eyes unashamedly, making her feel admired, appreciated, almost beautiful.

330

But he did not kiss her. Instead he distracted himself with a big grin, rose from the table, said, "Nos vamos, Señorita?" and led her across the plaza. They passed the mariachis, who were blasting forth some Mexican folk song at top volume, their singing punctuated with all sorts of yips and trills. Vance handed them a few coins as he and Maureen walked by.

"I'm pretty sure that was one of Pancho Villa's songs," he said as they waited for the streetcar to arrive. "I guess you could say it's an insult to Pershing, but after all, San Antonio is really Mexico, don't you think?"

It was still early, only eight o'clock, but he insisted on accompanying her home. As they rode down Roosevelt Avenue he begged her pardon and pulled out a pad and pencil to jot down some questions he'd just thought of for his interview tomorrow with the boy healer. He told her if he gained the confidence of the boy and his formidable mother he might be coming back to San Antonio two or three times this fall, and it would be a great delight if she would agree to see him again.

"Of course," she said.

"Good. I like you, you see. People tell me I'm rather a blowhard but I'm a good judge of character. And you have caught my attention, Miss Gilheaney."

He insisted on getting off the streetcar with her and walking her to her door. The house was dark.

"Your father isn't home?"

"He'll be in the studio. Out back."

"Well, I'll give you into his keeping, then."

He took her hand, squeezed it for a moment in both of his, and walked back in the night toward the streetcar stop. ★

Mary Guerrero Milligan

Mary Guerrero Milligan was raised on the Southside of San Antonio. She earned a BA in history and a MLS at the University of North Texas, where she was the first Latina to have her own radio program and was a founding member of that university's Mexican American Student Association. She has worked in university, public, and school libraries. A former chair of the south Texas region of the Texas Library Association, she has been TLA's "member of the month" and a member of the Texas Bluebonnet Award selection committee. She was also a member of the Texas State Library's "Task Force on Transforming Texas Libraries for the 21st Century." She has been the librarian at St. Luke's Episcopal School in San Antonio since 1986.

Working with her husband, Bryce Milligan, and poet Angela De Hoyos, she was a coeditor of two groundbreaking anthologies of Latina literature: *Daughters of the Fifth Sun: A Collection of Latina Fiction and Poetry* (Putnam/ Riverhead, 1995) and *¡Floricanto Sí! A Collection of Latina Poetry* (Penguin, 1998). Her stories, reviews, and essays have appeared in *Pax, Blue Mesa Review,* the *San Antonio Express-News*, and elsewhere, and have been included in the anthologies *Her Texas: Story, Image, Poem & Song* (Wings Press, 2015), *Entre Guadalupe y Malinche: Tejanas in Literature and Art* (University of Texas Press, 2015), and others.

This story takes place in the house of her grandmother, at 233 West Travis Street, one of the very few individual homes still standing in downtown San Antonio.

Lotería: La Rosa

GRANDMA'S HOUSE IS NOW A BARBERSHOP. I drive past wondering if I should take my son in for a haircut. I decide not to because he is very particular about his hair and this doesn't look like his kind of barbershop—a barbershop on a downtown San Antonio street with a red and white pole in front. And yet I haunt the house. My spirit has walked past the barbershop pole through the shop's walls past the hair clippings and scissors to my grandmother's kitchen.

I return again and again, as a little girl, to her kitchen. Standing in front of Grandma's kitchen table, I see her sitting with her two neighbors, lotería game boards in front of them. It looks like a grown-up birthday party, but Grandma says that Mexican bingo is *not* a children's game.

Playing for pennies, each player has three or four game boards and a handful of pinto beans for markers. The deck of cards is in the center of the table, face down. Grandma turns them over slowly, one at a time. I love looking at the different lotería cards. Each picture coloring my otherwise black-and-white memories. I stare at each beautiful picture, as real to me now as then. The brightly colored sandía still makes my mouth water, so perfectly ripe and juicy. Even now, whenever I pass a fruit vendor selling watermelons, I wonder if they could possibly be as sweet as la sandía in Grandma's kitchen.

I try to be patient as I wait for number forty-eight, la chalupa, to be called. Will she be called this game or will I have to sit through another until I see her again? Lovely and graceful in her narrow boat, I long to squeeze between her fruits and flowers and join her in her travels. Where is she going? Will she ever have room for me? Her card, more than any other, is alive for me. I can hear the gentle ripples as her boat glides through the water. Once when I touched her picture, my finger came away moist.

I often walk by the San Antonio River, and sometimes, when the water is especially calm, I can see the faint ripples of a narrow boat that has recently passed. Where is la chalupa going? Is anyone riding with her? Will she ever let me join her?

In Grandma's house, I am stripped of all that time has given me, able to revisit my earliest memories. Today I am waiting for a new lotería game to begin. It is a hot, sticky afternoon, but Grandma is refreshed from her nap and ready for a long session of bingo. Anticipation makes everyone silent. Except for the steady hum from the fan in the corner and the shuffling of the cards, the room is quiet and still. Pete in his tank-top undershirt and his wife Andréa in her brown print house dress watch my Grandmother carefully as she shuffles the cards—once, twice, three times. Placing the cards face down in the middle of the table signals the start of a new game.

The first card called is:

La Rosa

Waking up heavy with sleep in my grandmother's bedroom, I hear the sound of bells. The room is cold, but I am warm deep beneath the covers. The house is dark, except for two candles flickering on the altar in the next room. I can see Grandma's silhouette. She is kneeling in front of the candles, as still as her statues on the altar. While the shadows dance around the altar, I begin to doze, when I again hear the sounds that woke me up.

I know what it is: clip clop clip clop jingle jingle jingle. Wide awake, I throw off the covers, my heart pounding with excitement. "Quién viene? Santa Claus? Con reindeer?" Christmas Day is almost two weeks away, and I don't understand how this can be happening. Shivering with cold, I try to see out the window by the bed. The window is foggy from the cold, and I wipe it with my sleeve, making my arm feel wet and chilled, but I don't care. I will see Santa tonight.

"No, no, mija. Son los caballeros. Van a cantarle a la Virgen," answers my grandmother. Now that I have rubbed the mist from the window, I can see the horses clearly. Two rows of black and silver riders wearing huge sombreros ride slowly past us carrying guitars and trumpets. I hear their soft strumming intermingled with the horse hooves' ringing clatter against the paved street.

As the riders shrink into the night, Grandma explains that today is the day we sing las Mañanitas a la Virgen de Guadalupe. Before sunrise the riders will serenade la Virgen in front of the church. She tells me how special today is for la familia in Mexico. As I begin to get sleepy, I listen to her stories about visiting la Virgen with candles and roses. She reminds me that spring will soon be here and that her garden will be filled with many beautiful roses and, if I want and if I am good, I may choose any of her roses to give to la Virgen and to my teacher at school. Under the covers again, I drift back to sleep as the dawn begins to creep behind the office buildings, and the church bells begin to ring. I think about the rose bushes sleeping outside the bedroom window that will soon be filled with roses and I am not disappointed that it is still almost two weeks until Christmas.

The roses are long gone, yet their scent fills my mind. I walk through her garden, down her street, trying to recapture my lifeblood, but I stand in the middle of a parking lot. I am a barbershop ghost, searching.

Downtown was Grandma's neighborhood. We walked everywhere: to her work at El Teatro Alameda, to the Cathedral, to eat at El Bohemio, to visit the local curandera or to shop at El Mercado. An impatient walker, she refused to acknowledge traffic lights, racing across streets. She'd never wait and would walk against the light regardless of the traffic. I'd ask her why we were risking our lives. She would point to the red "DON'T WALK" and remind me in Spanish, "Yo soy Mexicana y . . . I—don't—read—English."

On bad weather days we'd take the Shopper's Special. Paying a nickel, we'd ride the slow-moving bus as it crawled its way through town. It was entertaining to listen to the passengers on the crowded ride: fast-talking viejitas, loud talking muchachos, English, Spanish, crying babies, giggling school girls in their Catholic school uniforms. And as soon as we were off the bus, Grandma would argue about how much faster it would have been to walk.

I loved our walks together. Grandma was not a silent walker. She talked as fast as she walked. No light conversations or playful chatter; instead, a steady catechism about the way I should live my life. While I explored her neighborhood, she'd explore my heart. Even now the noise, the color, the smell of downtown take me back to those walks.

Another cold, early morning. It is a little after sunrise when we enter El Bohemio. My mother and I have joined Grandma an hour earlier to help her finish cleaning the office buildings across the street. Now all three of us are ready for breakfast. The aromas remind me of my hunger while the mariachi music from the jukebox keeps me awake.

This morning Chorte is our waiter. He is my favorite as well as a friend of my grandmother. With an easy smile and a gentle manner, he shares his daily story with us. They are usually funny, and I eagerly await his new tale. I order my regular El Bohemio breakfast: one barbacoa taco and one chorizo con huevo taco. As we wait for our tacos, we sip our coffee. I drink some of Grandma's coffee from her small glass creamer. She always drinks sugary coffee with lots of milk. It is warm and sweet.

But this morning I don't like Chorte's story. It's about catching a pigeon in the park for last night's supper and I can't believe any of it. That he was able to catch it, or that he would want to or that he, my dear friend, could ever do such a thing. I try not to cry or show the pain I feel inside, but Grandma senses it and doesn't approve. After he leaves, Grandma is angry with me. She points out that the pigeons in the park are food to him, not pets, and that in Mexico where she and Chorte are from, people sometimes have to do worse. But what is worse than eating the park pigeons that come to you because you will feed them? She reminds me that barbacoa is a cow and chorizo is a pig and that farmers feed their animals lovingly right up to the time of their slaughter.

We finally get our tacos and now I am mad at Grandma for telling me that my wonderful breakfast might be some little girl's pet so I begin to eat my taco like a gringa. I take big bites right down the middle of the taco, eating it like a sandwich until it is split in half. Grandma watches me with growing displeasure. Telling me that I am eating it all wrong, she shows me the Mexicana way. She squeezes one end tight with her fingers to keep the juices in and bites from the opposite end. I laugh to myself as she demonstrates the proper way.

I try to retrace our walks: to the Cathedral, El Bohemio, back to her home. But like a puzzle with missing pieces, the picture is incomplete. Standing in front of her bedroom window, amid the long-dead rose bushes, I knock against her window, hoping to wake her up, but my hand goes through the wall. ★

ROBERT FLYNN

Robert Lopez Flynn is a professor emeritus, Trinity University, where he was a much beloved professor of English and creative writing for nearly forty years. Considered one of San Antonio's most important writers, he has always been generous of time and talent with the city's younger writers. His late wife, Jean, was the author of several historical works for children.

Flynn is the author of numerous books, including nine novels, among them *North To Yesterday* (Knopf, 1967), *In the House of the Lord* (Knopf, 1969), *The Sounds of Rescue, The Signs of Hope* (Knopf, 1970, TCU Press, 1988), and *Wanderer Springs* (TCU Press, 1987). He is also the author of a two-part documentary, *A Cowboy Legacy* (ABC-TV); a nonfiction narrative, *A Personal War in Vietnam* (Texas A&M, 1989); an oral history, *When I Was Just Your Age* (University of North Texas Press, 1992); and several collections of stories and essays. His critical study/philosophical rumination, *Lawful Abuse: How the Century of the Child Became the Century of the Corporation* was published by Wings Press in 2013. *Burying the Farm: A Memoir of Chillicothe, Texas,* was published as a limited edition, fine press chapbook (Wings Press, 2008). His not-for-normal-Sunday-School study of how the Bible got to be the way it is *Holy Literary License: The Almighty Publisher Chooses Fallible Mortals to Write, Edit, and Translate GodStory* (Wings, 2016).

North to Yesterday received awards from the Texas Institute of Letters and the National Cowboy Hall of Fame, and was named one of the Best Books of the Year by the *New York Times*. (It is also the funniest anti-cowboy novel ever written.) *Seasonal Rain* won the Texas Literary Festival Award. *Wanderer Springs* received a Spur Award from Western Writers of America. The list of awards is considerable. Flynn's work has been translated into a dozen languages. Flynn is a member (and past president) of The Texas Institute of Letters, The Writers Guild of America, Marine Corps Combat Correspondents, and PEN. In 1998, he received the Distinguished Achievement Award from the Texas Institute of Letters.

from *Wanderer Springs*

Rebecca answered the telephone when I called. 'Hi, Dad, just a minute," she said. "Hello, Dad," Maggie said, picking up the other telephone. "Can you hold on for a second?" I waited while Rebecca got her nail file and Maggie got a soft drink from the refrigerator. If you do not like waiting, you should not have children.

I told the girls I was going to Wanderer Springs and asked if they could go with me. Neither could. Maggie had a paper that was due, and Rebecca had a date to a football game and the most important party of the year after the game. Had the arrangements been reversed they both would have gone. Rebecca would have put off a paper as quickly as Maggie would have broken a date.

"I don't want to go and I'd really like someone to go with me," I pleaded.

"Why do you have to go if you don't want to go?" Rebecca asked. Rebecca, who had spent ten of her twenty years in Wanderer Springs, could not imagine that kind of belonging. Rebecca was whoever she wanted to be and if she belonged any place it was on the campus. When she came to San Antonio she tried to see everyone she knew, told delightful tales about weird professors, wild parties, and all the strange and bewildering people she knew, and she was gone. Rebecca was a butterfly, giving beauty and joy wherever she went but never lighting for long.

Maggie was a stray dog, radiating affection, saying little, happy to be with people she loved. She stood beside her grandmother in the kitchen listening to Mama talk of the mysteries of cooking and old age. She helped Rosa set the table and listened to the heartaches of husband and children. She sat on the porch with Gilbert, who said nothing. She talked to Manuel about the hurt and anger of broken dreams.

Rebecca ran through life tasting everything. Maggie absorbed. Rebecca was half past tomorrow; Maggie was half past yesterday. She had not cut her ties to any place. "Why do you have to go?" she asked, recognizing the irrelevance of Becky's conditional clause—if you don't want to.

I was going back for the reason man always returns—to find something he has lost. "Jesse Tooley died."

"Is that the woman who didn't hear her husband die in the yard?" Rebecca asked. With her lawyer's mind, Rebecca went for the jugular. Maggie would have asked if that was the woman who went deaf.

"Did I know her?" Maggie asked.

"I don't think so," I lied.

"Why did you say you had to go?" Rebecca asked. Maggie would never repeat a question I had avoided answering. Rebecca, like her mother, liked precision. Maggie took after me, believing that not everything had to be underlined.

"It's just something I have to do," I said. A mistake I had to make.

"How long are you going to be gone?" Maggie asked.

"Just a few days. I'll see you on the way back."

"How is Abuela?" asked Maggie, who insisted on being recognized as part Mexican. Rebecca seemed not to care either way.

"Your grandmother seems okay, but Rosa is worried about her."

"What else is new?" Rebecca asked. Although they lived in the same house, Rosa called her mother from work every day. Mama had given life to Rosa. It was a debt for which there was no forgiveness.

We talked about Rosa, who spent every day cleaning houses in Alamo Heights and Olmos Park, and her husband Gilbert, who was embarrassed that his wife worked as a maid. Especially when he was drinking. After Papa died, Gilbert should have been the head of the family and he tried, but Manuel was a talker. Manuel, Papa's youngest child, owned three or four cars, all of them sporting University of Texas decals and NOWHERE BUT SAN ANTONIO bumper stickers. Manuel never traded in a car, he gave it to a relative. Almost everyone in the family had one of Manuel's cars.

"Tío Manuel was here yesterday," Maggie said. Rebecca would not have mentioned it. Manuel had been arrested on drug charges when he lived in Wanderer Springs. The charges had been dropped and Manuel had become a successful and powerful man without seeming to work. "He took us to dinner." Manuel had given them stereos and color television sets and had offered them a car which I would not permit them to accept.

"What's Manuel doing these days?" I had reached the age where I had to ask my children to interpret for me the behavior of others, but I was not so much out of touch as out of patience.

Rebecca said nothing because she was a future lawyer. Maggie said nothing because she was protective toward her uncle, and because Manuel and I were no longer friends. "How is he doing?" I amended the question.

"Okay," Maggie said. "He said Gloria was already reading and she isn't six yet. She's going to be a doctor. Maria is still going to be an astronaut."

"Isn't anyone going to be a school teacher?"

"Poor Dad. How did you get in this family?" Rebecca asked.

"Your mother invited me," I said.

Although I hadn't been to Wanderer Springs in ten years, at one time the road had been the strongest cord in our lives, connecting us to Papa's illness, Rosa and Gilbert's fights, Manuel's anger. We had driven the road often, Delores and I, taking the children to visit their grandparents—going to San Antonio for Christmas with the car loaded with presents and Delores and the girls singing carols, returning home, the car filled with the things Delores could not get in Wanderer Springs, masa, corn shucks, a hog's head.

Except for Manuel, Delores's family did not visit us in Wanderer Springs. So that Delores would have some help when Rebecca was born, I had gone to San Antonio to get Rosa, who cleaned houses in Alamo Heights but refused to work in the far north suburbs of Castle Hills and Shavano Park. It was too far from the heart of San Antonio. There was too much space, too much room between houses; it was too far from stores and crowds. On the road to Delores in Wanderer Springs, Rosa was troubled by the distance, the emptiness. "How do you know where you are?" she asked. I had laughed. We did not identify with ice houses, or bus stops, or street corners. We identified with the land: the Tooley Place, Earl's Lake.

Rosa was homesick before we got to Wanderer Springs. She cried for Mama, Gilbert, her children, for crowds and noise. "Mama needs me," she said. After two days I put her on the bus that would return her to San Antonio.

After I got out of the army I had enrolled at a small state college near San Antonio because it had a reputation for being easy—I wasn't looking for a challenge—and because it was small, in a small town, and a long way from

Wanderer Springs. I had always known I would go to college. It was one of those things I understood without being told.

Delores said she had never thought of going to college until a high school teacher said, "Of course you're going to college. What excuse do you have for not going to college?" When Delores explained that her family had no money, the teacher said, "Let's get you a scholarship."

Even with her scholarship Delores had to convince her family. She was going to be the first of her family to graduate from high school and the thought of college was terrifying. Every one of them had told me the story of the day Delores came home and said she wanted to go to college.

"College," Mama said, as though she were saying the word for the first time. Mama had an enormous capacity for sharing the pains and joys of her children, smothering their tears and giggles in her ample bosom. What she clutched to her bosom now was emptiness. She had been part of every laugh, every sniffle, every heartbreak. College was beyond her understanding, beyond her sharing. Mama's broad, sensitive face was clouded with uncertainty and fear. "You should help your brother. Manuel should go to college and make a teacher." She said, "teeshur" in a soft, reverential way. Next to priest, teacher was the holiest word she knew.

"What do you want to go to college for?" Rosa asked. Everyone thought Rosa, with the long aristocratic face, light skin, and proud Spanish mouth, was the pretty one, the one who was meant to get married and have babies. In high school Rosa had worn a freshly ironed dress every day. She had dropped out of school to marry Gilbert, a war hero, and now she had two children, and a job cleaning and ironing in Alamo Heights. "Do you think college will teach you how to have kids?"

Gilbert, a big man whose dark handsome face was marred with scars on his eyebrow, his mouth, and his chin from fighting in ice houses when he was drunk, was so shy when sober as to be inarticulate. "Delores," he began, his face darkening with embarrassment, his eyes darting about as he searched for words. "Delores is smart."

"You going to be a nun?" Manuel asked. Manuel was a serious child who made As in school and read books at home until his mother told him to go outside and play.

"What do you know about it?" Rosa asked Gilbert. "You didn't even go to high school."

"I got a—a," Gilbert stuttered. Gilbert had passed the high school G.E.D. while in the Marines.

"You got a head for fighting, that's what you got," Rosa said. During the week Gilbert's slow tongue brought him scorn, but alcohol freed Gilbert from the anger and hurt and on the weekends he was the terror of the ice houses, and he took no abuse from Rosa.

"Delores thinks she is too good to get married and have babies," Rosa said.

"Delores wants babies," Mama said, horrified, as though Rosa had said Delores was lesbian.

"Delores wants—" Gilbert began tentatively.

"You don't know nothing about it," Rosa said.

"No fighting," Papa said. Papa was not as tall as Gilbert but he was strong. He had been the strongest man in Crystal City when he took his young bride and left the stoop labor of the fields to lift bags of cement and concrete forms in San Antonio. He sought the hardest jobs because they were the easiest to get, spoke English at work to get ahead, and English at home so that his children would have an advantage at school. Every year he found it more difficult to compete for jobs with younger men.

Papa was beginning to stoop and nagging pain had weakened his confidence and enthusiasm, but Papa was a proud man, too proud to admit that sometimes his muscles ached so that he had to drink alcohol in order to sleep. In his home Papa was boss. "College is expensive," he said. Papa, who had once promised his bride that their children could do anything, had learned to be cautious.

"I have a scholarship," Delores said. "I can get a campus job. I can pay my own way."

Papa studied the strong hands that were beginning to knot with arthritis. "Delores can go to college now, and when Manuel is ready, she can help him," he declared.

Mama cried and hugged Manuel and kissed his forehead as though he were leaving for college that day. Manuel beamed at Delores. Manuel wanted to go to college and now Delores could go too. Gilbert patted Delores on the back, struggling for words. Rosa hugged Papa. "I won't leave you Papa," she said.

Delores got a job in the college library and was in one of my classes, but I didn't speak to her. It wasn't that I was prejudiced against Mexicans. I was fearful of anything that was strange. Not only was she Mexican, she was from the city.

I listened to others talk about her. "Hot tamale," the frat men said, "and she doesn't wear too much makeup." "Mexican but she doesn't overdress," said the sorority sisters. I sat behind her in class. I studied in the library so I could watch her shelve books or smile at those who needed help.

There was a hint of the elegant savage about her—proud, graceful carriage, and when she stood on tiptoe to reach the top shelves, something caught in my throat. She was in the freedom of her youth before the knowledge of her sex laid its burden upon her. She had brown skin, and large dark eyes that flashed. Sometimes her eyes turned to me and I turned my attention to my books.

One day in Texas history she said, "Unless you're Mexican you can't understand what it's like to have a Ranger knock open your door and say, 'You that Meskin that's been causing trouble?'"

I think the other students had been as astounded as I. Even the professor was shocked. The Rangers were more than just historical heroes, they were religious giants of the Old Testament order with a pistol-pointing, "Thou art the man" righteousness. At the height of their glory they weren't law enforcement officers, they were dispensers of justice.

It was one of the things that I, along with the class and the professor, knew without knowing that we knew, until Delores brought it to our attention. No one in the class thanked her for it. Some defended the Rangers, some attacked the Mexicans. A young man from Louisiana yelled, "If you don't like the way we do things go back where you came from." Someone asked, "Why is she taking Texas history?" Mexicans, no matter where they were born, were outsiders. Why would they be interested in our history?

Delores might have forever remained a stranger had she not been attacked by the class. At that moment she became flesh and blood to me. One of "us." I knew what it was like to go from tacit acceptance to personal rejection. I apologized to her for the class. For not coming to her defense. I expected her to be humiliated.

"I'm Mexican so they say 'dumb Mexican,'" she said, finding the incident amusing. "If I weren't they'd say 'dumb broad.'" She was four years younger than I, had never been out of the state of Texas, knew little of what life had to offer but much of what it might require. All my life I had sought approval; Delores didn't expect it. Delores feared no one. I wanted her on my side.

I don't know at what point wanting her friendship, wanting her acceptance turned to wanting her love. As I had never known a Mexican American, I was forced to use the popular media as my guide to dating a Chicana at a time when misrepresentation had become an art form. Every night for a week I took Delores to a bar that featured Lone Star and loud guitars, and then parked outside her dorm. I wasn't trying to seduce her; I didn't think that possible. I wanted to be as close to her, to touch as much of her, to know as much of her as I could. It resembled wrestling. Delores said she wasn't going to see me any more.

"I thought you liked this."

"I hate this. I hate beer. I hate loud music. I hate it when people can't talk, when people aren't who they say the are."

I didn't know what she was talking about. "Who do you want me to be?"

"Be yourself. Is this what you do with your friends?"

I wasn't trying to impress my friends, and none was from the city. My friends sat under a tree and threw rocks in the river. We lay under the stars. We walked along country roads. Sometimes we talked.

"Do that with me," Delores said.

I took her to the cemetery, I'm not sure why. We walked among the graves and talked about the stories on the tombstones—those who had died young, those born in another state, another country, those whose lives were so entwined they shared a common stone. "You're fun to be with," she said. I was pleased and surprised. I had always been a sidekick.

We went swimming in the Guadalupe River and had a picnic on a small gravel island. I told her about Wanderer Springs and Dad living alone, hoping I would return, and how I wasn't sure I wanted to go back, and how I wanted to be a hero, and the only way was football and war. I told her that nothing I did could change the way the town felt about me.

Delores talked about Papa's pride and pain, about Mama's love and fear, about Rosa who wanted to be spoiled by love, and Gilbert who had failed her by not being the hero she thought she had married. In Korea he had been a Marine. In San Antonio he was a Mexican. Gilbert could not admit his failure, could not ask Rosa's forgiveness and punished her for not understanding. She talked about Manuel who was told in school that any boy could be president of the United States and was told out of school they did not mean him.

As she talked I listened to the music of her voice. Her words were soft with a strange tinkly intonation. Her lips slid effortlessly, wonderously over her teeth, and her silky eyelids slowly closed. I loved her. Sometimes I wonder if any human being knows what love is. Sometimes I think I recognize love only in retrospect, but at that moment I knew. And when I tried to get close to her, to touch her, to know her, to take her unto myself, it was not like wrestling, it was like sliding into myself and discovering who I was meant to be.

How does a man dare ask a woman to give up everything for him? That's what I asked Delores, not knowing what I was asking, not realizing how much I was asking her to give up. Her everything didn't seem like much to me. "Marry me," I said.

She shook her head and closed her eyes. "We're too different." I thought she meant our complexions, and I laughed at her. I teased her. I enumerated my prospects. She smiled. She kissed me. "I love you," she said, "But we are too different."

I went to San Antonio to meet Delores's family and prove that I was not prejudiced. Mama met us on the porch, crying into her apron. Gilbert sat on the porch drinking a beer which he lifted in greeting. Rosa, her children hiding in her skirt, stood beside Mama, arms spread, waiting to hug and kiss us both. Manuel stood at one side, waiting to be noticed. Papa waited at the door with dignity, and everyone crowded around to see him welcome me into his house.

I stayed with them, crowded as we were, in the house on Buena Vista. It wasn't just the house that was crowded—the streets were filled with people, the neighborhood, the corner grocery store. When Mama cooked, everyone crowded into the kitchen. When Papa went into the living room, everyone crowded into the living room. When Delores and I went into the back yard to talk, everyone followed.

The Hinojosas were courteous, friendly, generous. I was an honored guest but I was not one of them. When I looked at Delores I could see it in her eyes. I was not family. I thought it was the color of my eyes, the inflection of my words, the differences that made us charming or dull. It was years before I realized it was the color of strange practices, of unfamiliar places.

"Are you going to take Delores away?" Manuel asked.

He was so serious I laughed. I thought Delores would be embarrassed, that she would change the subject. She waited with the others for my answer. Behind her eyes I could see fear nibbling like mice behind a glass window. "Delores will always be your sister no matter who she marries or where she lives," I said.

Not even Delores thought I had answered the question.

I thought I had performed splendidly in my role of winsome suitor. I had showed surprise and delight at Mama's cooking, teased Delores about her tortillas, complimented Rosa on her house cleaning, helped Manuel with a school paper, gone to the ice house where I persuaded Gilbert to ignore a slight and come home for supper, and added just the right touch of modesty when telling Papa that I would soon graduate from college, that I could always get a job teaching, and that I would someday inherit a farm in northwest Texas. When we got back to school Delores told me she couldn't see me any more. "You are so funny," she said. "I will want you too much and I can't have you."

I promised to change. I promised to live in San Antonio, on Buena Vista Street, in the same house with Mama and Papa, Gilbert and Rosa, and Manuel. Delores closed her eyes and shook her head as though I was deliberately stupid. I was running out of time; I was going to graduate in a few months. I didn't have a trump so I played a wild card. I persuaded Delores to meet my family although I was afraid meeting Dad would convince her how different we really were. ★

Nan Cuba

Nan Cuba has been a mainstay of the San Antonio literary community for many years. She has taught at every level, and is now the writer-in-residence at Our Lady of the Lake University—the "Gem of the west side"—where she founded the MA/MFA Program in Literature, Creative Writing, and Social Justice. In the 1980s she founded Gemini Ink, a nonprofit literary center, which she directed for several years until she "retired to teach" in 2003.

Cuba is the author of *Body and Bread* (Engine Books, 2013), which received the PEN Southwest Award in Fiction and the Texas Institute of Letters Steven Turner Award for Best Work of First Fiction; it was also listed as one of "Ten Titles to Pick Up Now" in *O, Oprah's Magazine*, was a "Summer Books" choice from *Huffington Post*, and the *San Antonio Express-News* called it one of the "Best Books of 2013."

Her story, "Watching Alice Watch," was one of the Million Writers Award Notable Stories (*storySouth*), and "When Horses Fly" won the George Nixon Creative Writing Award for Best Prose from the Conference of College Teachers of English. As an investigative journalist, she reported on the causes of extraordinary violence in *LIFE*, *Third Coast*, and *D Magazine*. Cuba coedited *Art at our Doorstep: San Antonio Writers and Artists* (Trinity University Press, 2008). Other work has appeared in *Antioch Review, Harvard Review, Columbia, Chicago Tribune's Printer's Row*, and elsewhere. She has received a Dobie-Paisano Fellowship (Texas Institute of Letters and the University of Texas), an artist residency at Fundación Valparaiso in Spain, and was a finalist for the Humanities Texas Award for Individual Achievement.

Patriotism

Harriet was so mad, she thought she'd explode. She sat in front of the fireplace reading the paper. The elections were only a month away, and she was scared. How did her country get in this mess? Even though Gerald was still asleep, she talked as though he were sitting beside her.

"Oh, God," she said, crumpling the paper into her lap. She sipped coffee, leaned back, closed her eyes, pressed her lids. "What's wrong with those assholes in Congress? The more they scream, the less they get done." Somebody, she thought, should *do* something.

One article described a local rally. The accompanying picture, she noticed, showed people carrying signs with hideous messages and grotesque cartoon images. "Self-righteous radicals," she grumbled. She hit the photo with the back of her hand. If only she could knock some sense into them. *If only they'd listen.*

She jerked past the front page, snapping the paper into place. She read more headlines: Mexico's drug wars, kidnappings, journalists murdered. Iran could launch a nuclear attack. Palestine and Israel, infinite hatred. Oh no, a baby abandoned in an airplane bathroom. *Suffering, stupidity, violence*, but what could one person do? Candidates promised to fix everything before elections. Then did nothing. Or worse, they created bigger problems. Maybe she should write her own manifesto.

"Why do you read that crap?" Gerald said, his house shoes slapping on his way to the kitchen. "It only makes you crazy."

"Oh, come on. Can't you see that's exactly what's wrong?" She smiled, trying not to sound upset.

He kept walking.

"Smart people like you doing nothing." She followed after him. "Don't you care about what's happening to your country?"

"Get a grip," Gerald said, scratching his head, yawning. "It's too early."

"Say some new law made it *illegal* to complain about the government?" She rubbed his arm. "Who'd be crazy then, huh?"

"You're right," he said. "I'd probably kill somebody." He opened the refrigerator then closed it. "I can't do this every morning, Cheryl. I've got *real* problems." He started back toward the bedroom.

She tugged on his robe belt. "Wait a minute. You agree with *them*, don't you?" No wonder he refused to talk about the election. Why had it taken her so long to figure this out? She'd suspected but was afraid to admit they saw things so differently. She'd told herself he wasn't into politics. How could a person as good as Gerald be so wrong? It broke her heart to think he could believe such lies. But at least, *he* could be reasoned with. If she couldn't convince him, how could she talk to anybody? Persuading him would be a first step. She might not be able to change Congress, but she could sure help one voter see the truth.

"You don't want to do this." Gerald pried her fingers loose. "Please."

"I know you don't mean to, but you're hurting this country. Why can't you see that?"

"I love you, Cheryl. That's why I'm not having this conversation." He patted her shoulder. "Just let it go, okay?" He turned, his back retreating toward their bedroom.

She still felt the taps of his hand, placating. Like she was a child or, worse, a pet cat. Infuriating! "You can't really love me," she called. "You don't even know me." She understood that it was Gerald, but that body moving back down the hall didn't look like the man she'd lived with since they were kids. A catch in the stride, something different.

That night, when Gerald came home, they didn't speak. She interpreted his silence as condescension. He hunkered over his dinner plate, watching an old Bogart movie on TV. "Thanks, baby," he said afterward, pecking her on the forehead. She watched him put his greasy plate, glass, and silverware in the dishwasher. *Great*, she thought. She'd have to take them out, rinse and reload them. She carried the rest of the dishes to the kitchen, leaving everything in the sink. She tried to remember why she'd married him. Hot water flowed until steam fogged the window. *He could've been one of those saps in the photo at that rally. He'd probably carry a stupid sign, shove his arm in the air. He'd be shouting, his mouth wide open, its fleshy inside on display.* She filled the dishwasher then bleached the counter. *What if nothing could get through?*

She waited until he'd been asleep for an hour. While she brushed her teeth and changed clothes, his snoring rattled like a drum roll. Each breath's cadence brought her closer to tears. She stood over him, panting, dizzy, his smoker's breath an insult. She couldn't stand it any longer. *What's left when a person won't listen?* ★

GEOFF RIPS

Geoff Rips was born and raised in San Antonio, Texas. He is a former editor of the *Texas Observer* and has been a Soros Open Society Institute Fellow. He worked as the Freedom-to-Write Committee coordinator for PEN American Center and was the principal author of its report, *UnAmerican Activities* (City Lights Books, 1981). His 2008 novel, *The Truth*, from which this excerpt is taken, received the AWP (Association of Writers & Writing Programs) Award for the Novel. *The Truth* is an almost mythic work that relates the inner life of Chuy Pingarrón, a palsied hunchback who lives in a less-than-premium brothel amid a cast of oddly philosophical misfits. Rips is also the author of a collection of poetry, *The Calculus of Falling Bodies* (Wings Press, 2015).

Rips has worked with community organizations along the Texas/Mexico border to bring water and wastewater services to border colonias. He currently works for Texas Rio Grande Legal Aid. He is a member of the Texas Institute of Letters and PEN American Center and has published poetry, fiction, and journalism in various journals and newspapers over the years. He lives in Austin, Texas, with his wife, Nancy Maniscalco.

I EXPLAIN MYSELF

CALL ME CHUY. CHUY TESTIMONIO DE FELÍZ PINGARRÓN. I am the only known son of my mother, who did not refuse to claim me in the last minutes of her deathbed. And I'm not the only son, I'll wager on my soul, of my father who will wander faceless through the dark rooms of eternity. They also call me son of old Ofelia. They also call me worse than a cockroach. They also call me third post from the right. They call me anything they want. I don't hear them. They don't know me. They don't even know themselves, the way they come here willing to pay a woman to tell them not who they are but who they want to be. I can see it as I sit here on the front porch as they walk by me going into the house, refusing to see me, as if I were the last doubt they may have about themselves. As if we might have something in common. I see all those shoes and all those pairs of khaki pants with bulging flies that can barely contain their cargo. I see the way they walk up on the front porch already inclined in the angle used for falling into bed. And when they walk out the front door, I see the light breezes blowing through the new looseness of their pants. Some will stop here beside me on the way out to ask if my back is feeling better, just like that was the reason they came here in the first place—just to inquire about my health. And I will tell them, talking to their belts, No, the diseases of my back will never be improved. And to do this I have to point my knees toward the mimosa tree growing on the west side of the house. Then it will follow, through the painful course of the wandering pilgrimage of my spine, that my shoulders will be turned as if to face the approach of someone walking up the front porch from the street and my head will then be turned to confront the belt buckle that has just walked out the front door holding its precious vacuum. It's been like this for more than fifty years, the eternal wandering of my spine. And for the last six years or more there has also been the palsy, especially in the shaking of my left hand and the occasional refusal of my left leg to walk with its brother on the right. It's not so bad, this shaking. The only thing is when I go to take a piss, sometimes the palsy starts. That's when my water sprinkles everything except the target it's supposed to hit, in the same way that we often do something thinking it will lead somewhere and the place it leads is everywhere except the place we had in mind. That's when I come out of the bathroom looking like I'd just fallen into the sewer, and the women come up to me and say, So, Chuy, now you let the dogs piss on you. And I tell them, I don't need anyone else, not even dogs, for that.

But they're good to me, these women. When it's rainy weather a new spirit feeds into the twisting of my spine so that I feel like my backbone is no longer mine but instead has become a vine that carries me on its cruel winding through the trellis of my ribs and muscles. When it's rainy weather and my spine goes curling after raindrops, the women here take good care of me. Especially Eufamia. Especially Chabela. Especially Angelita famous for her hands. They call me to their beds without my asking for it. And then they take the oils containing herbs that were prescribed for me long ago and rub these oils all along the twisted spiral of my body—and I am forced to say spiral because at these times I can no longer be said to have a front and a back with which to face and leave the world. And sometimes they go on for hours, and they say it brings them luck to rub a body that is so much like the twisted chains of life.

And sometimes they do me other favors, though I don't require them so much anymore. But even a man who spends his life sitting on the front porch of a whorehouse has his desires. In the old days, when business was slow or they were on their day off, they used to invite me up to their beds, and in those days it was not uncommon for two or three to have me at one time because the twisting of my back was not without its compensations. And in my later years, the Midwife would tell me to go to bed with some of the newer women who were hesitating about some of the things they were asked to do in the course of an evening's work. She knew I could accommodate her. She told them, Chuy is the test for you. He is as far as you will ever need to go. If you have a customer who is more perverse than Chuy, then we throw him out. He's the standard of perversion that we use here to measure how far a girl must go. Worse than Chuy, then hasta nunca. This is what she says.

But to defend myself, I must say that what they call my perversions are nothing more than the natural conclusions of my own infirmities. And in these last years, I am not called to bed so much anyway. It's mostly just to rub my back or to hear me tell a story about the old days at this place. Except for Angelita, who calls me to her when she sees I have the palsy. She has even gotten me inside her and then tried certain tricks to get the palsy started. And sometimes it comes and sometimes it doesn't. It's hard to say whether it's her tricks that bring it on. She says she's never felt such excitement as when my palsy shakes her from inside. She says it must be what an earthquake feels like to a town. She is very kind. In general, I don't like the palsy. But when I am in Angelita's arms, I will suffer anything.

But I don't want to talk about myself. Who gives a shit about a man who can't look into the face of the woman he's making love to? A man so twisted that his words of love must be whispered to a wall while he looks for himself inside a woman. A man who, therefore, has come to look on walls with certain feelings of tenderness and holds a special affection for certain dark corners only a spider could love and certain dampness in the plaster that can make his flesh rise. Who cares about a man like that? Let him cry for mercy to the bricks. Let him tell his story to the baseboards of the hall. Let him grow so old and forgetful that there will be no record of him, not even in his own memory. I know that's what they say. So I won't talk about myself. Why do I want to leave a mark the way the dogs write their names in piss on every fence post and tree?

Besides, what is this life anyway? You come into this life and a few minutes later you walk out again. And either you have a stain on the inside of your pants or you leave a stain on someone else's bed or you may not have had it in you to bring about a stain at all. That's all life is—the buildup of desires until they're exploded, the way your pants fall off your bones one day in order to tell you that the next time they're zipped up you will be dead and in your coffin. So why should I bother to tell you about myself? It doesn't make a difference. But I will tell you some things. Not about myself but about the other people. Not because they make a difference either, but because it helps me get through all the minutes of my life here on this earth.

So I won't talk about myself. I am the son of a whore who never spoke of the mother before her. You can call me whatever you want. You can call me syphilitic dog. You can call me the one who sleeps with crabs every night of his life. You can call me the clap outright. Call me the dark emptiness that swallows the front porch light. Call me complete remorse. Call me no relief. Let me tell you this—even if a man becomes a great sword swallower, to himself he is still a fool.

I'll tell you who I am. I'm the one you've heard about. The one who one day woke up with an acquired taste for the sour stench of the sheets he was raised in. The one who one day, while hanging on a doorknob listening to the noises a woman makes while working, felt the pilot light turned on in the brick oven of his crotch. The one who went to piss in the presence of the women who used to wipe his ass and found an iron pipe behind the buttons of his pants that would not point in the direction he had trained it but instead turned to every corner of the bathroom as the new poles for its compass, the hot balloon that would not deflate even after spilling all its contents on his shoes, that would not fold up into its place behind the buttons but instead led him out of the bathroom like a bloodhound bewildered by a scent that whispers to it from every direction, that led him out into the hall followed by the tracks of his wet shoes and the coughing of the women, who had started laughing while they were rinsing out their mouths. I'm the one who woke up in the middle of the night with his nose buried in the dirty sheets and his body floundering in the puddle of its own fish smell.

I am Chuy The-Gray-Wing-of-Sadness Pingarrón, the one who one night woke up from the dream of childhood with moss growing up the insides of his legs and with the sudden understanding of what it means that his mother is a whore. I'm the one the story is about, the way it says the boy discovers the two main truths about the world in the same gunshot that begins the dog race to his manhood: the steamy truth about the way his mother earned their living for all those years he'd spent hanging onto doorknobs knowing everything a keyhole could reveal and understanding nothing and the more dangerous truth that now he could be counted among those who come to use her.

You know the rest of my story. How the boy steals the gold watch to pawn for his mother's bed. Only it was not a gold watch. It was one of my mother's shiny bracelets, the kind the customers steal all the time anyway to take back to their wives, saying, You are the only woman in my life. And I didn't pawn it either. I sold it outright to the hunchback at the market who sold it again for twice its value. And when I came back with the money later that night during the business hours and walked into the front room as we were not supposed to do at that time and walked up to my mother and put the money on her lap without saying anything, she slapped me across the face with such force I went flying across the room and into the fern plants the Midwife had growing by the door. My mother didn't say a word. And no one else in that room said anything either. I remember the silence sitting there like the rumor of someone's death. Then she grabbed my hand and took me with her to the upstairs rooms and closed the door behind us and told me, You are right. It's time you learned what it is to be a man like all the rest.

So that is who I am, the one who tried to recreate himself in the womb of

354

his own beginnings. Though that would be a crime larger than life itself: to be the one who brought another helpless soul into this world just to wait his turn to disappear again in sixty years. But you know the whole story already. I don't need to tell you anything. Let me say this, however. You may not like the way I live my life, but it's not up to us to judge the other people. That's what I think. We have enough trouble just watching over what we do ourselves. So I make judgments on no one. Not on my mother who always made sure I had clothes on and food to eat. Not on the ones who called her into the darkness of their lives. At least I'm not one of those who, instead of going directly to his mother's bed, walks out the door and comes back ten years later with a diamond ring on every finger and the death certificate of his father that he murdered, who goes to be with his mother before she figures out who it is and shoots her in the head before she can get up again. You can't say that about me. I judge nobody. I am who I am. Chuy Lies-That-Others-Tell-About-Me Pingarrón. But you knew all this about me already. One look at my face tells you everything.

Sometimes people call me crazy. They say I belong in the house for those who are insane and wandering through themselves. I tell them I already live there. I do that so they'll laugh and forget I'm here. I do that so they'll no longer see me and the twisted angles from which I view the world. I do that so they'll leave me to myself. But I also do that because it's not entirely untrue either. And I don't mean this whorehouse is different from the rest of the world in that regard. On the contrary, from the moment we take our mother's milk we are all infected with the syphilitic nature of this world. That's what kills you. It's not the cancer or the old age or someone's bullet. It's the venereal disease of life itself that claims you in the end. So when they tell me, Chuy, you are crazy, I say, I don't deny it. My madness is proceeding at its proper speed, I tell them. The speed of life and death is the proper speed, I say. And they laugh and walk off saying I am crazy. And I don't deny it. I know who I am.

The rest of the people who live here almost never think about these things the way they occur to me sitting for so long in the contagion of my own bones. But I think they would agree with me. I know this is the case with Angelita, whose hands could heal the wound of death itself, because I have discussed it with her, though she laughs all the time that we're talking, all the time that she's working out the barbs from the wire fence of my spine. She laughs but I know that she's listening because she's always listening. And she's thinking, too, like the time she told me that life means more to her because it is just out of reach than it would mean if she could hold it in her hands. And I know the Midwife thinks about these things because she's the one who makes sure the thick ball of the world is always sitting in our front room no matter what journeys into heaven or dances into hell are going on in the upstairs rooms. Many times I've seen her sitting surrounded by the business of the night, lost far inside herself. She's told me what she's found herself thinking at these times—what it is to bring life out of the darkness of a woman's womb in her office of a midwife, what it's like to preside over the configurations that men and women make looking for a way out through the shadows of the rooms of the second floor, what it's like to taste the world forever with the dark lips of a whore.

But if ever there was someone that I loved in this world of unfulfilled desires, if I've ever felt what the songs on the jukebox at Los Buddies speak of when they sing of love, then I've felt that for Angelita famous for her hands. If ever anyone has caused me to be someone besides myself, besides Chuy Flesh-Sold-On-Highways Pingarrón, the one to whom desires as they are known to others are unknown, if ever anyone has brought me a moment of forgetfulness of what it is to be an unfortunate galaxy made up of sixty years of dust, then that person is Angelita of the questioning heart, Angelita who cannot wear clothes, Angelita who denies the fact that she had parents, Angelita who lives naked in the upstairs rooms, who once told me, I feel naked when I'm wearing clothes, I can't recognize myself that way, I'm familiar only with my skin, though maybe it's sad that my own nakedness does not excite me as I have seen other people excited by the strangeness of their flesh, but that's of little consequence to me; all I know is that I am myself when I wear no clothes and look into a mirror, and when I'm dressed I can see that I'm lost inside someone else and anything can hurt me. Angelita who used to walk through the entire house with nothing on and go out into the street at night with people calling to her from their porches, Angelita, go and put some clothes on, you are too much with us. Who used to meet her customers in the front room with nothing on until her customers stopped coming and the Midwife had to tell her that she was not naked the way the other women were sometimes naked, that the men were frightened by the way she wore her nakedness, that it made them feel naked to all that they were hiding in their lives, that the eternal presence of her flesh was too much for them to bear the way they so often came there feeling like a pair of khaki breeches masquerading as a man, like a back that was losing its daily battle with the crates of lettuce or the highway tar or the cement blocks of an endless wall, that they came to her to forget all that they are and that they have never been and then she meets them with her unrelenting flesh and they are caught without a corner to hide in, without a shadow where they might seek refuge. Angelita who was forced to wear a satin dress when sitting in the front room and blamed the men for that, who spends most of her time upstairs naked with the white walls of her room where the men come knocking calling through the door, Angelita are you in bed and covered with a sheet? I'm coming for you. Angelita who more than the rest of us can look at herself in the mirror without the gentle shading of regret. Angelita who can bring the simple grace of her fingers to the difficult stairway of my spine, who tells me the trembling of my palsy is the greatest excitement of her life; this is what life is without clothes on, she whispers in my ear laughing; it's the joining of two bodies by an air hammer from above. Angelita who is forever standing by the window laughing at the boys walking home that way from school to see the revelations of her skin, at the girls walking that way to the store to peek into the future, at the men walking that way going home in order to see her laughing, at the women going to bingo walking that way just to see her. Angelita who says she has no last name. Angelita who was never born. Angelita who has a soul if anybody has one. Angelita who if I am capable of love I love. Angelita walking naked through every song in every juke box that I keep playing over and over night after night that I feel like this.

Some days I'm not myself. Not that I am someone else. But some days I'm not myself. On those days I wake up in the morning and sit up in bed and put my shoes on without the least resistance from my back and walk out of the house and forget entirely who I am. And the dogs I always feel like won't come near me then. They let me walk my own way, realizing I'm not the usual person who must suffer in this skin. On those days I walk away from this house, away from this block altogether. I walk the four or five blocks to Los Buddies Lounge and have a beer and sit in the booth thinking that maybe my life is suddenly becoming something that it never was and that my back will no longer be so much what it always has been and the palsy won't again return to my left side. I think these things, completely forgetting who it is I'm thinking about. And then sometimes I go eat a meal with the blind man at the Golden Star and think that now I'm a man that other people must speak directly to. Some days I fool myself in this way. And even going home I think my walking has some of the grace and ease that other people carry. But it doesn't last, this feeling. There's always something that gathers me up and returns me to the person I am. It might be a wind that shoots into my backbone from around the corner of a building and sews its silver thread through all the painful twisting of my body. Or it might be a dog that recognizes me before I recognize myself and lifts its leg beside my leg and bathes me in the yellow piss of who I am. Some days I'm not myself. But those days never last too long. Today I am myself entirely.

You see, these are modern times we live in. They have always been modern times. I tell you this. No matter how fast you are able to move along the unforgiving corridors of life always leading to a blank wall at the end, the world is moving faster. No matter which way you turn to escape your own existence, the world itself has turned that way already and all the other ways there are besides. That's why I live my life. There is nothing else to do. That's the only reason. Everyone claims to have his reasons, but, in truth, that's the only one. Even for those who think they go on living just to defy the dirty joke their own birth played on them. Even they are fooling themselves. The truth is, there is nothing else to do but live and live until you die and that is that. This is what I know. I also know that there is no one who can judge me. I am who I am. Let the world explain itself. That is all. As for me, I am Chuy Vidala-de-la-Vida Pingarrón. Call me one who refuses salvation. Call me sour mud. Call me the irritation of a moment. Call me what you like. Call me the one who is the same one he was the day before and who will always be the same even in his grave, the one to whom the burning fires of hell and the huisache trees of heaven make no difference. ★

Norma Elia Cantú

Born in Nuevo Laredo, Mexico, Norma Elia Cantú was raised in Laredo, Texas. Her novel, *Canícula: Snapshots of a Girlhood en la Frontera*, received the Aztlán Prize in 1996. Her most recent book is *Transcendental Train Yard* (Wings Press, 2015), a collection of bilingual poems, in Spanish and English, accompanied by color serigraphs created by Marta Sánchez.

She has published poetry, fiction, and scholarly essays. Other projects include coedited and edited works such as *Telling to Live: Latina Feminist Testimonios*; *Dancing across Borders: Danzas y Bailes Mexicanos*; *Paths to Discovery: Autobiographies of Chicanas with Careers in Mathematics, Science and Engineering*; *Moctezuma's Table: Rolando Briseño's Chicano and Mexicano Tablescapes*; *Chicana Traditions: Continuity and Change*; and *Ofrenda: Liliana Wilson's Art of Dissidence and Dreams*.

Cantú has received two Fulbright-Hays fellowships to do research in Spain. She was instrumental in the founding of the Literacy Volunteers Association (LVA); a feminist women's group, Las Mujeres; and a local chapter of Amnesty International. Formerly a professor at the University of Texas at San Antonio and at the University of Missouri in Kansas City, she is now the Norine R. and T. Frank Murchison Endowed Professor in Humanities at Trinity University, San Antonio, Texas.

La Chola

On a photo by Al Rendon of Ruby Nelda Peña, who was performing at the Teatro Guadalupe.

The camera captures her. Eyes as big as Texas, black liner, fake lashes at least an inch long. Chinese red lipstick, red fingernails. Big gold hoop earrings. Big hair. Teased bouffant. Stylish and just like her girlfriends'. Al has captured el caracter de la mujer that she is: strong and soft at once. Defiant but also a bit fearful; she knows her future. Sees it in her tías. Her mother dead too young, succumbed to cancer. La Chola fears cancer. Fears so many things: her boyfriend, her dad. Fears her uncles. Fears poverty. Fears illness. Fears old age. But most of all she fears them, the men who rule and decide for her. But maybe she'll show them all. Become *la reina del sur*. Her own boss. Take no shit from nobody, as she is wont to say.

You may judge her looks. Her clothes, the tattoos on her arm, her calf, her back. But you don't know her. Don't know who she is, where she belongs. She does. She knows far too much to let life cheat her. She knows life is short and must be lived to its fullest; perhaps it is a blessing that alcohol makes her sick. But mota doesn't. She smokes a bit. Now and then. Calms her nerves. Loosens her up to relax when things get to be too much.

La Ruby plays her well in the photo, this chola who lives in my imagination . . . ferrets out memories of cholas in my past. Sacudiendo el pasado. The chola from down the street in our barrio who one night sought refuge in our home. Papi was working the night shift so we were alone. Mami, Bueli, and the kids. We were already in bed. It was past midnight when she knocked at our door whispering Mami's name. She had been crying. Was frightened. She'd fought with her father who disapproved of her boyfriend. Of her chola ways. What to do? Why run, of course. Find solace at our home. She wept and Mami listened. Bueli counseled, stay. Go back in the morning. No. she wanted to go look for her boyfriend. To make sure he'd be there if her father refused to let her back in the house.

I don't know what happened to her. I was too young and the adults sheltered us. I probably went back to sleep in the big wrought iron bed where I slept with my sisters; Elsa, Laura, Leti. Under the heavy colcha with the wool batting Mami and Bueli handstitched under the pirul in our backyard all summer long. La Chola never came back; years later my aunt's niece by marriage, Susana, told us her story. How she always remembered how Mami and Bueli helped her that cold night when her future was on the line. I like to believe she went back to her family, married her boyfriend and they lived happily ever after. But the reality could well be otherwise. She eloped, ended up a battered wife whose husband reminded her how she had not been a virgin on her wedding night. Never believed her story of that fateful night.

The cholas of my youth like Rita. Teachers never understood La Rita with her blood red lipstick and the tiny cross tattooed on her hand although she wore bobby sox and loafers just like the rest of us; her pony tail bouncing with her walk. I can hear the swish of her crinoline; she wore her starched white blouse with pride, wore red lipstick, too. Chola, they called her; smart as a whip, but dropped out pregnant at sixteen. Abortion not an option and not just because it was illegal back then; we all knew someone who had died after a botched abortion in Nuevo Laredo. Others who had gone to San Antonio, if they had the money. Or to a clinic to give up the child for adoption. But not Rita. She wouldn't do any of that. She wanted to be a mom. To be loved and to love. She wanted to be a woman, respected. Married. So at sixteen she repeated the cycle; her mother, sixteen when Rita was born, now a grandmother at thirty-two. Hard not to judge women who believe that is the only way to be loved, to love. Love after all is the motor that drives desire, that drives a life to its ultimate end. Its goals and aspirations. It's not rare to see such genealogies of despair, of hope. Love drives. Options are few. Fate one might say. El destino.

Cholas. Colorful characters not immortalized in poems like pachucos are in "el louie." No. But still around, those 50s and 60s role models of defiant powerful women. Grandmothers now. They survived chismes. Survived cancer. Survived cheating husbands. Survived difficult childbirths. Survived life. These cholas are still around. Stigmatized: pot heads, loose women, huilas. They survived! The painting by Carmen Lomas Garza shows the blade in the chola's hair, only one of many dangers. Las cholas of my barrio, of your barrio, of the barrios of the past: in Tucson, in East Los, in Chicago, or the west side in San Anto. En todos los barrios de Aztlan. Las cholas in my barrio and from other barrios. Las cruces. Las lomas. El 13, el sal si puedes. The Westside. The Southside. In our history in our lore. They populate stories in our unwritten literature. Las cholas. Pachucas. Mujeres de fuerza. I salute you, your tenacity, your strength. How joyous your lives despite travail. Despite suffering. Desperate circumstances amid poverty and want. Loyal and loving beneath the rough. Al's photo renders homage to these fierce women. Living in a culture not always friendly but always there for them. A complex system of support and of oppression. Comadres. Amigas. Familia.

In memory of Wille Peña reads the mural of our Lady. La chola in black and white—in her red red blouse and red red lipstick remembers. She is waiting. ★

RICK RIORDAN

Rick Riordan was born and raised in San Antonio. He played guitar, simultaneously edited the Alamo Heights High School paper and its satirical "underground" alternative, read a lot of fantasy and mysteries, and began writing stories. He taught English and history in California before returning to teach the same subjects at the St. Mary's Hall middle school in San Antonio. While teaching, he began writing the Tres Navarre mystery series for adults, which received numerous awards, including the Edgar. In 2005, Riordan published the first of his wildly popular young adult novels, *The Lightning Thief*, based on stories he had told his own children. His several series of fantasy novels now include *Percy Jackson and the Olympians*, *The Kane Chronicles*, *The Heroes of Olympus*, *Magnus Chase and the Gods of Asgard*, and the *Trials of Apollo*. His novels—over 40 million of them—have achieved global popularity. Riordan now lives and writes in Boston. Most likely, Riordan is the best selling of all San Antonio authors—ever.

Big Red Tequila, the first of Riordan's mystery novels, won the 1998 Shamus Award for Best First Novel as well as the Anthony Award. In it, Tres Navarre has returned home to San Antonio to solve the twelve-year-old murder of his father, once the local sheriff—and to rescue his high school sweetheart from a difficult and dangerous situation. The title comes from a favorite (and awful) teenager's concoction of Big Red cream soda and cheap tequila.

---

from *Big Red Tequila*

"NOW I KNOW I'M IN LOVE," LILLIAN TOLD ME after she tasted her drink. The perfect margarita should be on the rocks, not frozen. Fresh-squeezed limes, never a mixer. Cointreau rather than triple sec. No tequila but Herradura Anejo, a brand that until a few years ago was only available across the border. All three ingredients in equal proportions. And without salt on the rim it might as well be a daiquiri.

I sat next to Lillian on the couch and tried mine. It had been a few years since I'd worked behind a bar, but the margarita was definitely passable.

"Well, it's not Big Red . . . " I said ruefully.

Lillian's smile was brilliant, a few new wrinkles etched around her eyes. "You can't have everything."

Her face had a little too much of everything, just as I remembered. Her eyes were slightly large, like a cat's, the irises flecked with too many browns and blues and grays to call them only green. Her mouth was wide, her nose so delicate it bordered on being sharp. Her light brown hair, which she now wore shoulder-length, had so many blond and red streaks it looked off-color. And she had too many freckles, especially noticeable now when she had a summer tan. Somehow it all worked to make her beautiful.

"It sounds like your day was hell, Tres. I'm impressed you're still standing."

"Nothing an enchilada dinner and a beautiful woman won't cure."

She took my hand. "Any one in particular?"

I thought about it. "Green or chicken mole."

She slapped me on the thigh and called me names.

We knew better than to try making reservations at Mi Tierra on a Saturday night. You just throw yourself into the crowd of tourists and native San Antonians in the front room, wave money, and hope you get a table in under an hour.

It was worth it. We got seats close to the bakery, where trays of cinnamon-smelling *pan dulce* in neon colors were brought out of the ovens every few minutes. The Christmas lights were still up along the walls, and the mariachis were as thick as flies, only much fatter. I threatened Lillian with having them play "Guantanamera" at our table unless she let me buy dinner.

She laughed. "A dirty trick. And me a successful businesswoman. "

She had promised to show me her gallery the next day. It was a small place in La Villita she co-owned with her old college mentor, Beau Karnau. They mostly sold Mexican folk art to tourists.

"And your own art?" I asked.

She looked down briefly, smiling still but not so much. Sore subject.

Ten years ago, when I left, Beau Karnau and Lillian had been talking big about her career—New York shows, museum exhibitions, changing the face of modern photographic art. As soon as the world rediscovered Beau's genius (which they'd apparently appreciated for about three months during the sixties) Lillian would ride his coattails to fame. Now, ten years later, Beau and Lillian were selling curios.

"I don't get as much time as I did in college," she said. "But soon. I have some new ideas."

I decided not to push it. After a large waiter with an even larger mustache came to take our order, Lillian changed subjects.

"How about you? Now that I've got you out here without a job, I mean. It can't be that easy without an investigator's license."

I shrugged. "Some legal firms like that—informal help for the messy jobs, no records on the payroll. I've got a few leads. Maia has lots of friends of friends."

The minute I said her name I wished I hadn't. It landed in the middle of the table between us like a brick. Lillian slowly licked some salt from the rim of her glass. There was no change in her face.

"You could always get a job evicting wayward tenants," she suggested.

"Or I could help sell art for you."

She gave me a lopsided smile. "When I have to pin a customer in a joint lock to buy my work, I'll know it's time to put down the camera and the paintbrush for good."

The waiter returned quickly with a bowl of butter and a basket the size of a top hat filled with handmade tortillas. Unfortunately Fernando Asante came up to our table right behind him.

"I'll be damned!" he said. "If it isn't Jack Navarre's boy. "

Before I could put down my half-buttered tortilla I was shaking hands with him, staring up at his weathered brown face and a row of smiling, gold-outlined teeth. Asante's hair was so thin and well greased, combed back from his forehead, that it could've been drawn on with a Marks-A-Lot.

I stood up, introducing Lillian to San Antonio's oldest city councilman. As if she didn't know who he was. As if anybody in town who read the *Express-*

News tabloid section didn't know.

"'Course," Asante said. "I remember Miss Cambridge. Fiesta Week. The Travis Center opening, with Dan Sheff."

Asante had a gift for names, and that one fell onto the table like another brick. Lillian winced a little. The councilman just smiled. I smiled back. An Anglo man had come up behind Asante and was waiting patiently with that distracted, brooding expression most bodyguards develop. About six feet, curly black hair, boots and jeans, T-shirt and linen jacket. Lots of muscles. He didn't smile.

"Councilman. You made it into the San Francisco paper a while back."

He did his best modest look. "The Travis Center opening. Millions in new revenue to the city. Friends called me up from all over the country, said they saw the coverage."

"Actually it was that piece about the secretary and you in Brackenridge Park."

Lillian suppressed a laugh by choking on her margarita. Asante's smile wavered momentarily, then came back different—more of a snarl. We were all quiet for a few seconds. I'd seen him give that look to my dad in the years they had been at each other's throats. I was downright proud to see it turned on me. I figured wherever my father was he would probably be biting the end off a new cigar and laughing his ass off about then.

Asante's large friend felt the change of mood, I guess. He moved around to the side of the table.

"Love to have you join us for dinner," I offered. "Double date?"

"No thanks, Jack," the councilman said. That was the second time today someone had called me by my father's name. It sounded strange.

"I hear you're in town for good." He didn't seem to like the sound of that. "It can be tough finding jobs down here. You have any trouble, let me know."

"Thanks."

"Least I can do." A politician's grin smoothed over his face again. "Not every day a Bexar County sheriff gets shot down. Your dad . . . that was a bad way to go."

Asante kept smiling. I was counting the gold caps on his teeth, wondering how hard they would be to break off.

"I always wished I could do something more for your family, Jack, but, well, you left town so fast. Like a jackrabbit, heard that shot and boom, you were in California."

A young orange-haired woman in a glittery dress came up behind Asante and waited at a respectful distance. Asante glanced back at her and nodded.

"Well," he said, patting his belly. "Dinnertime now. Like I said, you need anything, Jack, let me know. Nice to see you again, Miss Cambridge."

Asante's fan club followed him to a table nearby. My enchilada dinner was probably very good. I don't remember.

Around midnight Lillian and I drove back to her house with the VW top down. The stars were out and the air was as warm and clean as fresh laundry.

"I'm sorry about Asante," she said after a while.

I shrugged. "Don't be. Coming home is like that—you have to face the assholes too."

She had taken my hand by the time we pulled into her driveway. We sat there listening to the *conjunto* music from the house next door. The windows were lit up orange. Beers were being opened, loud talking in Spanish, Santiago Jimenez's accordion wailing out "Ay Te Dejo en San Antonio."

"Tonight was hard anyway," Lillian said. "We're going to need time to figure things out, I guess."

She raised my hand to her lips. I was looking at her, remembering the first time I had kissed her in this car, how she looked. She had been wearing a white sundress, her hair cut like Dorothy Hamill's. We had been sixteen, I think.

I kissed her now.

"I've been figuring things out for ten years," I told her. "It's got to get easier from here."

She looked at me for a long time with an expression I couldn't read. She almost decided to say something. Then she kissed me back.

It was hard to talk for a while, but I finally said: "Robert Johnson will be mad if I don't bring him these leftovers for dinner."

"Enchiladas for breakfast?" Lillian suggested.

We went inside. ★

CLAUDE STANUSH

Claude Stanush (1918-2011) was born in San Antonio, into a Polish family with deep roots in South Texas, having arrived in the 1850s. Stanush graduated from Central Catholic High School at age fifteen and graduated summa cum laude from St. Mary's University in 1939. He soon was writing for the *San Antonio Light*. In 1949, he moved to New York and planted himself outside the door of the editor of *LIFE Magazine*. After a week or so, the editor called him in and asked, "What are your qualifications?" Stanush replied, "Perseverance." He worked for thirteen years on the staff of *LIFE*. Accolades for his *LIFE* stories include awards from the World Council of Churches (for his work on the series "The World's Great Religions") and the American Association for the Advancement of Science (for his essay "The Geography of the Universe"). One of his *LIFE* stories inspired the film "The Lusty Men" (RKO Pictures), which *Premiere* magazine named an "unsung classic" of American cinema.

Stanush returned to San Antonio in 1962. For many years, until well past retirement age, he wrote a weekly column for the *San Antonio Express-News,*. He was a fearless but genial columnist, often focusing his commentary on public ethics. Some of those columns were gathered in *The World In My Head* (1984). As a freelance writer, he wrote short stories, essays, film scripts, and, in collaboration with his daughter Michele, a novel, *All Good Men* (Permanent Press, 2003). Awards for his fiction included a creative writing award from the National Endowment for the Arts as well as the Paisano Fellowship (given by the Texas Institute of Letters). He was a coscreenwriter on a feature film, *The Newton Boys* (20th Century Fox); and a cocreater of the documentary film, *The Newton Boys: Portrait of an Outlaw Gang* (with David Middleton), which won the gold medal in its category at both the Texas Film Festival and the International Film Festival in the Virgin Islands. A collection of his short fiction, *Sometimes It's New York*, was published in 2007 by Wings Press.

In "Live and Let Live," Stanush confronts a common Hill Country occurance—the presence of poisonous rattlesnakes and cottonmouth water mocassins. Whether to kill the "bad snakes" or not becomes an exquisite dilemma, pitting his upbringing against his adult morality.

Live and Let Live

The thing I was after lay at the edge of a stream-bed. It was unmistakable, stretched out full-length on some chalky-white stones—long and black and fat and stub-tailed.

I could feel my heart beating at my chest. I was in the kind of mood that, like flood water, overasserts itself until it finds its own level. Nervously, I began to look for the right kind of rock. Heavy enough to crush the skull. The locus of life. The vulnerable part.

There were plenty of rocks around; the creek bottom next to where the thing was sunning was nearly dry, except for one deep pocket of water. In May, when my family and I had come down from the city to spend our summer in the country, spring rain had filled the gravelly channel. The water moved slowly along, picking up speed where the land dropped away, until it plunged over the boulders with a frothy roar. But now, after a long summer's drought, there was only a trickle, barely enough to keep the stream alive—except for occasional pools.

The pocket of water in front of me was small, though likely the largest for a stretch of several miles. Which is precisely why *it* was here. A snake, too, has to eat.

At the pool's center it could have been four or five feet deep, maybe six; the clear, crystal-green water was deceptive. Within these bounds lived what might be considered a nice mess of fish—bass, catfish, perch, with enough minnows, if the tiny lifeline of water continued to flow, to sustain them until the heavy fall rains.

Within a few minutes, I found what I was looking for—a large gray stone, flat on the top and flat on the bottom, so it would land squarely. Grasping it firmly in my hand, I headed back toward the thing.

As it sensed my approach, it reared up half a foot. Devilish, that forked, sizzling tongue. Taunting me to come closer? Then it tilted its head back and popped its mouth wide open. Who said that black was the color of evil? Oh, yes, the body was black but that wasn't what gave the scene its horror. It was the white of the gaping mouth—the cottonmouth. Looking down that fibrous throat, rendered even more white by contrast with the dark body, I could almost see the milky-white venom dripping out of those white, curved fangs. That venom, injected into a leg, through those fangs, could kill one of our children. Or me or my wife.

I fingered the rock.

But why was my heart thumping so? What was so horrible about smashing a snake's head with a rock? Unlike my wife and children, all city-bred, I'd grown up in the country—snake country. As a boy, I had killed snakes innumerable times, hurling rock after rock until the job was done, with no more feeling than if I were throwing at a tin can. Back in those days, there were "good" snakes and "bad" snakes, just as there were "good" and "bad" people. A king snake was a good snake, primarily because it killed bad snakes. Coachwhips were also good snakes; one lived under our house and was a better mouser than the cat. Grass snakes were good snakes too—good for throwing at girls. The bad, meanwhile, were the pit vipers: rattlesnakes, copperheads, cottonmouth moccasins. And back in those days, everybody—even the kids—would kill a bad snake on sight, just as in the earlier days everybody would join in to hook up a horse-thief. The bad snakes all had fangs with deadly venom in them and unlike humans they didn't make distinctions between good and bad people, or even between animals and people: If you were walking along a well-worn animal trail, hunting for a milk cow, and a rattlesnake was coiled up waiting for a pack-rat to come bouncing by—well, my ten-year-old cousin died from a rattler bite on the calf of her little left leg. And the echo was still there in me, somewhere far down at the base of the brain: *You kill a bad snake on sight.*

I fingered the rock again. No question, I was going to kill this one if I could. Not necessarily with relish, but with a kind of righteous anger (was that the rub?) that I couldn't completely explain to myself if I tried, and that might even have had a certain pleasure mixed up with it.

But a snake doesn't deliberate. I had waited too long—and even before I could raise my hand, the cottonmouth was gone. Somewhere into the weeds.

I suppose I should have felt relieved. I didn't. I felt let down, cheated. Still, I wasn't about to plow into the underbrush after the snake. If there is anything that bothers me more than a bad snake, it's a bad snake in the grass. Instead, I trudged the half mile back up the dirt path that led to the house we'd rented for the summer, and I told my wife that I had almost killed a cottonmouth. Almost.

My wife was noncommittal. She didn't like snakes, any kind, bad or good. But even more she didn't like to see anything killed. Still, I knew the big cottonmouth would be back. It was as tied to those glistening fish within the pool of water as they were to the trickle of water coming from springs into the channel. It would be back, as certainly as the sun would rise the next morning. And so would I. The very next morning.

I set my alarm for 5:30.

I set the big, flat rock at the leg of our bed.

It was there, all right. Even in the faint pink of dawn, I could see it coursing slowly through the water like a giant arrow, sending diagonal ripples away from its body. But I wasn't about to enter the pool. No more than I was about to follow it into the weeds. This I know about cottonmouths: they can bite *in* the water, and they can bite *under* the water.

Then, as I was standing there deliberating, the most amazing thing happened. Out of the corner of my eye, on a crescent of land arcing out into the stream-bed, I saw two smaller moccasins slithering toward the water. They could have been the big one's children, or, if the big one was a male—which I certainly couldn't tell, but only hazarded a guess that he was by his size—one could have been his mate and the other his child. Makes no difference, really, except in the light of what followed. No sooner had they entered the water then the big one charged at them, first one and then the other; his mouth gaped open, flashing white.

I was spellbound. I had never seen anything like it in my life.

Facing the wrath of the big cottonmouth, the two smaller snakes then whipped around in the water and fled back onto the rocky shore where—sensing the danger over, I suppose—they stretched themselves out and began basking in the rising sun.

But that didn't suit the big one either. Shooting out of the water onto the shore himself, he approached the smaller snakes and again raised his head up and popped his fanged mouth wide open, this time also feinting lunges at them, as if to say: "This is only a warning. This is my territory! ..." Well, they didn't like that at all; who was he to order them off? —and so, rearing up themselves, they popped open their own mouths and lunged back at him—flashing white—and for a few moments it looked as if I was going to witness the damndest cottonmouth tangle anybody could imagine.

The two smaller ones, if they had understood teamwork, could probably have won. But apparently that's not how it works in the cottonmouth pecking order: I'd never seen a snake more angry than the big one, and by the sheer ferocity and power of his lunges he let the smaller two know that he wasn't taking any sass. He soon had them intimidated and crawling away.

By this time it was clear even to me that Big Daddy had staked out this pool with all the fish in it and all the frogs around it as his private pantry, and woe to anybody else, big or small, even of his own species, who disputed him! The drought, of course, had made it possible, and perhaps even necessary, looking at it from his point of view.

Though I still had the rock in my hand I had become so absorbed that I had almost forgotten about the weapon. It was only when the big cottonmouth slithered back to the edge of the water and lay there motionless, as if waiting for a big frog to come along that he could grab and swallow, that I remembered what I had come down to the water to do. It was a relatively easy target, stretched out with its stub-tail toward me. I raised my right arm.

No.

The damn thing had won my respect, if not my admiration. And if this were his private preserve, he'd be there again tomorrow, and the next day, and the day after that, performing no telling what extraordinary feats. For the time being, the simple wonder of it that was stirring within me surmounted my other feelings. I walked back home.

My wife said she was glad. "None of us are swimming down there now," she said, "so just let the snake be."

"That's not the way nature operates," I said back, reminding her that I had said my quest was over "for the time being." "If I don't get him eventually, something else will," and I told her about the time I came upon a turtle with a water moccasin in its mouth: The snake was writhing and twisting in a desperate effort to get its fangs into the soft, vulnerable part of the turtle, but it never did. The turtle bit him in two.

I thought my wife would be horrified by the story, but she wasn't. "That may be nature's ways," she said, "but that doesn't have to be a human's ways. Why kill when you don't have to? Just for the sake of killing? Do you find all this fun? Is that what this is to you—fun?"

"Sometimes," I argued, "when there's too much of something, man's got to help nature along. That old-timer who lives over at Horn's Bend told me there's more cottonmouths now than there ever was. He says everybody's 'citified' and nobody's killing the bad snakes anymore."

"Oh, how does that old man know if there's more snakes?" my wife asked over her shoulder as she left the living room for the kitchen. "You think he counted them?" Her voice was faint now, separated by a wall, but I could still hear her. "Remember how Mr. Thorndike used to swear a hundred times over that there were more deer way back when," she was saying, "and then we read that story in the paper where the Fish and Wildlife man said just the opposite. I don't know, but I wouldn't put too much count in one old man's memories."

She had a point. In fact, I began to remember certain people in my younger days who didn't kill snakes, even bad ones, on sight. There weren't many such people. Only a few. They were the exceptions. But there were some: men and women who lived so close to nature, among dogs and cats and horses and cows and owls and coons and bees and snakes, that they had acquired almost the senses and instincts of animals. If a single chicken was missing from their yard, they knew it at once, and whether a hawk or a coon had gotten it. In the mornings and evenings they never walked the animal trails where rattlesnakes were apt to be coiled and waiting. Even at night they walked through the wild grasses and weeds, knowing that snakes, at the sound of an approaching human, are likely to follow their instincts with regard to something larger and more powerful—that is, to keep moving. An old cowboy on our ranch, named Pablo Cruz, was one such person. On Saturday nights, because Pablo disdained bathtubs, he would walk half a mile through rattlesnake-infested grass and weeds to bathe in the stock tank. Never once was he bitten. What's more, the stock tank at night was usually chock-full of cottonmouths, but this didn't bother the old cowboy, not at all, he would have thought something was wrong with the water if it didn't have moccasins in it. He'd simply take off his shirt, swish it in the water several times to let the snakes know they better get over to the other side of the tank, then he'd sit down in the muddy water among the cow turds and enjoy himself infinitely more than if he were in a suite at the Waldorf-Astoria. . . .

Pablo did kill snakes, but only if and when they were an actual threat to him. My wife had a point. . . .

And yet the more I pondered it, the more I could see it wasn't all that simple. When I was a boy, we killed every bad snake on sight because we assumed they were all a threat: The one you killed might be the very one that would get you later, if you didn't get it first. Would the Big One make exceptions, or distinctions?

Tomorrow I'd do it! One more, one less, it does make a difference.

My wife was sweeping the porch. I asked her to come with me. "Sooner or later, you're going to have to get over your squeamishness."

She gave me a look. "*My* squeamishness?"

"Just come with me."

"If I thought there was really a reason for killing the thing," she said, "I'd go down there. But I don't."

"You want it to bite one of the children?"

"The children aren't going down there anymore. So you're the only one it could bite. I think you're asking for it, if you want my opinion."

Touché.

And so I puttered around the yard, digging up around the marigolds, looking for a rattlesnake under every plant. The children did play in the yard, and if there was a rattler in the yard, there was certainly a possibility it might bite them. Let her deny that!

After awhile, in the warm sun, the good earth crumbling between my fingers, I began to relax. It had been that way at the beginning of the summer. First, a kind of apprehension at the thought of living for three months with three relatively small children in the midst of poisonous snakes. ("Now, remember," I told them over and over again, because being kids, and city kids at that, I knew they'd forget it, "don't put your hands where you can't see. Stay away from the bushes. Swing a stick in front of you if you go out walking in the fields.") Then the panic at the boy's discovery of a rattler—two inches thick – coiled in the grass under a swing that hung from an oak limb right in front of the house, where the kids often played. For several days neither my wife nor I would let the children out of our sight. But, as nothing happened, as nobody got bitten, as the family became accustomed to the sight of snakes, as we fell into the easy rhythms of cool mornings and nights and soft breezes and green trees and tall native grasses swaying with the wind, all of us began to relax. . . . And after two months, and reading a dozen books on the life and habits of mockingbirds and bobwhites and armadillos and rattlers, we all began to feel a part of it. . . . The strangeness, the alien-ness, began to disappear. . . .

Still, as this particular day wore on, I began to brood, avoiding my wife by lying in the hammock and pretending to read. The house, an old rock one with big rooms and two fireplaces, sat on a rise overlooking half a mile of grasses and trees, the eye eventually stopping at a high limestone cliff at the base of which the stream ran. Lying in the hammock, eyes half-closed, lulled by breezes which came up a draw from the southeast, free from the customary pressures of work and social obligations, I could easily imagine how Adam and Eve must have felt living in the primeval Garden of Eden supposedly at peace with all creation. But weren't there serpents even then plotting to destroy their peace and joy and freedom? . . .

All a myth, my wife would say; particularly that part about the apple and God's condemning the serpent for his craftiness to crawl on his belly forever. Where's the good or evil in nature? Is the rattlesnake any more evil for eating the rabbit than the rabbit is good when eaten by humans (particularly as *hasenpfeffer*)? Are not good and evil simple human terms by which we separate that which supports us from that which threatens?

Yes, a rattler is dangerous if you step on it: But so are we! I thought of that early American flag: the one with the coiled snake and the words "Don't Tread on Me." My wife could have designed that flag.

But then, while I was lying in the hammock, having these secret thoughts, the front door of the house squeaked open and out came my wife, holding in her hand a tall highball glass. She began to move in my direction. Ah. Nothing I like better on a hot summer afternoon than a gin and tonic with a lime slice in it, smeared around the rim of the glass. . . .

Though didn't she know that the juice of that tree was reserved for the Gods?

"Thank you very much," I said.

"What are you reading?" she asked.

"The Bible."

"The Bible? Doesn't look like the Bible to me."

I took a sip. Delicious. How good it is! Except for somebody with cirrhosis of the liver. "There's always an exception," I said.

"What are you mumbling about?" she asked.

"Mumbling?"

"I hope it isn't more about that cottonmouth." And she took a handkerchief out of her shorts pocket and wiped the perspiration off her brow. I took another good sip. It was loosening my tongue. "Think about this," I said. "If you splash in the water a cottonmouth generally goes the other way, right? And if you walk through the grass and let a rattlesnake know you're coming, it generally crawls on out of your way, right? But not always; right?"

"Please. I'm going back in the house."

She did go back. But that didn't stop me. I was going to keep on talking, if only to myself. "It's the exceptions that cross you up. With snakes, with human beings, with everything. There's no absolute certainty."

A long sip this time.

In the late afternoon, as the shadows were lengthening, I went down to the pool, armed with my rock. I had wanted to take the boy with me; he was old enough now to know and, being a boy, might understand without a lot of explanations. But I decided against it. He really wouldn't understand, and it would be too complicated to explain. He'd think it was just another snake. One more, one less, what difference would it make?

The big fat cottonmouth was there, lying on the rocky bank, undisputed lord of his domain, and at my approach, as usual, he reared up and opened wide his white jaws. . . . Did I say, Undisputed Lord of His Domain? Well, I should have said, Undisputed except for me. Anyway, whatever was happening inside of him (adrenaline to the nervous system, venom squirting into the fangs), the adrenaline was certainly gushing inside of me, for my heart was beating wildly. . . .

Except now I knew why it was! . . .

And there was no way out. I had to take the risk!

I came to within a few feet of the thing, so frightened I could scarcely move, and it, sensing that the issue was no longer make-believe, no longer feinting and lunging and camouflage, but life or death, reared up to almost a third the length of its big body. It had power too!

Poison from those little sacs that sit right at the hinges of the snake's jaws, injected through the curved, hollow fangs into a main artery. . . .

But then . . . having reared up one fraction higher than the complicated laws of gravity permit—that is, one fraction beyond that invisible point where force and counter-force produce stability—it fell forward.

It landed flat, the mouth closed, the head exposed on the sun-bleached sacrificial stone . . .

I hurled the rock—with all the power and fury I could summon.

It landed squarely.

The body twisted and writhed. It rolled over and over on the ground, as if the coils were all in a knot and it was trying to untie itself.

But it was only the reflexes playing themselves out. The vital center, the locus of life, had been destroyed.

With a splash it convoluted into the water.

Immediately, in the crystal-clear liquid, I could see the long, contorted form surrounded by pinkish perch, yellow-bellied bass, whiskered catfish, hundreds of tiny silver-flashing minnows, the entire congregation of the pool, all pressing their noses against the black flesh tipped by the bloody-red head which now was beginning to color the water.

That night I writhed on the bed, and in my nightmare I saw a big fat cottonmouth, an exact duplicate of the one I had killed, pursuing me with its fanged mouth open; it went around and around the house, through one room after another, back into the city, along one street and down another, into my very bed, where I flailed futilely with my arms to ward off those hypodermic teeth. Hadn't I read story after story of how snakes always travel in pairs, like husband and wife, and if one is killed the mate will pursue the murderer forever, around the world if necessary, to avenge its death? Pure myth, I would have said in the daytime. But in the turmoil of troubled sleep, beware! The pursuing cottonmouth became retribution embodied, and I was consumed with guilt, not moral guilt but a kind of metaphysical guilt which kept asking me over and over again: Do you think you are God, to whom only belongs Absolute Knowledge, to whom only belongs the Absolute Power of Life and Death? . . .

No, no, I cried out.

Early the next morning, when the sun was just rising and casting its pink glow across the mirrored surface of the water, I was back, drawn there even in death by the fascination of the power that had once been in that long, black, stub-tailed form. But when I looked down into the water, glazed now by the slanting light of the rising sun, it was no longer that. I mean, no longer a black, full-fleshed form. Not even one with a bloody-red crushed head. All that remained was a long white skeleton—absolutely white; whiter I tell you than any white I have ever seen, with equally white ribs radiating from the spine like the thin, tiny wires of an electronic circuit. And along both sides of the long skeleton huddled dozens of tiny, silver-flecked minnows, their mouths pressed close to the vertebrae as they nibbled the last few remaining morsels of flesh.

How ironic! How just, I was tempted to add, in a nature where there is no good and no evil, where the big fish simply eat the smaller fish, the smaller fish eat the still smaller, and on down the line to the inconsequential tiny minnow which must wait in order to gorge itself on what is by nature beyond it, on the fortuitous exception to the rule. . . .

I shuddered at the sight of the calcified skeleton which only yesterday in the flushed flesh of life had held the power of life and death over those others imprisoned within the encapsulated pool. It was awful. Yet bewitching.

I couldn't resist racing back home to bring my wife and children back down to see it.

And my wife shuddered too, at the horror of it, but had to agree. It was a beautiful thing. The exquisite symmetry of the skeleton and the absolute whiteness of the white, if nothing else.

The boy got a long stick and wanted to fish it out so he could take it back to the city when school started again, and show it to his teacher.

"No!" I exclaimed, with more emotion than I knew I had left. "No, let it be."

Then my girls begged: "C'mon Daddy. Please. It's so pretty."

"No," I said. "It belongs here."

Belongs here, I said.

The next morning when I went down to the pool, still drawn by the vision of that white skeleton, the two smaller cottonmouths that had been driven off (at least, I presume they were the same) were there, stretched out full-length on some flat rocks at the edge of the stream-bed, with all the insouciance of ownership. At the sound of my approach they both reared up and popped opened their mouths, flashing white. . . .

One less, two more.

My God, I whispered to myself, what *is* the Law?

My heart suddenly went back to thump-thumping, thump-bump, thump-bump, so hard against the wall of my chest that I could actually hear it—and it only quieted when I turned around and headed back toward the house, resolved not to go down there again until we return for a weekend visit in autumn, when the rains have refilled the channel and restored the stream to its springtime vigor. ★

SANDRA CISNEROS

Sandra Cisneros arrived in San Antonio in 1983 to take the position of Literature Program Director at the Guadalupe Cultural Arts Center. The next year, her novelette *The House on Mango Street* was published by Arte Público Press. It has come to be considered a classic American coming-of-age novel, on a par with *The Catcher in the Rye*. In 1985, Cisneros received the Dobie-Paisano Fellowship (Texas Institute of Letters and the University of Texas), after which she held numerous residencies and fellowships around the country, always returning to live in the King William neighborhood in San Antonio.

By incorporating local places like Torres Taco Haven, the mural-covered Kwik-Wash, Tienda Guadalupe Folk Art store, and other locations into her fiction—many of these appear in "Bien Pretty"—she helped establish the neighborhood as a literary community of note. "Bien Pretty" appears in her collection *Woman Hollering Creek* (Random House, 1991), some of which was actually written in "her" window booth at Taco Haven on S. Presa Street, which she describes in this story.

Woman Hollering Creek earned the PEN Center West Award for Best Fiction, the Anisfield-Wolf Book Award, the Lannan Foundation Literary Award, among others, and was a *New York Times* and *Library Journal* "noteworthy book of the year." It was also short-listed as the Best Book of Fiction for 1991 by the *Los Angeles Times*.

Cisneros purchased a home at 735 E. Guenther Street, beside the river, in 1995. Two years later, she painted the house "periwinkle purple," which brought her into a much-publicized confrontation with the local Historic and Design Review Commission—and landed photos of her house in newspapers all across the country. As she wrote, "One day I painted my house tejano colors; the next day, my house is in all the news, cars swarming by, families having their photos taken in front of my purple casita as if it were the Alamo." While living in her purple house, she wrote her magnum opus, the novel *Caramelo* (Knopf, 2002).

Cisneros received a MacArthur "Genius" grant in 1995, with which she founded the Latino MacArthur Fellows, known as Los MacArturos, a group that has accomplished much in the area of community outreach and literacy. She also created the Macondo Foundation, an invitation-only group of "socially engaged writers," and the Alfredo Cisneros Del Moral Foundation, a grant-giving institution serving Texas writers. In short, she did a great deal for Latino/a writers and artists in general, and Tejana/o writers and artists in particular. In 2015, she sold her San Antonio home and moved to central Mexico. Her papers are archived at the Southwestern Writers Collection, Texas State University, San Marcos, Texas.

Born in Chicago in 1954, she studied at Loyola University (BA, English 1976) and the University of Iowa (MFA, Creative Writing 1978). Her books include *Bad Boys* (Mango Press, 1980), *My Wicked Wicked Ways* (Third Woman, 1987; Random House, 1992), *Loose Woman* (Knopf, 1994), *Hairs/Pelitos* (Knopf, 1994), *Have You Seen Marie?* (Knopf, 2012), and *A House of My Own: Stories from My Life* (Knopf, 2015). Her books have been translated into over a dozen languages.

Bien Pretty

> *Ya me voy,*
> *ay te dejo en Sun Antonio.*
> —Flaco Jiménez

He wasn't pretty unless you were in love with him. Then any time you met anyone with those same monkey eyes, that burnt-sugar skin, the face wider than it was long, well, you were in for it.

His family came from Michoacán. All *chaparritos,* every one of them—short even by Mexican standards—but to me he was perfect.

I'm to blame. Flavio Munguía was just ordinary Flavio until he met me. I filled up his head with a million and one *cariñitos.* Then he was ruined forever. Walked different. Looked people in the eye when he talked. Ran his eyes across every pair of *nalgas* and *chichis* he saw. I am sorry.

Once you tell a man he's pretty, there's no taking it back. They think they're pretty all the time, and I suppose, in a way, they are. It's got to do with believing it. Just the way I used to believe I was pretty. Before Flavio Munguía wore all my prettiness away.

Don't think I haven't noticed my girlfriends back home who got the good-lookers. They all look twice their age now, old from all the *corajes* exploding inside their hearts and bellies.

Because a pretty man is like a too-fancy car or a real good stereo or a microwave oven. Late or early, sooner or later, you're just asking for it. Know what I mean?

Flavio. He wrote poems and signed them "Rogelio Velasco." And maybe I would still be in love with him if he wasn't already married to two women, one in Tampico and the other in Matamoros. Well, that's what they say.

Who knows why the universe singled me out. Lupe Arredondo, stupid art thou amongst all women. Once I was as solid as a sailor on her sea legs, the days rolling steadily beneath me, and then—Flavio Munguía arrived.

Flavio entered my life via a pink circular rolled into a tube and wedged in the front gate curlicue:

$ SPECIAL $
PROMOTION
LA CUCARACHA APACHURRADA PEST CONTROL
OVER 10 YEARS OF EXPERIENCE

If you are Tired of **ROACHES** and Hate them like many People do,
but can't afford to pay a lot of Money $$$$ to have a house Free of
ROACHES ROACHES ROACHES!!! We will treat your kitchen,
behind and under your refrigerator and stove, inside your cabinets and
even exterminate your living room all for only $20.00. Don't be fooled
by the price. Call now. 555-2049 or Beeper #555-5912. We also kill
spiders, beetles, scorpions, ants, fleas, and many more insects.
!!So Don't Hesitate Call Us Now!!
You'll be glad you did call us. Thank you very much.
Your CUCARACHAS will be DEAD
(*$5.00 extra for each additional room)

A dead cockroach lying on its back followed as illustration.

It's because of the river and the palm and pecan trees and the humidity and all that we have so many palmetto bugs, roaches so big they look Pleistocene. I'd never seen anything like them before. We don't have bugs like that in California, at least not in the Bay. But like they say, everything's bigger and better in Texas, and that holds especially true for bugs.

So I live near the river in one of those houses with wood floors varnished the color of Coca-Cola. It isn't mine. It belongs to Irasema Izaura Coronado, a famous Texas poet who carries herself as if she is directly descended from Ixtaccíhuatl or something. Her husband is an honest-to-God Huichol *curandero*, and she's no slouch either, with a PhD from the Sorbonne.

A Fulbright whisked them to Nayarit for a year, and that's how I got to live here in the turquoise house on East Guenther, not exactly in the heart of the historic King William district—it's on the wrong side of South Alamo to qualify, the side where the peasantry lives—but close enough to the royal mansions that attract every hour on the hour the Pepto Bismol-pink tourist buses wearing sombreros.

I called La Cucaracha Apachurrada Pest Control the first month I house-sat Her Highness's home. I was sharing residence with:

> (8) Oaxacan black pottery pieces
> signed Diego Rivera monotype
> upright piano
> star-shaped piñiata
> (5) strings of red chile lights
> antique Spanish shawl
> St. Jacques Majeur Haitian voodoo banner
> cappuccino maker
> lemonwood Olinalá table
> replica of the goddess Coatlicue
> life-size papier-mâché skeleton signed by the Linares family
> Frida Kahlo altar
> punched tin Virgen de Guadalupe chandelier

bent-twig couch with Mexican sarape cushions
seventeenth-century Spanish *retablo*
tree-of-life candlestick
Santa Fe plate rack
(2) identical sets of vintage Talavera Mexican dishware
eye-of-God crucifix
knotty pine armoire
pie safe
death mask of Pancho Villa with mouth slightly open
Texana chair upholstered in cowskin with longhorn horns for
    the arms and legs
(7) Afghan throw rugs
iron bed with a mosquito net canopy

Beneath this veneer of Southwest funk, of lace and silk and porcelain, beyond the embroidered pillows that said DUERME, MI AMOR, the Egyptian cotton sheets and eyelet bedspread, the sigh of air that barely set the gauze bedroom curtains trembling, the blue garden, the pink hydrangea, the gilt-edged tea set, the abalone-handled silver, the obsidian hair combs, the sticky, cough-medicine-and-powdered-sugar scent of magnolia blossoms, there were, as well, the roaches.

I was afraid to open drawers. I never went into the kitchen after dark. They were the same Coca-Cola color as the floors, hard to spot unless they gave themselves away in panic.

The worst thing about them wasn't their size, nor the crunch they gave under a shoe, nor the yellow grease that oozed from their guts, nor the thin shells they shed translucent as popcorn hulls, nor the possibility they might be winged and fly into your hair, no.

What made them unbearable was this. The scuttling in the middle of the night. An ugly clubfoot grate like a dead thing being dragged across the floor, a louder-than-life munching during their cannibal rites, a nervous pitter, and then patter when they scurried across the Irish-linen table runners, leaving a trail of black droppings like coffee grounds, sticky feet rustling across the clean stack of typewriter paper in the desk drawer, my primed canvasses, the set of Wedgewood rose teacups, the lace Victorian wedding dress hanging on the bedroom wall, the dried baby's breath, the white wicker vanity, the cutwork pillowcases, your blue raven hair scented with Tres Flores brilliantine.

Flavio, it's true. The house charms me now as it did then. The folk art, the tangerine-colored walls, the *urracas* at sunset. But what would you have done if you were me? I'd driven all the way from northern California to central Texas with my past pared down to what could fit inside a van. A futon. A stainless-steel wok. My grandmother's *molcajete*. A pair of flamenco shoes with crooked heels. Eleven *huipiles*. Two *rebozos*—*de bolita y de seda*. My Tae Kwon Do uniform. My crystals and copal. A portable boom box and all my Latin tapes—Rubén Blades, Astor Piazolla, Gipsy Kings, Inti Illimani, Violeta Parra, Mercedes Sosa, Agustín Lara, Trio Los Panchos, Pedro Infante, Lydia Mendoza, Paco de Lucía, Lola Beltrán, Silvio Rodriguez, Celia Cruz, Juan Peña "El Lebrijano," Los Lobos, Lucha Villa, Dr. Loco and his Original Corrido Boogie Band.

Sure, I knew I was heading for trouble the day I agreed to come to Texas. But not even the *I Ching* warned me what I was in for when Flavio Munguía drove up in the pest-control van.

"TEX-as! What are you going to do *there?"* Beatriz Soliz asked this, a criminal lawyer by day, an Aztec dance instructor by night, and my closest *comadre* in all the world. Beatriz and I go back a long way. Back to the grape-boycott demonstrations in front of the Berkeley Safeway. And I mean the *first* grape strike.

"I thought I'd give Texas a year maybe. At least that. It can't be *that* bad."

"A year!!! Lupe, are you crazy? They still lynch Meskins down there. Everybody's got chain saws and gun racks and pickups and Confederate flags. Aren't you *scared?"*

"Girlfriend, you watch too many John Wayne movies."

To tell the truth, Texas *did* scare the hell out of me. All I knew about Texas was it was big. It was hot. And it was bad. Added to this was my mama's term *teja-NO-te* for *tejano*, which is sort of like "Texcessive," in a redneck kind of way. "It was one of those *teja-NO-tes* that started it," Mama would say. "You know how they are. Always looking for a fight."

I'd said yes to an art director's job at a community cultural center in San Antonio. Eduardo and I had split. For good. *C'est finis*. End of the road, buddy. *Adiós y suerte*. San Francisco is too small a town to go around dragging your three-legged heart. Café Picaro was off limits because it was Eddie's favorite. I stopped frequenting the Café Bohème too. Missed several good openings at La Galería. Not because I was afraid of running into Eddie, but because I was terrified of confronting *"la otra."* My nemesis, in other words. A financial consultant for Merrill Lynch. A blonde.

Eddie, who I'd supported with waitress jobs that summer we were both struggling to pay our college loans and the rent on that tiny apartment on Balmy—big enough when we were in love, but too small when love was scarce. Eddie, who I met the year before I started teaching at the community college, the year after he gave up community organizing and worked part-time as a paralegal. Eddie, who taught me how to salsa, who lectured me night and day about human rights in Guatemala, El Salvador, Chile, Argentina, South Africa, but never said a word about the rights of Blacks in Oakland, the kids of the Tenderloin, the women who shared his bed. Eduardo. My Eddie. That Eddie. With a blonde. He didn't even have the decency to pick a woman of color.

A month hadn't passed since I unpacked the van, but I'd already convinced myself San Antonio was a mistake. I couldn't understand how any Spanish priest in his right mind decided to sit right down in the middle of nowhere and build a mission with no large body of water for miles. I'd always lived near the ocean. I felt landlocked and dusty. Light so white it left me dizzy, sun bleached as an onion.

In the Bay, whenever I got depressed, I always drove out to Ocean Beach. Just to sit. And, I don't know, something about looking at water, how it just goes and goes and goes, something about that I found very soothing. As if somehow I were connected to every ripple that was sending itself out and out until it reached another shore.

But I hadn't found anything to replace it in San Antonio. I wondered what San Antonians did.

I was putting in sixty-hour work weeks at the arts center. No time left to create art when I came home. I'd made a bad habit of crumpling into the couch after work, drinking half a Corona and eating a bag of Hawaiian potato chips for dinner. All the lights in the house blazing when I woke in the middle of the night, hair crooked as a broom, face creased into a mean origami, clothes wrinkled as the citizens of bus stations.

The day the pink circulars appeared, I woke up from one of these naps to find a bug crunching away on Hawaiian chips and another pickled inside my beer bottle. I called La Cucaracha Apachurrada the next morning.

So while you are spraying baseboards, the hose hissing, the gold pump clicking, bending into cupboards, reaching under sinks, the leather utility belt slung loose around your hips, I'm thinking. Thinking you might be the perfect Prince Pop for a painting I've had kicking around in my brain.

I'd always wanted to do an updated version of the Prince Popocatépetl/ Princess Ixtaccíhuatl volcano myth, that tragic love story metamorphosized from classic to kitsch calendar art, like the ones you get at Carnicería Ximénez or Tortillería la Guadalupanita. Prince Popo, half-naked Indian warrior built like Johnny Weissmuller, crouched in grief beside his sleeping princess Ixtaccíhuatl, buxom as an Indian Jayne Mansfield. And behind them, echoing their silhouettes, their namesake volcanoes.

Hell, I could do better than that. It'd be fun. And you might be just the Prince Popo I've been waiting for with that face of a sleeping Olmec, the heavy Oriental eyes, the thick lips and wide nose, that profile carved from onyx. The more I think about it, the more I like the idea.

"Would you like to work for me as a model?"

"Excuse?"

"I mean I'm an artist. I need models. Sometimes. To model, you know. For a painting. I thought. You would be good. Because you have such a wonderful. Face."

Flavio laughed. I laughed too. We both laughed. We laughed and then we laughed some more. And when we were through with our laughing, he packed up his ant traps, spray tank, steel wool, clicked and latched and locked trays, toolboxes, slammed van doors shut. Laughed and drove away.

There is everything *but* a washer and dryer at the house on East Guenther. So every Sunday morning, I stuff all my dirty clothes into pillowcases and haul them out to the van, then drive over to the Kwik Wash on South Presa. I don't mind it, really. I almost like it, because across the street is Torres Taco Haven, "This Is Taco Country." I can load up five washers at a time if I get up early enough, go have a coffee and a Haven Taco—potatoes, chile, and cheese. Then a little later, throw everything in the dryer, and go back for a second cup of coffee and a Torres Special—bean, cheese, guacamole, and bacon, flour tortilla, please.

But one morning, in between the wash and dry cycles, while I ran out to reload the machines, someone had bogarted my table, the window booth next to the jukebox. I was about to get mad and say so, until I realized it was the Prince.

"Remember me? Six eighteen on Guenther."

He looked as if he couldn't remember what he was supposed to remember— then laughed that laugh, like blackbirds startled from the corn.

"Still a good joke, but I was serious. I really am a painter."

"And in reality I am a poet," he said. *"De poeta y loco todos tenemos un poco, ¿no?* But if you asked my mother she would say I'm more *loco* than *poeta*. Unfortunately, poetry only nourishes the heart and not the belly, so I work with my uncle as a bug assassin."

"Can I sit?"

"Please, please."

I ordered my second coffee and a Torres Special. A wide silence.

"What's your favorite course?"

"Art History."

"Nono nono nono nono NO," he said the way they do in Mexico—all the no's overflowing quickly quickly quickly like a fountain of champagne glasses. *"Horse,* not *course,"* and whinnied.

'Oh—horse. I don't know. Mr. Ed?" Stupid. I didn't know any horses. But Flavio smiled anyway the way he always would when I talked, as if admiring my teeth. "So. What. Will you model? Yes? I'd pay you, of course."

"Do I have to take off my clothes?"

"No, no. You just sit. Or stand there, or do whatever. Just pose. I have a studio in the garage. You'll get paid just for looking like you do."

"Well, what kind of story will I have to tell if I say no?" He wrote his name for me on a paper napkin in a tight tangle of curly black letters. "This is my uncle and aunt's number I'm giving you. I live with them."

"What's your name anyway?" I said, twisting the napkin right side up.

"Flavio. Flavio Munguía Galindo," he said, "to serve you."

Flavio's family was so poor, the best they hoped for their son was a job where he would keep his hands clean. How were they to know destiny would lead Flavio north to Corpus Christi as a dishwasher at a Luby's Cafeteria.

At least it was better than the month he'd worked as a shrimper with his cousin in Port Isabel. He still couldn't look at shrimp after that. You come home with your skin and clothes stinking of shrimp, you even start to sweat shrimp, you know. Your hands a mess from the nicks and cuts that never get a chance to heal—the salt water gets in your gloves, stinging and blistering them raw. And how working in the shrimp-processing factory is even worse—snapping those damn shrimp heads all day and the conveyor belt never ending. Your hands as soggy and swollen as ever, and your head about to split with the racket of the machinery.

Field work, he'd done that too. Cabbage, potatoes, onions. Potatoes is better than cabbage, and cabbage is better than onions. Potatoes is clean work. He liked potatoes. The fields in the spring, cool and pretty in the morning, you could think of lines of poetry as you worked, think and think and think, because they're just paying for this, right?, showing me his stubby hands, not this, touching his heart.

But onions belong to dogs and the Devil. The sacks balloon behind you in the row you're working, snipping and trimming whiskers and greens, and you gotta work fast to make any money, you use very sharp shears, see, and your fingers get nicked time and time again, and how dirty it all makes you feel—the taste of onions and dust in your mouth, your eyes stinging, and the click, click, clicking of the shears in the fields and in your head, long after you come home and have had two beers.

390

That's when Flavio remembered his mother's parting wish—A job where your fingernails are clean, *mi'jo*. At least that. And he headed to Corpus and the Luby's.

So when Flavio's Uncle Roland asked him to come to San Antonio and help him out with his exterminating business—You can learn a trade, a skill for life. Always gonna be bugs—Flavio accepted. Even if the poisons and insecticides gave him headaches, even if he had to crawl under houses and occasionally rinse his hair with a garden hose after accidentally discovering a cat's favorite litter spot, even if now and again he saw things he didn't want to see—a possum, a rat, a snake—at least that was better than scraping chicken-fried steak and mashed potatoes from plates, better than having to keep your hands all day in soapy water like a woman, only he used the word *vieja*, which is worse.

I sent a Polaroid of the Woolworth's across from the Alamo to Beatriz Soliz. A self-portrait of me having the Tuesday-Chili-Dog-Fries-Coke-$2.99-Special at the snakey S-shaped lunch counter. Wrote on the back of a Don't-Mess-with-Texas postcard: HAPPY

TO REPORT AM WORKING AGAIN. AS IN REAL WORK. NOT THE JOB THAT FEEDS MY HABIT—EATING. BUT THE THING THAT FEEDS THE SPIRIT. COME HOME RAGGEDY-ASSED, MEAN, BUT, DAMN, I'M PAINTING. EVERY OTHER SUNDAY. KICKING *NALGA* LOOKS LIKE. OR AT LEAST TRYING. *CUÍDATE*, GIRL. *ABRAZOS*, LUPE

So every other Sunday I dragged my butt out of bed and into the garage studio to try to make some worth of my life. Flavio always there before me, like if he was the one painting me.

What I liked best about working with Flavio were the stories. Sometimes while he was posing we'd have storytelling competitions. "Your Favorite Sadness." "The Ugliest Food You Ever Ate." "A Horrible Person." One that I remember was for the category "At Last—Justice." It was really his grandma's story, but he told it well.

My grandma Chavela was from here. San Antonio I mean to say. She had five husbands, and the second one was called Fito, for Filiberto. They had my Uncle Roland who at the time of this story was nine months old. They lived by the old farmers' market, over by Commerce and Santa Rosa, in a two-room apartment. My grandma said she had beautiful dishes, an antique cabinet, a small table, two chairs, a stove, a lantern, a cedar chest full of embroidered tablecloths and towels, and a three-piece bedroom set.

And so, one Sunday she felt like visiting her sister Eulalia, who lived on the other side of town. Her husband left a dollar and change on the table for her trolley, kissed her good-bye, and left. My grandma meant to take along a bag of sweets, because Eulalia was fond of Mexican candy—burnt-milk bars, pecan brittle, sugared pumpkin, glazed orange rind, and those pretty coconut squares dyed red, white, and green like the Mexican flag—so sweet you can never finish them.

So my grandma stopped at Mi Tierra Bakery. That's when she looks down the street, and who does she see but her husband kissing a woman. It looked as if their bodies were ironing each other's clothes, she said. My grandma waved at Fito. Fito waved at my grandma. Then my grandma walked back home with the baby, packed all her clothes, her set of beautiful dishes, her tablecloths and towels, and asked a neighbor to drive her to her sister Eulalia's. Turn here. Turn there. *What street are we on?* It doesn't matter—just do as I tell you.

The next day Fito came looking for her at Eulalia's, to explain to my grandma that the woman was just an old friend, someone he hadn't seen in a while, a long long time. Three days passed and my grandma Chavela, Eulalia, and baby Roland drove off to Cheyenne, Wyoming. They stayed there fourteen years.

Fito died in 1935 of cancer of the penis. I think it was syphilis. He used to manage a baseball team. He got hit in the crotch by a fastball.

I was explaining yin and yang. How sexual harmony put one in communion with the infinite forces of nature. The earth is yin, see, female, while heaven is male and yang. And the interaction of the two constitutes the whole shebang. You can't have one without the other. Otherwise shit is out of balance. Inhaling, exhaling. Moon, sun. Fire, water. Man, woman. All complementary forces occur in pairs.

"Ah," said Flavio, "like the *mexicano* word 'sky-earth' for the world."

"Where the hell did you learn that? The *Popul Vuh?*"

"No," Flavio said flatly. "My grandma Oralia."

I said, "This is a powerful time we're living in. We have to let go of our present way of life and search for our past, remember our destinies, so to speak. Like the *I Ching* says, returning to one's roots is returning to one's destiny."

Flavio didn't say anything, just stared at his beer for what seemed a long time. "You Americans have a strange way of thinking about time," he began. Before I could object to being lumped with the northern half of America, he went on. "You think old ages end, but that's not so. It's ridiculous to think one age has overcome another. American time is running alongside the calendar of the sun, even if your world doesn't know it."

Then, to add sting to the blow, he raised his beer bottle to his lips and added, "But what do I know, right? I'm just an exterminator."

Flavio said, "I don't know anything about this Tao business, but I believe love is always eternal. Even if eternity is only five minutes."

Flavio Munguía was coming for supper. I made a wonderful paella with brown rice and tofu and a pitcher of fresh sangria. Gipsy Kings were on the tape player. I wore my Lycra mini, a pair of silver cowboy boots, and a fringed shawl across my Danskin like Carmen in that film by Carlos Saura.

Over dinner I talked about how I once had my aura massaged by an Oakland *curandera*, Afro-Brazilian dance as a means of spiritual healing, where I might find good dim sum in San Antonio, and whether a white woman had any right to claim to be an Indian shamaness. Flavio talked about how Alex El Güero from work had won a Sony boom box that morning just by being the ninth caller on 107 FM K-Suave, how his Tía Tencha makes the best tripe soup ever no lie, how before leaving Corpus he and Johnny Canales from *El Show de Johnny Canales* had been like this until a bet over Los Bukis left them not speaking to each other, how every Thursday night he works out at a gym on Calaveras with aims to build himself a body better than Mil Mascara's, and is there an English equivalent for the term *la fulana?*

I served Jerez and played Astor Piazzolla. Flavio said he preferred "pure tango," classic and romantic like Gardel, not this cat-howling crap. He rolled back the Afghan rug, yanked me to my feet, demonstrated *la habanera, el fandango, la milonga,* and explained how each had contributed to birth *el tango.*

Then he ran outside to his truck, the backs of his thighs grazing my knees as he edged past me and the Olinalá coffee table. I felt all the hairs on my body sway as if I were an underwater plant and a current had set me in motion. Before I could steady myself he was popping a cassette into the tape player. A soft crackling. Then sugary notes rising like a blue satin banner held aloft by doves.

"Violín, violonchelo, piano, salterio. Music from the time of my *abuelos.* My grandma taught me the dances—*el chotis, cancán, los valses.* All part of that lost epoch," he said. "But that was long long ago, before the time all the dogs were named after Woodrow Wilson."

"Don't you know any indigenous dances?" I finally asked, "like *el baile de los viejitos?"*

Flavio rolled his eyes. That was the end of our dance lesson.

"Who dresses you?"

"Silver."

"What's that? A store or a horse?"

"Neither. Silver Galindo. My San Antonio cousin."

"What kind of name is Silver?"

"It's English," Flavio said, "for Silvestre."

I said, "What *you* are, sweetheart, is a product of American imperialism," and plucked at the alligator on his shirt.

"I don't have to dress in a sarape and sombrero to be Mexican," Flavio said. "I *know* who *I* am."

I wanted to leap across the table, throw the Oaxacan black pottery pieces across the room, swing from the punched tin chandelier, fire a pistol at his Reeboks, and force him to dance. I wanted to *be* Mexican at that moment, but it was true. I was not Mexican. Instead of the volley of insults I intended, all I managed to sling was a single clay pebble that dissolved on impact—*perro.*

"Dog." It wasn't even the word I'd meant to hurl.

You have, how do I say it, something. Something I can't even put my finger on. Some way of moving, of not moving, that belongs to no one but Flavio Munguía. As if your body and bones always remembered you were made by a God who loved you, the one Mama talked about in her stories.

God made men by baking them in an oven, but he forgot about the first batch, and that's how Black people were born. And then he was so anxious about the next batch, he took them out of the oven too soon, so that's how White people were made. But the third batch he let cook until they were golden-golden-golden, and, honey, that's you and me.

God made you from red clay, Flavio, with his hands. This face of yours like the little clay heads they unearth in Teotihuacán. Pinched this cheekbone, then that. Used obsidian flints for the eyes, those eyes dark as the sacrificial wells they cast virgins into. Selected hair thick as cat whiskers. Thought for a long time before deciding on this nose, elegant and wide. And the mouth, ah! Everything silent and powerful and very proud kneaded into the mouth. And then he blessed you, Flavio, with skin sweet as burnt-milk candy, smooth as river water. He made you *bien* pretty even if I didn't always know it. Yes, he did.

Romelia. Forever. That's what his arm said. Forever Romelia in ink once black that had paled to blue. Romelia. Romelia. Seven thin blue letters the color of a vein. "Romelia" said his forearm where the muscle swelled into a flat stone. "Romelia" it trembled when he held me. "Romelia" by the light of the votive lamp above the bed. But when I unbuttoned his shirt a bannered cross above his left nipple murmured "Elsa."

I'd never made love in Spanish before. I mean not with anyone whose *first* language was Spanish. There was crazy Graham, the anarchist labor organizer who'd taught me to eat jalapeños and swear like a truck mechanic, but he was Welsh and had learned his Spanish running guns to Bolivia.

And Eddie, sure. But Eddie and I were products of our American education. Anything tender always came off sounding like the subtitles to a Buñuel film.

But Flavio. When Flavio accidentally hammered his thumb, he never yelled

"Ouch!" he said "*¡Ay!*" The true test of a native Spanish speaker.

¡Ay! To make love in Spanish, in a manner as intricate and devout as la Alhambra. To have a lover sigh *mi vida, mi preciosa, mi chiquitita,* and whisper things in that language crooned to babies, that language murmured by grandmothers, those words that smelled like your house, like flour tortillas, and the inside of your daddy's hat, like everyone talking in the kitchen at the same time, or sleeping with the windows open, like sneaking cashews from the crumpled quarter-pound bag Mama always hid in her lingerie drawer after she went shopping with Daddy at the Sears.

That language. That sweep of palm leaves and fringed shawls. That startled fluttering, like the heart of a goldfinch or a fan. Nothing sounded dirty or hurtful or corny. How could I think of making love in English again? English with its starched *r*'s and *g*'s. English with its crisp linen syllables. English crunchy as apples, resilient and stiff as sailcloth.

But Spanish whirred like silk, rolled and puckered and hissed. I held Flavio close to me, in the mouth of my heart, inside my wrists. Incredible happiness. A sigh unfurled of its own accord, a groan heaved out from my chest so rusty and full of dust it frightened me. I was crying. It surprised us both. "My soul, did I hurt you?" Flavio said in that other language. I managed to bunch my mouth into a knot and shake my head "no" just as the next wave of sobs began. Flavio rocked me, and cooed, and rocked me. *Ya, ya, ya.* There, there, there.

I wanted to say so many things, but all I could think of was a line I'd read in the letters of Georgia O'Keeffe years ago and had forgotten until then. Flavio … did you ever feel like flowers?

We take my van and a beer. Flavio drives. Watching Flavio's profile, that beautiful Tarascan face of his, something that ought to be set in jade. We don't have to say anything the whole ride and it's fine, just take turns sharing the one beer, back and forth, back and forth, just looking at each other from the corner of the eye, just smiling from the corner of the mouth.

What's happened to me? Flavio was just Flavio, a man I wouldn't've looked at twice before. But now anyone who reminds me of him, any baby with that same cane-sugar skin, any moon-faced woman in line at the Handy Andy, or bag boy with tight hips carrying my groceries to the car, or child at the Kwik Wash with ears as delicate as the whorls of a sea mollusk, I find myself looking at, lingering over, appreciating. Henceforth and henceforth. Forever and ever. Ad infinitum.

When I was with Eddie, we'd be making love, and then out of nowhere I would think of the black-and-white label on the tube of titanium yellow paint. Or a plastic Mickey Mouse change purse I once had with crazy hypnotized eyes that blinked open/shut, open/shut when you wobbled it. Or a little scar shaped like a mitten on the chin of a boy named Eliberto Briseño whom I was madly in love with all through the fifth grade.

But with Flavio it's just the opposite. I might be working on a charcoal sketch, chewing on a pinch of a kneaded rubber eraser I've absentmindedly put in my mouth, and then suddenly I'm thinking about the thickness of Flavio's earlobes between my teeth. Or a wisp of violet smoke might rise from someone's cigarette at the Bar America, and remind me of that twist of sinew from wrist to elbow in Flavio's pretty arms. Or say Danny and Craig from Tienda Guadalupe Folk Art & Gifts are demonstrating how South American rain sticks work, and boom—there's Flavio's voice like the pull of the ocean when it drags everything with it back to its center—that kind of gravelly, charcoal and shell and glass rasp to it. Incredible.

Taco Haven was crowded the way it always is Sunday mornings, full of grandmothers and babies in their good clothes, boys with hair still wet from the morning bath, big husbands in tight shirts, and rowdy mamas slapping rude children to public decency.

Three security guards were vacating my window booth, and we grabbed it. Flavio ordered *chilaquiles* and I ordered breakfast tacos. We asked for quarters for the jukebox, same as always. Five songs 50 cents. I punched 132, "All My Ex's Live in Texas," George Strait; 140, "Soy Infeliz," Lola Beltrán; 233, "Polvo y Olvido," Lucha Villa; 118, "Mal Hombre," Lydia Mendoza; and number 167, "La Movidita," because I knew Flavio loved Flaco Jiménez. Flavio was no more quiet than usual, but midway through breakfast he announced, "My life, I have to go."

"We just got here."

"No. I mean me. I must go. To Mexico."

"What are you talking about?"

"My mother wrote me. I have compromises to attend to."

"But you're coming back. Right?"

"Only destiny knows."

A red dog with stiff fur tottered by the curb.

"What are you trying to tell me?"

The same red color as a cocoa doormat or those wooden-handled scrub brushes you buy at the Winn's.

"I mean I have family obligations." There was a long pause.

You could tell the dog was real sick. Big bald patches. Gummy eyes that bled like grapes.

"My mother writes that my sons—"

"Sons . . . How many?"

"Four. From my first. Three from my second."

"First. Second. What? Marriages?"

"No, only one marriage. The other doesn't count since we weren't married in a church."

"Christomatic."

Really it made you sick to look at the thing, hobbling about like that in jerky steps as if it were dancing backward and had only three legs.

"But this has nothing to do with you, Lupe. Look, you love your mother *and* your father, don't you?"

The dog was eating something, jaws working in spasmodic gulps. A bean-and-cheese taco, I think.

"Loving one person doesn't take away from loving another. It's that way with me with love. One has nothing to do with the other. In all seriousness and with all my heart I tell you this, Lupe."

Somebody must've felt sorry for it and tossed it a last meal, but the kind thing would've been to shoot it.

"So that's how it is."

"There is no other remedy. *La* yin *y el* yang, you know," Flavio said and meant it.

"Well, yeah," I said. And then because my Torres Special felt like it wanted to rise from my belly—"I think you better go now. I gotta get my clothes out of the dryer before they get wrinkled."

"*Es* cool," Flavio said, sliding out of the booth and my life. "*Ay te wacho*, I guess."

I looked for my rose-quartz crystal and visualized healing energy surrounding me. I lit copal and burned sage to purify the house. I put on a tape of Amazon flutes, Tibetan gongs, and Aztec ocarinas, tried to center on my seven chakras, and thought only positive thoughts, expressions of love, compassion, forgiveness. But after forty minutes I still had an uncontrollable desire to drive over to Flavio Munguía's house with my grandmother's *molcajete* and bash in his skull.

What kills me is your silence. So certain, so solid. Not a note, nor postcard. Not a phone call, no number I could reach you at. No address I could write to. Neither yes nor no.

Just the void. The days raw and wide as this drought-blue sky. Just this nothingness. That's what hurts.

Nothing wants to break from the eyes. When you're a kid, it's easy. You take one wooden step out in the hall dark and wait. The hallways of every house we ever lived in smelling of Pine-Sol and dirty-looking no matter how many Saturdays we scrubbed it. Chipped paint and ugly nicks and craters in the walls from a century of bikes and kids' shoes and downstairs tenants. The handrail old and never beautiful, not even the day it was new, I bet. Darkness soaked in the plaster and wood when the house was divided into apartments. Dust balls and hair in the corners where the broom didn't reach. And now and then, a mouse squeaking.

How I let the sounds, dark and full of dust and hairs, out of my throat and eyes, that sound mixed with spit and coughing and hiccups and bubbles of snot. And the sea trickling out of my eyes as if I'd always carried it inside me, like a seashell waiting to be cupped to an ear.

These days we run from the sun. Cross the street quick, get under an awning. Carry an umbrella like tightrope walkers. Red-white-and-blue-flowered nylon. Beige with green and red stripes. Faded maroon with an amber handle. Bus ladies slouched and fanning themselves with a newspaper and a bandanna.

Bad news. The sky is blue again today and will be blue again tomorrow. Herd of clouds big as longhorns passing mighty and grazing low. Heat like a husband asleep beside you, like someone breathing in your ear who you just want to shove once, good and hard, and say, "Quit it."

When I was doing collages, I bought a few "powders" from Casa Preciado Religious Articles, the Mexican voodoo shop on South Laredo. I remember I'd picked Te Tengo Amarrado y Claveteado and Regresa a Mí—just for the wrapper. But I found myself hunting around for them this morning, and when I couldn't find them, making a special trip back to that store that smells of chamomile and black bananas.

The votive candles are arranged like so. Church-sanctioned powers on one aisle—San Martín de Porres, Santo Niño de Atocha, el Sagrado Corazón, La Divina Providencia, Nuestra Señora de San Juan de los Lagos. Folk powers on another—El Gran General Pancho Villa, Ajo Macho/Garlic Macho, La Santísima Muerte/Blessed Death, Bingo Luck, Law Stay Away, Court Case Double Strength. Back to back, so as not to offend maybe. I chose a Yo Puedo Más Que Tú from the pagan side and a Virgen de Guadalupe from the Christian.

Magic oils, magic perfume and soaps, votive candles, *milagritos*, holy cards, magnet car-statuettes, plaster saints with eyelashes made from human hair, San Martín Caballero good-luck horseshoes, incense and copal, aloe vera bunched, blessed, bound with red string, and pinned above a door. Herbs stocked from floor to ceiling in labeled drawers.

AGUACATE, ALBAHACA, ALTAMISA, ANACAHUITE, BARBAS DE ELOTE, CEDRÓN DE CASTILLO, COYOTE, CHARRASQUILLA, CHOCOLATE DE INDIO, EUCALIPTO, FLOR DE ACOCOTILLO, FLOR DE AZAHAR, FLOR DE MIMBRE, FLOR DE TILA, FLOR DE ZEMPOAL, HIERBABUENA, HORMIGA, HUISACHE,

MANZANILLA, MARRUBIO, MIRTO, NOGAL, PALO AZUL, PASMO, PATA DE VACA, PIONÍA, PIRUL, RATÓN, TEPOZÁN, VÍBORA, ZAPOTE BLANCO, ZARZAMORA.

Snake, rat, ant, coyote, cow hoof. Were there actually dead animals tucked in a drawer? A skin wrapped in tissue paper, a dried ear, a paper cone of shriveled black alphabets, a bone ground to crystals in a baby-food jar. Or were they just herbs that *looked* like the animal?

These candles and *yerbas* and stuff, do they really work? The sisters Preciado pointed to a sign above their altar to Our Lady of the Remedies. *VENDEMOS, NO HACEMOS RECETAS.* WE SELL, WE DON'T PRESCRIBE.

I can be brave in the day, but nights are my Gethsemane. That pinch of the dog's teeth just as it nips. A mean South American itch somewhere I can't reach. The little hurricane of bathwater just before it slips inside the drain.

Seems like the world is spinning smooth without a bump or squeak except when love comes in. Then the whole machine just quits like a loud load of wash on imbalance—the buzzer singing to high heaven, the danger light flashing.

Not true. The world has always turned with its trail of tin cans rattling behind it. I have always been in love with a man.

Everything's like it was. Except for this. When I look in the mirror, I'm ugly. How come I never noticed before?

I was having *sopa tarasca* at El Mirador and reading Dear Abby. A letter from "Too Late," who wrote now that his father was dead, he was sorry he had never asked his forgiveness for having hurt him, he'd never told his father "I love you."

I pushed my bowl of soup away and blew my nose with my paper napkin. I'd never asked Flavio forgiveness for having hurt him. And yes, I'd never said "I love you." I'd never said it, though the words rattled in my head like *urracas* in the bamboo.

For weeks I lived with those two regrets like twin grains of sand embedded in my oyster heart, until one night listening to Carlos Gardel sing, *"Life is an absurd wound.*" I realized I had it wrong. Oh.

Today the Weber kettle in the backyard finally quit. Three days of thin white smoke like kite string. I'd stuffed in all of Flavio's letters and poems and photos and cards and all the sketches and studies I'd ever done of him, then lit a match. I didn't expect paper to take so long to burn, but it was a lot of layers. I had to keep poking it with a stick. I did save one poem, the last one he gave me before he left. Pretty in Spanish. But you'll have to take my word for it. In English it just sounds goofy.

The smell of paint was giving me headaches. I couldn't bring myself to look at my canvases. I'd turn on the TV. The Galavisión channel. Told myself I was looking for old Mexican movies. María Félix, Jorge Negrete, Pedro Infante, anything, please, where somebody's singing on a horse.

After a few days I'm watching the *telenovelas.* Avoiding board meetings, rushing home from work, stopping at Torres Taco Haven on the way and buying taquitos to go. Just so I could be seated in front of the screen in time to catch *Rosa Salvaje* with Verónica Castro as the savage Rose of the title. Or Daniela Romo in *Balada por un Amor.* Or Adela Noriega in *Dulce Desafío.* I watched them all. In the name of research.

I started dreaming of these Rosas and Briandas and Luceros. And in my dreams I'm slapping the heroine to her senses, because I want them to be women who make things happen, not women who things happen to. Not loves that are *tormentosos.* Not men powerful and passionate versus women either volatile and evil, or sweet and resigned. But women. Real women. The ones I've loved all my life. *If you don't like it* lárgate, *honey.* Those women. The ones I've known everywhere except on TV, in books and magazines. *Las* girlfriends. *Las comadres.* Our mamas and *tías.* Passionate *and* powerful, tender and volatile, brave. And, above all, fierce.

"*Bien* pretty, your shawl. You didn't buy it in San Antonio?" Centeno's Mexican Supermarket. The cashier was talking to me.

"No, it's Peruvian. Think I bought it in Santa Fe. Or New York. I don't remember."

"*Que* cute. You look real *mona.*"

Plastic hair combs with fringy flowers. Purple blouse crocheted out of shiny yarn, not tucked but worn over her jeans to hide a big stomach. I know—I do the same thing.

She's my age, but looks old. Tired. Never mind the red lips, the eye makeup that just makes her look sad. Those creases from the corner of the lip to the wing of the nostril from holding in anger, or tears. Or both. She's the one ringing up my *Vanidades.* "Extraordinary Issue." "Julio Confesses He's Looking for Love. " "Still Daddy's Girl?—Liberate Yourself!" "15 Ways to Say I Love You with Your Eyes." "The Incredible Wedding of Argentine Soccer Star Maradona (It Cost 3 Million U.S. Dollars!)" "*Summer by the Sea,* a Complete Novel by Corin Tellado."

"Libertad Palomares," she said, looking at the cover.

"*Amar es Vivir,*" I answered automatically as if it were my motto. Libertad Palomares. A big Venezuelan *telenovela* star. Big on crying. Every episode she weeps like a Magdalene. Not me. I couldn't cry if my life depended on it.

"Right she works her part real good?"

"I never miss an episode." That was the truth.

"Me neither. *Si Dios quiere* I'm going to get home in time today to watch it. It's getting good."

"Looks like it's going to finish pretty soon."

"Hope not. How much is this? I might buy one too. *Three-fifty! Bien* 'spensive."

Maybe once. Or maybe never. Maybe each time someone asks, *Wanna dance?* at Club Fandango. All for a Saturday night at Hacienda Salas Party House on South Mission Road. Or Lerma's Night Spot on Zarzamora. Making eyes at Ricky's Poco Loco Club or El Taconazo Lounge. Or maybe, like in my case, in my garage making art.

Amar es Vivir. What it comes down to for that woman at Centeno's and for me. It was enough to keep us tuning in every day at six-thirty, another episode, another thrill. To relive that living when the universe ran through the blood like river water. Alive. Not the weeks spent writing grant proposals, not the forty hours standing behind a cash register shoving cans of refried beans into plastic sacks. Hell, no. This wasn't what we were put on the planet for. Not ever.

Not Lola Beltrán sobbing *"Soy infeliz"* into her four *cervezas*. But Daniela Romo singing *"Ya no. Es verdad que te adoro, pero más me adoro yo."* I love you, honey, but I love me more.

One way or another. Even if it's only the lyrics to a stupid pop hit. We're going to right the world and live. I mean live our lives the way lives were meant to be lived. With the throat and wrists. With rage and desire, and joy and grief, and love till it hurts, maybe. But goddamn, girl. Live.

Went back to the twin volcano painting. Got a good idea and redid the whole thing. Prince Pop and Princess Ixta trade places. After all, who's to say the sleeping mountain isn't the prince, and the voyeur the princess, right? So I've done it my way. With Prince Popocatépetl lying on his back instead of the Princess. Of course, I had to make some anatomical adjustments in order to simulate the geographical silhouettes. I think I'm going to call it *El Pipi del Popo*. I kind of like it.

Everywhere I go, it's me and me. Half of me living my life, the other half watching me live it. Here it is January already. Sky wide as an ocean, shark-belly gray for days at a time, then all at once a blue so tender you can't remember how only months before the heat split you open like a pecan shell, you can't remember anything anymore.

Every sunset, I find myself rushing, cleaning the brushes, hurrying, my footsteps giving a light tap on each rung up the aluminum ladder to the garage roof.

Because *urracas* are arriving by the thousands from all directions and settling in the river trees. Trees leafless as sea anemones in this season, the birds in their branches dark and distinct as treble clefs, very crisp and noble and clean as if someone had cut them out of black paper with sharp scissors and glued them with library paste.

Urracas. Grackles. *Urracas*. Different ways of looking at the same bird. City calls them grackles, but I prefer *urracas*. That roll of the *r* making all the difference.

Urracas, then, big as crows, shiny as ravens, swooping and whooping it up like drunks at Fiesta. *Urracas* giving a sharp cry, a slippery rise up the scales, a quick stroke across a violin string. And then a splintery whistle that they loop and lasso from that box in their throat, and spit and chirrup and chook. *Chook-chook, chook-chook.*

Here and there a handful of starlings tossed across the sky. All swooping in one direction. Then another explosion of starlings very far away, like pepper. Wind rattling pecans from the trees. *Thunk, thunk.* Like bad kids throwing rocks at your house. The damp smell of the earth the same as tea boiling.

Urracas curving, descending on treetops. Wide wings against blue. Branch tips trembling when they land, quivering when they take off again. Those at the crown devoutly facing one direction toward a private Mecca.

And other charter members off and running, high high up. Some swooping in one direction and others crisscrossing. Like marching bands at halftime. This swoop never bumping into that. *Urracas* closer to earth, starlings higher up because they're smaller. Every day. Every sunset. And no one noticing except to look at the ground and say, "Who's gonna clean up this *shit*!"

All the while the sky is throbbing. Blue, violet, peach, not holding still for one second. The sun setting and setting, all the light in the world soft as nacre, a Canaletto, an apricot, an earlobe.

And every bird in the universe chittering, jabbering, clucking, chirruping, squawking, gurgling, going crazy because God-bless-it another day has ended, as if it never had yesterday and never will again tomorrow. Just because it's today, today. With no thought of the future or past. Today. Hurray. Hurray! ★

Acknowledgments

The editor wishes to thank the many helpful librarians at the San Antonio Public Library, the University of Texas at San Antonio, the Institute of Texan Cultures, the Daughters of the Republic of Texas Library at the Alamo, and elsewhere for their assistance over many years. Special thanks also for the wise counsel of readers Robert Bonazzi, Rosemary Catacalos, Bill Fisher, Lewis Fisher, Robert Flynn, John Igo, Carmen Tafolla, Juan Tejeda, Kathy Vargas, and Tomás Ybarra-Frausto; and to Ramón Vásquez of American Indians in Texas at the Spanish Colonial Missions.

Permissions

The editor also wishes to thank the following authors and publishers for permission to reprint these works:

Aitches, Mariana: "A Mother's October," "Winter Solstice," and "Fishing for Light" were published in *Fishing for Light* (Wings Press, 2009). Used by permission of the author.

Wendy Barker, "High Sky" was published in *Things of the Weather* (Pudding House Press, 2009); "Inheritance" was published in *Way of Whiteness* (Wings Press, 2000); "I'm Not Sure the Cherry is the 'Loveliest of Trees'" first appeared in *New Letters*, 2011; "Trash" was published in *Between Frames* (Pecan Grove Press, 2006). Used by permission of the author.

Robert Bonazzi, "Secret Missions," "Once In A Blue Moon," and "Intermezzi" are previously unpublished. Used by permission of the author.

Brandon, Jay: "A Jury of His Peers" is previously unpublished. Used by permission of the author.

Browne, Jenny: "The Man Who Gives Bad Directions in Downtown San Antonio" and "There's a Slow Green River I've Been Living By" were published in *The Second Reason* (University of Tampa Press, 2007). Used by permission of the author.

Cantú, Norma Elia: "La Chola" is previously unpublished. Used by permission of the author.

Cardona, Jacinto Jesús: "Pan Dulce" first appeared in *Mid-American Review,* XIII, No. 1; "Avocado Avenue" first appeared in *Puerto del Sol,* Spring 1992; "At The Wheel of a Blue Chevrolet" was published in *At The Wheel Of A Blue Chevrolet* (Amapola Pres, 1993); "Bar America," "Chicharras," and "Pan Dulce," were published in *Pan Dulce* (Chili Verde Press, 1998). Used by permission of the author.

Catacalos, Rosemary: "David Talamántez on the Last Day of Second Grade" was published in *Begin Here* (Wings Press, 2013); "Homesteaders," "La Casa," "Swallow Wings," and "Listen, Querido, They're Playing Our Song, or, Summer Ritual with a Poet Friend" were published in *Again for the First Time* (Tooth of Time, 1984; Wings Press, 2013). Used by permission of the author.

Cisneros, Sandra: "Bien Pretty" was first published in *Woman Hollering Creek and Other Stories* (Random House, 1991). Used by permission of the Susan Bergholz Literary Agency. This story is not included in the ebook edition of *Literary San Antonio.*

Clack, Cary: "Losing the Ice House" and "Bridging Cultures" were published (under different headlines) in the *San Antonio Express-News,* February 27, 2002, and February 29, 2004, respectively. Used by permission of the author.

Nan Cuba, "Patriotism" first appeared in *storySouth* (Spring 2013). Web. March (2013). Used by permission of the author.

De Hoyos, Angela: "Arise, Chicano!" was published in *Arise, Chicano!* (Backroom Books, 1975); "Hermano" was published in *Chicano Poems: For the Barrio* (M&A Editions, 1975); and "A Lesson in Semantics" was published in *Woman, Woman* (Arte Público Press, 1985). Used by permission of the author's estate and Moises Sandoval.

Flynn, Robert: from *Wanderer Springs* (TCU Press, 1987). Used by permission of the author.

Guerrero, Laurie Ann: "Sundays After Breakfast: A Lesson in Cotton Picking" was published as a broadside by printer Deborah Huacuja, and in *Palo Alto Review;* "Esperanza Tells Her Friends the Story of La Llorona" first appeared in *Feminist Studies*; both of these poems, as well as "Sundays After Breakfast: A Lesson in Speech" were published in *A Tongue in the Mouth of the Dying* (University of Notre Dame Press, 2013). Used by permission of the author.

Stephen Harrigan, from *Remember Ben Clayton* (Knopf, 2011). Used by permission of the author.

Houston, Sterling: "Driving Wheel" was first published in *High Yello Rose and Other Texas Plays* (Wings Press, 2011). Used by permission of the author (now deceased) and the Sterling Houston estate.

Jennings, Frank W.: "Naming San Antonio" was first published in *San Antonio, The Story of an Enchanted City* (*San Antonio Express News*, 1998). Used by permission of the author (now deceased).

Kellman, Steven G.: "The Yellow Rose of Texas" was first published in *The Journal of American Culture* (1984). Used by permission of the author and John Wiley & Sons, Inc.

Lanier, Sidney: "San Antonio de Bexar: An Historical Sketch" was first published in *San Antonio de Bexar: A Guide and History* (San Antonio: William Corner, 1890). Public domain.

LaVilla-Havelin, Jim: "Earl Abel's," "In the Courtyard," and "from *Some Trees*" are previously unpublished. Used by permission of the author.

Maverick, Sr., Maury: "The Wrong Side of the River" was first published in *Old Villita* (Works Progress Administration, 1939). Used by permission of Lynn Maverick Denzer.

Menchaca, Antonio: "After the Alamo . . . San Antonio, 1836-1842" originally appeared in *The Passing Show* (1908). The version here is from *Recollections of a Tejano Life: Antonio Menchaca in Texas History,* edited by Timothy Matovina and Jesús F. de la Teja (University of Texas Press, 2013).

Mendoza, Celeste Guzmán: "Tío Chucho would have you believe," "About Faith" and "Crooked pinky" were first published in *Beneath the Halo* (Wings Press, 2013). Used by permission of the author.

Milligan, Bryce: "O. Henry and The Bridge at the Heart of the City." An earlier version of this first appeared in the *San Antonio Express-News*. An earlier version of "San Antonio Nights" first appeared in *Daysleepers & Other Poems* (Corona, 1984); it has been reprinted numerous times. "Trusting Steel" was first published in *Working the Stone* (Wings Press, 1993). "Eós and the Train Horns" was published in *Take to the Highway: Arabesques for Travelers* (West End Press, 2016). Used by permission of the author.

Milligan, Mary Guerrero: "Lotería: La Rosa" was first published in *Blue Mesa Review* (No. 5, 1993). It has been included in several anthologies, including *Daughters of the Fifth Sun* (Riverhead, 1995) and *Her Texas: Story, Image, Poem & Song* (Wings Press, 2015). Used by permission of the author.

Josephina Niggli, "Saint's Day" is previously unpublished. It was discovered in Niggli's papers by Niggli biographer, Elizabeth Coonrod Martinez.

Nye, Naomi Shihab: "Will You Hold My Bullet, Please?" was published in *There Is No Long Distance Now* (Greenwillow/HarperCollins, 2011). "West Side" was published in *Hugging the Jukebox* (Breitenbush, 1982); "Because of Libraries We Can Say These Things" and "The Rider" were published in *Fuel* (Boa Editions, 1998); "Frankly" was published in *Transfer* (Boa Edition, 2011). Used by permission of the author.

Olmsted, Frederick Law: from *A Journey through Texas* was first published in *A Journey through Texas: Or a Saddle-Trip on the Southwestern Frontier.* (New York: Dix, Edwards & Co., 1857). Public domain.

Ortiz, Amalia: "Girl Strolls Down Nogalitos Street," "these hands which have never picked cotton," and "the night Ram died" were published in *Rant. Chant. Chisme.* (Wings Press, 2015). Used by permission of the author.

Parédez, Deborah: "Crape Myrtle, 1943" appeared in *Poet Lore* (October 2011); "St. Joske's" is previously unpublished; "Poem for the King William Dancers" and "Bustillo Drive Grocery" were first published in *This Side of Skin* (Wings Press, 2002); "Bustillo Drive Grocery" has been reprinted in several textbooks. Used by permission of the author.

Pike, Zebulon: "An Unexpected Fiesta" (1806), was first published in *An Account of the Expeditions to the Source of the Mississippi and Through Western Parts of Louisiana ... and a Tour Through the Interior Parts of New Spain* (Philadelphia: C & A. Conrad, 1810). Public domain.

Porter, William Sydney (O. Henry): "The Enchanted Kiss" was first published in *Roads of Destiny* (Doubleday, 1909). Public domain.

Riordan, Rick: from *Big Red Tequila* (Bantam, 1997). Used by permission of the author.

Geoff Rips: "I Explain Myself" first appeared in *New Directions 36* and was Chapter One in *The Truth* (Western Michigan University Press/New Issues, 2008). Used by permission of the author.

Russell, Jan Jarboe: an earlier version of "Letter from San Antonio: No Retreat! No Surrender!" was first published in *Texas Monthly,* October, 2010. Used by permission of the author.

Reposa, Carol Coffee: "Cicadas" was published in *Southwestern American Literature;* "Alamo Plaza at Night" and "Great Horned Owl" were published in *Facts of Life* (Browder Springs Press, 2002). Used by permission of the author.

Sánchez, Ricardo: "The Meaning of *Chicano*" was published in the *San Antonio Express-News,* May 29, 1988. Used by permission of the author (now deceased).

Stanush, Claude: "Live and Let Live" was published in *Sometimes It's New York* (Wings Press, 2006). Used by permission of the estate of Claude Stanush.

Tafolla, Carmen: "This River Here" and "Right in One Language" were published in *Sonnets and Salsa* (Wings Press, 2001); "San Antonio is a young Yanaguana woman" was published in *This River Here: Poems of San Antonio* (Wings Press, 2013). Used by permission of the author.

Tafolla, Santiago: from *A Life Crossing Borders: Memoir of a Mexican-American Confederate / Las memorias de un mexicoamericano en la Confederación*, edited by Carmen Tafolla and Laura Tafolla (Arte Público Press, 2010). Used by permission of Carmen Tafolla.

Vigil, Evangelina: "como embrujada" was published in *nade y nade* (M&A Editions, 1978); "was fun running 'round descalza" and "por la calle Zarzamora" were published in *Thirty an' Seen a Lot*, (Arte Público Press, 1982, 1985). Used by permission of the author.

Villanueva, Andrea Castañon (Madam Candelaria): "The Fall of the Alamo" first appeared in the *San Antonio Light*, February 19, 1899, with the headline "ALAMO MASSACRE: As Told by the Late Madam Candelaria. Her Vivid Story of the Great Battle, Where 177 Brave Men Met Death as True Heroes—Colonel Bowie Died in Her Arms—Blood Was Ankle Deep." Public domain.

INDEX